CW00728528

Joan Aiken
Omnibus

Joan Aiken Omnibus

The Wolves of Willoughby Chase
Black Hearts in Battersea
Night Birds on Nantucket

LEOPARD

This edition published in 1995 by Leopard Books,
20 Vauxhall Bridge Road, London SW1V 2SA,
an imprint of Random House Publishing Group Ltd

The Wolves of Willoughby Chase first published in 1962
by Jonathan Cape Ltd

Black Hearts in Battersea first published in 1965 by Jonathan Cape Ltd

Night Birds on Nantucket first published in 1966 by Jonathan Cape Ltd

ISBN 0 7529 0132 X

THE WOLVES OF WILLOUGHBY CHASE

For
John and Elizabeth and
Torquemada

Note

The action of this book takes place in a period of English history that never happened – shortly after the accession to the throne of Good King James III in 1832. At this time, the Channel Tunnel from Dover to Calais having been recently completed, a great many wolves, driven by severe winters, had migrated through the tunnel from Europe and Russia to the British Isles.

1

It was dusk – winter dusk. Snow lay white and shining over the pleated hills, and icicles hung from the forest trees. Snow lay piled on the dark road across Willoughby Wold, but from dawn men had been clearing it with brooms and shovels. There were hundreds of them at work, wrapped in sacking because of the bitter cold, and keeping together in groups for fear of the wolves, grown savage and reckless from hunger.

Snow lay thick, too, upon the roof of Willoughby Chase, the great house that stood on an open eminence in the heart of the wold. But for all that, the Chase looked an inviting home – a warm and welcoming stronghold. Its rosy herring-bone brick was bright and well-cared-for, its numerous turrets and battlements stood up sharp against the sky, and the crenellated balconies, corniced with snow, each held a golden square of window. The house was all alight within, and the joyous hubbub of its activity contrasted with the sombre sighing of the wind and the hideous howling of the wolves without.

In the nursery a little girl was impatiently dancing up and down before the great window, fourteen feet high, which faced out over the park and commanded the long black expanse of road.

'Will she be here soon, Pattern? Will she?' was her continual cry.

'We shall hear soon enough, I dare say, Miss Bonnie,' was the inevitable reply from her maid, who, on hands and knees in front of the fire, was folding and goffering the frills of twenty lace petticoats.

The little girl turned again to her impatient vigil She had climbed up on to the window-seat, the better to survey the snowy park, and was jumping on its well-sprung cushions, covered in crimson satin. Each time she bounced, she nearly hit the ceiling.

'Give over, Miss Bonnie, do,' said Pattern after a while. 'Look at the dust you're raising. I can hardly see my tongs. Come and sit by the fire. We shall hear soon enough when the train's due.'

Bonnie left her perch reluctantly enough and came to sit by the fire. She was a slender creature, small for her age, but rosy-cheeked, with a mass of tumbled black locks falling to her shoulders, and two brilliant blue eyes, equally ready to dance with laughter or flash with indignation. Her square chin also gave promise of a powerful and obstinate temper, not always perfectly controlled. But her mouth was sweet, and she could be very thoughtful on occasion – as now, when she sat gazing into the fire, piled high on its two carved alabaster wolfhounds.

'I hope the train hasn't been delayed by wolves,' she said presently.

'*Nonsense*, Miss Bonnie dear – don't worry your pretty head with thoughts like that,' replied Pattern. 'You know the porters and station-master have been practising with their muskets and fowling-pieces all the week.'

At that moment there was a commotion from downstairs, and Bonnie turned, her face alight with expectancy. As the noise of dogs barking, men shouting, and the doorbell clanging continued, she flew recklessly along the huge expanse of nursery floor, gleaming and polished as glass, and down the main staircase to the entrance hall. Her impetuosity brought her in a heap to the feet of an immensely tall, thin lady, clad from neck to toe in a travelling dress of swathed grey twill, with a stiff collar, dark glasses, and dull green buttoned boots. Bonnie's headlong rush nearly sent this person flying, and she recovered her balance with an exclamation of annoyance.

'Who is guilty of this unmannerly irruption?' she said, settling her glasses once more upon her nose. 'Can this hoydenish creature be my new pupil?'

'I – I beg your pardon!' Bonnie exclaimed, picking herself up.

'So I should hope! Am I right in supposing that you are Miss Green? I am Miss Slighcarp, your new governess. I am also your fourth cousin, once removed,' the lady added haughtily, as if she found the removal hardly sufficient.

'Oh,' Bonnie stammered, 'I didn't know – that is, I thought you were not expected until tomorrow. I was looking for my cousin Sylvia, who is arriving this evening.'

'I am aware of the fact,' Miss Slighcarp replied coldly, 'but that does not excuse bad manners. Where, pray, is your curtsy?'

Rather flustered, Bonie performed this formality with less than her usual grace.

'Lessons in deportment, I see, will need priority on our time-table,' Miss Slighcarp remarked, and she turned to look after the disposition of her luggage. 'You, sir! Do not stand there smirking and dawdling, but see that my valises are carried at once to my apartments, and that my maid is immediately in attendance to help me.'

James, the footman, who had been exchanging grimaces with the butler over the fact that he had received no tip, at once sprang to attention, and said:

'Your maid, miss? Did you bring a maid with you?'

'No, blockhead. The maid whom Lady Green will have appointed to wait on me.'

'Well, I suppose Miss Pattern will be helping you,' said James, scratching his head, and he shouldered one of the nine walrus-hide portmanteaux and staggered off to the service stairs.

'I will show you the way to your room,' said Bonnie eagerly, 'and when you are ready I will take you to see Papa and Mamma. I hope we shall love each other,' she continued, leading the way up the magnificent marble staircase, and along the portrait gallery. 'I shall have so much to show you – my collection of flint arrowheads and my semi-precious stones.'

Miss Slighcarp thinned her lips disapprovingly and

Bonnie, fearing that she had been forward, said no more of her pursuits.

'Here is your apartment,' she explained presently, opening a door and exhibiting a commodious set of rooms, cheerful with fires and furnished with elegant taste in gilt and mahogany. 'And here is my maid Pattern to help you.'

Miss Slighcarp drew down her brows at this, but acknowledged the remark by an inclination of her head. Pattern was already kneeling at the dressing-case and drawing out such articles as the governess might immediately need.

'I shall leave you, then, for the moment,' said Bonnie, preparing to go. She turned to add, 'Shall I come back in half an hour?' but was arrested by the sight of Miss Slighcarp snatching a heavy marble hairbrush from its rest and striking a savage blow at the maid, who had taken out a little case apparently containing letters and papers.

'Prying wretch! Who gave you permission to meddle with my letters?' she cried.

Bonnie sprang back in an instant, all her violent temper roused, and seized the brush from Miss Slighcarp's hand, hurling it recklessly through the plate-glass window. She picked up a jug of warm water which a housemaid had just brought, and dashed it full in the face of her new instructress.

Miss Slighcarp reeled under the impact – her bonnet came off, so did her grey hair, which, apparently, was a wig, leaving her bald, dripping, and livid with rage.

'Oh dear – I am so sorry!' said Bonnie in consternation. 'I did not mean to do that. My temper is a dreadful fault. But you must not strike Pattern. She is one of my best friends. Oh Pattern – help her!'

The maid assisted Miss Slighcarp to replace the damp wig and repair the damage done by the water, but her compressed lips and nostrils showed how little she relished the task. An angry red weal was rising on her cheek where the brush had struck her.

'Go!' said Miss Slighcarp to Bonnie, pointing at the door.

Bonnie was glad to do so. Half an hour later, though, she returned, having done her best in the meantime to wrestle with her rebellious temper.

'Shall I escort you to Mamma and Papa now?' she said, when the governess bade her enter. Miss Slighcarp had changed into another grey twill dress with a high white collar, and had laid aside her merino travelling-cloak.

She permitted Bonnie to lead her towards the apartments of her parents, having first locked up several drawers in which she had deposited papers, and placed the keys in a chatelaine at her belt.

Bonnie, whose indignation never lasted long, danced ahead cheerfully enough, pointing out to her companion the oubliette where Cousin Roger had slipped, the panel which concealed a secret staircase, the haunted portico, the priests' hole, and other features of her beloved home. Miss Slighcarp, however, as she followed, wore on her face an expression that boded little good towards her charge.

At length they paused before a pair of doors

grander than any they had yet passed, and Bonnie inquired of the attendant who stood before them if her parents were within. Receiving an affirmative answer, she joyfully entered and, running towards an elegant-looking lady and gentleman who were seated on an ottoman near the fireplace, exclaimed:

'Papa! Mamma! Such a surprise! Here is Miss Slighcarp, come a day earlier than expected!'

Miss Slighcarp advanced and made her salutations to her employers.

'I regret not having come up to London to make arrangements with you myself,' said Sir Willoughby, bowing easily to her, 'but my good friend and man of business Mr Gripe will have told you how we are situated – on the eve of a departure, with so much to attend to. I had been aware that we had a distant cousin – yourself, ma'am – living in London, and I entrusted Mr Gripe with the task of seeking you out and asking whether you would be willing to undertake the care of my estates and my child while we are abroad. My only other relative, my sister Jane, is, as perhaps you know, too frail and elderly for such a responsibility. I hope you and Bonnie will get on together famously.'

Here Miss Slighcarp, in a low and grating tone, told him the story of the hairbrush and the jug of water, omitting, however, her unprovoked assault in the first place upon poor Pattern. Sir Willoughby burst into laughter.

'Did she do that, the minx? Eh, you hussy!' and he lovingly pinched his daughter's cheek. 'Girls will be girls, Miss Slighcarp, and you must allow something for the natural high spirits and excitement attendant on your own arrival and the expected one of her cousin. I shall look to you to instil, in time, a more ladylike deportment into our wild sprite.'

Lady Green, who was dark-haired and sad-eyed, and who looked very ill, here raised her voice wearily and asked her husband if that were not a knock on the door. He called a summons impatiently, and the station-master entered – a black, dingy figure, twisting his cap in his hands.

'The down train is signalled, Squire,' he said, after bobbing his head in reverence to each of the persons present in the room. 'Is it your pleasure to let it proceed?'

'Surely, surely,' said Sir Willoughby. 'My little niece is aboard it — let it approach with all speed. How did you come from the station, my man? Walked? Let orders be given for Solly to drive you back in the chaise – with a suitable escort, of course – then he can wait there and bring back Miss Sylvia at the same time.'

'Oh, thank you indeed, sir,' said the man with heartfelt gratitude. 'Bless your noble heart! It would have taken me a weary while to walk those ten miles back, and it is freezing fast.'

'That's all right,' said Sir Willoughby heartily. 'Mustn't let Miss Sylvia die of cold on the train. Besides, the wolves might get you, and then the poor child would be held up on the train all night for want of the signal. Never do, eh? Well, Bonnie, what is it, miss?'

'Oh, Papa,' said Bonnie, who had been plucking at

his sleeve, 'may I go with Solly in the chaise to meet Sylvia? May I?'

'No indulgence should be permitted a child who has behaved as she has done,' remarked Miss Slighcarp.

'Oh, come, come, Miss Slighcarp, come, come, ma'am,' said Sir Willoughby good-naturedly. 'Young blood, you know. Besides, my Bonnie's as good a shot at a wolf as any of them. Run along, then, miss, but wrap up snug – remember you'll be several hours on the road.'

'Oh, thank you, Papa! Goodbye! Goodbye, Mamma dear, goodbye, Miss Slighcarp!' and she fondly kissed her parents and ran from the room to find her warmest bonnet and pelisse.

'Reckless, foolish indulgence,' muttered the governess, directing after Bonnie a look of the purest spite.

'But hey!' exclaimed Sir Willoughby, recalled to memory of Miss Slighcarp's presence by the sound though he missed the sense, of her words. 'If the train's only just signalled, how did you come, then, ma'am? You can't have flown here, hey?'

For the first time the governess showed signs of confusion.

'I – er – that is to say, a friend who was driving over from Blastburn kindly offered to bring me here with my baggage,' she at length replied.

A bell clanged through the apartment at that moment.

'The dressing-bell,' said Sir Willoughby, looking at a handsome gold watch, slung on a chain across his ample waist-coat. 'I apprehend, Miss Slighcarp, that you are fatigued from your journey and will not wish to dine with us. A meal will be served in your own apartments.'

He inclined his head in a dignified gesture of dismissal, which the governess had no option but to obey.

2

Two days before these events a very different scene had been enacted far away in London, where Bonnie's cousin Sylvia was being prepared for her journey.

Sylvia was an orphan, both her parents having been carried off by a fever when she was only an infant. She lived with her Aunt Jane, who was now becoming very aged and frail and had written to Sir Willoughby to suggest that he took on the care of the little girl. He had agreed at once to this proposal, for Sylvia, he knew, was delicate, and the country air would do her good. Besides, he welcomed the idea of her gentle companionship for his rather harum-scarum Bonnie.

Aunt Jane and Sylvia shared a room at the top of a house. It was in Park Lane, this being the only street in which Aunt Jane could consider living. Unfortunately, as she was very poor, she could afford to rent only a tiny attic in such a genteel district. The room was divided into two by a very beautiful, but old, curtain of white Chinese brocade. She and Sylvia each had half the room at night, Aunt Jane sleeping on the divan and Sylvia on the ottoman. During the daytime the curtain was drawn back and hung elegantly looped against the wall. They cooked their meals over the gas jet, and had baths in a large enamelled Chinese bowl, covered with dragons, an heirloom of Aunt Jane's. At other times it stood on a little occasional table by the door and was used for visiting cards.

They were making Sylvia's clothes.

Aunt Jane, with tears running down her face, had taken down the white curtain (which would no longer be needed) and was cutting it up. Fortunately

it was large enough to afford material for several chemises, petticoats, pantalettes, dresses, and even a bonnet. Aunt Jane, mopping her eyes with a tiny shred of the material, murmured:

'I do like to see a little girl dressed all in white.'

'I *wish* we needn't cut up your curtain, Auntie,' said Sylvia, who hated to see her aunt so distressed. 'When I'm thirty-five and come into my money, I shall buy you a whole set of white brocade curtains.'

'There's my angel,' her aunt replied, embracing her. 'But when you are thirty-five I shall be a hundred and three,' and she set to work making the tucks in a petticoat with thousands of tiny stitches. Sylvia sighed, and bent her fair head over another, with stitches almost equally tiny. She was a little depressed – though she would not dream of saying so – at the idea of wearing nothing but white, especially at her cousin Bonnie's, where everything was sure to be grand and handsome.

'Now let me think,' muttered Aunt Jane, sewing away like lightning. 'What can we use to make you a travelling-cloak?'

She paused for a moment and glanced round the room, at the lovingly tended pieces of Sheraton and Hepplewhite furniture, the antimacassars, the Persian screen across the gas-jet kitchen. The window curtains were too threadbare to use – and in any case one must have window curtains. At last she recollected an old green velvet shawl which they sometimes used as an extra bed-cover when it was very cold and they slept together on the ottoman.

'I can use my jet-trimmed mantle instead,' she said reassuringly to Sylvia. 'After all, one person cannot be so cold as two.'

By the day of departure, all the clothes had been finished. Nothing much could be done about Sylvia's shoes, which were deplorably shabby, but Aunt Jane blacked them with a mixture of soot and candle grease, and Sylvia's bonnet was trimmed with a white plume from the ostrich-feather fan which her aunt had carried at her coming-out ball. All Sylvia's belongings were neatly packed into an old carpetbag, and Aunt Jane had made her up a little packet of provisions for the journey, though with strict injunctions not to eat them if there were anyone else in the compartment.

'For ladies *never* eat in public.'

They were too poor to take a hackney-carriage to the station, and Aunt Jane always refused to travel in omnibuses, so they walked, carrying the bag between them. Fortunately the station was not far, nor the bag heavy.

Aunt Jane secured a corner seat for her charge, and put her under the care of the guard.

'Now remember, my dear child,' she said, kissing Sylvia and looking suspiciously round the empty compartment, 'never speak to strangers, tip all the servants immediately (I have put all the farthings from my reticule at the bottom of your valise); do not model yourself on your cousin Bonnie, who I believe is a dear good child but a little wild; give my fond regards to my brother Willoughby and tell him that I am in the pink of health and *amply* provided for;

and if anyone except the guard speaks to you, pull the communication cord.'

'Yes, Auntie,' replied Sylvia dutifully, embracing her. She felt a pang as she saw the frail old figure struggling away through the crowd, and wondered how her Aunt Jane would manage that evening without her little niece to adjust her curl-papers and read aloud a page of Dr Johnson's Dictionary.

Then all Sylvia's fears were aroused, for a strange man entered the compartment and sat down. He did not speak, however, and took no notice of her, and, the train shortly afterwards departing, her thoughts were diverted into a less apprehensive vein as she watched the unfamiliar houses with their lighted windows flying past.

It was to be a long journey – a night and a day. The hour of departure was six o'clock in the evening, and Sylvia knew that she did not arrive at her destination until about eight of the following evening. What strange forests, towns, mountains, and stretches of countryside would they not have passed by then, as the train proceeded at its steady fifteen miles an hour! She had never been out of London before, and watched eagerly from her window until they had left the houses behind, and she was driven to study the toes of her own shoes, so lovingly polished by Aunt Jane.

The thought of the old lady, carefully preparing for her solitary slumbers, was too much for Sylvia, and tears began to run silently down her cheeks, which she endeavoured to mop with her tiny handkerchief (made from a spare two inches of white brocade).

'Here, this won't do,' said a voice in her ear suddenly, and she looked up in alarm to see that the man at the other end of the compartment had moved along and was sitting opposite and staring at her. Sylvia gave her eyes a final dab and haughtily concentrated on her reflection in the dark window, but her heart was racing. Should she pull the communication cord? She stole a cautious glance at the man's reflection and saw that he was standing up, apparently extracting something from a large leather portmanteau. Then he turned towards her, holding something out: she looked round enough to see that it was a box of chocolates about a foot square by six inches deep, swathed around with violet ribbons.

'No, thank you,' said Sylvia, in as ladylike a tone as she could muster. 'I never touch chocolate.' All the same, she had to swallow rapidly a couple of times, for the tea which she had shared with Aunt Jane before the journey, although very refined, had not been substantial – two pieces of thin bread-and-butter, a cinnamon wafer, and a sliver of caraway cake.

She knew better, however, than to accept food from strangers, and as to opening her own little packet while he was in the carriage – that was out of the question. She shook her head again.

'Now come along – do,' said the man coaxingly. 'All little girls like sweeties, *I* know.'

'Sir,' said Sylvia coldly, 'if you speak to me again I shall be obliged to pull the communication cord.'

He sighed and put away the box. Her relief over

this was premature, however, for he turned round next minute with a confectioner's pasteboard carton filled with every imaginable variety of little cakes – there were jam tarts, maids of honour, lemon cheese cakes, Chelsea buns, and numerous little iced confections in brilliant and enticing colours.

'I always put up a bit of tiffin for a journey,' he murmured as if to himself, and, placing the box on the seat directly opposite Sylvia, he selected a cake covered with violet icing and bit into it. It appeared to be filled with jam. Sylvia looked straight ahead and ignored him, but again she had to swallow.

'Now my dear, how about one of these little odds and ends?' said the man. 'I can't possibly eat them all by myself – can I?'

Sylvia stood up and looked for the communication cord. It was out of her reach.

'Shall I pull it for you?' inquired her fellow-traveller politely, following the direction of her eyes upwards. Sylvia did not reply to him. She did not feel, though, that it would be ladylike to climb up on the seat or arm-rest to pull the cord herself, so she sat down again, biting her lip with anxiety. To her inexpressible relief the stranger, after eating three or four more cakes with every appearance of enjoyment, put the box back in his portmanteau, wrapped himself in a richly furred cloak, retired to his own corner, and shut his eyes. A subdued but regular snore soon issuing from his partly-opened mouth presently convinced Sylvia that he was asleep, and she began to breathe more freely. At length she brought out from concealment under her mantle her most treasured possession, and held it lovingly in her arms.

This was a doll named Annabelle, made of wood, not much larger than a candle, and plainly dressed, but extremely dear to Sylvia. She and Annabelle had no secrets from one another, and it was a great comfort to her to have this companion as the train rocked on through the unfamiliar dark.

Presently she grew drowsy and fell into uneasy slumber, but not for long; it was bitterly cold and her feet in their thin shoes felt like lumps of ice. She huddled into her corner and wrapped herself in the green cloak, envying her companion his thick furs and undisturbed repose, and wishing it were ladylike to curl her feet up beneath her on the seat. Unfortunately she knew better than that.

She dreamed, without being really asleep, of arctic seas, of monstrous tunnels through hillsides fringed with icicles. Her travelling companion, who had grown a long tail and a pair of horns, offered her cakes the size of grand pianos and coloured scarlet, blue, and green; when she bit into them she found they were made of snow.

She woke suddenly from one of these dreams to find that the train had stopped with a jerk.

'Oh! What is it? Where are we?' she exclaimed before she could stop herself.

'No need to alarm yourself, miss,' said her companion, looking unavailingly out of the black square of window. 'Wolves on the line, most likely – they often have trouble of that kind hereabouts.'

'Wolves!' Sylvia stared at him in terror.

'They don't often get into the train, though,' he added reassuringly. 'Two years ago they managed to climb into the guard's van and eat a pig, and once they got the engine-driver – another had to be sent in a relief-engine – but they don't often eat a passenger, I promise you.'

As if in contradiction of his words a sad and sinister howling now arose beyond the windows, and Sylvia, pressing her face against the dark pane, saw that they were passing through a thickly wooded region where snow lay deep on the ground. Across this white carpet she could just discern a ragged multitude pouring, out of which arose, from time to time, this terrible cry. She was almost petrified with fear and sat clutching Annabelle in a cold and trembling hand. At length she summoned up strength to whisper:

'Why don't we go on?'

'Oh, I expect there are too many of 'em on the line ahead,' the man answered carelessly. 'Can't just push through them, you see – the engine would be derailed in no time, and then we *should* be in a bad way. No, I expect we'll have to wait here till daylight now – the wolves get scared then, you know, and make for home. All that matters is that the driver shan't get eaten in the meantime – he'll keep 'em off by throwing lumps of coal at them I dare say.'

'Oh!' Sylvia exclaimed in irrepressible alarm, as a heavy body thudded suddenly against the window, and she had a momentary view of a pointed grey head, red slavering jaws, and pale eyes gleaming with ferocity.

'Oh, don't worry about that,' soothed her companion. 'They'll keep up that jumping against the windows for hours. They're not much danger, you know, singly; it's only in the whole pack you've got to watch out for 'em.'

Sylvia was not much comforted by this. She moved along to the middle of the seat and huddled there, glancing fearfully first to one side and then to the other. The strange man seemed quite undisturbed by the repeated onslaught of the wolves which followed. He took a pinch of snuff, remarked that it was all a great nuisance and they would be late, and composed himself to sleep again.

He had just begun to snore when a discomposing incident occurred. The window beside him, which must have been insecurely fastened, was not proof against the continuous impact of the frenzied and ravenous animals. The catch suddenly slipped, and the window fell open with a crash, its glass shivering into fragments.

Sylvia screamed. Another instant, and a wolf precipitated itself through the aperture thus formed. It turned snarling on the sleeping stranger, who started awake with an oath, and very adroitly flung his cloak over the animal. He then seized one of the shattered pieces of glass lying on the floor and stabbed the imprisoned beast through the cloak. It fell dead.

'Tush,' said Sylvia's companion, breathing heavily and passing his hand over his face. 'Unexpected – most.'

He extracted the dead wolf from the folds of the

cloak and tipped its body, with some exertion, out through the broken window. There was a chorus of snarling and yelping outside, and then the wolves seemed to take fright at the appearance of their dead comrade, for Sylvia saw them coursing away over the snow.

'Come, that's capital,' said the man. 'We'd better shift before they come back.'

'Shift?'

'Into another compartment,' he explained. 'Can't stay in this one now – too cold for one thing, and for another, have wolves popping in the whole time – nuisance. No, come along, now's the time to do it.'

Sylvia was most reluctant, and indeed almost too

terrified to accompany him, but she saw the force of his proposal and watched anxiously as he opened the door and glanced this way and that.

'Right! Just pass me out those bags, will you?' He had placed both his and hers ready on the seat. She passed them out. Holding them in one hand, he made his way sideways along the footboard to the next carriage door, which he opened. He tossed in the bags, returned for his cloak and rug, and finally reappeared and held out his hand to Sylvia.

'Come along now, my dear, if you don't want to be made into wolf-porridge,' he exclaimed with frightening joviality, and Sylvia timorously permitted him to assist her along the narrow ledge and into the next carriage. It was with a sense of unbounded relief and thankfulness that she heard him slam the door and make sure that the windows were securely fastened.

'Excellent,' he remarked with a smile at Sylvia which bared every tooth in his head. 'Now we can have another forty winks,' and he wrapped himself up again in his cloak, careless of any wolf gore that might remain on its folds, and shut his eyes.

Sylvia was too cold and terrified to sleep. She crouched, as before, in the middle of the seat – icy, shivering, and expecting at any minute to hear the wolves recommence their attack against the window.

'Here, we can't have this,' said a disapproving voice, and she turned to see the man awake again and scrutinizing her closely. 'Not warm enough, eh? Here . . .' and then as he saw her wince away from his cloak, he unstrapped a warm plaid travelling rug and insisted on wrapping her in it. Tired, frozen, and frightened, Sylvia was unable to resist him any longer.

'Put your feet up and lie down,' he ordered. 'That's right. Now shut your eyes. No more wolves for the time being – they've been scared away. Off to sleep with you.'

Sylvia was beginning to be deliciously warm. Her last recollection was of hearing his snores begin again.

3

When Sylvia woke, it was broad daylight and the train was running through a mountainous region, wooded here and there, and with but few and scattered dwellings. Her companion was already awake, and munching away at an enormous piece of cold sausage.

Sylvia felt herself to be nearly dead of hunger. She remembered Aunt Jane's precept, 'Never eat in front of strangers,' but surely Aunt Jane had not intended her to go for a whole night and a day without taking *some* refreshment? And moreover, the good soul could not have anticipated the dreadful perils that her niece was to encounter, perils which had left Sylvia so weak and faint that she felt she might never reach Willoughby Chase alive unless she could open her little packet and consume some of its contents. Perhaps, she thought, the shared adventure of the wolves formed some sort of an introduction to her fellow-traveller.

She pondered over this matter for some time and at length, driven by her ravenous appetite, and with many timorous glances at the strange man, she opened her carpet-bag and took from her parcel of food one or two of the little dry rolls her aunt had provided — rolls that contained in each a tiny sliver of ham, frail and thin as pink tissue paper. The remainder she put back for later in the day. After this frugal meal she felt greatly restored, and was not too discomposed when she saw that the man, having devoured his sausage down to the twisted end, was now smiling at her in a manner that was evidently intended to be the height of amiability.

'There! Now we both feel better,' he remarked.

'It was most kind of you, sir, to lend me your rug,' Sylvia faltered.

'Couldn't let you freeze to death, m'dear, could I? Not after you'd shown such pluck and spirit over the wolves. Some little gels would have screamed and cried, I can tell you!'

'Will they come back again?' inquired Sylvia, glancing anxiously out. The train was now running across a wide snowy plain, dazzlingly bright under the sun of a clear blue morning.

'Not till this evening,' he told her. 'When we get to the wolds at dusk you can depend on it there'll be wolves there to meet us. No need to worry, though.'

Sylvia looked her doubt of this statement, and he exclaimed, 'Pshaw! Wolves are cowardly brutes! They won't hurt you unless they outnumber you by more than ten to one. If you feel anxious about it I'll get my gun, though I don't generally use it for small fry.'

And to Sylvia's alarm he pulled down a canvas-wrapped bundle that she had taken for fishing-rods and took from it a long, heavy, glinting blue gun.

Opening a smaller bag he brought out a few cartridges and clapped them into the breech. Then, turning to Sylvia – she winced away in alarm – he said, 'Now, my dear, shall I give you a proof of my marksmanship? Shall I, eh?'

'Oh, no, sir, please don't! Please do not! Indeed, indeed, I am sure you can shoot extremely well!'

'Can't be sure till you have seen me! And it will pass the time for us both.'

So saying, he opened the window at one end of the compartment while Sylvia, with her hands to her ears, pressed herself as far as possible into a corner at the other end.

'Now then, what's there to shoot? Can't very well shoot cattle, though it would be a rare joke, ha ha! There's a bunny, bang! Got him – did you see him go head over heels?' Sylvia had seen no such thing, for her hands were over her eyes, and her nose buried in the red-and-black patterned upholstery.

'Now a rook – he's flapping along slowly, I'll wait till we catch him up – there! Tumbled down like a stone. The farmer'll wonder where he came from.'

He fired one or two more shots and then remarked, 'But I mustn't waste all my cartridges, must keep some for the wolves, what?' and put the gun back in its case, carefully cleaning it before he did so. The compartment was reeking with acrid blue smoke and Sylvia was nearly choking.

'There, I never asked if you'd like to try a shot,' the man said, 'but I fancy the gun would be a bit heavy for you, as you're on the small side – a lighter fowling-piece would be the thing for you.'

'Indeed, I hope I shall never need to shoot at all,' said Sylvia, horrified at the very possibility of such an idea.

'Never know when it might come in useful – my old mother used to say that every little girl should be able to cook, play the piano, sing, and shoot.'

Sylvia thought of Aunt Jane's very different catalogue of accomplishments for little girls, in which crewel-work, purse-netting, and making paper doilies took high place, and could not agree with him. The thought of Aunt Jane made her sad once more and she sighed deeply.

'Are you going far?' the man asked. 'Let's get acquainted. My name's Grimshaw – Josiah Grimshaw.'

Sylvia did not much wish to confide in him, but she felt that if she did not talk to him he might get bored and recommence shooting out of the window. Anything was preferable to that. Accordingly she told him her name, and that she was travelling to the house of her uncle, Sir Willoughby Green.

He expressed great interest in this.

'Ah yes, yes indeed. I've heard of Sir Willoughby. Richest man in five counties, isn't he?'

Sylvia knew nothing of that.

'And you'll have a fine time there, eh? Shall you be staying there long?'

'Oh yes. You see, my dear mamma and papa are dead, and so I am to live there now with my cousin Bonnie.'

'And your uncle and aunt will look after you,' he said, nodding.

'Oh, not for very long,' she told him. 'My poor aunt Sophia is very delicate, and it is necessary for my uncle to take her on a voyage south for her health, so they will be leaving very soon after I get there. My poor cousin Bonnie, how she will miss them! But we shall have a governess who is related to us, and of course there are many servants there to look after us. And I hope that Aunt Sophy will soon be better and come back to England – Aunt Jane says that she is so pretty and kind!'

He nodded again.

Afternoon was now come upon them – grey, with promise of more snow. The train had left the levels and was running into more upland country – waste, wide, and lonely, with not a living thing stirring across its bare and open expanses. It was bleak and forbidding, and Sylvia shivered a little, thinking what a long way there was yet to go before she reached her unknown destination.

The day dragged on. To her relief Mr Grimshaw presently fell asleep again and sat snoring in his corner. Sylvia took out Annabelle once more and showed her the landscape – it seemed to her that the poor doll looked somewhat startled and dismayed at the dreary prospect, which was not surprising, since her painted eyes had never before surveyed anything wilder than Hyde Park on a sunny morning.

'Never mind, Annabelle,' Sylvia said, comforting her, 'we'll be there soon, and there will be warm fires and many beautiful things to look at. I expect Bonnie will have many doll-friends for you to play with. Oh dear, I only hope they won't laugh at you in your funny little old pelisse!'

She felt rather self-reproachful about Annabelle's old clothes, but there really had not been a scrap of the white curtain left by the time her own outfit had been completed. She consoled herself and the doll as best she could, and presently sang some quiet songs in an undertone when it seemed fairly sure, judging by the loudness of Mr Grimshaw's snores, that she would not wake him with her singing.

At length darkness came, and poor Sylvia was dismayed by the sight, while it was yet dusk, of many animal shapes streaming in a broken formation across the snow. She heard again that lonely, heart-shaking cry of the wolves and wondered whether to waken Mr Grimshaw and tell him.

But the train chugged on its way without slowing, and the wolves came and went in the shadows of the trees, never approaching very near, so that she felt it would be cowardly to disturb him, and as long as there was no immediate danger she greatly preferred to let him sleep on.

It was now quite dark, and Sylvia wished very much that she had some means of knowing the time. Mr Grimshaw had a great gold watch in his waistcoat, but this was covered up, and she could not tell whether she was likely soon to reach her journey's end. She had been in readiness since twilight,with the last little hard roll eaten and the carpet-bag buckled up, and Annabelle safely tucked away under her cloak once more.

All at once there was a grinding jerk and the train

came with violent abruptness to a halt, the wheels screeching in protest and the windows almost starting from their frames.

'Oh, what has happened? What can it be?' cried Sylvia.

Mr Grimshaw leapt to his feet and reached upwards to pull down his portmanteau from the rack. But either from clumsiness or on account of the jolt with which the next coach struck theirs as it slid to a halt, he gave the case too vigorous a tug. It toppled forward and fell with a most appalling crash directly upon his head, felling him to the floor. He lay apparently stunned.

Sylvia was terrified. She sat utterly fixed for two or three seconds, and then rushed to the window, which had fallen open when the train stopped, and thrust out her head to see if there was anyone to whom she might appeal for help.

Greatly to her relief and joy, she discovered that they had actually stopped at a little forest station. Her portion of the train was at the extreme end of the platform, and the wildly swinging and flickering lamps did not enable her to read the name upon the notice-board, but she saw that a little group of persons carrying lamps and bundles were rapidly approaching down the length of the station, appearing to glance into each compartment in turn as they proceeded. She could not distinguish individuals of the group, but gathered an impression of urgency from their manner, an impression which was intensified by some indistinguishable shouts from the engine-driver, borne back on the wind.

'Help!' called Sylvia, leaning from her window. 'Help, please!'

She was afraid that her faint cry would not be heard, but at least one member of the group responded to it, for there was an answering halloo, and a small figure detached itself from the rest and darted forward.

'Sylvia! Is it you?'

Sylvia had hardly time to register more than a pair of bright, dark eyes, rosy cheeks, black locks escaping from under a little fur cap, before with a cry of 'Mind, now, Miss Bonnie, don't get so far ahead!' a man had come up and was busy undoing the fastening of the compartment door.

'Miss Sylvia, is it, miss? We'll soon have you out of there,' he called cheerily, wrestling with the frozen and snow-covered handle, while Bonnie somewhat impeded his activities, dancing up and down, blowing kisses to Sylvia, and crying, 'Poor dear Sylvia, you must be frozen! Never mind, you'll soon be warm and snug, we have a foot-warmer and ever so many blankets in the carriage. Oh, how I am going to love you! What fun we shall have!'

Sylvia responded heartily to these overtures, and then exclaimed urgently to the man, who had now undone the door, 'There is a gentleman here in need of assistance. I greatly fear that he has been stunned by his suitcase. Pray, pray, can you help him?'

'Let's have a look at him, then, miss,' the man said. 'You pop out with Miss Bonnie and let James take you back to the carriage. That will be safest for you.'

But Bonnie exclaimed, all interest, 'A man hurt?

Oh, the poor fellow! We must help him, Solly. We had better take him home.'

The other members of the group had come up by now, and there was clamour and discussion.

'What's to be done? Can't leave the poor gentleman in the train like that, 'tis another two hours to Blastburn and like as not he'd freeze to death.'

'Well, whatever you do,' said a whiskered man in a flat cap who appeared to be the station-master, 'do it quick, or the wolves'll settle the matter. Hark, I hear them now! We've not a moment to spare.' And an anxious toot from the engine-driver's whistle seemed to indicate that he was likewise of this opinion.

'Take him out, then,' cried Bonnie, 'put him in the carriage! I am sure my father would wish it.' And James and Solly agreeing, Mr Grimshaw and his luggage were lifted forth, together with Sylvia's carpet-bag, the door was slammed, and the guard waved his green lamp. Smoke and sparks puffed back on the wind as the engine heaved itself under way and the train slowly ground forward, the guard nimbly swung himself on board as the rear of the train passed them, and Sylvia, glancing back as she was hurried along the platform by Bonnie's eager hand, saw its serpent-line of lights disappear winding through the trees. Now the grinding and hissing of the engine was gone, Sylvia could hear the howls of wolves, distinct and frightening, and she understood the haste of the party to be gone.

She received a confused impression of the small station building, with its fringed canopy and scarlet-painted seats, as she was hustled through, and then they came to the neat little carriage in front of which six black horses were steaming, stamping, and shivering under their rugs, as impatient as the humans to be off.

'Lay him on the seat!' cried Bonnie. 'That's it, James! Now wrap a rug over him, so – is his luggage all there? Capital. Now Sylvia, spring in!' But poor Sylvia was too exhausted and cold to manage it, and James the footman lifted her carefully up and deposited her on the opposite seat, wrapping her in a beautiful soft blue merino rug and placing her feet upon a foot-warmer. Bonnie snuggled in beside her and cried, 'Now we can go!'

And indeed, it was only just in time. As James and Solly swung themselves up and the station staff dashed inside their little edifice, there was a chorus of yelps and howls, and the first of a considerable pack of wolves came loping into the station yard. There was a flash and a deafening report as James fired his musket among them. Solly whipped up the horses, who needed no whipping, and the carriage seemed almost to spring off the ground, so rapid was the motion with which it left the building and lights behind.

There had been a new fall of snow and their progress was silent as they flew over the carpeted ground, save for the muffled hoof-beats and the cry of the wolves behind them.

'Those poor men in the station!' exclaimed Sylvia. 'Will they be safe?'

'Oh yes,' Bonnie told her reassuringly. 'They have

plenty of ammunition. We always bring them some when we come, and food too – and the wolves can't get in. It's only troublesome when a train has to stop and people get out. But tell me about that poor man – what is the matter with him? Was he taken ill?'

'No, it was his portmanteau that fell on him and knocked him unconscious,' Sylvia explained. 'The train stopped with such a jerk.'

'Yes, the drivers always do that. You see, if the wolves notice a train slowing down, they are on the alert at once, and all start to run towards the station, so as to be there when the passengers get out. Consequently, if a train has to stop here, the driver goes as fast as he can till the very last moment, in order to deceive them into thinking that he is going straight through. But now tell me about yourself,' said Bonnie, affectionately passing an arm round Sylvia and making sure that she was well wrapped up. 'Did you have a pleasant journey? Are you hungry? Or thirsty?'

'Oh no, thank you. I had some provisions with me for the train. We had quite a pleasant journey. A wolf jumped into our compartment last night, but Mr Grimshaw – that gentleman – stabbed it to death and we moved into another compartment.'

'Is he a friend of yours?' Bonnie said, nodding over this incident.

'Oh dear no! I had never seen him before. Indeed, I did not like him *very* much,' Sylvia confessed. 'He seemed so strange, although I believe he meant to be kind.'

The two children were silent for a moment or two,

as the carriage galloped on its way. The soft rugs were delicious to Sylvia, and the grateful warmth of the foot-warmer as it struck upwards, gradually thawing her numbed and chilled feet, but the sweetest thing of all was the friendly pressure of Bonnie's hand and the loving brightness of her smile as she turned, every now and then, to scan her cousin.

'I can't believe you are really here at last!' she said. 'I wonder which of us is the taller? What delightful times we shall have! Oh, I can't wait to show you everything – the ponies – my father has bought a new little quiet one for you, in case you are not used to riding – and the hot-house flowers, and my collections, and the wolf-hounds. We shall have such games! And in the summer we can go for excursions on the wolds with the pony-trap. If only Mamma and Papa did not have to go away it would be quite perfect.'

She sighed.

'Poor Bonnie,' said Sylvia impulsively, squeezing her cousin's hand. 'Perhaps it will not have to be for very long.' She received a grateful pressure in return, and they were silent again, listening to the crunch of the wheels on the snow and the cry of the wolf-pack, now becoming fainter behind them in the distance.

There was something magical about this ride which Sylvia was to remember for the rest of her life – the dark, snow-scented air blowing constantly past them, the boundless wold and forest stretching away in all directions before and behind, the tramp and jingle of the horses, the snugness and security of the carriage, and above all Bonnie's happy welcoming presence beside her.

After a time Bonnie said, 'I wonder how that poor man is. What did you say was his name?'

'Mr Grimshaw.'

Bonnie leaned across and plucked gently at his hand. 'Mr Grimshaw? Mr Grimshaw? Are you any better?' But there was no reply. 'He must be unconscious still,' she said. 'I wish we had some restoratives to give him – however, we shall be at home in another hour. Pattern and Mrs Shubunkin will know what to do for him. Pattern is my maid – and oh! such a dear – and Mrs Shubunkin is the housekeeper.'

Presently Sylvia began to nod, and found her eyelids closing despite all her efforts to keep awake. But she had hardly more than dozed off when the carriage stopped with a clattering and a barking of dogs, and many shouts of greeting. Looking eagerly out of the window, she saw the great, rosy, glittering facade of Willoughby Chase, with every window shining a golden welcome. They had arrived.

Bonnie did not wait for James to open the carriage door. She had it unlatched in a moment and leaped out into the snow, turning to help her cousin with affectionate care. Sylvia was stiff and dazed with fatigue, and as Bonnie led her tenderly up the great curving flight of steps and into the hall she received only a vague impression of many lights and much warmth, people rushing hither and thither, and a kindly voice (that of Pattern, the maid) saying, 'Poor little dear, she is wearied to death. James, do you

carry her upstairs while I ask Mrs Shubunkin for a posset.'

The posset came, steaming, sweet, and delicious, and Pattern's gentle hands removed Sylvia's travelling clothes. Sylvia was too sleepy to study her surroundings before she was placed between soft, smooth sheets and sank deep into dreamless slumber.

Later in the night she awoke, and saw stars shining beyond the white curtain at her bed's foot. Suddenly she recalled Aunt Jane's voice, teaching her astronomy: 'There is Orion, Sylvia dear, and the constellation resembling a W is Cassiopeia.' Oh, poor Aunt Jane! Would she be lying awake too, watching the stars? Would she be warm enough under the jet-trimmed mantle? What would she do at breakfast-time with no niece to warm the teapot, brew the Bohea, and make the toast-gruel?

Tears began to run down Sylvia's cheeks and she drew a long breath, trying to suppress her silent sobs.

The next moment she heard feet patter across the carpet, and two small, comforting arms came round her neck. A cheek was rubbed lovingly against her wet one.

'What is it, Sylvia dear? Are you homesick? Shall I come into bed with you?'

Sylvia was on the point of revealing her worries about Aunt Jane. Then she realized that she must not. Aunt Jane's pride would not let her accept help from her brother, and so Sylvia must not disclose that she was lonely and cold and poor. But oh, somehow she must find a means of helping her aunt – she must! She must!

'Don't cry,' Bonnie whispered. 'This is your home now, and we shall do such delightful things together. I am sure I can make you happy.' She hugged Sylvia again, and, slipping into the bed, began telling her of all the plans she had, for sledging and skating, and picking primroses in spring, and days on the moors in summer. Sylvia could not help being cheered by this happy prospect, and soon both children fell asleep, the dark head and the fair on one pillow.

4

Next morning the children had breakfast together in the nursery, which was gay with the sunshine that sparkled on crystal and silver and found golden lights in the honey and quince preserve.

Miss Slighcarp, it seemed, was to take her meals in her own apartments, and of this Sylvia was glad, for when she met the governess after breakfast she found her a somewhat frightening lady, cold and severe and forbidding. However, Aunt Jane had taught Sylvia well, and in many respects it was found that she was ahead of Bonnie.

'You will have to work, miss,' said Miss Slighcarp curtly to Bonnie. 'You will have to work hard to catch up with your cousin.'

'I am glad,' said Bonnie, hugging Sylvia. 'I want to work hard. It is delightful that you are so clever, we shall study all sorts of interesting things, botany and Greek and the use of the globes.'

They did not do many lessons that morning. After they had lain on their backboards while Miss Slighcarp read them a short chapter of Egyptian history, they were dismissed to their own devices. Sir Willoughby and Lady Green would be departing at midday, and he wanted to instruct Miss Slighcarp in various matters relating to the running of the estate and household, of which she was to be in charge while he was away.

'Let us go and see how poor Mr Grimshaw is this morning,' Bonnie proposed. 'I am longing to take you to Mamma and Papa, but Miss Slighcarp is with them now. We will wait until she comes back.'

They ran along to the chamber where the unfortunate traveller had been placed, and found there an elderly whiskered gentleman, Dr Morne, in consultation with round, rosy Mrs Shubunkin, the housekeeper. They

curtsied to the doctor, who patted their heads absently.

'It is a most unusual case,' he was saying to Mrs Shubunkin. 'The poor gentleman has recovered consciousness, but he has clean lost all recollection of his name and address and who he is. I have ordered him some medicines, and he must be kept very quiet and remain in bed until his memory returns. I will go and speak to Sir Willoughby on the matter.'

'Perhaps if he were to see Sylvia he would remember the train journey,' Bonnie suggested. 'He told you his name, did he not, Sylvia?'

'Yes – Mr Grimshaw, Josiah Grimshaw.'

'It would be worth a trial,' the doctor agreed, and, a footman just then arriving to inform him that Sir Willoughby was at liberty, he left them, while the children ventured unescorted into Mr Grimshaw's chamber.

What was their surprise to discover that the patient was not in bed but up and standing by the fire, wrapped in a crimson plush dressing-gown! Moreover, he seemed to have been burning papers, for the fireplace was full of black ash, and the room of blue smoke. He started violently as they entered, slammed shut the lid of a small dispatch-box, and flung himself back into bed.

'What the deuce are you going here?' he growled. 'Who are you?'

'Don't you remember Sylvia, Mr Grimshaw?' said Bonnie. 'I am Bonnie Green, and Sylvia is my cousin who travelled with you on the train yesterday.'

'Never seen her in my life before. And name's not

Grimshaw,' he snapped. 'Don't know what it is, but not Grimshaw.'

'He's wandering, poor fellow,' whispered Bonnie. 'He must have got out of bed in delirium. We had best send Mrs Shubunkin to sit with him and see he does not do himself a mischief.'

Mr Grimshaw was plainly most displeased at their presence in his room, so they went off to tell the housekeeper that the invalid should not be left alone.

'Now come,' said Bonnie then, taking her cousin's hand, 'Papa and Mamma must be free now, for I saw Miss Slighcarp downstairs as we crossed the stair-head.

When they reached Lady Green's sitting-room, they found the doctor there speaking with Sir Willoughby.

'And so you will let this poor man remain here so long as he is in need of attention?' the doctor was saying. 'That is most kind of you, Sir Willoughby, and like your liberality.'

'Eh, well,' Sir Willoughby said, 'couldn't turn the poor fellow out into the snow, what? Plenty of room here. He can remain till he gets his wits back – till we return, if need be. Looking after him will give the servants something to do while we are away. You'll come in and see him from time to time, Morne?'

The doctor departed, promising careful attendance on the stranger and wishing Lady Green a speedy return to health.

'Nothing like a sea voyage, dear lady, to bring roses back to the cheeks.'

'And so this is Sylvia,' said Lady Green very kindly,

when the doctor had gone. 'I hope that you and Bonnie are going to be dear friends and look after one another when we are away.'

'Oh yes, Mamma!' Bonnie exclaimed. 'I love her already. We are going to be so happy together . . .'

Then her face fell and her bright colour faded, for at that moment Lady Green's maid entered the room with wraps and a travelling-mantle.

'Are you leaving *now* Mamma? So soon?'

'It wants but five minutes to midday, my child,' said Lady Green as she wearily allowed herself to be swathed in her cloak. Sylvia observed how thin her aunt's wrists were, how languid her beautiful dark eyes.

Silently the children followed downstairs in the bustle of departure. Servants darted here and there, mound upon mound of boxes went out to the chaise, Sir Willoughby tenderly supported his wife to the hall door. There she enveloped Bonnie in a long and loving embrace, had a warm kiss, too, for Sylvia, and, pale as death, allowed herself to be lifted into the carriage. They saw her face at the window, with her eyes fixed yearningly on Bonnie.

'It won't be long, Mamma,' Bonnie called. Her voice was strained and dry.

'Not long, my darling.'

'Be good children,' said Sir Willoughby hurriedly. 'Mind what Miss Slighcarp tells you, now.' He pressed a golden sovereign into each of their hands, and jumped quickly into the carriage after his wife. 'Ready, James!'

The whip cracked, the mettlesome horses blew

great clouds of steam into the frosty air, and they were off. The carriage whirled over the packed snow of the driveway, passed beyond a grove of leafless trees, and was lost to view.

Without a word, Bonnie turned on her heel and marched up the stairs and along the passages to the nursery. Sylvia followed, her heart swollen with compassion. She longed to say some comforting words, but could think of none.

'It may not be long, Bonnie,' she ventured at length.

Bonnie sat at the table, her hands tightly clenched together. 'I will not, I *will* not cry,' she was saying to herself.

At Sylvia's anxious, loving, compassionate voice she took heart a little, and gave her cousin a smile. 'After all,' she thought, 'I am lucky to have Papa and Mamma even if they have gone away; poor Sylvia has no one at all.'

'Come,' she said, jumping up, 'the sun is shining. I will show you some of the grounds. Let us go skating.'

'But Bonnie dear, I have no skates, and I do not know how.'

'Oh, it is the easiest thing in the world, I will soon show you; and as for skates, Papa thought of that already, look . . .' Bonnie pulled open a cupboard door and showed six pairs of white kid skating-boots, all different sizes. 'We knew your feet must be somewhere near the same size as mine, since we are the same age, so Papa had several different pairs made and we thought one of them was certain to fit.'

Sure enough, one of the pairs of boots fitted exactly. Sylvia was much struck by this thought on the part of her uncle, and astonished at the lavishness of having six pairs made for one to be chosen.

Likewise, Pattern pulled out a whole series of white fur caps and pelisses, and tried them against Sylvia until she found ones that fitted. 'I've hung your green velvet in the closet, miss,' she said. 'Green velvet's all very well for London, but you want something warmer in the country.'

Sylvia could not help a pang as she remembered the cutting of the green velvet shawl and saw the sumptuous pile of white fur; how she wished she might send one of the pelisses to Aunt Jane. But next moment Bonnie caught her hand and pulled her to the door.

'Don't go outside the park now, Miss Bonnie,' Pattern said.

'We won't,' Bonnie promised.

Snug in their furs, the two children ran out across the great snow-covered slope in front of the house, through the grove, and down to where a frozen river meandered across the park, after falling over two or three artificial cascades, now stiff and gleaming with icicles.

The children sat on a garden bench to put on their skates. Then, with much laughter and encouragement. Bonnie began to show Sylvia how to keep her balance on the ice.

'Why, Sylvia, you might have been born to it, you are a thousand times better than I was when I began.'

'Perhaps it is because Aunt Jane took such pains

teaching me to curtsy and dance the gavotte balancing Dr Johnson's Dictionary on my head,' Sylvia suggested, as she cautiously glided across to the opposite snow-piled bank and then hurriedly returned to the safety of Bonnie's helping hand.

'Whatever the reason, it is perfectly splendid! We can go right down the river to the end of the park, much farther skating than we can walking. The wolves, you see, cannot catch us on the ice.'

'Is the river frozen all the way down?'

'Yes, all the way to the sea. Oh, I can't wait for you to see this countryside in summer,' Bonnie said, as they skated carefully downstream. 'The river is not nearly so full then, it is just a shallow, rocky stream, and we bathe, and paddle, and the banks are covered with heather and rockrose, it is so pretty.'

'Is it far to the sea?'

'Oh, far — far. Fifty miles. First you come to Blastburn, which is a hideous town, all coal tips and ugly mills. Papa goes there sometimes on business. And then at the sea itself there is Rivermouth, where Papa and Mamma will go on board their ship the *Thessaly*.' Bonnie sighed and skated a few yards in silence. 'Why!' she exclaimed suddenly, 'is not that Miss Slighcarp over there? It is not very safe to go walking so near the park's boundary. The wolves have more than once been known to get in. I wonder if she knows, or if we should warn her?'

'Are you sure it is Miss Slighcarp?' said Sylvia, straining her eyes to study the grey figure walking beside a distant coppice.

'I think it is. Are you tired, Sylvia? Can you

manage another half-mile? If we continue down the river it will curve round and bring us near to her. I think we should remind her about the wolves.'

Sylvia protested that she was not at all tired, that she could easily skate for another hour, two hours if necessary, and, increasing their speed, the children hastened on down the frozen stream. The bank soon hid Miss Slighcarp from their sight.

'It is very imprudent of her,' Bonnie commented. 'I suppose, coming from London, she does not realize about the wolves.'

Sylvia, secretly, began to be a little anxious. They seemed to have come a very long way, the house was nearly out of sight across the rolling parkland, and when they rounded the curve of the river they saw that Miss Slighcarp had cut across another ridge and was almost as far from them as ever. Sylvia's legs and back, unused to this form of exercise, began to feel tired and to ache, but she valiantly strove to keep up with the sturdier Bonnie.

'Just round this next bend,' Bonnie encouraged her, 'and then we *must* meet her. If not, I do not know what we can do – we shall have reached the park boundary, and moreover, the river runs into woods here, and the ice is treacherous and full of broken branches.'

They passed the bend and saw a figure – but not the figure they expected. A stout woman in a red velvet jacket was walking away from them briskly into the wood. She was not Miss Slighcarp, nor in the least like her.

'It isn't she!' exclaimed Sylvia.

At the sound of her voice the woman swung round sharply and seemed to give them an angry look. Then she hurried on into the wood and disappeared. A moment later they heard the sound of horses' hoofs and the rumbling of carriage wheels.

'How peculiar! Can we have been mistaken? But no, we could not have confused a grey dress with a red one,' Sylvia said.

Bonnie was frowning. 'I do not understand it! What can a strange woman in a carriage have been doing in our woods? The road runs through there, but it goes nowhere save to the house.'

'Perhaps when we get back we shall find her. Perhaps she is a neighbour come calling,' Sylvia suggested.

Bonnie shook her head. 'There are no neighbours.' Then she seized Sylvia's arm. 'Look! *There* is Miss Slighcarp!' Sure enough, the grey figure they had first observed was now to be seen, far away behind them, walking swiftly in the direction of the house.

'She must have turned back when we were between the high banks,' Bonnie said repentantly. 'And I have brought you so far! Poor Sylvia, I am afraid that you are dreadfully tired.'

'Nonsense!' Sylvia said stoutly. 'We had to come. And I shall manage very well.'

But she was really well-nigh exhausted, and could not help skating more and more slowly. Bonnie bit her lip and looked anxious. The sky was becoming overcast with the promise of more snow, and, worse, it would not be long until dusk.

'I have done very wrong,' Bonnie said remorsefully. 'I should have made you turn back, and come on myself.'

'I should not have let you.'

A sudden wind got up, and sent loose snow from the banks in a scurry across the grey ice. One or two large flakes fell from the sky.

'Can you go a little faster?' Bonnie could not conceal the anxiety in her tone. 'Try, Sylvia!'

Sylvia exerted herself valiantly, but she was really so tired that she could hardly force her limbs to obey her.

'I am so stupid!' she said, half-laughing, half-crying. 'Suppose I sit here on the bank, Bonnie, while you go home for assistance?'

Bonnie looked as if she were half-considering this proposal when a low moaning sound rose in the distance, a sound familiar to Bonnie, and, since yesterday, full of terrible significance for Sylvia. It was the far-off cry of wolves.

'No, that is not to be thought of,' Bonnie said decisively. 'I have a better plan. We must take off our skates. Can you manage? Make haste, then!'

They sat on a clump of rush by the river's edge, and with chilled fingers tugged at the knots in their bootlaces. Sylvia shivered as once again the wolf-cry stole over the frozen parkland; it had been bad enough heard from the train, but *now*, when there was nothing between them and those pitiless legions, how dread it sounded!

The children stood up, slinging their skates round their necks.

'Now we must climb this little hill,' Bonnie said.

'Here, I'll take your hand. Can you run? Famous! Sylvia, you are the bravest creature in the world, and when we get home I shall give you my little ivory workbox to show how sorry I am for having led you into such a scrape.'

Sylvia did her best to smile at her cousin, having no breath to answer, and tried to stifle all doubts that they ever *would* get home.

Arrived at the top of the hill, Bonnie stood still and, as it seemed to Sylvia, wasted precious moments while she glanced keenly about her through the rapidly thickening snowstorm.

'Ah!' she cried presently. 'The temple of Hermes! We must go this way.' She tugged Sylvia at a run down the slope and across a wide intervening stretch of open ground towards a little pillared pavilion that stood on an artificial knoll against some dark trees. They had now put the river between them and the cry of the wolves, which was comforting, but Sylvia was dismayed to see that Bonnie was once more leading her away from the house.

'Where are we going, Bonnie?' she panted, fighting bravely to keep up.

'I have a friend who lives in the woods,' Bonnie returned. 'I only hope he is not away. Let us rest a moment here.'

They stood struggling to get their breath in the temple of Hermes, which was no more than a roof supported on slender columns.

'Oh, Bonnie, look, look!' Sylvia cried in uncontrollable alarm, pointing back the way they had come. Through the dusk they could just distinguish two small black dots at the top of the slope, which were soon joined by several others. After a moment all these dots began coursing swiftly down the hillside in their direction.

'There is not a moment to be lost,' Bonnie said urgently. 'Make haste, make haste!' Half-leading, half-supporting the exhausted Sylvia, she urged her on through the deepening wood. Here Bonnie seemed to know her way almost by instinct. She passed from tree to tree, scanning them, apparently, for signs invisible to her cousin.

'Here we are!' she exclaimed in a tone of unutterable thankfulness, and, to Sylvia's astonishment, she put her fingers to her lips and gave vent to a long, clear whistle. More surprising still, she was instantly answered by another whistle which seemed to come from the very ground beneath their feet.

A clear, ringing voice called, 'Here, Miss Bonnie! Here, quick!'

Sylvia found a lithe, bright-eyed boy beside her, helping her on. Taller than Bonnie, he was dressed entirely in skins. He wore a fur cap, carried a bow, and had a sheaf of arrows slung over his shoulder.

As the first of the wolf-pack found their track in the temple of Hermes and came raging after, along the clear scent, the boy turned, fitted an arrow to his bow, and sent it unerringly into the midst of the pursuers. One wolf fell, and his companions immediately hurled themselves upon him with starving ferocity.

'That gives us a breathing-space!' the boy exclaimed. 'Inside, Miss Bonnie! Don't lose a moment.'

With Bonnie tugging at her hand, and the boy guarding the rear, threatening the wolves with his bow, Sylvia found herself whisked down a long narrow path, or passage-way, snow-lined at first, then floored with dead leaves. It was dark, she was in a cave! And more curious still, she could feel a number of live creatures pushing against her legs, almost overbalancing her. They were soft and smooth, and she could hear an angry hissing coming from them which almost drowned the clamour of the wolves outside. She would have cried out in fright if she had had any breath left – and then she and Bonnie rounded a corner in the passage and saw before them the comfortable glow of a fire burning on a sandy hearth.

Heaped-up piles of ferns and dead leaves, covered with furs, lay against the cave walls, and on these Bonnie and Sylvia flung themselves, for even Bonnie could now acknowledge that she was nearly fainting from weariness.

'There!' said the boy, following them in. 'I've shut the gate. They'll not catch you this time! But what was you doing, Miss Bonnie, so far from the house on a night like this? It's not like you to take such a foolish risk.'

As Bonnie began explaining how it had come about, Sylvia was amazed to see a number of large white geese waddle after the boy into the cave. They looked rather threateningly out of their flat, black, beady eyes at Sylvia and Bonnie. One or two of them thrust out their necks and hissed, but the boy waved them back into the passage and flung them a handful of corn to keep them quiet.

Lulled by the flickering firelight and the long white necks weaving up and down in the entrance as the geese pecked their corn, Sylvia, who was half-stupefied by exhaustion, fell fast asleep.

When she awoke it was to the sound of voices. Bonnie was saying anxiously:

'But Simon, we cannot stay here all night! My dear Pattern will be so worried! She will be certain the wolves have got us. And Miss Slighcarp, too, will be concerned. Perhaps they have already sent the men out searching for us.'

'I'll have a look in a moment,' the boy returned. 'Now, if you'll wake your cousin, miss, the cakes are ready, and you'll both feel better on full stomachs than empty.'

He spoke with a pleasant country burr. Sylvia, lying drowsy on her heap of leaves, thought that his voice had a comfortable, brown, furry sound to it.

'Sylvia! Wake up!' Bonnie said. 'Here's Simon made us some delicious cakes. And if you are like me you are ravenous with hunger.'

'Indeed I am!' Rubbing her eyes and smiling, Sylvia brushed off the leaves and sat up.

The boy had separated the fire into two glowing hillocks. From between these he now pulled a flat stone on which were baking a number of little cakes. The two children ate them hungrily as soon as they were cool enough to hold. They were brown on the outside, white and floury within, and sweet to the taste.

'Your cakes are splendid, Simon,' Bonnie said. 'How do you make them?'

'From chestnut flour, Miss Bonnie. I gather up the chestnuts in the autumn and pound them to flour between two stones.'

While they were eating he went along the entrance-passage. In a minute he came back to say, 'Wolves have gone, and it's a fine, sharp night, all spiky with stars. No signs of men out searching, Miss Bonnie. It's my belief we'd best be off now while the way's clear. Do you think you can walk as far as the house now, Miss Sylvia?'

'Oh yes, yes! I feel perfectly rested,' declared Sylvia. But she was obliged to acknowledge when she

stood up that she still found herself stiff and tired, and would be unable to keep up a very fast pace.

'I have badly overtaxed your strength this first day,' exclaimed Bonnie self-reproachfully. 'Still, if you *can* walk, Sylvia, I think we should be off now and save our poor Pattern some hours of dreadful worry.'

'Certainly I can walk,' Sylvia said stoutly, 'let us start at once,' though inwardly her heart quailed somewhat at the thought of the wolves very likely still in the neighbourhood.

'A moment before we start.' The boy Simon dug in shallow sand at the side of the cave and brought out a large leather bottle and a horn drinking-cup. He gave the girls each a small drink from the bottle. It was strong, heady stuff, tasting of honey.

'That will hearten you for the walk,' he said.

'What is it, Simon?'

'Metheglin, miss. I make it in the summer from the heather honey.'

He picked up his bow and flung a few logs on the fire. The children resumed their furs, which they had taken off at their first entry into the warm cave.

'I do love your home, Simon!' Bonnie exclaimed. 'I hate to leave it!'

'*You*, miss?' he said, grinning. 'with your grand house and a different room for each day in the year?'

'Well, yes, of course I love that too, but this is so snug!'

Simon quieted the geese, who raised their necks and hissed as the children passed them.

'I wish I had another weapon to defend you with,'

he muttered. 'One bow is hardly sufficient for three. I will cut you a cudgel when we are outside, Miss Bonnie.'

'I know, Simon!' Bonnie cried. 'My old fowling-piece that I left here that rainy day last autumn! I have never thought of it since. Have you it still?'

'Of course I have,' he said, his face lighting up. 'And carefully oiled, too, with neat's-foot oil. It is in good order, Miss Bonnie. I am glad you reminded me of it — what a fool I was not to think of it before!'

He took it down from where it hung on the passage wall in a leather sack. Bonnie, somewhat to her cousin's alarm and amazement, handled the gun confidently and soon satisfied herself of its being in excellent order and ready to fire.

'Now let us be off,' she said gaily. 'I can keep the villains at a distance with this.'

They went out into the clear, sparkling night. The new snow, which had obliterated both their foot-prints and those of the wolves, made a crisp carpet beneath their feet. Bonnie and Simon kept a vigilant look-out for wolves, and Sylvia did too, though secretly she felt she was almost less afraid of the wolves than of her cousin Bonnie's gun. However, there was no occasion to use the fowling-piece, as the wolves appeared to have left that region for the moment, drawn away, doubtless, by some new quarry.

Their journey back to the house was quiet and uninterrupted.

'It is strange,' remarked Bonnie in a puzzled voice, 'that we do not see men out everywhere with lanterns searching for us. Why, the time I was late back from picking wild strawberries, my father had every man on the estate out with pitchforks and muskets!'

'Aye,' said Simon, 'but your father's from home now, isn't he, Miss Bonnie?'

'Yes he is,' answered Bonnie sighing. 'I suppose that is the reason.'

And she fell into rather a sad silence.

When they reached the great terrace, Bonnie suggested that they should go in by a side entrance, and thus avoid informing Miss Slighcarp of their return.

'For it is possible that Pattern, fearing her anger, has left her in ignorance that we were out,' she suggested thoughtfully. 'I believe Pattern is a little frightened of Miss Slighcarp.'

'I am sure *I* am,' Sylvia agreed. 'There is something so cold and glittering about her eyes, and then her voice is so disagreeable. I dare say that is the reason, Bonnie.'

As they passed a large, lighted window, Bonnie murmured, 'That is the great library, Sylvia, where my father keeps all his books and papers. I will show you over it tomorrow . . . Why, what a curious thing!' she exclaimed. For, glancing in as they walked by, they saw Miss Slighcarp, under the illumination of numerous candles, apparently hard at work searching through a mass of papers. There were papers on chairs, on tables, on the floor. Beyond her, at the far end of the room, similarly engaged, was a gentleman who looked amazingly like Mr Grimshaw. Could it be he? But at the slight noise made by their feet on the snow, Miss Slighcarp turned. She could not see the watchers, who were beyond the lighted area near the window, but she crossed with a decisive step and flung-to the heavy velvet curtains, shutting off the scene within.

'What can she be doing?' Bonnie exclaimed. 'And was not that Mr Grimshaw? Dr Morne said he should not get out of bed!'

'Perhaps she is familiarizing herself with the contents of your father's papers,' Sylvia suggested. 'Did you not say she was to look after the estate? And I am not *sure* that was Mr Grimshaw. We had hardly time to see.'

Arrived at the little postern door, they had scarcely knocked before it was flung open and Pattern had enveloped them in her arms.

'Oh, you naughty, naughty, precious children! How could you? How *could* you? Here's my poor heart been nearly broke in half with fright at thinking you was eaten by the wolves, and Miss Slighcarp saying no such thing, you'd come home soon, and me saying "Begging your pardon, miss, but you don't know this park and these wolves as I do," and begging, *begging* her to tell the men and sound the alarm, but no, my lady knows best what's to be done and it's my belief nothing ever *would* have been done till we found some boots and buttons of you in the snow and the rest all ate up by wolves if you hadn't come home all by yourselves, you good, wicked, precious, naughty lambs – *oh*!' and the faithful Pattern relieved herself by a burst of tears.

'Not by ourselves, Pattern,' said Bonnie, hugging her tightly. 'Simon brought us home. We *were* chased by wolves – though it wasn't exactly our fault – and he hid us in his cave till they were gone.'

'Never will I hear a word said against that boy. Some say he's a wicked, vagabond gipsy, but I say he's the best-hearted, trustiest . . . Ask him in, Miss Bonnie, and I'll give him the Christmas pudding that was too big to go in my lady's valise.'

But the silent Simon, overwhelmed, perhaps, by Pattern's flow of words, had melted away into the night without waiting to be thanked.

'Will he be all right?' breathed Sylvia, big-eyed with horror. 'Won't the wolves get him on the way home?'

'I don't believe they could ever catch him,' Bonnie reassured her. 'He can run so fast! Besides he has his bow, and then, too, he can climb trees and swing from branch to branch if they get near him.'

'Never mind about him, nothing ever hurts Simon,' bustled Pattern, half-pushing, half-pulling them up the little back stairs. 'Come on with you now till I get a posset inside you.'

Cold in spite of their furs, the children were glad to be sat down before a glowing fire in the night nursery, while Pattern scolded and clucked, and brushed the tangles out of their hair, brought in with her own hands the big silver bathtub filled with steaming water, in which bunches of lemon mint had been steeped, giving a deliciously fragrant scent, and bathed them each in turn, afterwards wrapping them in voluminous warm white flannel gowns.

Next she fetched little pipkins of hot, savoury soup, sternly saw every mouthful swallowed, and finally hustled them both into Bonnie's big, comfortable bed with the blue swans flying on its curtains.

'For if there's any nightmares about wolves, at least that way you'll be able to comfort each other,' she muttered. 'And as for Miss Slighcarp, let *her* rest in uncertainty till the morning, for I'm not going to her again. Coming home soon, indeed! As if such a thing were likely!'

And off she tiptoed, leaving a rose-scented nightlight burning and the peaceful crackle of the fire to lull them to sleep.

5

The next morning dawned grey and louring. Snow was falling fast out of the heavy sky, the flakes hurrying down like dirty feathers from a leaking mattress. Pattern let the children sleep late, and though when they woke she cosseted them by giving them breakfast in front of the nursery fire, it was not a happy meal. Sylvia felt stiff and tired from her unusual exertions the day before, while poor Bonnie was thinking every minute of her parents' absence: wondering how they had fared on their journey so far, noticing the sad, unaccustomed quietness of the house, which was generally filled with bustle – servants running to and fro, stamp of horses, and her father shouting his orders because he was too impatient to ring the bell.

Sylvia kindly tried to distract her by asking questions about Simon, the boy in the woods.

'Has he always lived in that cave, Bonnie? It seems so strange! Has he no father or mother?'

Bonnie shook her head. 'None that he knows of. He came to my father four or five years ago, one autumn day, and asked if he might live in that cave in the park; he said that he had been working for a farmer but the man ill-treated him and he had walked half across

England to get away from him. My father asked what he proposed to live on. He said, chestnuts and goose-eggs. He had a goose and a gander that he had reared from chicks. Papa took a fancy to him and told him that he might try it – there are hundreds of chestnut trees in the park – but he said Simon wasn't to come whining to him if he got hungry, he'd have to turn to and work for his living as a garden-boy.'

'And did he?'

'Work as a garden-boy? No, he lived on chestnuts and reared a great many geese. Mrs Shubunkin buys eggs from him, and every spring Simon drives his geese up to London and sells them at the Easter Fair. He gets on famously. Father often says he wishes he had as few worries.' Bonnie sighed.

'I wonder if he will always continue to live in the cave,' Sylvia was beginning, when Pattern came in to clear away the breakfast things.

'Now then, Miss Bonnie and Miss Sylvia, nearly lesson-time, my dearies, so make haste and get dressed.' They had been breakfasting in warm wadded satin dressing-gowns.

'This is not my frock, Pattern,' said Sylvia, looking admiringly at the clothes the maid had brought her. There was a soft, thick woollen dress in a beautiful deep shade of blue that exactly matched her eyes. 'It is a great deal prettier than anything of mine.'

'It's one I ran up for you yesterday, Miss Sylvia,' Pattern said kindly. 'My lady Green, bless her good heart, thought you might be needing some warmer dresses for the country, but didn't like to have anything made for you until she knew what colours suited you best. Before she left yesterday she bade me make up one out of this cloth, which she had ready with a number of others. There!' she added, fastening Sylvia's dress at the back and turning her round. 'If that doesn't bring out the colour of your eyes! And here's some ribbons to match for your hair.'

Sylvia's eyes none the less filled with tears at the thought that her aunt, so ill and grief-stricken at the idea of parting from her home, could still spare time for such thoughtfulness.

'Come along,' said Bonnie, who meanwhile had been hurriedly putting on a dark-red cashmere with a white lace collar, 'we shall be late for our lessons.'

The two children ran to the schoolroom while Pattern carefully folded and put away Sylvia's white dress.

Miss Slighcarp had not yet arrived, and the children beguiled the time by wandering round the room and looking at the many beautiful pictures that hung on its walls; then, as the governess still did not appear, Bonnie took Sylvia through a door leading out of the schoolroom into her toyroom.

This was a large and beautiful apartment, carpeted in blue, its walls white, its ceiling all a-sparkle with gilt stars. In it was every imaginable toy, and many that Sylvia never had imagined even in her most wistful dreams. Occupying the place of honour in the middle of the floor was a stately rocking-horse covered with real grey horsehair, and so cunningly carved that he seemed alive. His crystal eyes shone with intelligence.

'That's 'Dolphus,' said Bonnie, giving him a careless

hug as she passed. 'Then those are all the dolls, in that row of little chairs. The largest is Miranda, the smallest, at this end (she's my favourite) is Conchita.'

Sylvia's hand curled lovingly round Annabelle, hidden in her pocket, but she resolved not to introduce her to this galaxy of beauties until the kind Pattern had accomplished her promise and made a new dress for her from a left-over piece of the blue material. Then, Sylvia thought, Annabelle would be quite presentable, and some of the smaller dolls did not look at all proud.

'This is the dolls' house,' Bonnie said. 'Grown-ups aren't allowed inside, but you can come in, of course, Sylvia, whenever you like.'

The dolls' house, large enough to get into, was a cottage with real thatch (and real canaries nesting in it). There was a balcony, stairs, two storeys, a cooking-stove that really worked, and a lot of genuine Queen Anne furniture, including a beautiful walnut chest full of Queen Anne clothes that fitted the children.

Sylvia was trying a blue velvet cloak against her, and Bonnie was saying, 'Come and look at the other toys, you haven't seen half yet . . .' when they were interrupted by a cough from the schoolroom and hurriedly bundled the clothes back into the chest.

'I'll show you the rest this afternoon,' whispered Bonnie, waving her hand towards a large cupboard in the wall with double glass doors. Sylvia had a tantalizing glimpse of numerous variously-shaped brightly-coloured toys on its shelves as they ran back into the schoolroom.

'I'm so sorry we were not in the room to welcome

you, Miss Slighcarp,' Bonnie began in her impulsive way, and then she stopped abruptly. Sylvia noticed her turn extremely pale.

The governess, who had been examining some books on the shelves, swung round with equal abruptness. She seemed astonished to see them.

'Where have you been?' she demanded angrily, after an instant's pause.

'Why,' Sylvia faltered, 'merely in the next room, Miss Slighcarp.'

But Bonnie, with choking utterance, demanded, 'Why are you wearing my mother's dress?'

Sylvia had observed that Miss Slighcarp had on a draped gown of old gold velvet with ruby buttons, far grander than the grey twill she had worn the day before.

'Don't speak to me in that way, miss!' retorted Miss Slighcarp in a rage. 'You have been spoiled all your life, but we shall soon see who is going to be mistress now. Go to your place and sit down. Do not speak until you are spoken to.'

Bonnie paid not the slightest attention. 'Who said you could wear my mother's best gown?' she repeated. Sylvia, alarmed, had slipped into her place at the table, but Bonnie, reckless with indignation, stood in front of the governess, glaring at her.

'Everything in this house was left entirely to my personal disposition,' Miss Slighcarp said coldly.

'But not her clothes! Not to wear! How *dare* you? Take it off at once! It's no better than stealing!'

Two white dents had appeared on either side of Miss Slighcarp's nostrils.

'Another word and it's the dark cupboard and bread-and-water for you, miss,' she said fiercely.

'I don't care what you say!' Bonnie stamped her foot. 'Take off my mother's dress!'

Miss Slighcarp boxed Bonnie's ears, Bonnie seized Miss Slighcarp's wrists. In the confusion a bottle of ink was knocked off the table, spilling a long blue trail down the gold velvet skirt. Miss Slighcarp uttered an exclamation of fury.

'Insolent, ungovernable child! You shall suffer for this!' With iron strength she thrust Bonnie into a closet containing crayons, globes, and exercise books, and turned the key on her. Then she swept from the room.

Sylvia remained seated, aghast, for half a second. Then she ran to the cupboard door – but alas! Miss Slighcarp had taken the key with her.

'Bonnie! Bonnie! Are you all right? It's I, Sylvia.'

She could hear bitter sobs.

'Don't cry, Bonnie, please don't cry. I'll run after her and beg her to let you out. I dare say she will, once she has reflected. She can't have known it was your mother's *favourite* gown.'

Bonnie seemed not to have heard her. 'Mamma, Mamma!' Sylvia could hear her sobbing. 'Oh, why did you have to go away?'

How Sylvia longed to be able to batter down the cupboard door and get her arms round poor Bonnie! But the door was thick and massive, with a strong lock, quite beyond her power to move. Since she could not attract Bonnie's attention, she ran after Miss Slighcarp.

After vainly knocking at the governess's bedroom

door she went in without waiting for a summons (a deed of exceptional bravery for the timid Sylvia). Nobody was there. The ink-stained velvet dress lay flung carelessly on the floor, crushed and torn, so great had Miss Slighcarp's haste been to remove it.

Sylvia hurried out again and began to search through the huge house, wandering up this passage and down that, through galleries, into golden drawing-rooms, satin-hung boudoirs, billiard-rooms, ballrooms, croquet-rooms. At last she found the governess in the Great Hall, surrounded by servants.

Miss Slighcarp did not see Sylvia. She had changed into what was very plainly another of Lady Green's gowns, a rose-coloured crêpe with aiguillettes of diamonds on the shoulders. It did not fit her very exactly.

She seemed to be giving the servants their wages. Sylvia wondered why many of the maids were crying, and why the men looked in general angry and rebellious, until she realized that Miss Slighcarp was paying them off and dismissing them. When the last one had been given his little packet of money, she announced:

'Now, let but a glimpse of your faces be seen within ten miles of this house, and I shall send for the constables!' Then she added to a man who stood beside her, 'Ridiculous, quite ridiculous, to keep such a large establishment of idle good-for-nothings, kicking their heels, eating their heads off.'

'Just so, ma'am, just so,' he assented. Sylvia was amazed to recognize Mr Grimshaw, apparently quite restored to health, and in full possession of his faculties.

He held a small blunderbuss, and was waving it threateningly, to urge the departing servants out of the great doors and on their way into the snowstorm.

'What a strange thing!' thought Sylvia in astonishment. 'Can he be recovered? Or was he never really ill? Can he have known Miss Slighcarp before? He seemed so different on the train.'

At that moment she heard a familiar voice beside her, in the rapidly-thinning crowd of servants, and found Pattern at her elbow.

'Miss Sylvia, dear! Thank the good Lord I saw you. That wicked Jezebel is paying us all off and sending us away, but she needn't think *I'm* going to go and leave my darling Miss Bonnie. Do you and she come along to the little blue powder-room, Miss Sylvia, this afternoon at five, and we'll talk over what's best to be done.'

'But Bonnie can't! She's locked up!' gasped Sylvia. 'In the schoolroom cupboard!'

'She never has . . . ! *Oh*, what wouldn't I give to get my hands round that she-devil's throat,' muttered Pattern. 'That's because she knew Miss Bonnie would never stand tamely by and let her father's old servants be packed off into the snow. Let her out, Miss Sylvia! Let her out of it quick! She never could endure to be shut up.'

'But I can't! Miss Slighcarp has the key.'

'There's another – in the little mother-of-pearl cabinet in the ante-room where the javelins hang.'

Sylvia did not wait. She remembered how to find her way to the little ante-room, and she flew on winged feet to the mother-of-pearl cabinet. She found the key, ran to the school-room, opened the door, and in no time had her cheek pressed lovingly against Bonnie's tear-stained one.

'Oh, you poor precious! Oh, Bonnie, she's wicked, Miss Slighcarp's really wicked! She's dismissing all the servants.'

'What!' Bonnie was distracted from her own grief and indignation by the tale Sylvia poured out.

'Let us go at once,' she exclaimed, 'at *once*, and stop it!' But when they passed the big schoolroom window they saw the lonely procession of servants, far away, toiling across a snow-covered ridge in the park.

'We are too late,' said Sylvia in despair. Bonnie gazed after the tiny, distant figures, biting her lips.

'Is Pattern gone too?' she asked, turning to Sylvia.

'I believe not. I believe she means to hide somewhere about the house.' Sylvia told Bonnie of Pattern's wish to meet them that afternoon.

'Oh, she is good! She is faithful!' exclaimed Bonnie.

'But will it not be very dangerous for her?' Sylvia said doubtfully. 'Miss Slighcarp threatened to send for the constables if she saw any of the servants near the house. She might have Pattern sent to prison!'

'I do not believe Pattern would let herself be caught. There are so many secret hiding-places about the house. And in any case all the officers are our friends round here.'

At that moment the children were startled by the sound of approaching voices. One of them was Miss Slighcarp's. Sylvia turned pale.

'She must not find you out of the cupboard. Hide, quickly, Bonnie!'

She re-locked the cupboard door, and pocketed the

key. As there was no time to lose, the two children slipped behind the window-curtain. Miss Slighcarp entered with the footman, James.

'As I have done you the favour of keeping you on when all the others were dismissed, sirrah,' she was saying. 'you will have to work for your wages as never before.'

The blue velvet curtains behind which the children stood were pounced all over with tiny crystal disks, encircled with seed-pearls. The little disks formed miniature windows, and, setting her eye to one, Bonnie could see that James's good-natured face wore a sullen expression, which he was attempting to twist into an evil leer.

'First, you must take out and crate all these toys. Put them into packing-cases. They are to be sent away and sold. It is quite ridiculous to keep this amount of gaudy rubbish for the amusement of two children.'

'Yes, ma'am.'

'At dinner-time bring some bread-and-water on a tray for Miss Green, who is locked up in that cupboard.'

'Shall I let her out, ma'am?'

'Certainly not. She is a badly-behaved, ill-conditioned child, and must be disciplined. She may be let out this evening at half past eight. Here is the key.'

'Yes ma'am.'

'The other child, Miss Sylvia Green, may lunch in the schoolroom as usual. Plain food, mind. Nothing fancy. From now on the children are to make their own beds, sweep their own rooms, and wash their own plates and clothes.'

'Yes, ma'am.'

'After dinner I wish you to see to the grooming of the horses and ponies. They are all to be sold save four carriage horses.'

'The children's ponies as well, ma'am?'

'Certainly! I shall find more suitable occupations for the children than such idle and extravagant pursuits! Now I am going to be busy in the Estate Room. You may bring me a light luncheon at one o'clock: chicken, oyster patties, trifle, and a half-bottle of champagne.'

She swept out of the room. The moment she had gone James went quickly to the closet and unlocked it, saying in a low voice, 'She's gone now, Miss Bonnie, you can come out.'

He seemed greatly astonished to find the cupboard empty, but next minute the children ran out from behind the curtain.

'James, James!' cried Bonnie, 'what does it all mean? How dare she sell my toys, and Papa's horses? What is she doing it for?'

'Why, she's wicked!' Sylvia exclaimed indignantly. 'She's a fiend!'

'You're right, miss, she's a thorough wrong 'un,' said James gloomily, when he had got over the surprise of Bonnie's not being in the cupboard after all. 'How your pa came to be so deceived in her I'll never know.'

'But he had never met her! It was arranged that she should come here to look after us by his lawyer in London, Mr Gripe. And after all, she is a relative.'

'Ah, I see,' said James, scratching his head. 'Even so, it's a puzzle to me why Sir Willoughby didn't rumble her when he saw her. One look at her face would be enough to show the sort she is, you'd think. But I suppose he was worried over her ladyship.'

'But James, why is she dismissing the servants, and why has she kept you on?'

'Why, miss, I suppose she means to make hay while the sun shines – save the servants' wages and pop as much of your pa's money into her own pocket as she can while he's away. Then before he comes back, I suppose she'll be off. She's kept on three or four servants, just to look after her, like. The worst of it is, she's kept on all the untrustworthy ones, Groach, the keeper, and Marl, the steward that Sir Willoughby was giving another chance to after he was caught pilfering, and Prout, the under-groom that drinks – I dare say she liked the looks of their knavish faces. I saw how it was going, so I tried to make myself look as hangdog and sullen as I could, and the trick worked: she kept me on too. I couldn't abear to think of you, Miss Bonnie, and Miss Sylvia, being left all alone in the house with that harpy and such a pack of thieves. Poor Pattern had to go; in a mighty taking she was.'

'But she hasn't gone far,' Bonnie told him and explained about the scheme to meet in the little blue powder-room. James's face broke into a slow grin.

'I might ha' known she wouldn't be driven off so easily,' he said. 'Well, we'll have a proper old council then and decide what to do. In the meantime I'd better be getting on with packing up these things, Miss Bonnie, or I shall lose my place and not be able to help you.'

'Pack up my toys? But you *can't*!' exclaimed Bonnie in grief and horror, looking at her treasured things. 'Couldn't you hide them away in one of the attics?'

'Can't be, Miss Bonnie dear. She's going to go through 'em when they're in the boxes. I could save out a few, though, I dare say,' James said pityingly.

Half-distracted, Bonnie looked among her toys, trying to decide which she could bear to part with – 'Dolphus must go, for he would be missed, and so must the dolls' house and the bigger dolls, but she saved Conchita, her favourite, and an ivory paint-box as big as a tea-tray, and the skates, and some of the beautiful clothes from the dolls' house, while Sylvia mournfully sorted out the most interesting-looking and beautifully illustrated books from a large bookcase.

'Oh, and I must keep my little writing-desk, James, for I mean to write to Papa this very day and tell him how wicked Miss Slighcarp is. Then he'll soon come home.'

'I'll put the desk in the attic for you, miss,' promised James, 'but it's no use writing to your papa. Rather write to Mr Gripe.'

'Why, James?'

'Why, your papa's at sea now. His ship won't reach a port for three months.'

'Oh dear — nor it will,' said Bonnie sadly. 'and I don't know Mr Gripe's direction in London. What shall I do? For we can't, *can't* endure this dreadfulness for three months – and then it would be another three months before Papa could come home, even supposing Mamma was well again.'

Just then they heard Miss Slighcarp's step approaching once more, and her voice calling, 'James, come here. I need your help to move a heavy deed-box.'

'I must go, miss,' whispered James hurriedly. 'Don't let yourself be seen. I'll bring your luncheon up by and by.'

He hastened from the room.

The day passed unhappily. As Bonnie was supposed to be shut in the cupboard, she could not leave the schoolroom for fear of meeting Miss Slighcarp, and Sylvia would go nowhere without her. They tried various occupations, reading, sewing, drawing, but had not the heart to pursue them for long. At noon they heard Miss Slighcarp's voice in the passage outside. Bonnie whisked behind the curtain, but the governess did not come in. She was speaking to James again.

'Is that the young ladies' luncheon?'

'This is the bread-and-water for Miss Green, ma'am,' he answered respectfully. 'I'll fetch Miss Sylvia's tray when I've taken this in.'

'She's not to come out of the cupboard to eat it, mind.'

'No, ma'am.'

He appeared, grinning broadly, planked a dry-looking loaf and a jug of water on the table, and then whispered, 'Don't touch it, Miss Bonnie. Just as soon as the old cat's out of the way I'll bring something better!' And, sure enough, ten minutes later, he returned carrying a tray covered with a cloth which, when taken off, revealed two dear little roast partridges with bread sauce, red-currant jelly, and vegetables.

'You'll not starve while I'm here to see after you,' he whispered.

The children ate hungrily, and later James came back with a dish of trifle and took away the meat dishes, carefully covering them again with the cloth before venturing into the corridor.

'I wish I knew where the secret passage came out,' he murmured. 'Porson, the old steward, always used to say there was a sliding panel in this room and a passage that led down to the dairy. With that she-dragon on the prowl it would be rare and useful to have a secret way into here. You might have a bit of a search for it, Miss Bonnie.'

'We'll begin at once!' exclaimed Bonnie. 'It will be something to pass the time.'

The moment James had taken away the pudding-plates they began testing the walls for hidden springs.

'You start by the door, Sylvia, and I'll begin at the fireplace, and we'll each do two sides of the room,' Bonnie suggested.

It was a big room, its walls covered in white linenfold panelling, decorated with carved garlands of roses painted blue. The children carefully pushed, pulled, and pressed each wooden rose, without result. An hour, two hours went by, and they were becoming disheartened and beginning to feel that the story of the secret passage must have been merely an idle tale, when Sylvia suggested:

'We haven't tried the fireplace, Bonnie. Do you suppose it possible that part of the mantlepiece should be false?'

'Clever girl!' said Bonnie, giving her a hug. 'Let us try it at once.'

The mantel was large, and beautifully carved from some foreign stone with a grey, satiny surface. It extended for several feet on either side of the fireplace to form two wide panels on which were carved deer with elaborately branching antlers. The children ran to these and began fingering the antlers and trying to move them. Suddenly Sylvia gave an exclamation – as she pushed the deer's head to one side the whole panel slid away into the wall, leaving a dark aperture like a low, narrow doorway.

'You've found it!' breathed Bonnie. 'Oh, what fun this is! Let us go in at once and see where it leads. Sylvia, you are the cleverest creature in the world, and I do not know what I should have done if you had not been here to keep me company. I could not have borne it!'

She was about to dart into the hole when the more prudent Sylvia said, 'Should we not take lighted candles? I have heard that the air in this kind of disused passage is sometimes very foul and will put out a flame. If we had candles we should be warned in time.'

'Very true! I did not think.' Bonnie ran to a cupboard which held wax tapers in long silver holders and brought two each, which they kindled at the fire. Then they slipped cautiously through the narrow opening, Bonnie leading the way.

'We had better shut the panel behind us,' she said. 'Only imagine if Miss Slighcarp should come into the schoolroom and find it open!'

'What if we cannot open it again from the inside?'
'Perhaps it will be possible to leave just a crack.'
Unfortunately the panel proved to be on some sort of spring. As soon as Sylvia touched it, it rolled smoothly shut. A small plaster knob seemed intended to open it from the inside, but when Bonnie rather impatiently pressed this, it crumbled away in her hand.

'How vexatious!' she said.

Sylvia was alarmed at the thought that they might have immured themselves for life, but Bonnie whispered stoutly:

'Never mind! The passage must come out somewhere, and if we are shut up, at least it is no worse than being shut up by Miss Slighcarp.'

They tiptoed along, through thick, shuffling dust.

The passage was exceedingly narrow, and presently led them down a flight of steep steps. It was not pitch dark; a tiny hole let in a glimmer of daylight, and, placing her eye to these holes, Bonnie was able to discover their whereabouts.

'Now we are behind the Great Hall, I can see the coats of arms. This is the silver-gilt ante-room. Now we are looking into the armoury, those are gun-barrels. Imagine this passage having been here all this time and my never knowing of it! Oh, how I wish Papa and Mamma were at home! What famous times we should have, jumping out and surprising them! And we should discover a whole lot of secrets by overhearing people's private conversations.'

'Would that be honourable?' Sylvia doubtfully whispered.

'Perhaps not with Papa and Mamma, but it would be quite another matter with Miss Slighcarp. I mean to listen to *her* all I can!'

They soon had an opportunity to do so, for the next peep-hole looked into the library, and when Bonnie put her eye to it she saw the governess in close consultation with Mr Grimshaw. They were at the far end of the large room, and at first out of earshot, but they soon moved nearer to the unseen watchers.

'Poke up the fire, Josiah,' said Miss Slighcarp, who was studying a large parchment. 'This must be burnt at once, now that we have succeeded in finding it.' The children heard Mr Grimshaw stirring up the logs, and realized that they must be standing beside the fireplace and that their spyhole was probably concealed in the chimneypiece. It was possible that there was another opening panel, similar to that in the schoolroom, but they were careful not to try pressing any projections, having no wish to be brought suddenly face to face with their enemies.

'Take the bellows and blow it into a blaze,' Miss Slighcarp said. She was reading the document carefully.'What a good thing Sir Willoughby was careless enough to leave his will at home instead of keeping it with Mr Gripe. It has saved us a deal of trouble.'

'Indeed, yes,' said Mr Grimshaw comfortably. 'And is it as you thought – does he leave everything to the child?'

'Almost everything,' said Miss Slighcarp. She read on with compressed lips. 'There is a legacy of twenty thousand pounds a year to his niece, a few hundred to me in gratitude for my services – pah! – and some trifling bequests to servants. Mention, too, of his sister Jane, my distant cousin. Is she likely to come poking her nose and being troublesome?'

'Not a fear of it,' Mr Grimshaw answered. 'I made inquiries about her when I was in London. She is extremely elderly and unworldly; moreover, she is frail and unlikely to last long. She will never interfere with our management of the estate.'

'Excellent. I will burn this will then – there, on the fire it goes – and you must set to work at once to forge another, leaving *everything* to me. Have you practised the signature sufficiently?'

'I could do it with my left hand,' Mr Grimshaw said. 'I have copied it from every document in this room.' He drew a chair to a table at a little distance, pulled a piece of parchment towards him, and began slowly and carefully writing on it.

Miss Slighcarp, meanwhile, was tearing up and burning a great many other documents. 'The more confusion his affairs are found to be in, the better,' she observed. 'It will give us the more time to make our plans.'

'You sound very certain that he – that *the event* will take place. Suppose he should, after all, return?'

'My dear Josiah,' said Miss Slighcarp meaningfully, 'the master to whom I spoke was very certain about the state of the vessel. He said she could not last another voyage. But even if that plan should miscarry, what then! Sir W. cannot be back before a year is up. We shall have ample warning of his return and can be clear away and embarked for the colonies before he arrives. We shall never be caught.'

'What of the children? You will not keep them here?'

'Not for long. They can go to Gertrude,' said Miss Slighcarp ominously. 'She will soon knock the nonsense out of them. Now, do not disturb me. I must master the details of this deed.' She picked up another document and began studying it absorbedly.

The children tiptoed on.

'Bonnie,' said Sylvia rather fearfully after a few moments, when she judged that they were well out of earshot of the library and its inmates. 'what did Miss Slighcarp mean when she referred to the *event*? And why was she burning my uncle's will?'

'I am not certain,' confessed Bonnie, who was pale and frowning over this new evidence of Miss Slighcarp's knavery, 'but it is plain that she means nothing but wickedness.'

Sylvia glanced in a troubled way at her cousin. It was evident that Bonnie did not wish to pursue the matter, and they went on in silence for a while. They came to another spyhole, which looked on to a passage, and then they found themselves up against a blank wall. The secret corridor appeared to have come to a dead end.

Even Bonnie's heart sank, for the candles were perilously low, when they heard the clink of dishes, and a familiar voice, that of James, broke into song so close beside them that they might have been touching him.

'As I was a walking one morning for pleasure,
I spied a young—'

'Knock on the wall!' Bonnie whispered to Sylvia, and both children began banging on the panel as hard as they could. The song broke off abruptly.

'James! James! It's us, in here behind the panel! Can you let us out?'

'Laws, miss, you gave me a fright,' James's voice said. 'I thought it was the hobgoblin for sure.'

They heard him fumbling on the wall, and tapped again, to show him where they were. Suddenly there came a click, and bright cold light and icy air rushed into their hiding-place.

'I always wondered why that great knob was there on the wall,' James said. 'Well, laws, miss! To think of your really finding the secret passage. That's champion, that is!'

They stepped out, and found themselves in the dairy, a brick-floored, slate-shelved room with several sinks, where some of the dish-washing was done. An outside door led from it to the stable-yard, and they could see the whiteness of the new-fallen snow.

Since this entrance, too, appeared to have no means of opening it from the inside, James arranged to leave it open, artfully moving a tall cupboard so that it partly obscured the doorway, and hanging a quantity of horse-blankets and other draperies to hide the remainder.

'Now at least no one need get shut up inside,' said Bonnie. 'The bother of it is that we can do nothing of the sort in the schoolroom. It would look too queer. The person in the passage will simply have to knock on the panel until somebody in the room lets them out.'

'But supposing it was Miss Slighcarp in the room!'

'Goose! Of course we should have to make sure before knocking that she was not in the room. I dare say there is a spyhole.'

'Do you go back along the passage now and look,' suggested Sylvia, 'and I will return to the schoolroom by the back stairs and let you out.'

This was agreed to, and Sylvia hastened away, glancing, as she passed the open door, at the stable clock to make sure that they would not be late for their meeting with Pattern. But it still lacked half an hour of five o'clock, the time appointed for the meeting.

Most unfortunately, as she neared the schoolroom door, she saw the gaunt, bony form of Miss Slighcarp approaching from the other direction, carrying in her arms a pile of linen. Sylvia was greatly alarmed when the governess swept before her into the schoolroom and deposited her burden on the table. What if Bonnie, not realizing that the governess was in the room, should have the imprudence to knock on the panel and ask to be let out of the secret passage?

'Now, miss,' said Miss Slighcarp coldly – since the departure of her employers she had made no slightest pretence of being pleasant to either of the two children – 'since I am at present too busy to occupy myself with teaching you, I have brought you a task so you shan't be idle. All these sheets and pillow-cases require mending. To work at once, please! If they are not finished by tomorrow you will come under my severe displeasure. Small stitches, mind.'

'Yes, ma'am,' said Sylvia, trembling, trying to keep her eyes from wandering towards the fireplace.

'I have a good mind to set that insolent child in the cupboard to this work too . . .' Miss Slighcarp muttered. She moved to the cupboard door, feeling in the reticule attached to the sash of her dress. Sylvia gasped with fright. 'How very provoking! I gave the key to James.' Sylvia let out a long, quivering breath of relief. 'Miss Green!' the governess said, rapping on the door of the cupboard. 'I trust you are repenting of your outrageous behaviour?'

There was no reply from within the cupboard.

'Spirit not broken yet?' Miss Slighcarp moved away from the door. 'Well, it will be bread-and-water for you until it is. On thinking the matter over, the light in that cupboard would not be sufficient to permit her to mend the linen.'

This was no more than the truth, Sylvia reflected, for it must be pitch dark inside the cupboard.

Just as Miss Slighcarp was about to leave the schoolroom a loud, unmistakable rap sounded from inside the fireplace. Sylvia, pale with fright, sprang to the fender and began rattling the poker and tongs noisily, pretending to poke up the fire and put a few more pieces of coal on it. The governess paused suspiciously.

'What was that noise?'

'Noise, ma'am?' said Sylvia innocently.

'Something that sounded like a tap on the wall.'

'It was this piece of coal, Miss Slighcarp, that fell into the grate.' Sylvia spoke as loudly as she could, and rattled the fire-irons more than ever. Miss

Slighcarp seemed convinced, and left, after a sharp glance round to make sure that James had obeyed her command to pack up all the children's toys. Fortunately this had been done. The schoolroom and toyroom looked bleak and bare enough with all the gaily-coloured games and playthings removed, but Sylvia comforted herself by recollecting the hidden store up in the attic.

As soon as Miss Slighcarp was safely gone, Sylvia ran to the secret panel and with trembling hands pressed the carved deer's head, praying that she had remembered the correct prong on the antlers. To her unbounded relief the stone panel slid back as before, and Bonnie, black, dusty, laughing, and triumphant, fell out into her arms.

'Oh, is not this fun? Oh, what a narrow squeak! I had quite thought you were alone in the room, for neither of you had spoken for several moments before I tapped. Is it not provoking, there is no spyhole in this room? The first one looks out on the upstairs landing. But it is possible to hear voices from inside the passage, so long as somebody is speaking. What a mercy that you were so clever with the poker and tongs, Sylvia!'

6

At five o'clock the two children stole cautiously to the little blue powder-room, which, luckily, was in a remote wing of the great house, where Miss Slighcarp was not likely to make her way. Pattern was there already, and greeted them with tears and embraces.

'Oh, Miss Bonnie, Miss Sylvia, my dears! What's to become of us, that's what I should like to know, with that wicked woman in charge of the house?'

'*We* shall be all right,' said Bonnie stoutly. 'She can't do anything very dreadful to us, but oh, Pattern, what about *you*? She will have you sent to prison if she catches you here.'

'She won't catch me,' said Pattern confidently. 'I crept in by the apple-room door when the other servants left, and I've fixed myself up in the little south attic on the fourth floor as snug as you please. My fine lady will never set foot up there, you may be certain. And I'll be able to creep down from there and help you with your dressing and put you to bed and look after your things, my poor lambs! Oh that I should live to see such a wicked day!'

'But Pattern, how will you live?' Bonnie was beginning, when James came quickly and quietly into the room.

'What a lark!' he said. 'The old cat nearly caught me – met me in the long gallery – and asked what I was doing. I said, going to see all the windows were shut for the night, and she said, "Yes, that's right, we want no thieving servants creeping back under cover of dark." Thieving! I'd like to know what she thinks she is!'

The children told him Pattern's plan and he approved it heartily.

'For I don't trust Miss Slighcarp not to starve these young ones or do something underhand if we're not there to keep an eye on them,' he said. 'I'll look after their meals, Miss Pattern, if you see they're snug and mended and cared for. But, Miss Bonnie dear, you'd best write off to your papa's lawyer the very first thing, and tell him what's afoot here.'

'But I don't know his address, James!'

'Eh, that's awkward,' said James, scratching his head. 'Who can you write to, then?'

'How about Aunt Jane?' Bonnie suggested to Sylvia. 'She will surely know Mr Gripe's address, for I have heard Papa say that Mr Gripe is in charge of her money.'

'Ye-es,' said Sylvia doubtfully, 'but Aunt Jane is so old, and so *very* frail, that I am afraid the news would be a dreadful, dreadful shock to her. It might make her ill, and then she is all on her own . . .'

'No, you are right,' said Bonnie decisively. 'It is not to be thought of. I know! We will write to Dr Morne.

He promised that he would come from time to time, in any case, so there would be nothing odd about asking him over. And very likely he will know Mr Gripe's direction in London.'

'Or perhaps he can get the magistrates to commit Miss Slighcarp to prison,' said James. 'That is a champion notion of yours, Miss Bonnie. Do you write the letter and I will ride over with it as soon as I get a chance.'

'I will wait for a few days,' suggested Bonnie, 'just so that Miss Slighcarp shan't be suspicious, and then will pretend to have the toothache.'

A distant bell sounded, and James sprang up. 'There! The old cat wants me for something and I must run. I'll be up to the schoolroom by and by with your suppers.' And he hastened away.

Left with Pattern, the children told her how they had discovered the secret passage leading to the schoolroom, and she was delighted.

'I can come up that way to dress and undress you, and take your things away for washing,' she said. 'What a mercy of providence!'

'Only you must take care never to tap on the panel unless you are sure Miss Slighcarp is not in the room,' Bonnie said chuckling.

'In any case, let us hope it need not be for long. Dr Morne will soon settle her when you tell him what's going on here.'

'Hark! There's the stable clock chiming the hour, Sylvia,' said Bonnie. 'I believe we should go back to the schoolroom so that presently James can come and let me out of the cupboard. It would be terrible if

Miss Slighcarp were to accompany him and find me not there!'

During the next few weeks the children became half-accustomed to their strange new life. They hardly saw Miss Slighcarp and Mr Grimshaw, who were too busy discovering what they could make away with from Sir Willoughby's property to have much time for the children. James and Pattern cared for them, bringing their meals and protecting them from contact with the other servants, who were a rough, untrustworthy lot. Several times the secret panel proved exceedingly useful when Miss Slighcarp approached the schoolroom on her daily visit of inspection, and Pattern, busy performing some service for the children, hastily darted through it.

There was little enough to do. They dared not be seen skating, and the snowy weather kept them near the house. But one day Prout, the under-groom, finding Bonnie crying for her pony in the empty stable, whispered to her that he had not sold the ponies, only taken them to one of the farms on the estate, and that when the weather was better they might go over there and have a ride. This news cheered Bonnie a good deal; to lose her pony, Feathers, and the new one that had been bought for Sylvia, on top of everything else, had been almost more than she could bear.

At last she decided that she could write to Dr Morne without incurring suspicion. For a whole day she went about with her face tied up in a shawl, complaining that it ached, and that evening she crept up to the attic where her little desk was hidden and composed a note in her best handwriting, with advice from Sylvia.

Dear Doctor,

Will you please come to see us, as we don't think Papa would like the things that are happening here and we can't write to him for he is on board Ship. Miss Slycarp, our wicked Governess, has dismissed all the good old Servants and is making herself into a Tyrant. She wears Mamma's dresses and Mr Grimshaw is in League with her and they drink champagne every Day.

Yours respectfully,

BONNIE GREEN AND SYLVIA GREEN.

Alas! next morning when Bonnie gave James this carefully written note a dreadful thing happened. James had the note in his hand when he met Miss Slighcarp – who seemed to have the knack of appearing always just where she was not wanted – and her sharp eyes immediately fastened upon it.

'What is that, James?'

'Miss Bonnie has the toothache, ma'am. She wrote a note asking Dr Morne if he would be so kind as to send her a poultice for it.'

'I see. There is a heavy deed-box in the library I want moved, James. Come and attend to it, please, before you deliver the note.'

Unwillingly James followed.

'Put that note on the table,' she said, giving Mr Grimshaw, who was in the library, a significant look as she did so.

While James was struggling to put the heavy box exactly where Miss Slighcarp required it, under a confusing rain of contradictory instructions, Mr Grimshaw quickly glanced at the direction on the note, and then, with his gift for imitating handwriting, copied the address on to a similar envelope with a blank sheet of paper inside. When James's back was turned for an instant he very adroitly exchanged one note for the other.

'There, then,' said Miss Slighcarp. 'Be off with you, sirrah, and don't loiter on the way or stop to drink porter in the doctor's kitchen.'

The instant James was out of the room she opened the letter, and her brow darkened as she read it.

'This must be dealt with,' she muttered. 'I must dispose of these children without delay!' And she showed the letter to Mr Grimshaw.

'Artful little minxes!' he exclaimed. 'You are right! The children cannot be allowed to stay here.'

'When can we move them? Tonight?'

He nodded.

James hurriedly saddled one of the carriage horses that remained in the stable, armed himself with a pair of pistols in the saddle-holsters and one stuck in his belt, and made off at a gallop for the residence of Dr Morne, who lived some five miles beyond the park boundary.

Unfortunately when he reached his destination it was only to discover that the doctor had been called from home on an urgent case – a fire in the town of Blastburn in which several people had been injured – and was not expected home that evening. James

dared not linger, though he had been intending to reinforce Bonnie's note by himself telling the doctor how bad things were at the Chase. He could only deliver the letter and come away, leaving a message with the doctor's housekeeper imploring Dr Morne to visit Miss Bonnie as soon as possible. Then he made his way homewards. A wolf-pack picked up his trail and followed him, but his horse, its hoofs winged by fear, kept well ahead, and James discouraged the pursuit by sending a couple of balls into the midst of the wolves, who fell back and decided to look for easier prey.

The dull, dark afternoon passed slowly by. The children worked fitfully at their tasks of mending. Bonnie was no longer locked up, but Miss Slighcarp made it plain that she was still in disgrace, never speaking to her, and giving her cold and sinister looks.

The sound of a horse's hoofs had drawn both children to the window on one occasion, when Miss Slighcarp came suddenly into the room.

'Back to your work, young ladies,' she said angrily. 'Whom did you expect to see, pray?'

'I thought – that is, we did not expect – ' Sylvia faltered. 'It is James, returning from his errand.'

'So!' Miss Slighcarp gave them again that strange glance, and then left them, after commenting unfavourably upon their needlework. She returned to the library, where she rang for James and gave him orders that utterly puzzled him.

'The carriage?' he muttered, scratching his head. 'What can she want the carriage for, at *such* a time?'

Dusk, and then dark, came, and bedtime drew near. The children had long since abandoned their sewing and were sitting on the hearthrug, with arms entwined, in a somewhat sorrowful silence, gazing at the glowing coals which cast their dim illumination over the bare room.

'It is too late, I fear. Dr Morne will never come today,' Bonnie said sighing.

There was a gentle tap on the secret panel.

'Pattern! It is Pattern!' said Sylvia, jumping up, and she made haste to press the spring. Pattern came bustling out with a tray on which were two silver bowls of steaming bread-and-milk, besides little dishes of candied quince and plum.

'Here's your supper, my lambs! Now eat that while it's hot, and I'll be warming your beds and night-things. Thank the good providence old Pattern's here to see you don't go to bed cold and starving.'

When the last spoonful was eaten she hustled them into their warm blue flannel nightgowns, and saw them tucked up in bed. 'There, my ducks! Sweet dreams guard your rest,' she said, and gave each a good-night hug. At this moment they heard Miss Slighcarp's brisk heavy steps coming along the passage.

'Lawks-a-me!' gasped Pattern. She snatched up the tray and was through the secret door in a flash. Just as it clicked behind her Miss Slighcarp entered through the other door, carrying a lamp.

'In bed already?' she said. She sounded displeased. The children lay wondering what fault she could find with such praiseworthy punctuality.

'Well, you must just get up again!' she snapped, dumping the lamp on the dressing-table. 'Get up, dress yourselves, and pack a valise with a change of clothing. You are going on a journey.'

A journey? The children stared at each other, aghast. They could not discuss the matter, however, as Miss Slighcarp remained in the room, sorting through their clothes and deciding what they were to take with them. Sylvia noticed that she put out only their oldest and plainest things. She herself was given none of the new clothes that Pattern had been making her, but only those made from Aunt Jane's white curtain.

'Wh-where are we going, Miss Slighcarp?' she presently ventured. Bonnie had such a vehement dislike of the governess that she would never address Miss Slighcarp unless obliged to do so.

'To school.'

'To school? But are you not then going to teach us, ma'am?'

'I have not the leisure,' Miss Slighcarp said sharply. 'The estate affairs are in such a sad tangle that it will take me all my time to straighten them. You are to go to the school of a friend of mine in Blastburn.'

'But Mamma and Papa would never agree to such a thing!' Bonnie burst out indignantly.

'Whether they would or whether they would not is of no importance, young lady.'

'Why do you say that?' asked Bonnie, filled with a nameless dread.

'Because I had a message this afternoon to say that the *Thessaly*, the ship on which your mamma and papa set sail, has been sunk off the coast of Spain. You are an orphan, Miss Green, like your cousin, and from now on it is I who have the sole say in your affairs. I am your guardian.'

Bonnie gave one sharp cry – 'Papa! Mamma!' – and then sank down, trembling, on the sofa, burying her face in her hands.

Miss Slighcarp looked at her with a strange sort of triumph, and then left the room, carrying the valise, and bidding them both be ready in five minutes.

As soon as she was gone, Bonnie sprang upright again. 'It is not true! It can't be! She said it just to torment me! But oh,' she cried, 'what if it is true, Sylvia? *Could* it be true?'

How could poor Sylvia tell? She tried to comfort Bonnie, tried to assure her that it must be lies, but all the time a dreadful doubt and fear lay in her own heart. If Bonnie's parents were no more, then their only protectors were gone. She thought with grief of cheerful, good-hearted Sir Willoughby and kind, gentle Lady Green. To whom, now, could they turn?

Before the five minutes were more than half gone Miss Slighcarp had come back to hasten them. With a vigilant eye she escorted them down the stairs and through a postern door to the stable-yard, where the carriage was waiting, with the horses harnessed and steaming in the frosty night air.

Sleepy and shivering, they hardly had strength to protest when Mr Grimshaw, who was there, hoisted each into the carriage, and then handed up Miss Slighcarp, who sat grimly between them.

'Well, a pleasant journey, ma'am,' he cried gaily. 'Mind the wolves don't get you, ha ha!'

'I'd like to see the wolf that would tackle me,' snapped Miss Slighcarp, and then, to James on the box, 'You may start, sirrah!' They rattled out of the yard and were soon crossing the dark and snowy expanses of the park.

They had gone about a mile when they spied the lights of another carriage coming towards them. It drew to a halt as it came abreast of them.

''Tis the doctor, ma'am,' said James.

'Young ladies!' said Miss Slighcarp sharply. They caught sight of her face by the swaying carriage light; the look on it was so forbidding that it made them shiver. 'One word from either of you, and you'll have me to reckon with! Remember that you are now going to a place where Miss Green of Willoughby Chase is not of the slightest consequence. You can cry all day in a coal-cellar and no one will take notice of you, if I choose that it shall be so. Hold your tongues, therefore! Not a sound from you while I speak to the doctor.'

'Is that Miss Slighcarp?' the doctor called.

'Dr Morne? What brings you out at this time of night?' She spoke with false cordiality.

'I received a strange message, ma'am – most strange, a blank sheet of paper, and an urgent summons to the Chase. Is everybody ill? Can nobody write?'

'Oh Doctor,' she said, sweet as syrup, 'I'm afraid it must be some prank of those dreadful children. They are *so* naughty and high-spirited.' (Here she gave both children a fierce pinch.) 'There is nobody ill at the Chase, Doctor. I most *deeply* regret that you should have been called out for nothing. Let me give you ten guineas instead of your usual five.'

There was a chink of coins as she leaned out of the dim coach and obscured the doctor's view of its interior.

He rumbled, dissatisfied. 'Very odd, very. Can't say it's like Bonnie to do such a thing. Must be the other little minx. Don't care for being called out on false errands. However, very kind of you, ma'am. Say no more about it.'

Still grumbling to himself, he turned his horses. Miss Slighcarp gave him a few minutes' start and then told James to make all possible speed towards Blastburn.

The rest of the journey passed in silence. Both children were utterly cast down at this failure of their plan, and Bonnie was almost numb with grief and despair over the news about her parents. Try as she would to control herself, tear after tear slipped from under her eyelids, and the utmost that she could achieve was that she wept in silence. She was too proud to let Miss Slighcarp guess her misery. Sylvia guessed it, and longed to comfort her, but the bony bulk of the governess was between them.

Long before the end of the trip they were almost dead of cold, and their feet were like lumps of ice, for Miss Slighcarp had all the fur carriage rugs wrapped round herself, and the children had to make do without. They were too cold for sleep, and could almost have wished for an attack by wolves, but, save for an occasional distant howl, their passage was undisturbed. It seemed that Miss Slighcarp was right when she said that the wolves feared to attack her.

At last they drew near the great smoky lights and fearsome fiery glare of Blastburn, where the huge slag-heaps stood outlined like black pyramids against the red sky.

They clattered through a black and cobbled town where the people seemed to work all night, for the streets were thronged, although it was so late, and presently drew up in a dark street on the farthest outskirts.

Miss Slighcarp alighted first, and Sylvia had just time to breathe hurriedly to James, as he lifted her down, 'You'll tell Pattern where we are gone, James? She'll be so worried,' and to receive his nod, before the governess pushed them along a narrow gravel path towards the front door of a high, dark house.

She rang a bell whose echoes they heard far within, harsh and jangling. Almost at once the door flew open.

7

The door was opened by a thin, dirty child in a brown pinafore with one white front pocket on which was stitched a large number six. Bonnie and Sylvia were not certain if the child was a boy or a girl until Miss Slighcarp said, 'It's you, is it, Lucy? Where is Mrs Brisket?'

'In here, please, miss,' Lucy said with a frightened gasp, and opened a door on one side of the entrance hall. Miss Slighcarp swept through, turning her head to say to Bonnie and Sylvia, 'Wait there. Don't speak or fidget.' Then they heard her voice beyond the door:

'Gertrude. It is I. Our plans are going excellently.' Somebody shut the door and they could hear nothing further. The little girl, Lucy, regarded the new arrivals for a moment, her finger in her mouth, before picking up a broom several inches taller than herself and beginning to sweep the floor.

'Are you a pupil here?' Bonnie asked her curiously.

The brown pinafore looked like some kind of uniform – but why was her hair cut so short, even shorter than a boy's? And why was she doing housework?

'Hush!' whispered Lucy. Her eyes flicked in terror towards the closed door. 'She'll half kill me if she hears me speak!'

'Who?' breathed Bonnie.

'*Her*. Mrs Brisket.'

Bonnie looked as if she was on the point of asking more questions, but Sylvia hushed her, not wishing to get Lucy into trouble, and Lucy herself resolutely turned her back and went on with her work, stirring up a cloud of dust in the dim and stuffy hall.

Suddenly Sylvia had the feeling that they were being watched. She raised her eyes and saw someone standing by the banister rail at the top of the ill-lit stairs, staring down at them. Meeting Sylvia's eyes, this person slowly descended towards them.

She was a girl of about fifteen, tall and thin, with a pale, handsome, sharp-featured face. She walked with a slouch, and was very richly dressed in velvet, with a band of fur round her jacket and several bracelets. She carried a pair of silver skates.

She walked up to Bonnie and Sylvia, surveying them coolly and insolently. She made no remark or friendly gesture of greeting; merely looked them up and down, and then, with a sudden quick movement, tugged off Sylvia's white fur cap and tried it on herself. It was too small.

'Hm,' she said coldly. 'What a nuisance you're not bigger.' She dropped the cap disdainfully on the floor. Sylvia's lips parted in indignation; even she, mild and good-tempered as she was, would have protested had she not noticed Lucy's face behind the girl's elbow, grimacing at her in an agony of alarm, evidently warning her not to object to this treatment.

Wordlessly, she picked up the beautiful white cap, its fur dusty from the heap of sweepings on to which it had fallen, and stood stroking it while the girl said carelessly to Lucy:

'Is my mother in there?'

'Yes, Miss Diana. Talking to Miss Slighcarp.'

'Oh, *that* old harridan.' She pushed open the door and they heard her say, 'Ma, I'm going out. There's a fair, and all-night skating on the river. Give me five guineas.' She reappeared in the doorway jingling coins in her hand, turned her head to say, 'If either of the new girls is good at mending, make her sew up my satin petticoat. It's split.' Then she pushed haughtily past them and went out, slamming the front door.

Miss Slighcarp summoned Bonnie and Sylvia to be inspected by their new instructress. As soon as they saw her they recognized the lady whom they had seen driving her carriage near the boundaries of Willoughby Chase. She was a tall, massive, smartly-dressed woman, her big-knuckled hands loaded with rings flashing red and yellow, rubies and topazes. She glanced at the children irritably. Her eyes were yellow as the stones in her rings, yellow as the eyes of a tiger, and she looked as if she could be bad-tempered.

'These are the children, Gertrude,' Miss Slighcarp said. 'That one' – pointing to Sylvia – 'is tractable enough, though lazy and whining and disposed to malinger. This one' – indicating Bonnie – 'is

thoroughly insolent and ungovernable, and will need constant checking and keeping down.'

'I'm not!'

'She's not!' burst from Bonnie and Sylvia simultaneously, but Mrs Brisket checked them with a glare from her yellow eyes.

'Speak before you're spoken to in this house, young ladies, and you'll get a touch of the strap and lose your supper. So let's have no more of it.'

They were silent, but Bonnie's eyes flashed dangerously.

'Both, as you can see,' continued Miss Slighcarp as if there had been no interruption, 'have been grossly spoilt and over-indulged.'

'They'll soon have that nonsense knocked out of them here,' said Mrs Brisket.

Miss Slighcarp rose. 'I am leaving them in good hands, Gertrude,' she said. 'I am very busy just at present, as you know, but when next we meet I hope *you* will be coming to visit *me*. You have helped me in the past, Gertrude, and soon I shall be in a position to help *you*.'

She said this last very significantly. Bonnie's and Sylvia's eyes met. Was Miss Slighcarp intending to take complete possession of Willoughby Chase? Sylvia felt something like despair come over her, but Bonnie clenched her hands indomitably.

Mrs Brisket ushered Miss Slighcarp out and saw her to the carriage. When it had gone, with a clattering of hoofs and a flashing of lamps, she returned to the children.

'We have no names here,' she said sternly. 'You,'

to Sylvia, 'will be number ninety-eight, you number ninety-nine. Come, make haste, the others are in bed long ago except for the night-workers.'

She led them through the hall — where the little girl Lucy swept frenziedly as soon as Mrs Brisket appeared, though it was plain she was dropping with sleepiness — and up flight after flight of steep, uncarpeted stairs. On the fourth floor she pushed Bonnie through a doorway, hissing, 'The bed near the door,' and raised the candle she carried long enough to show a large, bare room, crammed with small iron cots, on which children lay sleeping, sometimes two to a cot. One bed, by the door, was still vacant.

Sylvia had just time to whisper 'Good night!' before she was hustled up to the floor above and thrust into a similar bedroom. She undressed in the pitch dark and fumbled her way into the bed, which was narrow, hard, and inadequately covered. 'I'll never get to sleep,' she thought, as she lay shivering miserably, trying to summon up courage to thrust her feet into the chilly depths of the bed. She could hear the mill hooters wail, and iron wheels clang on the cobbles; somewhere a church clock struck midnight. The whole of her short stay among the riches and splendours of Willoughby Chase seemed like a dream.

'Oh how I wish I was still with Aunt Jane,' she thought unhappily. 'But then I should not have met Bonnie, dear Bonnie!' She turned over, hugging the too-thin, too-narrow blanket round her. Suddenly a hand touched her cheek and a voice whispered, 'Sylvia, is that you?'

'Bonnie!'

'I had to come and make sure you were all right.'

Sylvia thought remorsefully how selfish she had been, lying and pitying herself while Bonnie had courageously dared the perils of the dark house to come and see her.

'Yes, I'm all right, quite all right!' she whispered. She reached out and hugged Bonnie. 'Run back to bed quickly, someone may catch you!' She felt sure that in this place the punishment for getting out of bed would be dire.

'Just came to make sure,' said Bonnie. 'Don't worry, Sylvia, we'll keep each other company, it won't be too bad. And if we don't like it, well then we'll run away.'

Though she said this so stoutly, her heart sank. Where could they run to, with Miss Slighcarp in occupation at Willoughby Chase?

'See you in the morning!'

'See you in the morning!'

With the memory of Bonnie's comforting presence, Sylvia at last found the courage to push her feet down to the cold bottom of the bed and go to sleep. But Bonnie lay awake for hour after hour, hearing the city clocks strike, and the wail of the factory hooters, and the rumble of wheels.

'What shall we do?' she thought again and again. 'What shall we do?'

In the morning they discovered why the beds near the door were the last to be occupied. While the sky outside was still black as midnight and the frosty stars still shone, a tall girl thrust a great bell through the door and clanged it deafeningly up and down until every shivering inmate of the room had thrown back her covers, jumped to the floor, and begun dressing.

Dazed and startled, Sylvia nearly fell out of bed.

'Where do we wash?' she whispered to the girl by the next bed.

'Hush! You mustn't speak,' the girl said, and pointed.

Sylvia saw a tin basin in one corner of the room, with a bucket beneath it. The biggest girl in the room broke the ice in the basin by giving it a sharp crack with her hairbrush, then they all washed in order of size. Sylvia was last. When it came to her turn there was no more than a trickle of dirty, icy water left in the basin. She could not bring herself to touch it. She was about to start plaiting her hair when the big girl who had washed first said:

'Wait, you! Julia, fetch the shears.'

'Yes, Alice.' The child who had told Sylvia not to talk ran from the room, and came back in a moment with an enormous pair of garden shears. Before Sylvia realized what was to happen, or had time to protest, Alice had seized hold of her pretty fair plaits and lopped them off, one after the other. Then she chopped the remainder of Sylvia's hair off as short as possible, leaving it in a ragged, uneven fringe round her head. There was no mirror in the room, so Sylvia could not see quite how bad it looked.

'What do you mean by cutting off my hair?' she gasped.

'Hush! It's the rule. Mrs Brisket doesn't allow long hair. Now get into line.'

The other crop-haired, overalled children were in line already. Alice pushed Sylvia into place at the back, took up her own position at the front, and led them downstairs. Sylvia caught a glimpse of Bonnie at the end of another line which joined theirs. Bonnie's hair, too, had been cut, and she, like Sylvia, had been given a brown overall to wear, with a number on the pocket. She looked almost unrecognizable, like a thin dark-haired boy. She gave Sylvia a wry grin.

The files had assembled round tables in a large, cold, stone-floored room. They stood waiting while three or four weary, grimy, exhausted-looking children, among whom was Lucy, brought round bowls which proved to contain thin, grey, steaming porridge. It was eaten without milk or sugar. After it they each had a small chunk of stale bread, with the merest scrape of dripping, and that was the end of breakfast.

At this moment Mrs Brisket entered the room, and the whole school stood up. Mrs Brisket said grace, and then looked sharply round.

'Where are the new girls?' she demanded. Bonnie and Sylvia were pushed forward from their places at different tables towards the rear of the room.

She scowled at them. 'I am told that you left your beds and communicated last night. For that you will both miss your dinners.'

Who could have heard them, Sylvia wondered. Then she caught sight of the big girl, Alice, who had cut off her hair. On Alice's rather lumpish, stupid face was a smug expression.

'Sylvia didn't do a thing! It was I who went to talk to her!' Bonnie exclaimed.'

'Silence, miss! I will not have this insolence! You can miss your tea too. Perhaps that will teach you respect.

'Now, tasks. Number ninety-eight will work in the laundry. Eighteen, show her what to do. Ninety-nine, you will be in the kitchen, under cook. She will see that you don't give any trouble.'

'There will be an inspection by the Education Officer this afternoon, so I want you all in the classroom at two o'clock sharp. Eighteen and ninety-eight, you must see that the night-workers are waked in time.'

She left the hall, and the children dispersed quickly and silently to their various tasks. Sylvia was led off by a thin, wiry, but quite friendly-looking girl of fifteen or so, who whispered that her name was Emma.

'Don't we do any lessons?' murmured Sylvia.

'Hush! Wait till we're in the laundry, then we can talk.'

The laundry was a large external room, stone-floored and bitterly cold, built out from the back of the house. It contained many large zinc washtubs, scrubbing-boards, two huge iron wringers, and a great mound of coarse calico sheets and house-linen waiting to be washed. Eight or nine other children came with them and set to work doggedly, sorting the linen and filling the tubs at an outside pump, the handle of which creaked so loudly that conversation could be pursued under cover of its noise.

'Don't, whatever you do, let *her* hear you talking,' warned Emma. 'We're only allowed to say necessary things to each other.'

Her obviously referred to Mrs Brisket.

Emma gave Sylvia a tub, a pile of sheets, and a bar of rough yellow soap.

'But do the parents allow their children to be made to work like this?' Sylvia asked in bewilderment.

'They are all orphans. This is a charity school, and Mrs Brisket gets some money for running it. But as well she makes us do all the work, and take in outside work too. We do the washing for half Blastburn. Then when the Education Officer comes round we go into the classrooms and pretend to be learning lessons.'

'Do you like it here?' asked Sylvia, struggling to drag a bunch of heavy dripping cloth out of the cold water.

Emma glanced round cautiously, but no one else was very near, and the pump handle was going full blast. Leaning nearer she whispered:

'It's a horrible place! But don't let anyone hear you say so! The school is full of tale-bearers. Everyone is always hungry – and Mrs Brisket rewards anyone who carries her a tale against another person. She gives them a bit of cheese. She has a big laundry-basket in her room full of bits of cheese, ready cut up.'

So that was why Alice had reported on Bonnie's midnight visit. Sylvia herself, who was still just as hungry after breakfast as before it, felt her mouth watering at the thought of those bits of cheese.

When the sheets had been painfully scrubbed and rinsed three times by hands that were red and sore from the harsh soap and icy water, Emma showed Sylvia how to use the wringer.

'Never touch it with your hands. One girl lost her fingers in it. Now we always poke the sheets through with a stick.'

She dumped the wrung-out sheets into a basket and carried them out to the yard behind the house, where there were long rows of henhouses and many washing-lines. When the sheets were hung up, she and Sylvia returned to the central heap for a new lot.

The morning seemed endless. Sylvia was soon almost exhausted from the heavy work, and soaked through with icy water from the wringer, which sprayed anybody who was using it.

Presently the bell went for dinner. Sylvia had hoped that as she and Bonnie were both to miss their meal, they might at least meet and talk somewhere. But she learned that people punished in this way were obliged to stand at the back of the dining-room and watch everybody else eat. Mrs Brisket sat at the head table eating grilled trout and plum pudding, and there was no chance to move a finger without being seen by her.

Bonnie looked tired and rebellious. She had a smear of coal-dust on one cheek, a cut finger, and grease-spots on her overall, but she grinned at Sylvia encouragingly. At the end of the meal she seized the moment when all the benches were nosily pushed back to whisper:

'It wasn't much of a meal to miss, anyway!'

Nor had it been. One thin slice of cold fat pork, a piece of beetroot, and a small withered apple.

After dinner Bonnie was summoned back to the scullery to help with the washing-up, while Sylvia and Emma went round with a bell to wake the night-workers. Then Sylvia realized that, as the beds were insufficient for the number of children in the school, half of them slept by night and half by day. The night-workers were always dropping with fatigue, as they were liable to be roused for duties in the daytime too, but just the same they were envied, as they performed their tasks without the fierce supervision of Mrs Brisket.

It was a hard job to waken them. One by one they were clanged out of their slumbers and dragged from their beds. At two o'clock sharp the whole school, yawning and shivering, stood lined up in the heatless classrooms.

At half past two Mrs Brisket came round with the Inspector. The children were well trained. As the door opened into each classroom they burst out in chorus:

'A! B! C! D! E! F! G!' and so on, until the visitors had left.

In the next room it would be, 'One! Two! Three! Four! Five!'

'Ah, I see they are getting on with their reading and arithmetic, ma'am,' said Mr Friendshipp, the Inspector, comfortably.

'Yes, Mr Friendshipp. As you see.'

'As I might have expected, in such a well-run establishment as yours, ma'am.'

'And now, Mr Friendshipp,' said Mrs Brisket, when they had passed through the last room, where Bonnie and Sylvia were standing, 'come and have a small glass of port wine to keep out the chill.'

After tea, which Bonnie missed, the children were set to mending. The meal had consisted of another small wedge of bread, dry this time, and a cup of water. Sylvia had contrived to save a half of her morsel of bread for Bonnie, and she pushed it into Bonnie's hand later, as they sat working in the biggest classroom, huddled together for warmth. This was the only time of day when they were allowed to talk to each other a little.

'The cook's a tartar!' whispered Bonnie. 'If you say a word she hits you with the frying-pan, or anything that's handy. And the kitchen is filthy – I'd sooner work in a pigsty. We can't stay here, Sylvia.'

'No we can't,' breathed Sylvia in heartfelt agreement. 'But how can we possibly get away? And where would we go?'

'I'll think of some plan,' said Bonnie with invincible optimism. 'And you think too, Sylvia. Think, for all you are worth.'

Sylvia nodded. Then she whispered, 'Hush, Diana Brisket's looking at us,' and bent her head over the enormous rent in the satin petticoat which she was endeavouring to repair.

They had already learned that Diana Brisket was someone to dread. Her sharp eyes were everywhere, ready to catch the slightest fault, which she would then shrilly report to her mother, and her bony fingers were clever to prod or pinch or twist as she passed on stairs or landing. She was cordially hated by the whole school.

After they had sewed or mended for two hours they were put to sorting bristles for broom-making, while Mrs Brisket read aloud a chapter of the Bible to them. Then there was supper – a choice of bluish skim milk or a cup of thin potato soup – and then they were sent to bed, most of them so bone-weary that in spite of hunger and the thin coverings they fell into bed and slept at once the dreamless sleep of exhaustion.

8

Bonnie did not last long in the kitchen. The second time that the cook hit her with the frying-pan, Bonnie picked up a sauce-boat full of rancid gravy and dashed it in the cook's face.

There was a fierce struggle, but the cook, one Mrs Moleskin, a large, stout woman with a savage temper, at last thrust Bonnie into the broom cupboard and reported her to Mrs Brisket.

Mrs Moleskin was used to having a dozen terrified small slaves running hither and thither at her beck and call, and announced that she would not have Bonnie working under her. Accordingly, after a punishment which consisted of losing all her meals for two days, Bonnie was put on to doing the outside work, which was considered a terrible degradation.

In fact, she did not mind it half so much as being in the squalid kitchen. Outside work meant fetching in coal and kindling, lighting fires, sweeping the front and back steps, cleaning windows and doorknobs, digging the front garden, and looking after the poultry.

Bonnie, who was as strong as a pony, bore her two days' starvation with stoical fortitude. Twice Sylvia slipped her a piece of bread, but the second time she was caught by Alice, who snatched the bread and ate it herself, subsequently reporting the affair to Mrs Brisket. Sylvia then had to forgo her own supper, and after that Bonnie would not let her sacrifice herself.

One dark, foggy afternoon when Bonnie, shivering in her thin overall, was sweeping snow off the front path, she suddenly heard a familiar whisper from the other side of the front railings.

'Miss Bonnie! Miss Bonnie!'

'Simon!' she cried out joyfully, almost dropping the broom in her surprise.

'Miss Bonnie, why ever are you doing work like that?'

'Hush!' breathed Bonnie, looking back at the house to make sure that Mrs Brisket was not watching from one of the windows. 'They've sent us to school here, Simon, but it's more like a prison. We can't stand it, we're going to run away.'

'I should think so, too,' said Simon with indignation. 'Sweeping paths, indeed! And in that thin apron! It's downright wicked.'

'But Simon, what are you doing in Blastburn?'

'Came in to sell my geese of course,' he said winking cheerfully. 'But to tell the truth, I was looking for you, Miss Bonnie. James and Pattern asked me to come. We was all uneasy about you and Miss Sylvia. What'll I tell them?'

At that moment a coal-cart appeared and stopped outside the house. The coal-man banged on the front door, shouting, 'Coal up! Coal up! Coal up!'

Mrs Brisket came out and ordered thirty sacks.

'Here, you,' she said sharply to Bonnie. 'Help the man carry them to the coal-cellar. Who is that boy?'
She eyed Simon suspiciously.

'Geese for sale, geese for sale. Anybody want my fine fat geese?' he called, displaying the two geese he was carrying under his arms.

Mrs Brisket's eyes lit up. She strode down the garden to the gate and prodded the two geese with a knowing finger.

'I'll give you five shillings each for them, boy.'

'Ten!' said Simon.

'Ridiculous! Not a penny more than seven shillings!'

'Fifteen shillings the pair, ma'am – and it's a special price for you because I never can resist a handsome lady,' said Simon impudently.

'Guttersnipe!' said Mrs Brisket.

But she paid over the fifteen shillings and told Bonnie to put the two geese in the fowl-run. In fact, the price was a ridiculously low one, as she well knew.

'I'll carry in your coal for a brown, ma'am,' Simon suggested.

'Very well.' She dug in her purse for another coin. 'You can help the girl – the School Inspector is coming to dinner in half an hour, and I don't want children running to and fro and getting in the way when he arrives.'

Simon picked up one of the sacks without more ado and humped it across the garden to the coal-cellar entrance, a flap-door directly under Mrs Brisket's drawing-room window. Mrs Brisket unlocked the door and he tipped the coal down the chute and ran back for another load. By the time he returned Mrs Brisket had gone indoors, leaving the key in the lock.

Simon glanced round to make sure that he was unobserved. The coal-man, considering that his help was not necessary, had climbed back on to the seat of his cart and gone to sleep. Simon scooped a handful of snow aside and, pulling a knife out of his pocket, carved from the ground a hunk of yellow clay which he warmed and rubbed in his hands until it was soft. Taking the large key from the cellar lock, he pressed it vigorously into the clay, first on one side, then on the other, until he had two clear impressions of it. Then he put the key back in the lock, whipped off his muffler, damped it with snow, and wrapped it carefully round the lump of clay, which he placed under some bushes.

By the time Bonnie came running back from shutting up the geese, he was hard at work carrying his fifth sack of coal.

'Don't you try to carry one, Miss Bonnie!' he said with horror, as she went matter-of-factly to the cart. 'They're far and away too heavy for you.'

'I'll take them in the wheelbarrow,' Bonnie said, and fetched it from the shed. 'Mrs Brisket would dock me of my supper if she looked out and saw that I was letting you do all the work.'

'Does she do that?' Simon was horrified. 'Does she starve you?'

'Not me,' Bonnie said cheefully. 'I soon found out what to do. When she cuts one of my meals I make up on raw eggs. I didn't much like them at first, but when you're really hungry it's surprising what you enjoy.'

'You mustn't stay here!' Simon exclaimed.

'Will you help us to run away, Simon?'

'That I will!'

'But, Simon, if we're to escape we shall need some clothes. That's what has been worrying me. She has taken our own things, and our purses with our money, so that we can't buy other things, and if we walked about in these overalls everyone would know that we were escaped from the orphan-school.'

'I'll bring you clothes,' he promised.

'Boys' things would be best. I go to feed the hens every evening at six. You could meet me then, by the henhouses, as soon as you've got the clothes. If you went to Pattern, I'm sure she could give you something.

'The difficulty will be to get Sylvia out of the house, for she never has an excuse to come outside except in the morning when she's hanging up washing, and it would be too dangerous then.'

'Wait till next week and I'll have a key made to get you out. Can you get into the coal-cellar from inside?'

Bonnie nodded. 'All too easily. She locks us into it as punishment quite often.'

'Then I will give you a key to the outside door, and you will only have to contrive to be locked in.'

Bonnie flung her arms round his neck. 'Simon, you are wonderful! Now I must fly back or I shall be punished for loitering.'

Simon watched until she had run indoors. Then he

shied the last lump of coal to wake the driver of the cart from his beery slumbers, carefully took his piece of clay from its hiding-place in the laurel bushes and, holding it as if it were the most precious gold, walked swiftly away to find the nearest locksmith.

Sylvia was obliged to miss her tea. She had been given a dress of Diana Brisket's to mend, and the task had taxed even her skilful needle, so disgracefully torn were its delicate flounces. Her head ached, and her cold fingers were less nimble than usual: consequently the dress was not finished when Diana wanted it. She flew into a passion, slapped Sylvia, and told her mother that number ninety-eight was lazy and refused to work. In consequence, Sylvia had to stand at the back of the dining-room with the other wrongdoers at tea-time, while Bonnie burned with sympathetic fury.

During sewing-time after tea, Bonnie chose a moment when Mrs Brisket was out of the room, crept round to Sylvia, and pressed something into her hand.

'Eat it, quick, before she comes back!'

Sylvia looked at what was in her hand and saw with amazement that it was a little cake, crisp and hot from the bakery.

'Where did you get it, Bonnie?'

'It must be from Simon! I found two of them in the nesting-boxes when I went to collect the eggs. If I'd known that horrid wretch Diana would make you miss your tea, I'd have saved mine for you, too.'

And she whispered to Sylvia the news of Simon's plan for them.

Sylvia was pale already, but she became paler still with excitement.

'Escape? Oh, Bonnie, how wonderful! Here, you finish this cake. I think I'm too excited to eat it.' And she coughed.

'No, you must eat it, Sylvia. You had no tea.'

'I can't, my throat is too sore. Where shall we go, Bonnie?'

'Well,' Bonnie whispered, frowning, 'we can't very well go back to Willoughby Chase, for they'd search for us there at once. And if James and Pattern tried to help us they'd get into trouble. What do you say to trying to get to London to see Aunt Jane?'

'Oh, Bonnie, *yes*! Dearest Aunt Jane, how I long to know if she is all right.' Sylvia spoke with such enthusiasm that she coughed again. 'But how shall we get there, Bonnie? It is such a long way, and we have no money for train tickets.'

'I have thought of that. Very soon Simon will be driving his geese up to London for the Easter Fair at Smithfield Market. Easter falls at the end of April this year, and he will want at least two months to get there – '

' – And we could go with him!'

'Hush,' whispered Bonnie, for at this moment the door opened and Mrs Brisket re-entered the room. She cast her usual suspicious glance round the assembled children before beginning to read aloud from a volume of sermons, and they bent their heads and pretended to busy themselves over their work.

Every night that week, when Bonnie went to feed the hens and collect the eggs, her pleasantest task of the day, she felt a tremor of excitement. Would the key and clothes be there? But Tuesday, Wednesday, Thursday, and Friday evenings went by without her discovering anything unexpected in the henhouse.

On Saturday there was another inspection by the Education Officer, this time in the morning. He had really come to invite Mrs Brisket to dine with him next day, but she always seized the opportunity of showing him how well-behaved and biddable her pupils were, and she had them all standing in rows for a hour before his arrival. The strain of this was too much for poor Sylvia. Drenched through every day with cold water in the icy, draughty laundry, she had taken a bad cold and was flushed, heavy-eyed, and feverish. Just as the Inspector entered the room where she stood, she fainted quietly away.

'That child, ma'am, is ill,' said Mr Friendshipp, pointing to her with his cane.

'Very likely it is all a pretence!' exclaimed Mrs Brisket, looking at Sylvia with dislike. But on inspection it was plain that Sylvia's illness was genuine enough, and Mrs Brisket angrily directed two of the big girls to put her to bed in a small room on the ground floor, where sick children were kept so that they should not give the infection to others. A basin of cold porridge was dumped in her room and, as she was much too ill to eat it, she would have fared badly had Bonnie not come to her aid.

Bonnie, discovering at dinner-time that Sylvia was missing, whispered to the friendly Emma to ask where she was.

'Ill, in the little locker-room.'

'Ill?' Bonnie turned pale. She had suspected for several days that Sylvia was ailing, though Sylvia always stoutly denied it.

If she was ill, how could they escape? On the other hand, if they did not escape, what would become of Sylvia? It was not impossible, Bonnie thought, that she might *die* of neglect and ill-attention in this horrible place.

With great daring Bonnie took a chance when Mrs Brisket was inspecting the dormitories upstairs, and ran in to visit Sylvia, whom she found conscious, but dreadfully weak, flushed, and coughing. A cup of cold water stood by her bedside.

'Here!' whispered Bonnie, 'here, Sylvia, swallow this down. It's not much, but at least it's nourishing and warm!' And she pulled from her pocket an egg, only five minutes laid, tossed the water from the cup out of the window, broke the egg into it, and beat it up with her finger.

'I'm sorry, Sylvia, that it's so disgusting, but it will do you good.'

Sylvia gazed with horror at the nauseous mess, but Bonnie's bright, pleading eyes compelled her to swallow it, and it slipped more easily than she had expected down her sore throat. Then, hearing Mrs Brisket descending the upper stairs, Bonnie covered Sylvia as warmly as she could, gave her a quick hug, and dashed silently away.

That evening, when Bonnie fed the hens and searched for eggs, she put her hand beneath one warm, protesting feathery body and felt something hard and long among the eggs — a key! She pulled it out and found attached to it a label, which said, in Pattern's printed script:

'Tomorrow night at ten. Look under the straw-bales.'

Bonnie ran to the bales of straw which were kept for the nesting-boxes and found behind them two warm suits of clothes, a boy's, with breeches and waistcoat, and a girl's, with a thick woollen skirt and petticoat. Both were of coarse material such as tinker children wear, but well and stoutly made, and both had beautiful thick sheepskin jackets, lined with their own wool. In the pocket of each jacket was a golden guinea.

Bonnie guessed that the boy's was for her and the girl's for Sylvia.

'For Sylvia could never be got to look like a boy. Oh, how clever and good Simon is! He must have got Pattern to help him. But will Sylvia be able to travel? We *must* manage it somehow!'

She bit her lips with worry.

Snatching the opportunity while it was dark and there was nobody about, Bonnie carried the two bundles of clothes indoors and hid them in the coal-cellar behind a large mound of coal while she was supposed to be filling Mrs Brisket's evening coal-scuttle and making up her fire.

During the evening she seized another chance to take a fresh egg to Sylvia and whisper the news to her. Poor Sylvia dutifully swallowed the egg and tried to be excited by the plan, but she felt so weak and ill that she was sure she would never manage the escape, though she dared not tell Bonnie this. Bonnie could see for herself, though, how frail Sylvia looked, and she became more worried than ever.

Sunday passed in the usual tasks.

Mrs Brisket departed after ten to the party at Mr Friendshipp's, leaving the school in charge of her daughter Diana, who, as her custom was, immediately began to bully and harry the children, making them fetch and carry for her, iron her clothes, curl her hair, and polish her shoes. Mrs Brisket had forbidden her to leave the house, but she had no intention of staying in, and was proposing to visit a bazaar on the other side of the town, having calmly taken some money from her mother's purse.

'Here! You!' she called, seeing Bonnie hurrying past. 'Where are you going with that hangdog look? Come here!'

Bonnie came, as if unwillingly.

'What have you got in your pocket?'

Bonnie made no reply.

Diana thrust in her hand and let out a shriek of disgust. She withdrew it and stared at her fingers, which were dripping with egg-yolk.

'Thief! Miserable little thief! Stealing the eggs from my mother's henhouse!' She raised the dripping hand and slapped Bonnie's face with it.

Six months ago Bonnie would have slapped her back, and heartily, but she was learning patience and self-command. To be embroiled in a struggle with Diana was not part of her plan, though she longed to box the girl's ears.

'I was taking it to Sylvia,' she said steadily. 'Your

mother is starving her to death. She has had nothing to eat all day but two raw onions.'

'Is that any business of yours? Very well,' said Diana, white with temper, 'since you think you can look after Sylvia so well, you *shall* look after her.

You can look after each other in the coal-cellar. Alice, help me shut them in.'

Alice, and a couple of the larger, worse-natured girls, willingly did so. Others remonstrated, as Bonnie was pushed, and Sylvia, still in her night-clothes, half carried into the dark, dirty place.

'You shouldn't do it, Miss Diana. Sylvia's ill – it will make her worse,' exclaimed Emma.

'Hold your tongue! Who asked *you* to interfere?' shouted Diana, and slapped her. The door was locked, and the key put in its accustomed place on Mrs Brisket's parlour mantelpiece. Then, after making sure that everyone was in a properly cowed frame of mind, Diana wrapped herself in a velvet cloak and went out to the bazaar, locking the front door and taking the key with her.

Meanwhile Bonnie, in the coal-cellar, was congratulating herself on the success of her idea as she swiftly helped to dress the trembling, shivering Sylvia in her new warm clothes.

'There, Sylvia! Now don't cry, there's a lamb, for I feel sure Simon will have some good plan and will be able to take us to a place where you can be properly cared for. Don't cry!'

But Sylvia was too weak to hold back her tears. She sat obediently on a large lump of coal while Bonnie prepared to change her own clothes. But before she could do so there was a creaking of the lock and the door softly opened – not the door to the garden, but the one through which they had been thrust in. A head poked round it – Emma's.

'Bonnie! Sylvia! Are you all right? Can you come

out and get warm! Diana's out and Alice has gone to bed.'

Bonnie felt the tears prick her eyes at this courageous kindness on the part of Emma. But how ill-timed it was! At any minute Simon might arrive, and she did not want anyone to know that he was helping with their escape.

She whispered to Sylvia, 'Wait there, Sylvia, for two minutes, only two minutes, and then I'll be back,' and ran swiftly to the cellar door.

Outside stood Emma and a large number of children, all deathly silent, in the passage that led from the kitchen. One of them pointed upwards, meaning that they must make no sound for fear of Alice.

Bonnie was amazed and touched. She had had no idea how popular her bright face and friendly ways had made her with the other children, in the fairly short time she had been at Mrs Brisket's.

Impulsively she hugged Emma.

'Emma, I won't forget this! If ever I get away from this hateful place' (and oh, I pray it will be tonight, she said to herself), 'I'll send back somehow and get you out too. But Sylvia and I mustn't leave the cellar. If Mrs Brisket or Diana came back you would get into dreadful trouble.'

She looked at the children's anxious, eager faces and wished that she could do something for them. Suddenly she had an idea. She ran to Mrs Brisket's parlour and brought out the large hamper of cheese which the headmistress kept for rewarding tale-bearers.

'Here! Quick, girls! Eat this up!' She tossed out the chunks of cheese in double handfuls to the ravenous children.

'Cheese!'

'Oh, Bonnie!'

'Cheese!'

'Wonderful cheese!'

They had gobbled up most of the savoury lumps before Emma suddenly exclaimed, 'But what will Mrs Brisket say?'

'I'll take care of that,' said Bonnie grandly. She had been scribbling on a sheet of paper. 'This is to pay for the cheese,' and she now signed it with her name, fetched the guinea piece from her jacket pocket and put it with the paper on Mrs Brisket's writing-desk.

'There! She'll be angry, but she will see that I am the one to blame. Now, Emma, you must lock us up in the cellar again and put back the key. Yes!' as Emma protested, 'I promise that will be best in the end,' and she nodded vigorously to show that she meant it, and went back into the cellar.

With great reluctance Emma locked the door again. Instantly Bonnie flung off her brown overall and hustled on her boy's clothes, which felt very thick and strange, but comfortable.

'Oh, how funny I must look! I wish we could see ourselves. Here, Sylvia, I saved a piece of cheese for you. Try to eat it. It will give you some strength. We must take our aprons with us. It won't do to leave them behind, or they will guess that we have got other clothes and may be in disguise.' She bundled them up and tucked them in her capacious pockets.

'Now for the key!'

Just for one awful moment it seemed as if the somewhat roughly-made key would not open the outer door. However,wrapping a fold of her jacket over it and wrenching it with both hands, Bonnie got it round, and raised the flap. A gust of snowflakes blew into her face. 'Good, it's snowing, so much the better. We shan't leave any footprints. Now, Sylvia, you had better have my coat as well as your own.' She buttoned it on to her cousin, who was really too ill and weak to make any objection, and half-pulled, half-hoisted her up the slope down which the coal was poured. Then, swiftly, she re-locked the door, put the key in her pocket, and urged Sylvia towards the gate with an arm round her shoulders.

'We can hide in a laurel bush,' she whispered. 'There's a thick one beside the front railings. Then if Mrs Brisket or Diana should come back, they won't see us. I can hear the town clock striking ten – Simon should be here at any moment.'

And indeed, as they reached the railings, they heard his voice whispering, 'Miss Bonnie? Miss Sylvia? Is that you?'

'Yes, it's us!' Bonnie called back quietly, and ran to open the gate.

9

'Sylvia's ill!' Bonnie muttered to Simon as soon as they were outside the gate. 'She can hardly walk! I think we shall have to carry her.'

'No, she can go in the cart,' Simon whispered back, and then Bonnie saw that he had with him a beautiful little cart, drawn by a donkey.

Her eyes lit up with delight. 'Why, it's the very thing! Isn't it the one from Willoughby that we use for picnics – '

'Hush. Yes!' whispered Simon. 'Let's get away quick, and then I'll explain.'

Between them they lifted the trembling, shivering Sylvia into the cart. She gave a little protesting moan as she came into contact with something soft that seemed alive.

'What is it?' breathed Bonnie.

'The geese! They won't hurt her. There are quilts and mattresses underneath.'

Swiftly and skilfully Simon disposed Sylvia in the cart, on a warm mattress, covered with several quilts. Thirty sleepy, grumbling geese were pushed unceremoniously to one side and then, when Sylvia was settled, allowed to perch all over and round her until only her face was showing.

'There! They'll keep her famously warm.'

And in fact the warmth of the mattress and quilts and the soft feathery bodies on top was such that in two minutes Sylvia was in a deep sleep, and never even felt the cart begin to move.

'Will you ride too, Miss Bonnie?'

'No, I'll walk at the head with you, Simon.'

'Let's be off, then.'

They hastened away. Simon had tied rags round the wheels and they went silently over the cobbled road. The only sound was the tippety-tap of the donkey's feet.

When they had turned several corners, and put several streets between them and Mrs Brisket's school, both Simon and Bonnie breathed more freely.

'No one will remark us now,' said Bonnie, as they passed into a wide, naphtha-lighted street in the middle of the town, where, although it was nearly midnight, trams still clanged up and down, and pit and factory workers trudged to and fro in their clogs.

'Certainly no one would take you for Miss Bonnie Green,' said Simon, chuckling. 'You make a proper boy in those things, haircut and all. Here, I brought these for you.' He turned, sank an arm into the cart and rummaged among the geese, and brought out two sheep's-wool-lined caps, one of which he carefully placed over Sylvia's sleeping head. The other he gave to Bonnie, who gratefully pulled it on, for the snow was now falling thick and fast.

'Miss Pattern made them for you; they weren't finished in time to leave with the other things.'

'Pattern? Oh, did she make the clothes?'

'Yes, she did, when she heard I was going to help you, and James found the donkey and cart – Miss Slighcarp was going to have sold them, but James told her they belonged to parson and hid them away. I reckoned it would be just the thing for our journey. And Miss Pattern gave me a saucepan and a fry-pan and some cups and plates and a great pie – they're all in the back, under the seat. We'll have a bite to eat presently – I dare say you're clemmed, Miss Bonnie – but not till we're out of the town.'

'Where is Pattern?' asked Bonnie.

'She's gone back to live with her mother at the lodge. She sent her dear love but didn't dare ask you to call in, for Miss Slighcarp passes there every day and there's only the one room, as you know. If there's a search for you they'd be bound to go there. It's best Pattern should not have seen you.'

'And is James still at the house?'

'Yes. He gave me the guineas to put in your pockets out of his wages – and gracious knows they're little enough now.'

'I've spent mine already, Simon,' confessed Bonnie, and told what she had done.

Simon shook his head at her, but all he said was, ''Twas like you, Miss Bonnie.'

'Simon, it's ridiculous to go on calling me miss. Just call me plain Bonnie.'

Simon grinned, but answered indirectly, 'Have you

got that coal-cellar key with you? Here's a good place to get rid of it.'

They were crossing the bridge over the wide river, with its busy traffic of coal barges and wool wherries. When Bonnie produced the key and the two overalls, he made them into a bundle with a bit of string, weighted it with a cobble, and threw the whole thing into the river. Then they went on with light hearts.

The town presently gave way to country. Not much could be seen in the dark, but Bonnie caught dim glimpses of snow-covered slag-heaps, with here and there a great pit-wheel or chimney. Then they passed fields, enclosed in dry-stone walls. After a while they were climbing up a long, slow ascent, the beginning of the wolds.

'You'd best have a bit of a sleep now,' Simon suggested to Bonnie after a couple of hours had passed. 'We're safe away, and 'twill be morning by and by.'

'What about the wolves, though?' Bonnie said. 'Shan't we be in danger from them? I'd better help you keep a look-out. Have you brought a gun?'

'Ay, I've my bow, and James gave me your fowling-piece. It's in the cart. But I doubt we'll not be troubled by wolves; it's turned March now, and with spring coming they'll be moving farther north. We're not likely to see any of them once we're over Great Whinside.'

'What shall we do about Sylvia, Simon? She ought to stop somewhere till she's well enough for the journey.'

'I've been thinking that, and I know the very place. We'll reach it about six in the morning. You get in the cart and have a nap now.'

'All right, I will,' said Bonnie, who was beginning to be very sleepy, 'if you're sure the donkey can stand the load.' She patted the donkey's nose.

'Caroline's pulled heavier loads than that.'

So the cart was halted, and Bonnie, carefully, so as not to wake Sylvia, scrambled in and made a nest for herself among the feather quilts and the warm, drowsy geese. Soon she, too, was asleep.

When Bonnie woke she lay wondering for a moment where she was. There was no clanging bell, no complaining voices, and instead of shivering under her one thin blanket she was deliciously comfortable and warm.

A cool breeze blew over her face, the cart jolted, and then she remembered what had been happening and said softly, 'Simon?'

His voice came from somewhere in front. 'Yes?'

'Stop the cart a moment, I want to get out.'

'Not worth it,' he said. 'We're nearly there.'

Bonnie wriggled to a sitting position and looked about her. The sky was still mostly dark, but daylight was slowly growing in the east. Thin fronds of green and lemon-yellow were beginning to uncurl among masses of inky cloud. When Bonnie looked back she could see that they had come over a great ridge of hills, whose tops were still lost in the blackness of the sky to the north. Ahead of them was a little dale, and loops of the white road were visible leading down to it over rolling folds of moor. A tremendous hush lay over the whole countryside. Even the birds were not awake yet.

'That's where we'll have our breakfast.' Simon pointed ahead. 'That's Herondale. We're way off the main road now. No one's likely to come looking for us here.'

He began to whistle a soft tune as he walked, and Bonnie, curling up even more snugly, watched in great contentment as the lemon-yellow sky changed to orange and then to red, and presently the sun burst up in a blaze of gold.

'Simon.'

'What is it?'

'There's no snow here.'

'Often it's like that,' he said nodding. 'We've left snow t'other side of Whinside. Down in Herondale it'll be warm.'

Presently they came to the last steep descent into the valley, and Simon then allowed Bonnie to get out of the cart while he adjusted the drag on the wheels to stop it running downhill too fast. All this time Sylvia slept. She stirred a little as they reached the foot of the hill and walked through a fringe of rowan trees into a tiny village consisting of three or four cottages round a green, with a couple of outlying farms.

'We'll go to the forge,' said Simon, and led the donkey across the green to a low building under a great walnut tree.

Bonnie fell back and walked beside the cart, smiling at Sylvia's puzzled, sleepy face. The geese were beginning to stir and stretch their long necks, and at first sight of them Sylvia looked slightly alarmed, but when she saw Bonnie she smiled too, and shut her eyes again.

'Smith's up,' said Simon. A thread of smoke dribbled from the forge chimney, and they could see a red glow over the stable-door in front, while the noise of bellows came in a regular wheezing roar.

Simon called over the forge door.

'Mr Wilderness!'

The roaring stopped and there was a clink. Then a face appeared over the half door and the smith came out. He was an immensely tall man, wearing a blackened leather apron. Bonnie couldn't help smiling, he looked so like a large, gentle, white-haired lion, with a pair of dark eyes like those of a collie dog, half-hidden by the locks of white hair that fell over his forehead.

'Eh, it's you, Simon me boy? What road can I help you?'

'Caroline's loosed a shoe,' said Simon, patting the donkey, 'and as well as that we'd like your advice about the little lass here. She's not well.'

'Childer come afore donkeys,' Mr Wilderness said. He moved over beside the cart and looked down at Sylvia's face among the geese. 'Eh, a pretty little fair lass she be. What's amiss with her?'

'She's got a cough and a sore throat and a fever,' explained Bonnie.

The smith gazed at Bonnie wide-eyed.

'And th'art another of 'em, bless me! Who'd ha' thought it? I took thee for a boy in that rig. Well, she's sleeping fair in a goosefeather bed, tha can't better that. Are they goosefeathers?' he said to Simon.

'Stuffed the quilts and mattresses myself,' said Simon nodding, 'My own geese.'

'Champion! Goose grease for chilblains, goosefeathers for a chill. We'll leave her in the cart.'

'Shouldn't she be put to bed?' Bonnie said doubtfully.

'Nay, where, lass? I've only the forge and the kitchen, where I sleep mysen. Nay, we'll put her, cart and all, in the shippen, she'll be gradely there.'

He led them round the corner of the forge and showed them how to back the cart into a big barn with double doors on each side. When he opened these, sunlight poured into the place and revealed that it was half-full of hay, and lined along the walls with lambing pens made from hurdles. A tremendous baaing and bleating came from these and, walking along, Bonnie saw with delight that each pen contained a sheep and one, two, or three lambs.

'There's nought like lying wi' sheep two-three days for a chesty cough,' pronounced Mr Wilderness. 'The breath of sheep has a powerful virtue in it. That and a brew of my cherry-bark syrup with maybe a spoonful of honey in it, and a plateful or two of good porridge, will set her to rights better than the grandest doctor in the kingdom. Put her in the sun there, lad. When sun gets round we can open t'other doors and let him in that side. Now for a bite o' breakfast. I'm fair clemmed, and happen you'll be the same, if you've walked all the way fro' Blastburn.'

'We've a pie and some victuals,' Simon said.

'Nay, lad, save thy pie for later. Porridge is on the forge fire this minute, and what's better nor that?'

The geese had climbed and fluttered out of the cart, and were busy foraging in the hay. Bonnie, after making sure that Sylvia was well covered and had gone back to sleep, was glad to come into the smith's clean little kitchen, which opened off the smithy and was as warm as an oven. They sat down at a table covered with a checked red-and-white cloth.

Mr Wilderness's porridge was very different from that served in Mrs Brisket's school. It was eaten with brown sugar from a big blue bag, and with dollops of thick yellow cream provided by Mr Wilderness's two red cows, who stood sociably outside the kitchen door while breakfast was going on, and licked the nose of Caroline the donkey.

After the porridge they had great slices of sizzling bacon and cups of scalding brown tea.

Then the smith prepared a draught of his cherry-bark medicine, syrupy golden stuff with a wonderful aromatic scent, and took it out to Sylvia, who was stirring drowsily. She swallowed it down, smiled a sleepy no-thank-you to an offer of porridge and cream, and closed her eyes again.

'Ay, sleep's the best cure of all,' said Mr Wilderness. 'You look as if you could do wi' a bit too, my lass.'

Bonnie did begin to feel that she could do nothing but yawn, and so Simon made her a nest in the hay and covered her with one of his goosefeather quilts. Here in the sun amid the comfortable creaking of the geese and the baaing chorus of the sheep she too fell into a long and dreamless sleep.

They stayed with Mr Wilderness for three days, until he pronounced Sylvia better and fit to travel.

In the meantime Simon helped the smith by blowing the fire and carving wooden handles for the farm implements he made. Bonnie washed all his curtains, tablecloths, and sheets, and, aided by Simon, did a grand spring-clean of the cottage.

'Two months ago I shouldn't have known how to do this,' she said cheerfully, beating mats on the village green. 'Going to Mrs Brisket's at least taught me housework and how to look after hens.'

Mr Wilderness was sorry to lose them when they went. 'If tha'd ha' stayed another two-three weeks th' birds would ha' been nesting, and th' primroses all showing their little pink faces. Herondale's a gradely place i' springtime.'

'*Pink* faces?' said Bonnie disbelievingly. 'Don't you mean yellow?'

'Nay, they're pink round here, lass, and the geraniums is blue.'

But even with this inducement they wanted to press on to London. They left with many farewells, promising that they would call in on the return journey, or come over as soon as they were safely back at Willoughby Chase.

The journey to London took them nearly two months. They had to go at goose-pace, for in the day-time the geese flew out of the cart and wandered along as they chose, pecking any edible thing by the road-side, and, as Simon explained, 'There's no sense in hurrying the geese or by the time we reach Smithfield they'll be thin and scrawny, and nobody will buy 'em.'

'Anyway,' said Bonnie, 'supposing Mrs Brisket and Miss Slighcarp have set people searching for us, the search will surely have died down by the end of two months.'

So they made their leisurely way, picking flowers, of which they found more and more as spring advanced and they travelled farther south, watching birds, and stopping to bathe and splash in moorland brooks.

At night they usually camped near a farm, sleeping in or under the cart in their warm goosefeather quilts. If it rained, farmers offered them shelter in barn or haymow. Often a kindly farmer's wife invited them in for a plate of stew and sped them on their way with a baking of pasties and apple dumplings. In return, Sylvia did exquisite darning, Bonnie helped with housework, and Simon, who could turn his hand to anything, ploughed, or milked, or sawed wood, or mended broken tools.

Pattern had smuggled one or two books and Bonnie's paintbox from the attic out to the cart with the food and clothes, and these were a great resource on rainy evenings in the hay. They read aloud to each other, and Simon, who had never bothered about reading before, learned how, and even pronounced it quite a handy accomplishment. He also took a keen pleasure in making use of Bonnie's box of colours, and sometimes could hardly be torn away from some view of a crag or waterfall that he was busy sketching. The girls would wander slowly on with Caroline, the cart, and the geese, until Simon, finished at last, caught them up at a run with the colour-box under his arm and the painting held out at arm's length to dry.

Sylvia and Bonnie thought his pictures very beautiful, but Simon was always dissatisfied with them, and would give them away to any passer-by who admired them. Several times people pressed money on him for them, and once, when they were stopping overnight in a little village named Beckside, the landlord of the inn, the Snake and Ladder, who had seen one of the sketches, asked if Simon would repaint his faded inn-sign. So they spent a pleasant day at the village, feeding like gamecocks at the innkeeper's table on roast duck and apple cheesecake, while Simon painted a gorgeous green-and-gold serpent twined in the rungs of a pruning-ladder.

'Should you like to be a painter, do you think, Simon?' Sylvia asked.

'I might,' he confessed. 'I'd never thought of such a trade before. Eh, though, but there's a lot to learn! And I doubt I'd never have the money for a teacher.'

Bonnie opened her lips to speak, and then checked herself, sighing.

Late in April they came to the top of Hampstead Hill, among the grey old houses and the young green trees.

At the foot of the hill they could see the village of Chalk Farm, and, far away, the great city of London spread out, with its blue veil of smoke and its myriads of spires and chimneys. Sylvia felt a quickening of her heart to think she was so close to her dear Aunt Jane again. How pleased the old lady would be to see her beloved little niece!

They camped that night on Hampstead Heath near a tribe of gipsies – and indeed they looked like gipsies themselves. Bonnie and Simon were as brown as berries and their black locks were decidedly in want of cutting, while even Sylvia would hardly have been recognized for the thin, pale, fair child who had set out to Willoughby Chase so many months ago. Her cheeks were pink, and her hair, though not its original length yet, was thick and shining and reached to her shoulders.

They found an obliging dairyman in Hampstead Village who was willing to keep Caroline and the cart for them in his stable, and next day they drove the geese down into London.

'You girls had best not come to Smithfield Market,'

said Simon. 'It's a rough, wild place, not fit for little maids.'

'I've been thinking,' suggested Bonnie, 'how would it be if we tried to find Mr Gripe's office while you are at the Market? Sylvia, can you tell us where lawyers' offices in London are usually to be found?'

Sylvia said she thought they were in the region of Chancery Lane. Having inquired the way of a constable, therefore, the girls accompanied Simon as far as Lincoln's Inn Fields, and there he left them with Goosey and Gandey, the two parent geese, who were never sold, while he went on to dispose of the rest of the flock.

Bonnie and Sylvia wandered along outside the houses that surrounded the Fields and saw on brass door-plates the names of many attorneys, barristers, and Commissioners for Oaths, but nowhere that of Mr Gripe.

At about midday when, tired, they were lying sunning themselves on the grass, and eating sliced beef and lemon tarts procured at a near-by cookshop, Bonnie suddenly exclaimed:

'Look, Sylvia, look! Isn't that Mr Grimshaw?'

A portly, middle-aged man was walking across the grass towards a near-by archway. Sylvia scrutinized him closely and whispered.

'Yes! I am almost sure it is he! If he would but turn his head this way!'

'We must follow him and find out,' Bonnie said decisively. 'If he, too, is in London we shall have to be on our guard.'

The two children got up and, calling their geese,

walked fast, but not so as to attract his attention, after the gentleman in question. He passed through the archway, descended some steps, and turned into a small street, where he stopped outside one of the houses.

'Perhaps it is his residence,' whispered Sylvia.

They approached slowly. Unfortunately a large black cat was seated on the pavement, and if there was one animal that Goosey abominated, it was a cat. He set up a vociferous honking and cackling, and the gentleman, in the act of ringing the doorbell, turned his head and looked at the two girls. His eyes passed over Bonnie, but he stared very sharply at Sylvia for an instant – then the door opened and he was admitted.

'Oh mercy!' exclaimed Sylvia, 'do you think he recognized me? For it was *undoubtedly* Mr Grimshaw! I could not have sat so long opposite him in the train and been mistaken.'

'I am not certain if he knew you,' said Bonnie uneasily. 'It is possible. You are not so sunburned as Simon or I. We had better not remain in this vicinity.'

They were turning to go when Bonnie's quick eyes caught sight of the brass plate by the door that Mr Grimshaw had entered.

'Look Sylvia! Abednego Gripe, Attorney. Father's man of business! Is not that a lucky chance!'

'Is it so lucky?' said Sylvia doubtfully, as they retraced their steps along the street. 'I do not like the fact that Mr Grimshaw has gone to see him. Why can he have done so, do you suppose?'

'No, you are right,' Bonnie answered thoughtfully.

'It is very queer. At all events, we must not go to see Mr Gripe while Mr Grimshaw is there. We had best wait until we have seen Aunt Jane and asked her advice.'

They remounted the steps and saw Simon crossing Lincoln's Inn Fields. He waved to them triumphantly.

'Twenty-two pounds, girls! They fetched fourteen and eightpence each!' he called as soon as he came within earshot. 'We are rich!'

'Heavens, what a lot of money!' breathed Sylvia.

'Let us be off to Aunt Jane at once,' said Bonnie.

'Shall you want me to come?' asked Simon diffidently.'

'Gracious, yes! Why ever not?'

'I'm only poor and rough –'

'Oh, what nonsense,' said Bonnie, seizing his hand. 'You can't come all this way with us and then desert us now, just when things might turn out better! Sylvia, tell us how to get from here to Park Lane.'

They finished their four-hundred-mile journey riding on the open upper deck of one of the new horse-drawn omnibuses, geese and all, though Sylvia did rather shudder to think what Aunt Jane would say to this, should she chance to be looking out of her window when they arrived. Aunt Jane had many times told Sylvia that *no* lady *ever* rode in an omnibus, and more particularly not on the upstairs deck.

'I feel half-afraid,' confessed Sylvia, laughing, looking up at the familiar tall house with its Grecian columns on either side of the door and white window-boxes filled with lobelia. 'Look, Bonnie, that is our window — the attic one, right up in the roof.'

'The window-box flowers are withered,' commented Simon.

'So they are. That is not like Aunt Jane,' said Sylvia, puzzled. 'She usually waters them so carefully.'

The main door to the house stood open, and they went in silence up the stairs – up, up again, and still up. As they passed a door on the fourth-floor landing, it flew open and a young man's head popped out exclaiming, 'Is that the grocer? Have you brought my pies and turpentine? Oh – ' in disappointment, as he saw Simon and Bonnie and the geese. Sylvia had impatiently gone on ahead. The young man eyed them in surprise a moment, then shut his door again.

They caught up with Sylvia on the top landing. She was already tapping at Aunt Jane's attic door.

'It is strange! She does not answer!'

'Perhaps she's out shopping?' suggested Simon.

'But she always takes tea at this time of day.' (It was five o'clock.)

'She could not have moved away?' Bonnie said with a sinking heart.

'No,' exclaimed Sylvia in relief, 'here is the spare door-key that she always keeps under the oilcloth in case by some mischance she should lose her other one. She must be out, after all. We will go in and surprise her on her return.'

She opened the door with the key, and, cautioning them by laying her finger on her lips, tiptoed in. Bonnie and Simon rather shyly followed and stood hesitating in the tiny hallway, while Sylvia went on into the one room which served Aunt Jane for kitchen, parlour, and bedroom.

Suddenly they heard Sylvia give a faint cry, and she came back to them, white and frightened.

'What is it, Sylvia?' said Bonnie anxiously.

'It is Aunt Jane! Oh, I think she must be dreadfully ill, or in a faint – she is there, and so thin and pale and hardly breathing! Come, come quickly!'

They hastened after her, Simon pausing but a moment to shut the geese out on the landing. They saw the poor old lady stretched on her bed under the jet-trimmed mantle. Her eyes were closed, and her breathing was rapid and shallow. 'Aunt Jane?' whispered Sylvia. 'It is I, Sylvia!' There was no reply.

10

All three children retreated on to the landing once more. It seemed dreadful to stay in the little close room and talk about Aunt Jane with her quite unconscious of their presence. Sylvia noticed that the window was shut, the dishes unwashed. A thick layer of dust covered everything.

'What do you think is the matter with her?' Sylvia said, her voice quavering.

'I don't know,' said Bonnie decidedly, 'but whatever it is, we must get a doctor to her at once.'

'Yes, Bonnie, how sensible of you! But where shall we find one?'

'Has Aunt Jane no regular doctor?'

'She always said she could not afford one,' said Sylvia, dissolving into tears. 'She always said all her ailments could be cured by P-Parkinson's Penny Pink Pills.'

'Now come, Sylvia, don't get into those crying ways again,' Bonnie began, sounding cross because she was so worried, when Simon interposed:

'I think I saw a doctor's plate on the floor below. Wait a moment and I'll go down and make certain.'

He pushed past the geese, who were roosting on the stairs, and ran down to the landing below. Sure enough, by the door out of which the head had popped was a notice: **GABRIEL FIELD** – *PHYSICIAN AND CHIRURGEON.*

Simon knocked. A voice shouted, 'Come in, it's not locked,' and so he pushed open the door and looked into a room which was in a considerable degree of confusion. Several shelves along the walls bore a clutter of bottles, phials, and surgical implements; a large table was covered with brushes, jars, and tubes of paint, while the floor was almost equally littered with stacks of canvases and piles of medical books.

The young man who had looked out before stood with a paint-brush in his hand, considering a half-finished painting on a large easel.

'Oh, it's you again, is it?' he said, seeing Simon's perplexed face come round the door. 'What d'you want?'

Simon found something reassuring in his rather brusque manner.

'Please, are you Doctor Field, sir?'

'Yes, I am.'

'The old lady upstairs is very ill. Could you come and look at her?'

'Certainly. Just a moment while I wash my hands.'

While Doctor Field was washing, and fetching a black bag of medicines from his bedroom, Simon stared at the picture on the easel.

'Like it?' said the doctor, coming back.

'Yes,' said Simon. 'I do, very much. But I'm not sure about this bottom right-hand corner. It seems a bit too dark.'

The doctor gave him a surprised look before

waving him out of the door and hurrying upstairs. He brushed past the two girls and the geese without comment, and made his way in to Aunt Jane's bedside. 'One of you two girls come and help me,' he said, so Sylvia went, while the other two remained on the landing in a silence of anxiety and suspense.

They had to wait some time, while Dr Field made a thorough examination of Aunt Jane. Then he and Sylvia came out on to the landing again.

'She's your aunt, is she?' he said sharply. 'Well, you've been neglecting her. She's suffering from malnutrition.' As none of them appeared to understand this word he added impatiently, 'Under-nourishment. She's been starving herself.'

Sylvia began to cry quietly.

'Oh, poor, *poor* Aunt Jane! I should never have left her.'

'I'm to blame, too,' said the doctor angrily. 'I saw her coming upstairs, a couple of weeks ago, with her shopping – one egg and an apple. I should have guessed.'

'What does she need, sir?' said Simon quietly. 'I'll go out and get it.'

'Firstly, champagne. She's too weak to take anything else at the moment. You needn't bother about that, I've a bottle in my room. Then beef-tea, eggs, milk, butter, honey.'

'We'll go and get them,' said Bonnie. 'Come on, Simon. I saw a basket in Aunt Jane's parlour. Sylvia, you stay with the doctor and see to the champagne. Can you direct us to the nearet market, sir? We have only just come to London and don't know our way about.'

Dr Field told them how to find the nearest market, and they ran off with their basket, while Sylvia helped administer a few teaspoonfuls of champagne to Aunt Jane, tipping it between her motionless lips.

'You're the old lady's niece, are you?' the doctor said. 'I've only been in this house a month. I thought she had no kin at all. It's high time she was properly looked after.'

Sylvia considered the doctor. He had a kind, sensible face, and she was inclined to confide the whole story to him and ask his advice, but thought she had better wait till the others returned.

Simon and Bonnie soon came back. They were loaded, for, as well as the food, Simon was carrying a small sack of coal, and Bonnie had a blanket and a fleecy shawl.

While they were out they had had a short, brisk argument.'

'Simon, this is your money we're spending – your year's money. We shouldn't be doing it.'

'Oh, fiddlesticks!' he said uncomfortably. 'Anybody would do all they could to help that poor old lady.'

'Well, I shall pay you back as soon as I possibly can, Simon, if I ever get my own home and money back, but otherwise you do understand you'll have to wait till I can earn some money, and gracious knows how many months that will be!'

'Oh, get along with you, girl, you're wasting time,' said Simon good-naturedly.

Dr Field suggested that they should do their cooking downstairs in his room in order not to disturb the invalid, so Bonnie, first borrowing Aunt Jane's cookery book, set about scraping some beef and putting it to simmer with carrots and a teaspoonful of brandy. Simon lit a fire in Aunt Jane's room, and Sylvia tiptoed about cleaning the place and setting it to rights. Every now and then Dr Field came and administered another teaspoonful of champagne, and presently he reported with satisfaction an improvement in the patient's breathing and a tinge of colour in her cheeks.

'Your cousin's cooked you a meal,' he said to Sylvia and Simon after a while. 'Better come down and eat it in my room.'

They realized they had not eaten all day, and were glad to come down. Bonnie had cooked a great panful of bacon and eggs, which she cordially invited the doctor to share.

'Are you all cousins?' said he, when they were eating, among the paints and bottles of medicine.

'Oh no. Sylvia and I are, but Simon's no relation.'

'Where are all your parents?'

They looked at each other, and, without the need for discussion, decided that they could trust the doctor. Bonnie told him the whole story, ending with the sight of Mr Grimshaw at the lawyer's office that morning. 'And oh, sir,' she ended, with tears in her eyes, 'can you tell me if the ship my parents sailed in truly sank? *Truly?*'

'What was its name?'

'The *Thessaly*.'

'Yes, my poor child,' he said sadly. 'I wish I could tell you otherwise, but I read the report in *The Times* myself. It was said that the captain should never have set sail, knowing the dangerous state of the ship's hull. It was said that someone must have paid him handsomely to do so, and it was rumoured that he himself had escaped in a small boat, some hours before the wreck.'

Bonnie could not speak for a moment. She turned away to the window and bit her lip.

Dr Field went on hastily to break the unhappy silence:

'The whole business sounds to me like a plot, hatched up beforehand between this Miss Slighcarp of yours, who's evidently a thorough wrong 'un, and her precious friends Grimshaw and Mrs Brisket. Whether Gripe the lawyer has a hand in it too we can't be sure, but I've a friend who's a lawyer, and as soon as old Miss Green's fit to be left I'll go and see him, and ask him what he knows about Gripe.'

'Oh, *could* you, sir? Thank you indeed.'

Their faces of gratitude evidently touched his heart, for he said gruffly, 'A couple of you can bed down here if you like. I've plenty of cushions. Just shift some of those books and pictures and the skeleton off the sofa.' (Sylvia gave a faint scream. She had not noticed the skeleton before.) 'One of you should sleep upstairs with the old lady. And you'd better all get yourselves a wash and brush-up. You look as if you can do with it.'

The beef-tea was ready now, and Sylvia, with the

doctor's help, fed some of it to Aunt Jane through a straw. She opened her eyes once or twice, but seemed hardly conscious of her surroundings yet.

With the aid of a couple of the doctor's blankets Sylvia made herself up a couch for the night by the side of Aunt Jane's bed. They were all tired, and went to sleep as soon as they lay down.

In the middle of the night Sylvia awoke. She had left a nightlight burning, and by its faint glimmer she saw that Aunt Jane had raised herself on her pillows and was looking wonderingly about her.

'Mind, Auntie,' said Sylvia, springing up. 'You'll uncover yourself!'

Carefully she arranged the woolly shawl round her aunt's shoulders again.

'It *is* Sylvia! But no,' said Aunt Jane mournfully. 'I have so often dreamed that she came back. This must be just another dream.'

'No it isn't!' said Sylvia, forgetting to be careful in her joy and giving her aunt an impetuous hug, 'it really is me, come back to look after you. And I've brought Bonnie too.'

'Sylvia, my precious child,' Aunt Jane murmured, and two tears slipped down her cheeks.

'Now, Aunt dear, you *mustn't*! You must get strong quickly. Please try to sip some of this,' said Sylvia, who had been hastily heating up the beef-tea over the nightlight.

Aunt Jane sipped it, and soon, for she was still very weak, she slipped off to sleep, holding Sylvia's hand. Sylvia, too, began to doze, leaning against her aunt's bed, half-awake and half-dreaming.

She dreamed that she was on top of a mountain, the black ridge that they had crossed before they reached Herondale. She saw Miss Slighcarp coming up from Blastburn at the head of a pack of wolves. Sylvia was dumb with fright. She was unable to move. Nearer and nearer Miss Slighcarp came, tramp, tramp, tramp . . .

Suddenly Sylvia was awake. And listening. And there *were* footsteps coming up the stairs.

She lay palpitating, with her heart hot against her ribs. Who could it be? The night was still black dark. No light showed under the door. If it was the doctor, surely he would be carrying a light? The steps were very slow, very cautious, as if whoever it was wanted to make as little sound as possible. Sylvia knew that she must move – she *must* –

A frantic cackling, hissing, and honking broke out on the stairs. There was a yell, a thud, more cackling, pandemonium!

'What is it?' said Aunt Jane drowsily.

'Oh, what can it be?' cried Sylvia, pale with terror. But the noise had shaken her out of her paralysis, and she seized a candle, lit it at the nightlight, and ran to the door.

The scene that met her eyes when she held the door open was a strange one. At the top of the stairs were two indignant geese, still hissing and arching their necks for battle. Prone on the stairs, head down, and cursing volubly, was Mr Grimshaw. Simon held one of his arms and Bonnie the other.

Dr Field, in a dressing-gown, looking sleepy and considerably annoyed, was emerging from his front

door holding a piece of rope, with which he proceeded to tie Mr Grimshaw's hands and ankles.

'Breaking into people's houses at three in the morning,' he muttered. 'That's really a bit high! It's bad enough having children and geese camped all over the place.'

'It was lucky the geese sounded the alarm,' said Bonnie, pale, but clutching Mr Grimshaw gamely.

'True,' Dr Field agreed. 'Now, lock him in the broom-closet. Good. I'll just run down and bolt the outside door, then perhaps we can have a bit more sleep. We'll get to the bottom of all this in the morning.'

Yawning, they all went back to bed, but Sylvia declared she was too scared to sleep without Bonnie, and so they brought up more of the doctor's cushions and made a double pallet beside Aunt Jane's bed.

11

Dr Field's face at breakfast next morning was grim, and the children were all rather silent. The unseen presence of Mr Grimshaw in the broom-cupboard put a damper on their spirits.

'What do you suppose he was trying to *do*?' whispered Bonnie.

'Oh, very likely just see if you were there,' said Dr Field doubtfully . 'Or try to frighten the old lady into handing you over if you should turn up later. At all events, you and the geese between you put an effective stop to him. I shall take him straight to Bow Street after breakfast and put him in charge of the constables.'

Luckily Aunt Jane was a great deal better this morning. After the doctor had inspected her, he pronounced that she might be given a little warm gruel and some tea and dry toast, which Bonnie and Sylvia prepared. Aunt Jane greeted Bonnie kindly and declared that she would never have recognized her – which was very probable, as the last time she had seen Bonnie had been at her christening. Then Sylvia announced that she would remain with the old lady while the rest of the party went off with the prisoner; the very sight of Mr Grimshaw, she said, made her feel sick with fright. Dr Field considered this to be a sensible plan, and he told Simon to go out and whistle for a hackney-cab.

Mr Grimshaw was released from his closet, but his bonds were not untied. He was sulky, threatening, and lachrymose by turns; in the same breath he begged for mercy and then swore he would get even with them.

'That's enough, my man. You can spare your breath,' said Dr Field, and showed him a blunderbuss, ready primed, which he had taken out of his desk drawer. At sight of this weapon Mr Grimshaw relapsed into a cowed silence.

'Shall I get my fowling-piece?' exclaimed Bonnie, and then remembered that it was with the cart in Hampstead.

Dr Field looked slightly startled but said he thought one weapon should be sufficient to keep the scoundrel in order.

At this moment Simon came back to report that a cab was waiting below, and after a solicitous farewell to Aunt Jane and Sylvia, bidding the latter keep the door locked and admit nobody, they took their departure.

At Bow Street they waited only a very few minutes while the doctor haled his prisoner into the Constabulary Office; he soon reappeared, accompanied by a couple of burly, sharp-looking individuals who marched Grimshaw between them, and they all piled into the cab again.

'Where is he to be taken now?' said Bonnie.

'We shall go to Mr Gripe's office for some explanation of Grimshaw's behaviour,' Dr Field told her. 'He has said that he worked for Mr Gripe.'

They were soon back in the region of Lincoln's Inn Fields, and drove up to the house that Bonnie and Sylvia had seen the day before. A scared-looking clerk, hardly more than a boy, admitted them into a waiting-room, and next moment a thin, agitated, grey-haired man hurried into the room, exclaiming, 'What can I do for you gentlemen? I am Abednego Gripe.'

He appeared excessively surprised to see the children and the manacled Mr Grimshaw. Bonnie soon decided that he could not have hatched a dark plot to obtain possession of Willoughby Chase – he looked too kind and harmless.

One of the Bow Street officers spoke up.

'I am Sam Cardigan, sir, an officer of the constabulary. Here is my card. Can you identify this person here?' indicating Mr Grimshaw.

'Why yes,' said Mr Gripe, looking at Mr Grimshaw with distaste. 'His name is Grimshaw. He was a clerk in my office until he was dismissed for forgery.'

'Aha!' said the other Bow Street officer, whose name was Spock.

'Have you ever seen him since you dismissed him?' said Dr Field.

'No indeed. He would have a very cold reception in this office.'

'And yet he was seen entering here yesterday,' snapped Cardigan.

Mr Gripe seemed surprised. 'Not to my knowledge.'

Cardigan looked thunderously disbelieving and

was about to burst out with his suspicions of Mr Gripe, when the little clerk who had let the party in, and who had been standing in the doorway with eyes like saucers, piped up:

'Please, sir, I saw him.'

Mr Grimshaw darted a furious look at this speaker.

'Who are you?' said Cardigan.

'Please sir, Marmot, a clerk. Yesterday while Mr Gripe was out having dinner, th-that gentleman as is tied up there came and asked me to give him the address of Miss Jane Green, sister to Sir Willoughby.'

'And you gave it him?'

'Yes, sir. He said he wished to take her some dividends.'

'Dividends, indeed!' growled Dr Field. 'Wanted to murder her more probably.'

'Certainly not,' said Grimshaw, pale with fright. 'I merely wished to ascertain from her if these children, who are the runaway wards of a friend of mine, had taken shelter with her.'

'At three o'clock in the morning? A fine story! More likely you wanted to terrify her into signing some document giving you power over the children. And what about this Letitia Slighcarp?' continued Dr Field, glaring at the lawyer. 'Were you responsible for sending that female fiend to feather her nest at Willoughby Chase?'

Mr Gripe looked very much alarmed. 'She is a distant relation of Sir Willoughby. She came with the highest references,' he began. 'From the Duchess of Kensington. I have them still.' He pulled out a drawer in a cabinet and produced a paper. Cardigan scanned it.

'A patent forgery,' he said at once. 'I have seen the Duchess's signature on many documents and it is utterly unlike this.'

'Then I have been duped!' cried Mr Gripe, growing paler still. 'But what can have been the object of this deceit?'

'Why,' said Bonnie indignantly, 'Miss Slighcarp has taken our whole house for her own, dismissed all the servants, sent me and my cousin to live in a school that is no better than a workhouse or prison, and treated us with miserable cruelty! And I believe, too, she and Mr Grimshaw had some hand in seeing that Papa and Mamma set sail on a ship that was known to be likely to sink!'

'This is a bad business, a very bad business,' said Mr Gripe.

'No, no!' cried Mr Grimshaw, now nearly dead of terror. 'We were not responsible for that! The ship was sunk by an unscrupulous owner to obtain the insurance. It was when I learned – through a friend who was a shipping clerk – that they were to sail on the *Thessaly*, that the plan took shape. I had seen Sir Willoughby's letter to Mr Gripe, asking him to seek out his cousin Letitia Slighcarp, as an instructress for his daughter and so – and so – '

'And so you conspired with Miss Slighcarp and forged her credentials,' said Mr Gripe angrily. 'It is all very plain, sir! Take him away, gentlemen! Take him away and keep him fast until he can appear before a magistrate.'

'After that it was very dull,' said Bonnie, reporting the scene to Sylvia later. 'I had to tell the Bow Street officers every single thing I could remember that Miss Slighcarp had done, and the clerk wrote it all down, and Mr Gripe looked more and more shocked, especially when I told what I had seen when we looked through the hole in the secret panel and watched them tearing up Papa's will and all the other documents.

'And the end of it all is, Sylvia, that Mr Grimshaw is committed to prison until the Assizes, when he will stand his trial for fraud, and the Bow Street officers are to go to Willoughby tomorrow to seize Miss Slighcarp!'

'How surprised she will be!' exclaimed Sylvia with lively pleasure. 'I almost wish I could be there to see!'

'But, Sylvia, you are to be there! They most particularly requested that you and I should be taken too, to act as witnesses.'

'But who will look after Aunt Jane?' inquired Sylvia anxiously.

'Dr Field has said that he would procure a nurse for a few days. And it need be for only two – you can return directly Miss Slighcarp is apprehended. And Sylvia, as soon as Aunt Jane is well enough to travel, I have asked Mr Gripe to arrange that she shall come and live at Willoughby, and be our guardian.'

'Oh *yes*!' exclaimed Sylvia, her face brightening, 'what a splendid plan, Bonnie!'

It was a gay and lively party that assembled in the train next day – very different from that earlier and sorrowful departure when Sylvia had taken leave of Aunt Jane. A special coupé compartment had been chartered, and the Bow Street officers had no objection to Simon and his geese travelling in it as well. Dr

Field was remaining to keep an eye on Aunt Jane, but he bade the children a cordial farewell and invited them to come and sleep in his apartment again when they returned to take Aunt Jane to Willoughby. Mr Gripe the lawyer was with them, and had given his clerk instructions to procure a luncheon hamper from which came the most savoury smells. Sylvia smiled faintly as she thought of the other tiny food-packet and Mr Grimshaw's sumptuous jam-filled cakes.

'I suppose he only pretended to have forgotten who he was when the portmanteau fell on him', she said to Bonnie.

'So that he would be taken to Willoughby,' said Bonnie, nodding. 'How I wish that we had left him in the train!'

'Still, he did save me from the wolves.'

There were no wolves to be seen on this journey. The packs had all retreated to the bleak north country, and the train ran through smiling pasture-lands, all astir with sheep and lambs, or through green and golden woods carpeted with bluebells.

The day passed gaily, with songs and story-telling – even the dry Mr Gripe proved to know a number of amusing tales – and in between the laughter and chat Cardigan and Spock, the Bow Street officers, busily wrote down in their notebooks more and more of the dreadful deeds of Miss Slighcarp recounted to them by Bonnie and Sylvia.

They reached Willoughby Station at dawn. Mr Gripe had written to one of the inns at Blastburn for a chaise and it was there to meet them.

'How different this road seems,' said Sylvia, as they

set off at a gallop. 'Last time I travelled along it there were wolves and snow and it was cold and dark – now I see primroses everywhere and I am so hot in these clothes that I can hardly breathe.'

They were still wearing the tinker children's clothes Pattern had made them, for there had been no time in London to get any others made. Mr Gripe's eye winced when it encountered them, for he liked children to look neat and nicely dressed.

'Let us hope that Miss Slighcarp has not got rid of all our own clothes,' said Bonnie.

When they reached the boundary of Willoughby Park they saw an enormous notice, new since they had left. It said:

WILLOUGHBY CHASE SCHOOL

A select Seminary for the Daughters of
Gentlemen and the Nobility
Boarders and Parlour Boarders
Principals: MISS L. SLIGHCARP AND MRS BRISKET

'What impertinence!' gasped Bonnie. 'Can she really have made our home into a school?'

'This is worse even than I had feared,' said Mr Gripe grimly, as the chaise turned into the gateway.

They took the longer and more roundabout road that led to the back of the house, for the Bow Street officers wanted to surprise Miss Slighcarp.

'Didn't you say there was a secret passage, miss?' Sam Cardigan said to Bonnie.

'Yes, and a priests' hole and an oubliette –'

'Very good. Couldn't be better. We'll put some ginger in the good lady's gravy.'

He explained his plan to Mr Gripe and the children, and then they knocked at the back door. It was opened by James.

'Miss Bonnie! Miss Sylvia!' he exclaimed, scarlet with joy and surprise. They both flung themselves on him and hugged him.

'James, dear James! Are you all right? Is Pattern all right? What is going on here?'

'Terrible doings, miss – '

'Now, now,' said Sam Cardigan. 'Pleasure at seeing old acquaintance all very well, but business is business. We must get under cover. My man, where can this carriage be concealed?'

'It can go in the coach-house, sir,' James told him. 'There's only Miss Slighcarp's landau now.'

The carriage was hastily put away, and the conspirators took refuge in the dairy.

'Now James,' said Bonnie, dancing with excitement, 'you must go and tell Miss Slighcarp that Sylvia and I have come back, and that we are *very* sad and sorry for having run away. Don't say anything about these gentlemen.'

'Yes, miss,' said James, his eyes beginning to twinkle. 'She's teaching just now, up in the schoolroom. The pupils study for an hour before breakfast.'

'Is the entrance to the secret passage still open, James? Has Miss Slighcarp ever discovered it?'

'No to the second and yes to the first, Miss Bonnie,' said James, and pulled aside the cupboard and horse-blankets which he had arranged to conceal the opening.

'Capital! Go to her quickly, then, James! Tell her we are starving!'

'You don't look it, begging your pardon, miss,' said James, grinning, and left the room. Mr Gripe and the two Bow Street officers squeezed their way into the secret passage. Simon, who had left his geese in the stable-yard, hesitated, but Mr Gripe said, 'Come on, come on, boy. The more witnesses, the better,' so he followed.

Bonnie and Sylvia spent the time while they waited for James's return in artistically dirtying and untidying each other, rubbing dust and coal on their faces, rumpling their hair, and making themselves look as dejected and orphanly as possible.

James came back with a long face.

'You're to come up to the schoolroom, young ladies. At once.'

He led the way, and they followed in silence. The house bore traces everywhere of its new use as a school. On the crystal chandelier in the ballroom ropes had been slung for climbing, and the billiards-table had been exchanged for backboards. The portraits of ancestors in the long gallery had been replaced by notice-boards and the gold-leaf and ormolu tables were covered with chalk-powder and ink-stains.

Even though they knew they had good friends close at hand, the children could not control a certain swelled and breathless feeling in the region of their midriffs as they approached the schoolroom door.

James tapped at the door and in response to Miss Slighcarp's 'Come in' opened it and stood aside to let the children through.

A quick glance showed them that all the furniture had been removed and that the room was filled with desks. The more senior children from Mrs Brisket's school were sitting at them, with expressions varying from nervous excitement to petrifaction on their faces.

Miss Slighcarp stood on a raised platform by a blackboard. She had a long wooden pointer in her hand. Mrs Brisket was there, too, sitting at the instructress's desk. She wore a stern and forbidding expression, but on Miss Slighcarp's face there was a look of triumph.

'So!' she said – a long, hissing exhalation. 'So, you have returned! – Come here.'

They advanced, slowly and trembling, until they stood below the platform. Miss Slighcarp was so tall that they had almost to lean back to look up at her.

'P-please take us back into your school, Miss Slighcarp,' faltered Bonnie. 'We're so cold and tired and hungry.'

Into Sylvia's mind came a sudden recollection of the grouse pies and apricots they had eaten on the train. She bit her lip, and tried to look sorrowful.

Behind them, James quietly poked the fire, but no one noticed him. All eyes were on the returning truants.

'Hungry!' said Miss Slighcarp. 'You'll be hungrier still before I've done with you. Do you think you can run away, spend two months idling and playing on the moors, return when it suits you, and then expect to be given roast beef and pudding? You'll have no food for three days! Perhaps that will teach you something. And

you shall both be beaten, and we'll see what a taste of the dungeons will do for your spirit. James, go and get the dungeon keys.'

'No, miss,' said James firmly. 'I obey some of your orders because I've got no alternative, but help to put children in those dungeons I can't and won't. It's not Christian.' And he left the room, shutting the door sharply behind him.

'I'll get the keys, Letitia,' said Mrs Brisket, rising ponderously. 'You can be administering chastisement, meanwhile.'

Miss Slighcarp came down from her platform. 'Miss Green,' she said, and her eyes were so glittering with fury that even Bonnie quailed, 'put out your hand.'

Bonnie took a step backward. Miss Slighcarp followed her, and raised the pointer menacingly. The children at the desks drew a tremulous breath. But just as the pointer came swishing down, the chimneypiece panel flew open, and Mr Gripe, stepping out, seized hold of Miss Slighcarp's arm.

For a moment she was utterly dumbfounded. Then, in wrath she exclaimed:

'Who are you, sir? Let me go at once! What are you doing in my house?'

'In your house, ma'am? In *your* house? Don't you remember me, Miss Slighcarp?' said Mr Gripe. 'I was the attorney instructed by your distant relative, Sir Willoughby Green, to seek you out and offer you the position of instructress to his daughter. You brought with you a testimonial from the Duchess of Kensington. Don't you remember?'

Miss Slighcarp turned pale.

'And who gave you permission, woman,' suddenly thundered Mr Gripe, 'to turn this house into a boarding school? Who said you could use these children with villainous cruelty, beat them, starve them, and lock them in dungeons? Oh, it's no use to protest, I've been behind that panel and heard every word you've uttered.'

'It was only a joke,' faltered Miss Slighcarp. 'I had no intention of really shutting them in the dungeons.'

At this moment Mrs Brisket re-entered the room holding a bunch of enormous rusty keys.

'We can't use the upper dungeons, Letitia,' she began briskly, 'for Lucy and Emma are occupying them. I have brought the lower . . .'

Then she saw Mr Gripe, and behind him the two Bow Street officers. Her jaw dropped, and she was stricken to silence.

'Only a joke, indeed?' said Mr Gripe harshly. 'Mr Cardigan, place these two females under arrest, if you please. Until it is convenient to remove them to jail, you may as well avail yourself of the dungeon keys so obligingly put at your disposal.'

'You can't do this! You've no right!' shrieked the enraged Miss Slighcarp, struggling in the grip of Cardigan. 'I have papers signed by Sir Willoughby empowering me to do as I please with this property in the event of his death, and appointing me guardian of the children – '

'Papers signed by Sir Willoughby. Pish!' said Mr Gripe scornfully. 'You may as well know, ma'am, that your accomplice Grimshaw, who is already in prison, has confessed to the whole plot.'

At this news all the fight went out of Mrs Brisket,

and she allowed herself to be manacled by Spock, only muttering, 'Grimshaw's a fool, a paltry, whining fool.'

But Miss Slighcarp still gave battle.

'I tell you,' she shouted, 'I saw Sir Willoughby before he departed and he himself left me full powers – '

At this moment a heavy tread resounded along the passage, and they heard a voice exclaiming:

'What the *devil's* all this? Desks, blackboards, carpet taken up – has m'house been turned into a reformatory?'

The door burst open and in marched – Sir Willoughby Green! Behind him stood James, grinning for joy.

Bonnie turned absolutely pale with incredulity, stood so for a moment, motionless and wide-eyed, then, uttering one cry – *'Papa!'* – she flung herself into her father's arms.

'Well, minx? Have you missed us, eh? Have you been a good girl and minded your book? I can see you haven't,' he said, surveying her lovingly. 'Rosy as a pippin and brown as a berry. I can see you've been out of doors all day long instead of sewing your sampler and learning your *je ne sais quoi*. And Sylvia too – eh, my word, what a change from the little white mouse we left here! Well, well, well, girls will be girls! But what's all this, ma'am,' he continued, addressing Miss Slighcarp threateningly, 'what's all this hugger-mugger? I never gave you permission to turn Willoughby Chase into a school, no, damme I didn't! Being my fourth cousin doesn't give you such rights as that.'

'But, sir,' interjected Mr Gripe, who, at first silent with amazement, had now got his breath back, 'Sir

Willoughby! This is joyful indeed! We had all supposed you drowned when the *Thessaly* sank.'

Sir Willoughby burst into a fit of laughter.

'Ay, so they told me at your office! We have been travelling close behind you, Mr Gripe – I visited your place of business yesterday, learned you had just departed for Willoughby, and, since Lady Green was anxious to get back as soon as may be, and relieve the children's anxiety, we hired a special train and came post-haste after you.'

'But were you not in the shipwreck then, Sir Willoughby?'

The reply to this question was lost in Bonnie's rapturous cry – 'Is Mamma here too? *Is* she?'

'Why yes, miss, and ettling to see you, I'll be bound!'

Before the words had left his mouth Bonnie was out of the door. Sylvia, from a nice sense of delicacy, did not follow her cousin. She thought that Bonnie and her mother should be allowed those first few blissful moments of reunion alone together.

Sir Willoughby and Mr Gripe had retired to a corner of the schoolroom and Mr Gripe was talking hard, while Sir Willoughby listened with his blue eyes bulging, occasionally exclaiming, 'Why damme! For sheer, cool, calm, impertinent effrontery – why, bless my soul!' Once he wheeled round to his niece and said, 'Is it really true, Sylvia? Did Miss Slighcarp do these things?'

'Yes, sir, indeed she did,' said Sylvia.

'Then hanging's too good for you, ma'am,' he growled at Miss Slighcarp. 'Have her taken to the dungeons, Gripe. When these two excellent fellows have breakfasted they can take her and the other harpy off to prison.'

'Oh sir . . .' said Sylvia.

'Well, miss puss?'

'May I go with them to the dungeons, sir? I believe there are two children who have been put down there by Miss Slighcarp, and they will be so cold and unhappy and frightened!'

'Are there, by Joshua! We'll all go,' said Sir Willoughby.

Sylvia had never visited the dungeons at Willoughby Chase. They were a dismal and frightening quarter, never entered by the present owner and his family, though in days gone by they had been extensively employed by ancestors of Sir Willoughby.

Down dark, dank, weed-encrusted steps they trod, and along narrow, rock-hewn passages, where the only sound beside the echo of their own footfalls was the drip of water. Sylvia shudderd when she remembered Miss Slighcarp's expressed intention of imprisoning herself and Bonnie down here.

'Oh, do let us hasten,' she implored. 'Poor Lucy and Emma must be nearly frozen with cold and fear.'

'Upon my soul,' muttered Mr Gripe. 'This passes everything. Fancy putting children in a place like this!'

Miss Slighcarp and Mrs Brisket trod along in the rear of their captors, silent and sullen, looking neither to right nor to left.

The plight of Lucy and Emma was not quite so bad as it might have been. This was owing to the kind-hearted James, who, though he could not release them, had contrived to pass through their bars a number of warm blankets and a quantity of kindling and some tapers, to enable them to light a fire, and he had also kept them supplied with food out of his own meagre rations.

But they were cold and miserable enough, and their astonishment and joy at the sight of Sylvia was touching to behold.

Sylvia danced up and down outside the bars with impatience while James found the right key, and then she hurried them off upstairs, without waiting to see Miss Slighcarp locked in their place.

'Come, come quickly, and get warm by a fire.

Pattern shall make you a posset – or no, I forget, Pattern is probably not here yet, but I think I know how it is done.'

However, they had no more than reached the Great Hall when they were greeted with an ecstatic cry from Bonnie.

'Sylvia! Emma! Lucy! Come and see Mamma! Oh, she is so different! So much better!'

They went rather shyly into the salon, where Pattern, who had been summoned by Simon at full gallop on one of the coach-horses, bustled about in joyful tears and served everybody with cups of frothing hot chocolate.

'Well,' a gay voice exclaimed, 'where's my second daughter?' And in swept someone whom Sylvia would hardly have recognized for the frail, languid Lady Green, so blooming, beautiful, and bright-eyed did she appear. She embraced Sylvia, cordially made welcome the two poor prisoners, and declared:

'Now I want to hear all your story, every word, from the very beginning! I am proud of you both – and as for that Miss Slighcarp, cousin of your father's though she be, I hope she is sent to Botany Bay!'

'But Aunt Sophy,' said Sylvia, 'your tale must be so much more adventurous than ours! Were you not shipwrecked?'

'Yes, indeed we were!' said Lady Green laughing, 'and your uncle and I spent six very tedious days drifting in a rowing-boat, our only fare being a monotonous choice of grapes or oranges, of which there happened to be a large crate in the dinghy, fortunately for us. We were then picked up by a small and *most* insanitary fishing-boat, manned by a set of fellows as picturesque as they were unwashed, who none of them spoke a word of English. They would carry us nowhere but to their home port, which turned out to be the Canary Islands. On *this* boat we received nothing to eat but sardines in olive oil. I am surprised these shocks and privations did not carry me off, but Sir Willoughby maintains they were the saving of me, for from the time of the wreck my health began to pick up. On reaching the Canaries we determined to come home by the next mail-ship, but they only visit these islands every three months or so, and one had just left. We had to wait a weary time, but the peace and the sunshine during our enforced stay completed my cure, as you see.'

'Oh how glad I am you came home and didn't go on round the world!' cried Bonnie.

Sir Willoughby marched in, beaming. 'Well, well,' he said, 'has Madam Hen found her chicks, eh? But as for the state your house is in, my lady, I hardly dare describe it to you. We shall have to have it completely redecorated. And what's to be done with all these poor orphans?'

'Oh Papa,' said Bonnie, bursting with excitement. 'I have a plan for them!'

'You have, have you, hussy? What is it, then?'

'Don't you think Aunt Jane could come and live in the Dower House, just across the park, and run a school for them? Aunt Jane loves children!'

'What, Aunt Jane run a school? At her age?'

'Aunt Jane is very independent,' Bonnie said. 'She wouldn't want to feel she was living on charity. But she could have people to help her – *kind* people. And she could teach the girls beautiful embroidery!'

Lucy and Emma looked so wistful at the thought of this bliss that Sir Willoughby promised to consider it.

A happy party sat down to dine in the Great Hall that night. Spock and Cardigan, the Bow Street officials, had already left to commit their prisoners to the nearest jail, and the ruffianly gang of servants kept on by Miss Slighcarp had been summarily dismissed. Simon, riding about the countryside, had taken the news of Sir Willoughby's return to all the old servants, Solly and Timon and John Groom and Mrs Shubunkin, and they had come hastening back.

The orphans, still dazed at their good fortune, sat at a table of their own, eating roast turkey and kindly averting their gaze from the pale cheeks and red eyes of Diana Brisket, who, having been in a position to bully and hector as much as she pleased, was now reduced to a state where she had not a friend to stand by her. Mrs Brisket had sold the school in Blastburn and so Diana had nowhere to go and was forced, willy-nilly, to stay with the orphans (where, it may be said in passing, wholesome discipline and the example of Aunt Jane's unselfish nature soon wrought an improvement in her character). Some of the parlour boarders and daughters of the nobility and gentry had been fetched away by their parents, such as lived near enough, and the rest were awaiting removal.

Simon sat between Bonnie and Sylvia. Sir Willoughby gave him some very kindly looks. He had heard by now of Simon's brave part in rescuing the girls both from the wolves and from Mrs Brisket's dreadful establishment, and of his help with Aunt Jane's illness. The money he had spent had been returned to him with interest.

'It looks as if we're going to have an adopted son as well as an adopted daughter,' said Sir Willoughby. 'Hey, my boy? What shall we do with you, then? Put you through school?'

'No thank you, Sir Willoughby,' said Simon gratefully but firmly. 'School wouldn't suit me at all.'

'What then? Can't just run wild.'

'I'm going to be a painter,' Simon explained. 'Dr Field said I showed great promise, and he told me I could stay with him and go to one of the famous London art schools.'

'Oh Simon,' said Bonnie, dismayed, 'and leave Willoughby?'

'I'll come back every holidays,' he told her. 'Remember we promised to go and see Mr Wilderness! I want to paint a picture of Great Whinside from the dale – oh, and a hundred other places round here.'

'Sensible lad,' approved Sir Willoughby. 'Well, always remember, whenever you come back, there's a warm welcome for you at Willoughby Chase.'

'Thank you, Sir Willoughby,' said Simon beaming. 'And now if you'll excuse me, I think I ought to be returning to my cave. I want to see how my bees are getting on.'

'Good night, Simon,' cried Bonnie and Sylvia, 'we shall come and see you tomorrow.'

Bonnie yawned.

'It's long past these children's bedtime,' said Sir Willoughby, 'and they were travelling all night. Off with you now – I dare say your mother will be up by and by to say good night to you in bed.'

Their own room had been hastily prepared for them and they were glad to tumble between the fine silken sheets. 'And oh, Bonnie,' called Sylvia, '*have* you seen the pretty dresses Pattern has been making for us?'

'I've grown accustomed to boys' clothes,' grumbled Bonnie.

'Oh, what nonsense, miss!' said Pattern scoldingly, and ruined the effect by giving Bonnie a hug. 'There now, go to sleep, you blessed pair, and don't let either of you move a muscle till you're called. We've had quite enough to worry about today, with everything at sixes and sevens, and no servants to speak of, and a hundred orphans to feed. Mind! You're not to speak a word till eight o'clock. You're not even to dream!'

'Dream,' murmured Bonnie sleepily, 'we can't help dreaming, Pattern. We've so much to dream *about* — the wolves, and Miss Slighcarp, and walking to London, and helping poor Aunt Jane, and Mamma and Papa adrift in a boat full of oranges and grapes . . .' Her voice trailed away into sleep.

Light after light in the windows of the great house was extinguished, until at length it stood dark and silent. And though the house had witnessed many strange scenes, wolf-hunts and wine-drinking and weddings and wars, it is doubtful whether during its whole history any of its inmates had had such adventures as those of Sylvia and Bonnie Green.

BLACK HEARTS
IN
BATTERSEA

For
Jessica and Joanna

Note

The action of this book takes place in the same period as that of *The Wolves of Willoughby Chase*: the reign of King James III, in the earlier part of the nineteenth century, when England was still sadly plagued by wolves. A family tree of the Dukes of Battersea will be found on page 109.

1

On a fine warm evening in late summer, over a hundred years ago, a boy might have been seen leading a donkey across Southwark Bridge in the City of London. The boy, who appeared to be about fifteen, was bright-eyed and black-haired, and looked as if he had spent most of his life out of doors; he carried a knapsack, and wore rough, warm garments of frieze. Both boy and donkey seemed a little bewildered by the crowds round about them: the streets were thronged with people strolling in the sunshine after their day's work.

Halfway across the bridge the boy paused, took an extra turn of the donkey's halter round his wrist, and pulled out of his pouch a grubby and much-handled letter, which he proceeded to study for the twentieth time.

> Come and stay with me for as long as you like, my dear Simon. I have lately moved from Park Lane to lodgings that are less expensive, but sufficiently comfortable and commodious for us both. I have two rooms on the top floor of this house, which belongs to a Mr and Mrs Twite.

The Twites are an unattractive family, but I see little enough of them. Moreover, the windows command a handsome view of the river and St Paul's Cathedral. I have spoken of you to Dr Furnace, the Principal of the Art Academy in Chelsea where I sometimes study, and he is willing to accept you as a pupil. Through my visits to this Academy I have made another most interesting acquaintance to whom I wish to introduce you. More of this when we meet.

Yours, Gabriel Field, M.D.

P.S. Kindly remember me to Sir Willoughby and Lady Green, Miss Bonnie and Miss Sylvia Green, and all other friends in Yorkshire.

The letter was addressed from Rose Alley, Southwark, London.

The boy named Simon looked about him somewhat doubtfully and, after a moment's hesitation, accosted an elderly and rather frail-looking man with sparse locks who was walking slowly across the bridge.

'I wonder, sir,' he said politely, 'if you can direct me to Rose Alley? I believe it is not far from here.'

The old man looked at him vaguely, stroking his beard with an unsteady hand.

'Rose Alley, now? Rose Alley, dear me. The name is indeed familiar . . .'

His hand stopped stroking and his eyes roamed vacantly past Simon. 'Is that your beast?' he asked absently, his gaze lighting on the donkey. 'Ah, I remember when I was a lad in the forest of Epping, I had a donkey; used to carry home bundles of firewood for a penny a load . . .' His voice trailed off.

'Rose Alley, sir,' Simon said gently. 'I am searching for the lodgings of a Dr Field.'

'Dr Field, my boy?'

'Yes, sir, Dr Gabriel Field.'

'That name, too, seems familiar. Dear me, now, dear me. Was it Dr Field who put the bread poultice on my knee;' He advanced his knee and stared at it, seeming mildly surprised to find that the bread poultice was no longer there with Dr Field's bill attached to it.

Simon, watching him, had not noticed an extremely dirty urchin who had been hovering near them. This individual, a sharp-looking boy of eleven or twelve who seemed to be dressed in nothing but one very large pair of trousers (he had cut holes in the sides for his arms) now jostled against Simon, contriving at the same moment to tread on his toes, flip his nose, and snatch Dr Field's letter out of his hand. He then ran off, singing in a loud, rude manner:

'Simple Simon came to town,
Riding on a moke.
Donkey wouldn't go,
Wasn't that a joke?'

'Hey!' shouted Simon angrily. How did the boy know his name? 'Give back that letter!'

He started in pursuit, but the boy, thumbing his nose derisively, crumpled up the letter and tossed it over the rail into the water. Then he disappeared into the crowd.

'Eh, deary me,' said the old man, sighing in a discouraged manner. 'The young people grow rougher and ruder every day. Now, what was it you were saying, my boy? You wanted the address of a Dr Poultice? A strange name, a strange name – very. So far as I know there's no Dr Poultice in these parts.'

'No, Dr *Field* – Dr Gabriel Field in Rose Alley,' said Simon, still vainly trying to catch a glimpse of the boy.

'Dr Alley? Never heard of him. Now, when I was a lad in the forest of Epping there was a Dr Marble . . .'

Simon saw that he would get no good out of the old man, so he thanked him politely and walked on across the bridge.

'Did I hear you say you wanted Rose Alley?' said a voice in his ear. He turned with relief and saw a smallish, brisk-looking woman with pale-blue eyes and pale sandy hair and a bonnet that was most ingeniously ornamented with vegetables. A small bunch of carrots decorated the brim, a couple of lettuce leaves curled up rakishly at one side, and a veritable diadem of radishes was twined tastefully round the back.

'Yes, Dr Field's lodgings in Rose Alley,' said Simon, relieved to find someone who looked able to answer his question, for though the little woman's bonnet was eccentric, her mouth was decided and her eyes were very sharp.

'Don't know any Dr Field, but I can tell you the best way to get to Rose Alley,' she said, and reeled off a set of directions so complicated that Simon had much ado to get them into his head. He thanked her and hurried on, repeating, 'Two miles down Southwark Bridge Road, past the Elephant and Castle Inn, past Newington Butts, through Camberwell, then take a left turning and a right fork . . .'

But hey! he said to himself when he had gone half a mile, didn't Dr Field say that from his window he had a view of the river Thames? And of St Paul's Cathedral?

He turned round. St Paul's Cathedral had been in view while he stood on Southwark Bridge. But now it was out of sight.

That woman must have been wrong, Simon thought, beginning to retrace his steps. She must have been thinking of some other Rose Alley. I'll go back until I am once more within sight of St Paul's and the river, and ask somebody else. What a place this London is for confusion!

He presently reached the bridge once again, and this time was luckier in his adviser. A studious-looking young man with a bag of books said he was going to Rose Alley himself. He led Simon off the bridge, round a couple of corners, and into a tiny cobbled lane giving directly on to the river-front. There were but half a dozen tall, narrow, shabby houses on either side, and at the far end a patch of thistly grass sloped down to the water.

Simon had forgotten the number of the house where Dr Field lodged, but when he asked which belonged to Mr and Mrs Twite the young man pointed to the last house on the right, Number Eight, which stood with its back to the bridge and its side to the river.

Simon tethered his donkey to some broken railings and knocked on the door, which was in need of a coat of paint.

For a long time there was no reply. He knocked again, louder. At that, a window flew open and a child's head popped out.

'There's nobody in but me,' she snapped. 'Whose donkey is that?'

'Mine. Is this the house of Mr and Mrs Twite?'

'Yes, it is. I'm Miss Twite,' the brat said with a haughty air 'What d'you want?'

'I'm looking for Dr Field.'

'There's no Dr Field here. Can your donkey gallop? What's its name?'

'Caroline. Do you mean Dr Field is out?' The child looked thoroughly unreliable and Simon was not sure whether to believe her.

'Can your donkey gallop?' she repeated.

'If you'll come down and answer the door I'll give you a ride on her,' said Simon. She vanished like lightning and reappeared in the doorway. She was a shrewish-looking little creature of perhaps eight or nine, with sharp eyes of a pale washed-out blue and no eyebrows or eyelashes to speak of. Her straw-coloured hair was stringy and sticky with jam and she wore a dirty satin dress two sizes too small for her.

'Is Dr Field out? Do you know when he'll be back?' Simon said again.

She took no notice of his question but walked up to the donkey and untied it. 'Lift me on its back,' she ordered. Simon good-naturedly did so, urged the reluctant Caroline to a trot, and led her to the end of Rose Alley and back. Miss Twite hung on to the saddle uttering loud exclamations:

'Mind out! Not so fast, you're shaking me! She's bumping, make her slow down! Oo, your saddle's hard!'

When they arrived back at Number Eight she cried, 'Give me another ride!'

'Not till you tell me when Dr Field will be back.'

'Don't know.'

'Well, where are your father and mother?'

'They've gone to Vauxhall Gardens with Penny and Grandpa and Aunty Tinty and they won't be back till midnight past.'

'Why aren't you with them?'

'Acos I threw Penny's hat on the fire,' she said, bursting into giggles. 'Oo, how they did scold! Pa walloped me with a slipper – leastways he tried to – and Ma said I mightn't go out and Penny pinched me. Spiteful cat.'

'Who's minding you?'

'I'm minding myself. Give me another ride!'

'Not just now. The donkey's tired, she and I have come all the way from Yorkshire this week. If you're good you shall have another ride later, perhaps.' Simon was learning cunning. But Miss Twite looked at him with a knowing, weary eye and said:

'Gammon! I know yer "later perhaps"!'

'Would you like to give the donkey some carrots?' Simon said, visited with inspiration.

'Don't mind.'

He pulled a handful of carrots out of the pannier and broke them up.

Miss Twite was delighted with the privilege of feeding Caroline, and almost shed her world-weary air. Seeing her absorbed, Simon quietly walked through the front door of the house and up a steep and dirty flight of stairs, past several landings. At the top of the house two doors faced one another. Simon remembered that Dr Field had said there were two rooms; doubtless both of these were his. But no reply came from either door when he tapped; it appeared that the child had been speaking the truth and Dr Field was indeed out.

It could surely do no harm to wait for him here, however, Simon thought. By this time he was decidedly weary, and a kitten, which had been asleep in his knapsack, at this moment woke up and mewed to be released.

Simon opened one of the doors and looked through into the room beyond.

As soon as he saw the window he recognized the view that Dr Field had described – the river, and Southwark Bridge, and an expanse of mud gleaming pink in the sunset below the tethered barges. Beyond towered the dome of St Paul's. But, strangely enough, the room, which had a faintly familiar smell, did not contain a single stick of furniture.

Perhaps this room is for me and I am to buy my

own things, Simon thought, and re-crossed the landing, remembering with a grin Dr Field's lodgings in Park Lane, where painting-equipment – easels, palettes, and bottles of turpentine – jostled pills and medicine phials, while a skeleton lounged on the sofa.

But the other room, too, was bare. It did contain a little furniture – a bed, table and chair, and a worn strip of drugget on the floor – but there were no covers on the bed and it was plain that this room, too, was unoccupied.

Simon scratched his head. Could he have made a mistake? But no, Dr Field had distinctly written 'Mr and Mrs Twite, Rose Alley, Southwark', and here, sure enough, was the Twite house in Rose Alley. Here was the top room with the view of St Paul's. The only thing lacking was Dr Field himself. Perhaps he had not yet moved from his other lodgings? And yet Simon had received the letter with the new address a full two months ago, and had then written to Rose Alley saying when he proposed to arrive. Could something have changed or delayed the doctor's plans? Simon ran down the stairs again, resolved on trying to get a little more help from young Miss Twite.

He arrived none too soon for poor Caroline. Having finished the carrots – Simon observed traces of carrot on the child's face and deduced that the donkey had not received a full ration – Miss Twite had contrived to clamber on to Caroline's back from the railings. Using a rusty old umbrella she was urging the donkey at a fast trot along Rose Alley.

Simon ran after them and grabbed the bridle.

'You little wretch!' he remarked. 'Didn't you hear me say Caroline was tired?'

'Fiddlestick!' said Miss Twite. 'There's plenty of go in her yet.' She raised the umbrella, and Simon twitched it neatly out of her hand.

'So there would be in you if I beat you with an umbrella.'

'Are you going to? I'll tell my Pa if you do!' Miss Twite eyed him alertly.

Simon couldn't help laughing; she looked so like an ugly, scrawny little bird, ready to hop out of the way if danger threatened. He led Caroline back to her pasturage and dumped Miss Twite on the steps of Number Eight.

'Now then, tell me once and for all – where is Dr Field?'

'What Dr Field? I don't know any Dr Field?'

'You said just now he was out.'

'I only said that to get a ride,' said Miss Twite, bursting into a fit of laughter and throwing herself from side to side in the ecstasy of her amusement. 'I've never met Dr Field in my life.'

'But he was going to move here – I'm sure he *did* move here,' said Simon, remembering the words in the doctor's letter – 'The Twites are an unattractive family, but I see little enough of them . . .' Didn't that sound as if he were already moved in? And this specimen of the Twite family was unattractive enough, heaven knows!

'There's no Dr Field living here and never has been,' said the child definitely.

'Who lives in your top rooms?'

'They're empty.'

'Are you sure Dr Field isn't coming soon?'

'I tell you, no!' She stamped her foot. 'Stop talking about Dr Field! Can I have another ride?'

'No, you can *not*,' said Simon, exasperated. He wondered what he had better do. If only Mr or Mrs Twite were here, they might be able to throw some light on this puzzling situation.

'Is that a kitty in your knapsack?' said Miss Twite. 'Why do you keep it there? Let it out. Let me see it!'

'If I let you see it,' said Simon cautiously, 'will you let me stay the night? I could sleep in your top room. I'll pay you, of course,' he added quickly.

She hesitated, chewing a strand of her stringy hair. 'Dunno what Ma or Pa would say. They might beat me. And what 'bout the donkey? Where'll she go?'

'I'll find a place for her.' There was a row of little shops round the corner – greengrocer's, butcher's, dairy. Simon thought it probable that he could find lodgings for Caroline behind one of them. He was not going to risk leaving her tethered in the street with this child about.

'Will you promise to give me another ride tomorrow?'

'Yes.'

'But Pa only lets by the week,' she said swiftly. 'It's twelve and six the week, boots and washing extry, and a shilling a day fires in winter. If you stayed the week you could give me a ride every day.'

'All right, you little madam,' said Simon, rapidly reckoning how long his small stock of money would last.

'Hand over the twelve and six, then.'

'Not likely! I'll give that to your father.'

She accepted this defeat with a grin and said, 'Show me the kitty, then.'

'First I want to buy some food and find a place for the donkey. You'd better be putting sheets on the bed.' Miss Twite made a grimace but trailed indoors, leaving the front door ajar.

When he had bought milk and eggs at the dairy, Simon arranged to stable Caroline with the milk roundsman's pony for half a crown a week, this sum to be reduced if she was ever borrowed for the milk deliveries. Simon was not quite satisfied with this arrangement – the sour-looking dairywoman had too strong a resemblance to young Miss Twite for his taste, and he wondered if they were related – but it would do for the time being.

He purchased a quantity of cold ham and a loaf of bread and then returned to Rose Alley where the door of Number Eight still stood open.

Surprisingly enough, young Miss Twite had taken a pair of sheets and blankets up to the top room and was rather carelessly throwing them over the bed.

'*Now* let's see the kitty,' she said.

Simons kitten was equally eager to be let out from its travelling-quarters, and gave a mighty stretch before mewing loudly for bread-and-milk.

'I suppose you're hungry too,' Simon said, noticing Miss Twite's hopeful looks at the loaf.

'Aren't I jist? Ma said I was to miss my dinner on account of burning Penny's hat – spiteful thing.'

'Who's Penny?' Simon asked, cutting her a slice.

'My sister. Oo, she's a horrible girl. She's sixteen. Her real name's Pen-el-o-pe.' She mouthed it out disgustedly.

'What's yours?'

'Dido.'

'I never heard that name before.'

'It's after a barge. So's Penny. Can I have another bit?'

He gave her another, noticing that she had already eaten most of the ham.

'Can I take the kitty down and play in the street?'

'No, I'm going to bed now, and so's the kitty. Tell your father that I've taken the room for a week and I'm waiting for Dr Field.'

'I tell you,' she said, turning in the doorway for emphasis, 'there *ain't* any Dr Field. There never *has* been any Dr Field.'

Simon shrugged and waited till she had gone. Then he went across into the room that faced on to the river and stared out of the window. It was nearly dark by now, and the opposite bank glittered with lights, some low down by the water, some high up on St Paul's. Barges glided upstream with the tide, letting out mournful hoots. Dr Field had been here, Dr Field had seen this view. Dr Field must be somewhere. But where?

Simon soon went to sleep, though the mattress was hard and the bedding scanty. At about one in the morning, however, he and the kitten, who was asleep on his chest, were awakened by very loud singing and the slamming of several doors downstairs.

Presently, as the singer apparently mounted several flights of stairs, the words of the song could be distinguished:

'My Bonnie lies over the North Sea,
My Bonnie lies over in Hanover,
My Bonnie lies over the North Sea,
Oh, why won't they bring that young man over?
Bring back, bring back,
Oh, bring back my Georgie to me, to me . . .'

Simon realized that the singer must be one of the Georgians, or Hanoverians as they were sometimes called, who wanted to dethrone King James and bring back the Pretender, young Prince George of Hanover. He couldn't help wondering if the singer were aware of his rashness in thus making known his political feelings, for since the long and hard-fought Hanoverian wars had secured King James III on the throne, the mood of the country was strongly anti-Georgian and anybody who proclaimed his sympathy for the Pretender was liable to be ducked in the nearest horsepond, if not haled off to the Tower for treason.

'Abednego!' cried a sharp female voice. 'Abednego, will you hold your hush this instant! Hold your hush and come downstairs – I've your night cap a-warming and a hot salamander in the bed – and besides, you'll wake the neighbours!'

'Neighbours be blowed!' roared the voice of the singer. 'What do I care about the neighbours? I need solitude. I need to commune with Nature. I'm going to sleep up in the top room. Mind I'm not called in the morning till eleven past when you can bring me a mug of warm ale and a piece of toast.'

The steps came, very unsteadily, up the last flight of stairs. The kitten prudently retired under the bed just before the door burst open and a man lurched into the room.

He carried a candle which, after several false tries, he succeeded in placing on the table, muttering to himself:

'Cursed Picts and Jacobites! They've moved it again. Every time I leave the house those Picts and Jacobites creep in and shift the furniture.'

He turned towards the bed and for the first time saw Simon sitting up and staring at him.

'A Pict!' he shrieked. 'Help! Ella! There's a Pict got into the house! Bring the poker and the axe! Quick!'

'Don't talk fiddlesticks,' the lady called up the stairs. 'There's nothing up top that shouldn't be there – as I should know. Didn't I scrub up there with bath-brick for days together? I'll Pict you!'

'Are you Mr Twite?' Simon said, hoping to reassure the man.

'Ella! It speaks! It's a Pict and it speaks!'

'Hold your hush or I'll lambast you with the salamander!' she shouted.

But as the man made no attempt to hold his hush but continued to shriek and to beseech Ella to bring the poker and the axe, there came at length the sound of more feet on the stairs and a lady entered the room carrying, not the axe, but a warming-pan filled with hot coals, which she shook threateningly.

'Come along down this minute, Abednego, or I'll give you such a rousting!' she snapped, and then she saw Simon. Her mouth and eyes opened very wide, and she almost dropped the warming-pan, but, retaining her hold on it, shortened her grip and advanced towards the bed in a very intimidating manner.

'And who might *you* be?' she said.

'If you please, ma'am, my name is Simon, and I rented your top rooms from your daughter Dido this evening – if you're Mrs Twite, that is?' Simon said.

'I'm Mrs Twite, all right,' she said ominously. 'And what's more, *I'm* the one that lets rooms in this house, and so I'll tell that young good-for-nothing

baggage. Renting rooms to all and sundry! We might have been murdered in our beds!'

Simon reflected that it looked much more as if he would be the one to be murdered in his bed. Mrs Twite was standing beside the bed with the warming-pan held over him menacingly; at any moment, it seemed, she might drop the whole panful of hot coals on his legs.

She was a large, imposing woman, with a quantity of gingerish fair hair all done up in curl-papers so that her head was a strange and fearsome shape.

In order to show this good intentions as quickly as possible Simon got out his money, which he had stowed under the pillow, and offered Mrs Twite five half-crowns.

'I understand the room is twelve and six a week,' he said.

'Boots and washing extra!' she snapped, her eyes going as sharp as bradawls at sight of the money. 'And it'll be another half-crown for arriving at dead of night and nearly frightening Mr. Twite into convulsions. And even then I'm not sure the room's free. What do you say, Mr Twite?'

Mr Twite had calmed down as soon as his lady entered, and had wandered to a corner where he stood balancing himself alternately on his toes and his heels, singing in a plantive manner:

'Picts and pixies, come and stay, come and stay,
Come, come, and pay, pay, pay.'

When his wife asked his opinion he answered, 'Oh,

very well, my dear, if he has money he can stay. *I've* no objection if you are satisfied. What is a Pict or two under one's roof, to be sure?'

Simon handed over the extra half-crown and was just about to raise the matter of Dr Field when Mr Twite burst into song again (to the tune, this time, of 'I had a good home and I left') and carolled:

'A Pict, a Pict, she rented the room to a Pict,
And I think she ought to be kicked.'

'Come along, my dove,' he said, interrupting himself. 'The Pict wants to get some sleep and I'm for the downy myself.' Picking up the candle he urged his wife to the door.

'I thought you wanted to commune with Nature,' she said acidly, pocketing the money.

'Nature will have to wait till the morning,' Mr Twite replied, with a magnificent gesture towards the window, which had the unfortunate effect of blowing out the candle. The Twites made their way downstairs by the glow of the warming-pan.

Simon and the kitten settled to sleep once more and there were no further disturbances.

2

When Simon woke next morning he lay for a few minutes wondering where he was. It seemed strange to wake in a bed, in a room, in the middle of a city. He was used to waking in a cave in the woods, or, in summer, to sleeping out under the trees, being roused by the birds to lie looking up at the green canopy overhead. He felt uneasy so far away from the grass and trees of the forest home where he had lived for the past five years.

Outside in the street, he could hear wheels and voices; the kitten was awake and mewing for its breakfast. After Simon had fed it with the last of the milk, he wandered across the landing to the empty room and gazed out of the window. The tide was nearly full and the Thames was a bustle of activity. Simon watched the shipping, absorbed, until a whole series of church clocks striking culminated in the solemn boom of St Paul's itself, and reminded him that he could not stand here all day gazing while time slipped by. It was still needful to discover Dr Field's whereabouts, and to earn some money.

Kind, wealthy Sir Willoughby Green, who had befriended Simon in Yorkshire, had offered to pay his art-school fees, but Simon had no intention of being beholden if he could avoid it, and proposed to look for work which would provide enough money for his tuition as well as food and rent. He had a considerable fund of quiet pride, and had purposely waited to leave Willoughby Chase until the Green family were away on a visit. Thus he had been spared a sad farewell, and had also avoided the risk of hurting Sir Willoughby's feelings by refusing the money which he knew that liberal-hearted gentleman would have pressed on him.

Munching a piece of bread, Simon tucked the kitten into the bosom of his frieze jacket; then he ran softly downstairs. The house was silent – evidently the Twites were still asleep. Simon resolved that he would not wait till they woke to question them about Dr Field, but would go to the Academy of Art which he was to attend – where Dr Field also studied – to ask for the doctor's address. Unfortunately Simon did not know the name of the Academy, but he remembered that it was in Chelsea.

He stole past the closed doors of the Twites, resolving that when he returned in the evening he would move the furniture from the room where he had slept into the one overlooking the river; it had a pleasanter view, and appeared to be in a superior state of cleanliness.

Opening the front door Simon found Dido Twite sitting on the front steps, kicking her heels discontentedly. She was wearing the same stained dress that she had had on yesterday, and did not appear to have washed her face or brushed her hair since Simon had last seen her.

'Hallo!' she said alertly. 'Where are you going?'

'Out,' said Simon. He had no intention of retailing all his doings to her and having them discussed by the Twite family.

Dido's face fell. 'What about my donkey-ride?' she said, looking at him from under where her brows would have been had she had any.

Although she was an unattractive brat, she had such a forlorn, neglected air that Simon's heart softened. 'All right,' he said. 'I'll get Caroline and give you a ride if you'll do something for me while I'm fetching her.'

'What?' said Dido suspiciously.

'Wash your face.' He went whistling up the street.

After he had given Dido her ride he asked, 'What time is your father likely to get up?'

'Not till noon – perhaps not till three or four. Pa works evenings and sleeps all day – if Penny or I wake him he throws his hoboy at us.'

Simon could not imagine what a hoboy might be, but it seemed plain that no information was to be had from Mr Twite until the evening.

'Well, goodbye. I'll see you when I come home. What do you do with yourself all day? Do you go to school?'

'No,' she said peevishly. 'Sometimes Pa teaches me the hoboy or Aunt Tinty sets me sums. Uncle Buckle used to teach me but he doesn't any more. Mostly I does tasks for Ma – peel the spuds, sweep the stairs, stoke the furnace – '

'Furnace!' exclaimed Simon. 'That was the name!'

'What name?'

'Oh, nothing that concerns you. The Principal of the Art Academy where I am to learn painting.'

He had thrown the information over his shoulder as he walked away, not thinking that it could be of any possible interest to Dido Twite. He would have been surprised to see the sudden flash of alert calculation in her eyes.

Simon asked his way through the streets till he reached Chelsea – no very great distance, as it proved. Here he inquired of a man in the uniform of a beadle where he would find an Academy of Art presided over by a Dr Furnace.

The beadle scratched his head.

'Dr Furnace?' he said. 'Can't say as I recall the name.'

Simon's heart sank. Was Dr Furnace to prove as elusive as Dr Field? But then the beadle turned and shouted, 'Dan!' to a man who was just emerging from an arched gateway leading a horse and gaily painted dustcart with a cracked wheel.

'Hallo?' replied this man. 'What's the row?'

'Young cove here wants Furnace's Art Academy. Know what he means?'

Both men turned and stared at Simon. The man called Dan, who was dressed in moleskin clothes from cap to leggings, slowly chewed a straw to its end, spat, and then said:

'Furnace's Academy? Ah! I knows what he means. He means Rivière's.'

'Ah,' said the beadle wisely. 'That's what you mean, me boy. You means Rivière's.'

'Is that far from here?' said Simon, his hopes rising.

'Matter o' ten minutes' walk,' said Dan. 'Going that way meself. I'll take you.'

'Thank you, sir.'

They strolled off, Dan leading the horse.

'I'm going to me brother-in-law's,' Dan explained. 'Does the smithying and wheelwrighting for the parish. Nice line o' business.'

Simon was interested. He had worked for a blacksmith himself and knew a fair amount about the wheelwright's trade.

'There must be plenty of customers for a wheelwright in London,' he said, looking about him. 'I've never seen so many different kinds of carriages before. Where I come from it's mostly closed coaches and farm carts.'

'Countryfied sort o' stuff,' said Dan pityingly. 'No art in it – and mind you, there's a lot of art in the coachmaker's trade. You get the length *without* the 'ighth, it looks poky and old-fashioned, to my mind, but, contrariwise, you get the 'ighth without enough body and it looks a reg'lar hurrah's-nest. Now *there's* a lovely bit o' bodywork – see that barouche coming along – the plum-coloured one with the olive-drab outwork? Ah, very racy, that is – Duke o' Battersea's trot-box; know it well. Seen it at me brother-in-law's for repair: cracked panel.'

Simon turned and saw an elegantly turned-out vehicle in which was seated an elderly lady dressed in the height of fashion with waterfalls of diamonds ornamenting her apple-peel satin gown, and a tremendous ostrich-plume head-dress. She was accompanied by a pretty young girl who held a reticule, two billiard-cues, a large shopping basket, and a small spaniel.

'Why!' Simon exclaimed. 'That's *Sophie*!'

His voice rang across the street and the young girl turned her head sharply. But just then a high closed carriage came between Simon and the barouche and, a succession of other traffic following after, no second view of the girl could be obtained.

'I know that girl! She's a friend of mine!' Simon said, overjoyed. He looked at Dan with shining eyes.

'Ah, Duchess's lady's-maid, maybe? Nice-looking young gel. Very good position – good family to work for. Duke very affable sort o' gentleman – when he comes out o' those everlasting experiments of his. Bugs, chemicals, mice – queer set-out for a lord. But his lady's a proper lady, so I've been told. O' course young Lord Bakerloo ain't up to much.'

'Where does he live – the Duke of Battersea?' asked Simon, who had not been paying much attention.

'Battersea Castle o' course – when the family's in London. Places in the country too, nat'rally. Dorset, Yorkshire – that where you met the gel? Now, here's me brother-in-law's establishment, and, down by the river, that big place with the pillars is Rivière's.'

Dan's brother-in-law's place was almost as impressive as the Art Academy beyond. Inside the big double gates (over which ran the legend 'Cobb's Coaches' in gold) was a wide yard containing every conceivable kind of coach, carriage, phaeton, barouche, landau, chariot, and curricle, in every imaginable state of disrepair. A shed at the side contained a forge, with bellows roaring and sparks blowing, while elsewhere lathes turned, carpenters hammered, and chips flew.

'Do you suppose I could get work here?' Simon asked impulsively. 'Of an evening – when I've finished at the Academy?'

'No 'arm in asking, is there? Always plenty to do at Sam Cobb's, that I do know. Depends what you can do, dunnit?'

Dan led his dustcart through the gates and then lifted up his voice and bawled, *'Sam!'*

A large, cheerful man came towards them.

'Why, bless me!' he exclaimed. 'If it's not old Dan back again. I don't know what you do to your cart, Dan, I don't indeed. I believe it's fast driving. *I* believe you're out of an evening carriage-racing on the Brighton road. You can't expect the parish dustcarts to stand up to it, Dan, no you can't, me boy.'

Dan took these pleasantries agreeably, and asked after his sister Flossie. Then he said, 'Here's a young cove, Sam, as wants a bit of evening work. Any use to you?'

'Any use to me?' said Mr Cobb, summing up Simon with a shrewd but friendly eye. 'Depends what he can do, eh? Looks a well-set-up young' un. What can you do, young' un? Can you carpenter?'

'Yes,' said Simon.

'Done any blacksmith's work?'

'Yes,' said Simon.

'Used to horses?'

'Yes,'said Simon

'Ever tried your hand at ornamental painting?' said Mr Cobb, gesturing towards a little greengrocer's cart, newly and beautifully ornamented with roses and lettuces. 'This sort o' thing? Or emblazoning?' He waved at a carriage with a coat-of-arms on the panel.

'I can paint a bit,' said Simon. 'That's why I've come to London – to study painting.'

'Proper all-rounder, ennee?' said Mr Cobb, rolling his eyes in admiration.

'You'd best take him on, Sam, then you'll be able to retire,' Dan remarked.

'Well, I like a young 'un who has confidence in hisself. I like a bit o' spunk. And dear knows there's plenty of work. Tell you what, young 'un, you come round here this evening, fiveish, and I'll see what you can do. Agreeable?'

'Very, thank you, sir,' Simon answered cheerfully. 'And thank *you*, for setting me on my way,' he said to Dan, who winked at him in a friendly manner.

'Goodbye, young 'un. Now then, Dan,' said Mr Cobb, 'it's early, to be sure, but there's such a nip in the air these misty mornings; what do you say to a little drop of Organ-Grinder's Oil?'

Simon felt somewhat nervous as he approached the Academy, but was encouraged to find that, on a nearer view, it presented a less imposing aspect. Some ingenious spirit had hit on the notion of suspending clothes-lines between the Grecian columns supporting the roof, and from these dangled a great many socks, shirts, and other garments, while all round the marble fountain in front of the Academy knelt or squatted young persons of both sexes busily engaged in washing various articles of apparel.

Simon approached a young man who was scrubbing a pair of red socks with a bar of yellow soap and said:

'Can you tell me, please, where I shall find Dr Furnace?'

The young man rinsed his socks, held them up, sniffed them, glanced at the sun, and said:

'About ten o'clock, is it? He'll be having breakfast. In his room on the first floor.'

He sniffed his socks again, remarked that they still smelt of paint, and set to rubbing them once more.

Simon walked on, wondering if the young man kept his paints in his socks. In the doorway a sudden recollection hit him. Paint! That was the smell that had seemed so familiar at the top front room at Mrs Twite's. Of course, it was paint! Then – Simon stopped, assailed by suspicion – was that why Mrs Twite had been scrubbing with bath-brick? To remove the smell of paint? Why?

Pondering this, Simon sat down on the first convenient object he found – a stone statue of a lion, half finished – to unravel the matter a little further.

Dido said Dr Field had not been at the Twites'. But the rooms were as he had described them, the address was as he had given it, and the room smelt of paint, which suggested that he had occupied it.

Perhaps, Simon thought, perhaps he had fallen out with the Twites – had had something stolen, or found the house too dirty, or objected to being woken at one in the morning by Hanoverian songs.

He had complained, taken his leave, and moved away. The Twites, annoyed at losing a lodger, had contrived an elaborate pretence that no Dr Field had ever lived with them . . .'

Somehow Simon found it hard to believe this. For one thing, Dr Field was far from fussy, and, provided he was furnished with privacy and a good light for painting, was unlikely to object if his neighbours practised cannibalism or played the bass drum all day so long as they let him alone. And secondly, why should the Twites bother to make such a pretence about a trivial matter? Half a dozen people – neighbours, patients, local tradesmen – would be able to give their story the lie.

Then it occurred to Simon that he had not yet heard what Mr or Mrs Twite had to say; he had only had Dido's version. Perhaps the whole mystery was just her nonsense, and when he got back that night he would be handed a piece of paper with Dr Field's address on it.

Cheered by this reasonable notion, Simon stood up and crossed the entrance hall. A large double flight of marble stairs faced him, and between them stood a statue of a man in a huge wig, dressed in knee-breeches and a painter's smock. He held a marble paintbrush and was engaged in painting a marble picture on a marble easel. The back of the easel bore an inscription:

MARIUS RIVIÈRE
1759-1819
Founded this Academy

Simon noticed, when he was high enough up the stairs to be able to look over the marble gentleman's shoulder, that someone had painted a picture of a pink pig wearing a blue bow on the marble canvas.

Opposite the top of the stairs he saw a door labelled 'Principal'. Rather timidly he knocked on it, and an impatient voice shouted, 'Alors – entrez!'

Walking in, Simon found himself in a medium-sized room that was overpoweringly warm and smelt strongly of garlic and coffee and turpentine. The warmth came from two braziers full of glowing charcoal, on one of which a kettle steamed briskly. The room was so untidy – littered with stacks of canvases, baskets of fruit, wood-carvings, strings of onions hanging from the ceiling, easels with pictures on them, statues – that at first Simon did not see the little man who had told him to come in. But after a moment the same irascible voice said:

'Eh bien! Shut the door, if you please, and declare yourself!'

'Are – are you Dr Furnace, please, sir?' Simon said hesitantly.

'*Furrneaux*, if you please, *Furrneaux* – I cannot endure the English pronunciation.'

Dr Furnace or Furneaux was hardly more than three feet six inches high, and extraordinarily whiskery. As he rose up from behind his desk he reminded Simon irresistibly of a prawn. His whiskers waved, his hands waved, a pair of snapping black eyes took in every inch of Simon from his dusty shoes to the kitten's face poking inquisitively out of his jacket.

'And so, and so?' Dr Furneaux said impatiently. 'Who may you be?'

'If you please, sir, my name is Simon, and I believe Dr Field spoke about me – '

'Ah, yes, Gabriel Field. A boy named Simon. Attendez – '

Dr Furneaux waved his antennae imperatively, darted over to a cupboard, returned with a coffee-pot, tipped coffee into it from a blue paper bag, poured in hot water, produced cups from a tea-chest and sugar from another blue bag.

'Now we wait a moment. A boy named Simon, yes. Gabriel Field mentioned you, yes. In a moment I shall see what you can do. You are hungry?' he said, looking sternly at Simon. 'Take the bread off that brazier – zere, blockhead! – and find some plates and some butter. In ze brown jar, of course!' as Simon, bewildered, looked uncertainly about him. The brown earthenware jar resembled something from the Arabian Nights and could easily have held Ali Baba and a couple of thieves.

'So, now we eat,' said Dr Furneaux, breaking eight inches off a loaf shaped like a rolling-pin and handing it to Simon.

'I will pour ze coffee in a moment. Tell me about my good friend Dr Gabriel Field – how is it wiss him?'

'Dr Field?' Simon stammered, absently taking a large bite of the crisp bread which flew into crumbs all round him, 'but h-haven't you seen him? I thought he would be here.'

'Not since my jour de fête in July,' said Dr

Furneaux, carefully pouring coffee into two cups and handing one to Simon.

'But then, but –'

'He said you were to live wiss him. Are you not, then?'

'He seems to have moved. He is not at the address he sent –'

'Chose assez étonnante,' Dr Furneaux muttered to himself. 'Can Dr Field be in debt? Escaping his creditors? Or in prison? He would have told me . . .'

'He wrote inviting me to come and live with him, sir,' Simon said. 'He would have said if he was planning to move –'

'Well, no doubt he has been called away on ze private affairs. He will return. One sing is certain, he will come back here. Now, you have eaten? Ze little one, he has eaten too?' Dr Furneaux nodded benevolently at the kitten which was licking up some crumbs of bread and butter from the dusty floor. 'It is well. To work, zen! I wish to see you draw.' He handed Simon a stick of charcoal.

'Yes, sir.' Simon took the charcoal with a trembling hand. 'Wh-where shall I draw?'

Dr Furneaux's whiskered gaze roved round the room. There was not a clean canvas nor an empty space in it. 'Draw on zat wall,' the Doctor said, waving at the wall to his right, which was invitingly bare and white.

'All over it, sir?'

'Of course.'

'What shall I draw?'

'Oh – anysing you have seen in ze last few days.'

As usual when Simon started drawing, he was carried away into a world of his own. People knocked and entered and consulted Dr Furneaux, waited for assistance, went away again; some of them stared at Simon, others took no notice. Dr Furnaux himself came and went, darting out to conduct a class, or back to criticize the efforts of a private pupil. At intervals he made more coffee, and from time to time offered a cup of it – or a piece of bread, apple, grape, or sausage – to Simon. He ignored Simon's work, preferring, apparently, to wait till it was finished.

Towards noon a boy a little younger than Simon came in escorted by a tall, thin man.

'Mon Dieu!' Dr Furneaux groaned to himself at sight of them. Then he stood up and waved them forward.

'My dear young Justin – my dearest friend's grandson! And the sage Mr Buckle. Enchanté de vous voir. Mr Buckle – do yourself ze kindness to sit down. Let us see what you have been working at ziss week, my dear Justin.'

The boy did not speak, but hunched his shoulders and looked depressed, while the man addressed as Mr Buckle – a sandy-haired, pale-eyed individual dressed in rusty black – laid a small pile of drawings on the desk.

Neither the man nor the boy took any notice of Simon, who observed that the boy looked positively ill with apprehension as Dr Furneaux examined his work. He was a sickly-looking lad, very richly dressed, but the olive-green velvet of his jacket went badly with his pale, spotty cheeks, and the plumed hat which he had taken off revealed lank, stringy hair.

It was plain that he wished himself a thousand miles away.

Dr Furneaux looked slowly and carefully through the pile of drawings. Once or twice he seemed about to burst out with some remark, but restrained himself; when he reached the last, however, his feelings became too much for him and he exploded with rage.

'How can you, how *can* you bring such stuff to show to *me*, Jean-Jacques Furneaux, Principal of ze Rivière Académie? Ziz, *zis* is what I sink of zese *abominable* drawings!'

With considerable difficulty he tore the whole batch across and across, scattering pieces of paper all about him, his whiskers quivering, his eyes snapping with rage. Although so small, he was a formidable spectacle. The boy, Justin, seemed ready to melt into the ground with terror as bits of paper flew like autumn leaves. Simon watched with awe and apprehension. If Dr Furneaux was so severe with a familiar pupil, grandson of an old friend, what was his own reception likely to be?

The only person who thoroughly enjoyed the scene was the kitten, who darted out and chased the fluttering scraps of paper round Dr Furneaux's feet. The sight of him appeared to calm the fiery little Principal. He stopped hissing and stamping, stared at the kitten, snapped his fingers, took several deep breaths, and walked briskly two or three times up and down the room, neatly avoiding all the obstacles. At last he said:

'I have been too harsh. I do not mean to alarm you, my dear boy. No, no, I hope I treat my best friend's grandson better zan zat. But zere must, zere *must* be a painter hidden in ze grandson of Marius Rivière. We shall wr-rrench him out, n'est-ce-pas? Now – you shall draw somesing simple –'

His eye roamed about the room and alighted on the kitten. 'You shall draw zat cat! Of the most simple, no? Here –' He swept everything – plates, bread, papers, and ink – off his desk in disorder, found a stack of clean paper, and beckoned to Justin. Here, my dear boy. Here is charcoal, here is crayon.

Now – *draw*! I shall return in two hours' time. Come, my dear Mr Buckle. Justin will be easier if we leave him alone.'

He took the arm of Mr Buckle who moved reluctantly towards the door. 'Who is that?' he asked sourly, pointing to the legs of Simon, who was lying on his stomach behind the Arabian Nights jar, drawing cobblestones.

'Zat?' Dr Furneaux shrugged. 'Nobody. A boy from nowhere. He will not disturb Justin – his mind is engr-rossed in drawing.'

The door closed behind them.

Simon felt sorry for Justin – it seemed unreasonable to expect the boy to be a painter just because his grandfather had been one and founded the Academy.

People, surely, did not always take after their grandfathers? Perhaps I'm lucky, Simon thought for the first time, not to know who my parents or grandparents were.

After working diligently for another half-hour, he stood up and stretched to rest his cramped muscles. The kitten greeted him with a loud squeak of pleasure and ran up his leg. But the boy, Justin, took no notice – he was sitting at the desk, slumped foward with his face in his hands, the picture of dejection. He had not even started to draw.

'I say, cheer up,' Simon said sympathetically. 'It can't be as bad as that, surely?'

Justin hunched one shoulder away from him.

'Oh, *you're* all right,' he said with the rudeness of misery. 'Nobody cares how *you* draw. But just because my grandfather was a painter and started this place, everyone expects me to be wonderful. Why should I learn to paint? I'm going to be a duke. Dukes don't paint.'

'I say, are you though?' Simon said with interest. 'I've never met a duke.'

'And I daresay you never will,' Justin said listlessly. Just at that moment the kitten climbed across from Simon's leg to the desk and began playing with a ball of charcoal eraser. Justin made a rather hopeless attempt at sketching it, but it would not oblige him by staying still, and, after jabbing a few crude scrawls, he exclaimed furiously, 'Oh, curse and confound the little brute!' and hurled the charcoal across the room. The kitten sat down at once and stared at him with large reproving eyes.

'Quick, now's your chance while he's still,' Simon urged encouragingly. 'Try again.'

'I can't draw live things!' snapped Justin. 'A kitten hasn't any shape – it's all fuzzy!' He angrily scribbled a matchstick cat – four legs, two ears, and a tail – then rubbed it out with his fist and drew the same fist over his eyes, leaving a damp, charcoaly smear on his cheek.

'No,' said Simon patiently, '*look* at the kitten. Look at its shape and then draw that – never mind if what you draw doesn't look like a cat. Here –' He picked up another bit of charcoal and, without taking the tip off the paper, quickly drew an outline – quite carelessly, it seemed, but Justin gasped as the shape of the kitten fairly leaped out of the paper. 'I could never do that,' he said with grudging admiration.

'Yes you could – try!'

Advising, coaxing, half guiding Justin's hand, Simon made him produce a rough, free drawing which was certainly a great deal better than his previous work.

'You ought to feel the kitten all over,' Simon suggested. 'Feel the way its bones go. It looks fluffy, but it's not like a wig – it has a hard shape under the fur.'

'I shall never be able to draw,' Justin said pettishly. 'Why should I? It's not my nature. Besides, it's not the occupation of a gentleman.'

Simon opened his eyes wide.

'But drawing is one of the best things in the world! I can't think how you can live in London and not want to draw! Everything is so beautiful and so interesting I could be drawing for ever. And it is so useful; it helps you to remember what you have seen.'

He glanced towards his own picture on the wall and Justin's eyes followed listlessly. Not much was visible from where they stood, but a face could be seen, and Justin said at once:

'Why, that's Dido Twite.'

'Do you know her?' Simon was a little surprised that a future duke should be acquainted with such a guttersnipe.

'Buckle, my tutor, used to lodge with her family and we called there once,' Justin said indifferently. 'I thought her a vilely impertinent brat.'

'I lodge there now,' Simon explained.

'Will you help me some more?' Justin said. 'I expect old Fur-nose may come back soon.'

The kitten had settled again, and Simon helped Justin with more sketches.

'Don't rely on how you think it ought to look,' he repeated patiently, over and over. 'Ask your eyes and make them tell your hand – Look, his legs bend this way, not the way you have them –' And, as Justin rubbed out his line and obediently redrew it, he asked, 'Why did your tutor leave the Twite house? Where is he living now?'

'With me, at Battersea Castle,' Justin said, bored. 'My uncle – he's my guardian; my parents are dead – he arranged it. I'd been doing lessons with Buckle in the mornings, but now he lives in and works as my uncle's steward too, and I have him on top of me all day long prosing and preaching about my duty as a future duke, and I hate it, hate it, hate it!'

He jabbed his charcoal angrily at the paper and it snapped. Simon was disappointed. He had hoped the reason why Buckle left the Twite household might give him some clue as to Dr Field's departure. He was about to put a further question when they heard voices outside. With a hasty gesture Justin waved him back to his corner behind the big jar and laid a finger on his lips. The door opened and Dr Furneaux burst in briskly, whiskers waving.

'Eh bien, well, let us see how you have been getting on,' he demanded, bustling round the desk to look at Justin's drawings.

'Pas mal!' he declared. 'Pas mal du tout! You see – when you work wiss your head and do not merely s-scamp through ze drawing, all comes different! Ziss here, and ziss –' he poked the sketches – 'is a r-r-real artist's line. Here, not so good.' Justin met his eyes nervously. 'I am please wiss you my boy, very please. Now I wish you to do some painting.'

Justin turned pale at the idea, but Mr Buckle, who had followed Dr Furneaux into the room, interposed hastily, 'I am afraid that won't be possible today, Dr Furneaux. His Grace the Duke is expecting Lord Bakerloo to meet him at three on His Grace's barge to view the Chelsea Regatta.'

'Barges – regattas,' Dr Furneaux grumbled. 'A true painter does not sink of anysing but *painting*! Eh bien, be off, zen, if you muss, but bring me more drawings – more, more! – and better zan zese, next time you come.'

Justin and Mr Buckle nipped quickly out of the room almost before Dr Furneaux had finished speaking. The little Principal sat down at his desk, sighing heavily like a grampus.

Then the kitten, who had been investigating a dangling string of onions, managed to dislodge the whole lot and bring them crashing down on to himself. He bounded away, stiff-legged with fright. Simon burst out laughing.

'Tiens!' declared Dr Furneaux. 'It is ze doctor's boy. I had forgotten you, mon gars. Voyons, what have you been doing all zis time?'

Simon scrambled up, dusting charcoal from his knees, and Dr Furneaux picked his way through the furniture until he could survey the whole drawing, which now occupied about seven foot square. Simon tried in vain to make out the Doctor's reactions from his expression. Dr Furneaux looked at the picture carefully for about five minutes without saying a word; sometimes he scrutinized some detail with his whiskers almost touching the charcoal, sometimes he stepped back as far as possible to observe the picture from a distance.

Simon had drawn several scenes, one in front of the other. In the foreground was Dido Twite, perched on the donkey; her pert sparrow's looks contrasting with its sleepy expression as she urged it along Rose Alley. To the right lay Mr Cobb's yard, full of broken coaches, with the beaming Mr Cobb leaning against a wheel, about to sip his mug of Organ-Grinder's Oil, and his men hard at work behind him.

'Wiss whom have you studied drawing before?' Dr Furneaux asked sharply.

'With no one, sir. Dr Field told me one or two things – that's all . . .'

Dr Furneaux continued to study the picture and now rapped out a series of fierce questions: why had Simon placed this object there, that figure here, why had he drawn the man's leg like this, the steps thus, the donkey like that?

'I don't know, sir,' Simon kept saying in bewilderment. 'It seemed as if it ought to go that way.'

He was beginning to be afraid that Dr Furneaux must be angry when the little man amazed him by suddenly giving him a tremendous hug. Bristly whiskers nearly smothered him and the smell of garlic was overpowering.

'You are a good, good boy!' the Doctor declared. 'I am going to make a painter of you, but only if you work wiss every particle of yourself!'

'Yes, sir,' Simon said faintly. All at once he felt excessively tired and hungry, his head ached, his arms and legs were stiff, he seemed to have been drawing in the stuffy room for half his lifetime.

'You will go now. You will come back tomorrow morning. Wiss you you will bring charcoal, brushes, oil-paints – here, I give you ziss list – and palette. Zese sings you buy at a shop and at one shop only; zat is Bonnetiers in the King's Road.'

'Yes, sir. How – how much will they cost?' Simon asked, doing feverish sums in his head, wondering how soon Mr Cobb would pay him for his work, how much he would get, how late the paint shop stayed open.

Dr Furneaux looked at him sharply and said:

'For ziss time, you pay nossing. Here, I give you ziss note to Madame Bonnetier –'

'Oh, thank you – thank you, sir! And my fees? How much –'

'Never mind zat for ze moment. We shall see, later. Now, go, go! Do you sink ze Pr-r-rincipal of ze Académie has nossing to do but talk to you all day?' Dr Furneaux plainly hated to be thanked. 'Ah, bah, it is nossing. I, too, was once a poor ragged boy – *I*! Take ze little one, too.'

He grabbed the kitten, which was on his desk again, and held it out. As he did so his eye fell on Justin's drawings. He checked a moment, his mouth open, then shut. He stared at Simon as if about to ask something, then evidently changed his mind, sighed, and gestured him to go.

'He knew,' Simon said to himself. 'He knew I'd been helping Justin. I wonder if he was angry?'

3

When Simon returned to Rose Alley that evening it was late. He had been to the paint shop and bought beautiful new fat glistening tubes of paint, soft smooth brushes, and a glossy palette. Then he had returned to Mr Cobb's yard where he was given about five jobs to do in quick succession – replacing a cracked panel in a barouche, mending a broken axle-tree, turning a new spoke and putting it in a chariot-wheel, shoeing a pony, and bending an iron wheel-tread. By the end of this gruelling stint he was nearly dead of fatigue, and ravenous, but it was worth it, for Mr Cobb, clapping him on the shoulder, pronounced him a prime all-rounder, paid him a guinea then and there, with the promise of as much work as he wanted, and invited him up for a dish of pigs' pettitoes and onions with Mrs Cobb and young Miss Cobb, who lived in a neat little apartment up a flight of steps over the coach-house at the back of the yard.

When he got home to Rose Alley he found Dido Twite swinging on the broken rails in front of the house.

'Why've you bin such a long time?' she greeted him.

'Working,' said Simon.

'Watch me do a handstand. What you bin working at?'

'All sorts of things.' He was very weary and disinclined for the company of this fidget of a child, but she seemed so delighted to see him that he lingered a minute or two, kindly admiring her antics.

'There's a circus coming to Southwark Friday week. D'you think they'd take me as a tumbler?'

'I'm not sure,' Simon said cautiously. 'Anyway you don't want to leave home, do you?'

'Don't I jist? Will you take me to the circus?'

'I may not be here still,' said Simon, who had been offered lodgings at the Cobbs', and was inclined to move nearer to Rivière's Academy. Dido's face fell and she gazed at him open-mouthed. 'Where can I get a wash?' he went on.

'Washus at the back,' Dido said automatically. 'Hot water's tuppence a bucket. Why won't you be here?'

'I may move to Chelsea. I'm going in now. Goodbye.'

He ran whistling upstairs. From behind a closed door on the first floor came long, breathy, mournful notes. He heard Dido scurry up behind him and burst through the door crying, 'Pa! *Pa!* Stop playing and listen.'

Simon went on up to his own room, fed the kitten, and rummaged among the things in his pack for a small towel and a lump of soap he had made himself from wood-ash and goose-grease. Presently he ran downstairs again. As he neared the bottom a voice above him called, 'Hey!'

He looked up and saw Dido hanging upside-down over the stair-rail. She dropped a slice of bread-and-jam which landed jam-side downwards on his head.

'Now look what you've done, you wretched brat!' said Simon crossly. He made a grab for her through the rail, but she retreated, screeching with laughter and mock alarm.

'Oo, you don't half look a sight! Jellyboy, jelly-boy!'

'Just wait till I get you!' Simon threatened.

'What's it matter, you're going to wash anyway.'

Simon reflected that this was true, and went out to the wash-house, which was in a lean-to at the back of the house. A fire burned under a large copper in a brick bunker; the water in the copper was steaming. In a corner behind a screen stood a tin bath, with a shower pan supported on iron legs above it. Simon poured hot water into the bath. He pulled the string of the shower and hot water sluiced down on him and washed the jam out of his hair. He was soaping himself enjoyably when the wash-house door opened.

'Go away!' Simon shouted apprehensively. 'I'm in the bath.'

Dido's face came poking round the door. 'It's only me,' she reassured him.

Simon scowled over the top of the screen. 'Well, be off! It's not polite to come in when someone's bathing.'

She skipped across the room. 'Shall I take your clothes? You *would* look a nut-case then!'

'Don't you dare!'

'Well, will you give me a ride tomorrow?'

'All right.'

She put his clothes down and retreated, turning in the doorway to say, 'Pa says you're to come and have a dish of tea when you're ready.'

Simon hurried out of the bath as soon as she had gone and put his clothes on again. While he was emptying the water in canfuls down a grated drain he head voices apparently coming from the roof. This puzzled him until he realized that the chimney of the copper acted as a conductor for sound. What he could hear was the voices of Mr and Mrs Twite in their upstairs parlour.

'. . . very annoying that he found his way here,' Mrs Twite was saying irritably.

Mr Twite replied in a rumble of which nothing could be heard but the words, 'Dido . . . most unfortunate.'

'Eustace says' – her voice came clearer, as if she had stepped towards the chimney-piece – 'best stay here under our eye for the time being.'

'I'm sure *I* don't care,' her husband replied rather shrilly. 'It's only *my* house, after all. It's all one to me if Eustace and his ideas land us in the –'

'Quiet, Abednego! It's only for six weeks or so, in any case. Only till we can dispose of him by means of the dark dew. And you may be sure that we'll be handsomely rewarded when the Cause triumphs.'

'Yes?' he said sourly. 'We haven't had any reward for our other trouble yet, have we? I'm put upon, that's what it is. I'm put upon! All I want is to follow art and play my hoboy, but what happens?' He must have been walking across the room, for his words became fainter and Simon could hear nothing but a distant mumble in which the word 'paint' was alone distinguishable.

He returned to his room with all his suspicions aroused once more. What – or who – was the cause of the 'other trouble'? And was he himself the object of the Twites' conversation? And who was Eustace? And, even more mysterious, what was the dark dew by means of which somebody was to be disposed of? Poison? The Twites looked a shifty, havey-cavey lot, but he found it hard to believe they were poisoners.

The mournful music had begun again, but it stopped when he tapped at the Twites' door.

'Come in, come in, my dear young feller,' boomed Mr Twite, who in daylight proved to be a scraggy individual, thin and bony, with a wisp of hair and a wisp of beard and curiously wandering eyes that never stayed in one position very long. 'Settling, are you?' he went on. 'Capital, capital. All one happy family here, aren't we, Penny? Aren't we, Dido? Aren't we, Ella, my dear?'

The young lady addressed as Penny replied listlessly, 'Yes, Pa,' and did not lift her eyes from a copy of the *Gentlewoman's Magazine* which she was studying. Dido, toasting bread at the fire, caught Simon's eye and pulled a face. Mrs Twite, pouring hot water into a teapot, snapped, 'Hold your hush, Abednego, and fetch the cordial.'

Mr Twite meekly laid down the large wooden instrument on which he had been playing – Simon guessed it to be his hoboy – and took a dusty black bottle out of a cupboard.

Mrs Twite turned to Simon, all smiles. 'Sit down, Mr Thingummy, sit down. Don't stand on ceremony here. Dido – *move!* You'll take a dish of tea, I hope?'

'Thank you, ma'am.' Simon had already done very well at the Cobbs', but in order to be polite he accepted tea and toast.

'And a dash of mountain dew in it?' said Mr Twite with the black bottle.

'No, thank you,' Simon said firmly. He wondered if this could be the dark dew, but decided it was not after Mr Twite had adminstered a large dram to himself and his lady, and a small one to Penelope. After a few sips of tea Mr Twite, who had been looking rather gloomy, cheered up amazingly and began singing:

> 'Oh, it's dabbling in the dew that makes the
> barmaids fair,
> With their dewy, dewy eyes and their brassy,
> brassy hair!'

'Now, my dear boy,' Mrs Twite said to Simon, 'we want to hear *all* about you.'

'Yes,' agreed Mr Twite, putting down the dew-bottle, we want to hear *all* about you!'

'*All* about you,' murmured Penelope, without raising her eyes fron the magazine, and even Dido piped up, '*All* about you,' and dropped a fistful of toast crumbs down Simon's neck.

'Oh, there's not much to tell –' Simon began, but Mrs Twite would have none of this.

'Dear boy, there must be. *Where* have you come

from? *Who* do you know? *What* are you going to do all day long in London?'

Question by question she drew from Simon all there was to know about him. At the age of three he had been found wandering in the village of Loose Chippings in Yorkshire. Nobody claimed him and, mysteriously, he could not speak a word of English, so he was sent to the Poor Farm, where unlucky orphans were starved and neglected by the overseer, Gloober, whose only interest was in the half-crown per head per week he was paid by the parish. Here Simon survived as best he could for five years – he would not have endured it for so long, he said, had he not made a friend there whom he was reluctant to leave – until at the age of eight he decided to run away and live by himself in the woods.

'And that has been my life ever since,' he concluded, 'until last year I met Dr Field and he said I should learn to paint, which I have long wanted to do.'

'But what a *romantic* tale!' exclaimed Mrs Twite, casting her eyes up. 'Is it not, Abednego? And did you never hear what happened to your friend?'

'Oh, she's in London too,' Simon said happily. 'I had the good luck to see her today. But about Dr Field – I wrote to him, to this address, saying when I should arrive. Was my letter not delivered here?'

'Never, dear boy.'

'And Dr Field has not been here?'

'Neither hide nor hair of him,' declared Mr Twite. 'Now is not that a curious thing? But of course there are many, *many* Rose Alleys in London and I daresay we shall find that your Dr Field is living at one of the *others* and, when you discover which one, then you will be happily reunited. Depend upon it, that is the explanation. Do you not agree, my dove?'

'Undoubtedly,' agreeed Mrs Twite. 'But in the meantime, my dear Mr Thingummy, you mustn't *think* of moving away. We've begun to look on you as one of us, haven't we, girls?'

'Yes,' yawned Penelope, bored, looking at a picture of a lady's dolman with bugled ruching.

'Besides, if you moved away and Dr Field *should*

chance to make his way here, think what a misfortune if you missed one another!'

'Then you are expecting him?' Simon said hopefully.

'Never heard of him till today, dear boy. But if *you* are looking for *him*, it stands to reason that *he* must be looking for *you*, doesn't it?'

'I suppose so,' Simon said doubtfully. He glanced about, half hoping for some trace of Dr Field's presence. The room was large and extremely shabby; it contained several down-at-bottom armchairs, a

table covered with dingy red plush, a potted palm in a brass pot, and a pianoforte with several of its yellowed keys missing.

'You play?' said Mr Twite, following the direction of Simon's eyes to the piano. 'You are a follower of Terpsy-core?'

'No,' said Simon, without the least notion as to who Terpsy-core could be.

'All my family sing and play. My dear wife, the triangle. My sister-in-law, the violoncello. Dido, the hoboy like myself. Penelope and my father-in-law, the pianoforte. Penelope, my dear, you shall play and sing for us, to welcome our young friend into our circle.'

'No I shan't, Pa,' said Penelope shortly, and returned to her reading. Simon thought her a disagreeable girl. She was pale and, like Dido, had straw-coloured hair which was elaborately dressed in ringlets. She wore a showy gown adorned with floss and spangles. She caught Simon's eye, gave him a scornful glance, yawned again, and said, 'Isn't anyone coming in tonight?'

Simon excused himself, explaining the he had to be up early.

'Now you won't *think* of moving, dear boy, will you?' Mrs Twite gave him a toothy smile. 'We might even – *even* – see our way to lowering your rent.' She thought this over and added, 'Washing water reduced to three-halfpence a bucket.'

'Thank you.' Simon wondered why the Twites, last night not at all keen to have a lodger, were now so anxious to persuade him to stay.

He was at the door, about to say good night, when it opened smartly in his face and a woman walked in carrying a violoncello. She was looking behind her as she walked, and she called to somebody behind her, 'Put them in the kitchen, Tod, do. Mind you don't drop the cabbages.' She turned to Mrs Twite and added, 'There's cabbages, Ella, and as nice a basket of potatoes as you'll find this side of the Garden.'

'Thank you, Tinty,' Mrs Twite said, looking a little flustered. 'This is our new lodger, Mr Thingummy. My sister Mrs Grotch.'

'Good evening,' Simon said. Mrs Grotch, too, appeared disconcerted, but nodded stiffly. On his way up to bed Simon glanced down the stairs and saw the boy, Tod, stagger into the Twites' kitchen with a heavy load of mixed vegetables. Simon's suspicions were confirmed. For Tod was the boy who had snatched his letter on Southwark Bridge and Mrs Grotch, or Aunt Tinty, was the little woman who had misdirected him. A slow plodding step was now audible coming up the stairs from the front door. Simon lingered, waiting to see if his last guess was right, and was rewarded. For the old man who came into view, pulling himself up laboriously by the handrail and pausing to take a long quavering breath on each step, was the same white-bearded elder whom he had last seen on Southwark Bridge talking about his youth in the forest of Epping.

4

When Simon woke next day he heard the rain beating against his window. He opened the casement and a wild gust of wind surged about the room, so he shut it again hastily. As on the previous day, when he went downstairs, the Twite family seemed wrapped in slumber. However, his arrival at the front door coincided with the postman's knock, and a cascade of letters shot through the slot. Miss Penelope Twite instantly darted out of a near-by door, snatched up the letters, yawning, and gave Simon a hostile glance. She was wearing a faded gingham wrapper, her hair was in curl-papers, and she seemed in a very irritable humour. As she retired again Simon heard her say snappishly:

'*You* can do it tomorrow morning –'

then there was a stifled grunt and a creak of springs as if someone had jumped back into bed, slamming the door behind them.

Simon went out wondering if the Twites had a particular reason for not wanting him to see the mail. In case there might be a letter for Dr Field? However, as soon as he stepped outside he was obliged to direct all his energy to keeping himself upright and the kitten dry in the wild gusts of wind and rain that seemed threatening to knock him off his feet. He was glad that it was not far to the Academy, and thankful to gain the shelter of its great portico. Here he was approached by the young man whom he had seen yesterday washing socks.

'Hallo, my cocky,' said this individual. 'Old Fur-nose told me to watch out for you. So here's poor old Gus, eyes like cannon balls from lack of sleep, hoisted from the downy before the Chelsea cocks have left their watery nests – particular watery this morning, wasn't it, Fothers? Ugh!' he added, shuddering. '*Eight o'clock!* To think such a time exists! There ought to be a law against it, so there should!'

'I'm sorry if I've kept you waiting, sir,' Simon apologized.

'We've only just this minute got here,' interposed the young man with Gus whom he had addressed as Fothers. 'We've orders to take you to the Mausoleum, but I daresay you could do with a cup of coffee first?'

'Here, young 'un, just hold that bit of tinder, will you?' Gus pulled out flint and steel and a handful of carpenters' shavings from his pouch and soon expeditiously kindled a small fire under the shelter of the portico.

Meanwhile, Fothers had run down to the river-shore – only a stone's throw from the Academy – and returned with an armful of driftwood and tarry splinters, damp, to be sure, but ready to blaze up with a little encouragement. In no time a handsome fire was burning, over which Fothers dexterously slung a tin paint-pot full of water. 'No cooking at our lodgings,' he explained, tossing in a handful of coffee, 'ever since Gus started a fire and nearly burnt the landlady in her bed. So we have breakfast here.'

'Pity I didn't succeed in frizzling the old skinflint,' Gus remarked morosely, dropping three eggs into the coffee-pot. 'Seven minutes for mine, Fothers. I fancy 'em hard. Hey, you, whatsyourname! have you any bread on you?'

'Yes, sir.' Simon had purchased a long loaf and a sausage on the way to Chelsea. He was delighted to contribute to the meal.

'Ah, that's good, devilish good,' exclaimed Gus, his eyes lighting up. 'I haven't had my grinders in a bit of solid prog for three days; had just about enough of nibbling old Mrs Gropp's parsley and spring onions from her window-boxes. But you mustn't call us 'Sir', young 'un, we're only poor students, same as yourself. This is Democracy Hall, this is.'

While he waited for his egg to boil he pulled a cake of soap from his pocket, held it out in the rain a moment, rubbed up a lather on his jaw, and then, with a palette knife which he drew from his painter's satchel, calmly proceeded to shave, using the lid of the coffee-tin as a mirror. By the time he had done, Fothers, who had been timing the eggs with a large turnip-watch, pronounced them ready.

Simon, who was wet and chilled, found himself very glad of the drink of hot coffee. He noticed that his new friends, though they were plainly very hungry, showed great delicacy in eating only sparingly of his bread and sausage. He pressed more on them.

'No, thank'ee, young 'un,' said Fotheringham. 'You'll be wanting it yourself come dinner-time. Sausages don't grow on trees in London, you know, and they aren't giving away any half-crowns yet, that I've heard. Come along, now, and I'll show you the way to the Mausoleum.'

This proved to be an enormous room containing a regular forest of statues: sitting, standing, lying, in marble, metal, and granite, they seemed as if they had sprouted from the floor like mustard-and-cress.

'Old Fur-nose always makes you start by drawing these,' Gus explained.

'*All* of them?' Simon looked round in alarm.

'Bless you, no! Depends if he likes you – then he moves you on quick enough. *You'll* be all right – anyone could tell he'd taken quite a shine to you.'

'Thank you!' Simon called after them as they left. Presently Dr Furneaux came bustling in, directed Simon to draw a statue of a lady who appeared to be wearing noting but a fish-net, uttered words of instruction and encouragment in his ear, and then surged round the room, praising, scolding, and exhorting the other students.

The day passed quickly. As usual when Simon drew he hardly noticed the passage of time. The kitten foraged among the statues and received a share of bread and sausage at dinnertime. At last the light began to fade, and Simon rubbed his stiff hand.

'Enough, enough, now, boy,' exclaimed Dr Furneaux, materializing beside him like a whiskery ghost in the dusk. 'Ze ozzers zey all pack up and finish long ago. To draw in ze dark is to r-rruin ze eyes. Away wiss you and come back matinalement, in good time, tomorrow morning.'

He peered at Simon's drawing, said, 'Good boy,' and bustled away. Simon went off to Mr Cobb's yard, where he worked hard at splicing shafts for a couple of hours. Mr Cobb himself was in the smithy, superintending the shoeing of an excitable little bay mare. Presently he came out, rubbing the sweat off his brow.

'Proper handful she be,' he said with a grin. 'Artful as a curricle-load o' monkeys. She come in a-hobbling from her cast shoe, and now she've lamed the young feller as brought her – kicked him on the knee-cap and he's limping like a tinker's moke. He allus was an unhandy chap, was my wife's cousin Jem.'

Another explosion of whinnies came from the forge. The little mare danced out, making circles round the smith who was leading her. Another man followed, limping and cursing.

'Here, Jem, boy, you'd best goo up to Floss. Ask her to rub some liniment on that knee,' Mr Cobb said. 'If a knee like that goes proud on you, you'll be lame for months. I dessay his Grace the Dook won't mind waiting for the mare.'

' 'Tain't his Grace,' Jem said sulkily. 'It's for my young Lord Whippersnapper. Nothing would please his fancy but he must go riding by torchlight in the park, and no other mount in the stable but this one would do for him to set his lordly seat on. Dang me, was there ever such a pother when 'twas found she'd a shoe loose! Nowt would serve but I must take and have her shod this instant. And he's waiting for her now.' He moved to take the mare's bridle, limped again heavily, and let out an involuntary groan.

'You bide here-along, Jem, boy,' said Mr Cobb concernedly. 'One o' the others can take the filly back.'

'I'll go!' said Simon instantly, putting a finished shaft with a pile of others. 'Where shall I take her?'

'Ah, that's me boy! 'Twon't take you but a minute. Only a step from here it be. Duke o' Battersea's stables. Goo in the back way, through the tunnel, ask for Mr Waters, he's the head groom, give him my compliments, and say my Floss is putting a tar poultice on Jem's knee and he'll be right as rain before Goose Friday.'

'Is the boy trustworthy?' Jem asked, shooting a doubtful glance at Simon. 'He won't take the filly over to Smithfield and sell her for cat's meat?'

'Trustworthy as my old mother,' said Mr Cobb heartily. 'Come on now, Jem, boy, what you need is a drop of Organ-Grinder's Oil.' He helped the limping Jem up the stairs, shouting for Flossie to get out the tar and a large saucepan.

Simon tucked the kitten into his jacket, took the mare's bridle from the smith, and led her out of the gate and along the river-bank to Chelsea Bridge. Beyond, across the river, was the noble pile of Battersea Castle.

Gus had pointed out the Castle that morning while they were breakfasting. Simon had been delighted to learn that the place where his friend Sophie lived was so near, and had been planning to go to the servants' entrance as soon as possible and ask to see her. Returning the mare offered an excellent opportunity and he had seized it at once.

He paused a moment, gazing in awe at the huge mass of buildings composing the Castle. It stood close to the river; on either side and to the rear stretched the extensive park and gardens, filled with splendid trees, fountains and beds of brilliant flowers in shades of pink, crimson, or scarlet. The Castle itself was built of pink granite, and enclosed completely a smaller, older building which the present Duke's father had considered too insignificant for his town residence. The new Castle had taken forty years to build; three architects and hundreds of men had worked day and night, and the old Duke had personally selected every block of sunset-coloured stone that went to its construction. 'I want it to look like a great half-open rose,' he declared to the architects, who were fired with enthusiasm by this romantic fancy. It was begun as a wedding-present to the Duke's wife, whose name was Rosamond, but unfortunately she died some nine years before it was completed. 'Never mind, it will do for her memorial instead,' said the grief-stricken but practical widower. The work went on. At last the final block was laid in place. The Duke, by now very old, went out in his barouche and drove slowly along the river-bank to consider the effect.

He paused midway for a long time, then gave his opinion. 'It looks like a cod cutlet covered in shrimp sauce,' he said, drove home, took to his bed and died. But his son, the fifth and present Duke, who had been born and brought up in the Castle, lived in it contentedly enough, and was only heard to utter one complaint about it. 'It's too dry,' he said. 'Not enough mildew.' For the fifth Duke was a keen natural scientist, and moulds were one of his passions.

At this time of day the great pink structure was lit by a circle of blazing gas flambeaux, which vied with the smoky rose-colour of the London sunset and were reflected in the river below.

Glancing about him, Simon noticed a sign at the foot of the bridge: 'Battersea Castle. Tradesmen and Servants Turn Left.' Obediently he turned, and found the entrance to a large tunnel which ran under the river. The mare went forward confidently into it with ears pricked; plainly she knew her way home and was not startled by the booming echoes which her hoofbeats called out from the curving walls. The tunnel was not dark, for gas-lamps hung at regular intervals from the roof, but it was rather damp; rain from the morning's storm had collected on the floor in large pools. Towards the middle one of these extended for some twenty feet.

Simon, leading the mare, splashed unconcernedly through; having lived in the woods for years he was not worried by a trifle like wet feet. But he saw a girl some way ahead of him pause at the edge of the large puddle; then a man, who had been walking some paces behind her, overtook her and picked her up to carry her through. When the man was well into the middle of the pool, however, he evidently began to tickle the girl, for she screamed and struggled. Simon, approaching, heard him say:

'You'd best promise to come with me to the bear-baiting on Saturday or I'll drop you in. One – two – three –'

'I'll do no such thing!" exclaimed the girl with spirit. 'You know I can't abide the bear-baiting.'

'Then I'll drop you.'

'Oh!' exclaimed the girl furiously. *'How* I'd box your ears if my hands weren't full of grapes and thistles. Will you stop being so provoking and let me get on! My lady's waiting for these things.'

'I shan't budge till you promise.'

Neither of the pair had noticed Simon: their voices

had covered the sound of the mare's hoofs. He recognized the girl as Sophie and was about to come to her aid when there was an unexpected interruption.

A painter's cradle had been slung from the roof, and an elderly man who had been lying on it, attentively regarding the stonework, suddenly loosed a rope, letting himself down with a rattle of pulleys, until he dangled in front of the disputing couple.

'Midwink!' he barked. 'Leave the girl alone!'

The man was so startled that he almost dropped Sophie.

'Y-y-yes, of course, sir!' he gulped.

'Put her down! No, not there, dolt – ' for Midwink made as if to deposit Sophie in the pool – 'take her along to the dry road.'

'Certainly, certainly, sir.'

'And don't let me see you up to such tricks again, or you'll go back to Chippings and stay there.'

'Oh, no, sir! Please don't send me back there, please!'

'Well, behave yourself!' said the man on the cradle severely, and he hauled on the pulley and shot up to the roof again muttering, 'Where had I got to? Aha, what have we here? Something of definite mycological interest, I feel positive.'

The man Midwink carried Sophie across the pool and put her down. Then he noticed Simon and gave him a malevolent look. He was a hatchet-faced individual, dressed in black plush with buckled shoes and a stiff white collar. There was something mean, shifty, and bad-tempered about his appearance; he looked as if he would be a nasty customer to cross.

'Who might *you* be?' he said, eyeing Simon up and down, at the same moment as Sophie cried out in joyful recognition, '*Simon!* It's Simon! How in the world did you get here?'

'I've brought the bay mare from Mr Cobb,' Simon said.

'Horseflesh is not my province,' Midwink remarked loftily. 'You'd best take the mare to the stables.'

'I'll show you the way,' Sophie said. 'I'm going there myself. But Simon, how amazing it is that you should be in London. *Oh,* I am so pleased! I was beginning to fear we should never see each other again.'

'I see you've found a *friend*, Miss Fine-Airs,' sneered Midwink. 'Nice sort of riff-raff you slight decent folk for, I must say! What would her Grace think if she saw you consorting with horse-yobs and gutter-boys – there wouldn't be so much of "my pretty Sophie" then!'

'Oh, be quiet, Midwink – I do not find you interesting at all!' snapped Sophie.

Simon chuckled quietly to himself. Sophie's speech was so very characteristic that he wondered how he could have forgotten it. She had a trick of rattling out her words very fast and clearly, like a handful of beads dropped on a plate. He wondered where he had recently heard somebody else speak in the same way.

'*I* know when I'm not wanted,' said Midwink sourly. 'But you'd best guard your tongue, Madam Sophie – a pretty face isn't the only passport to fortune here, as you may find!'

'Who's he?' asked Simon, as Midwink walked ahead of them and took a turning to the right.

'Oh, he is the Duke's valet – he is of no account,' Sophie said impatiently. 'He would be turned off if it were not for his knack of tying cravats. The Duke has grown too short-sighted to tie his own, and Midwink is the only person who can arrange them to his liking. But tell me, how do you come to be in London? Did you ever go back to Gloober's Poor Farm? What have you been doing all these years? Oh, there is so *much* to ask you! But I must run to my lady with these things – she is waiting for them. Can we meet tomorrow – it is my evening off. Are you free then? Ah, that is good, excellent, I will meet you, where? Not too near the Castle or Midwink may come bothering – Cobb's yard? Yes, indeed I know it, that will do very well. Now, here are the stables and there is Mr Waters. Good evening, Mr Waters. Here is my friend Simon who has brought back your horse.'

'That ain't no horse, Miss Sophie, that's as neat a little filly as yourself,' said Mr Waters.

'Ah, bah, horses and fillies are all the same to me! Simon, it is *wonderful* to see you again. Now I must fly. Till tomorrow!' She stood on tiptoe to give Simon a quick peck on the cheek, then ran off with her basket.

'And where's Jem Suds got to?' asked Mr Waters. 'Come up, my beauty, then, hold still while I put a saddle on your pernickety back.'

Simon explained about the kicked knee and Mr Cobb's tar poultice.

'That lad's born to get his neck broke,' sighed Mr

Waters, tightening a girth. 'Ah, there's his young lordship. You just brought the mare back in time – '

'Aren't you ready yet, Waters?' called an irritable voice, and a boy came out of a doorway. Simon recognized Justin, the unwilling art student. He swung himself rather clumsily into the saddle, then looked down at Simon. 'Oh, hallo,' he said carelessly. 'What are you doing here?' He did not, however, wait for an answer, but gave a flip with his crop and trotted across the stable-yard and out through a gateway that led into the park.

'Wait, your lordship!' called Waters. 'I've got Firefly saddled. I'll be with you directly.' He led out another mount, but Justin impatiently called back, 'I don't want you, Waters, I want to be on my own,' set spurs to the mare, and galloped off into the dusk.

'Pesky young brat!' growled Waters. 'He knows he's not allowed out alone. Now I suppose I shall have to chase him all over the park, afore he breaks his neck.'

'Who was that?' Simon asked.

'Young Lord Bakerloo, the Dook's nevvy. He's the heir, as his Grace never had none o' his own . . . Goodbye, my lad. Thank you for bringing back the filly,' Waters called as he rode out of the gate.

Simon made his way back through the tunnel.

The elderly gentleman was still slung up on his painter's cradle halfway along, gazing at the roof through a magnifying glass. Simon had forgotten about him and was rather startled at being addressed by a voice above his head as he waded through the largest puddle.

'It's rather damp down there, isn't it?'

'It *is* rather damp,' Simon agreed, pausing and looking up politely.

'You find it inconvenient?' the old man asked, betraying a certain anxiety.

'Bless you, no!' Simon said cheerfully

The man brightened up at once.

'You don't mind a bit of damp? You're a boy after my own heart! *I* don't mind damp either. In fact I *like* damp. You don't find it troublesome? That's excellent – excellent.'

'I suppose it's a bit of a nuisance for females,' Simon suggested, thinking of Sophie's white cambric skirts. The man's face fell.

'For females? You think it is? Yes, perhaps – perhaps.' He sighed. 'Still, you yourself don't object to it – that's very gratifying. It's always gratifying to find a kindred spirit. Do you, I wonder, play chess?'

'Yes, I do, sir,' said Simon, who had been taught to play by Dr Field.

'You do? But that's capital – famous!' The old gentleman looked radiant. 'We must certainly meet again. You must come and play chess with me. Will you?'

'Why, certainly, sir,' said Simon, who began to believe the old gentleman must be a trifle cracked. Still, he seemed a harmless old boy, and quite kindly disposed. 'When shall I come?'

'Let me think. Not tomorrow night, dinner with the Prince of Wales. Night after, Royal Society, lecture on moss. Night after that, tennis with the

Archbishop. Indoor, of course. Night after, Almack's with Henrietta. Devilish dull, but she enjoys it. Night after, ball at Carlton House. Stuffy affairs, can't be helped, must put in an appearance. Night after, billiards with the Lord Chief Justice. How about today week?'

'That would be quite all right for me, sir,' said Simon. 'Where shall I come?'

'Oh I'm always around and about,' the man said, waving a hand vaguely. 'Anyone will tell you where to find me. Any time after nine. That's excellent – really delightful.' He pulled on a rope and his cradle moved away.

'Excuse me, sir – whom shall I ask for?' Simon called after him.

'Just ask for Battersea,' the man's voice came faintly back.

Battersea? Battersea? He *must* be cracked, Simon decided. No doubt by that day week he would have forgotten all about the invitation. Perhaps Sophie would know who he was, and whether the invitation should be taken seriously or not. Sophie was so shrewd and cheerful and kind-hearted – what a comfort it was to have found her again!

Leaving the tunnel, Simon swung on towards Vauxhall Bridge, whistling happily. If only he could find Dr Field, life in London would not be so bad!

5

Next day, chancing to wake early, Simon looked out of his front window into Rose Alley and saw his unfortunate donkey, Caroline, struggling to pull an outrageously heavy milk-cart loaded with churns, and being encouraged thereto by the shrewish dairy woman, who was beating her with a curtain-pole.

Simon threw on his clothes and ran down to the street.

'Hey!' he shouted after the milkwoman. She turned, scowling, and snapped: 'Penny a gill, and only if you've got your own jug.'

'I don't want milk,' Simon said (indeed it looked very blue and watery), 'I want my donkey.' And before she could object, he kicked a brick under the wheel of the cart and slipped the relieved Caroline out from between the shafts. In two days she seemed to have grown noticeably thinner and to have acquired several weals.

'I'm not leaving her with you a minute longer,' Simon told the woman. 'You ought to be ashamed to treat her so.'

'I suppose you are the President of the Royal

Humane Society,' she sneered. Then she turned and bawled, 'Tod! Bring the mule.'

'Coming, Aunt Poke,' called a voice, and the boy Tod appeared leading a scraggy mule with one hand and holding his trousers round his neck with the other. He put out his tongue at Simon and remarked, 'What price cat's meat?'

It was still very early, and Simon decided this would be a good time to make inquiries about Dr Field at the shops in the neighbourhood. There was a greengrocer's next to the dairy, adorned with piles of wizened radishes and bunches of drooping parsley. He saw Mrs Grotch, Aunt Tinty, watering these with dirty water from a battered can. Guessing that he would get no help from her he passed to the next shop a bakery.

'Can you tell me if a Dr Gabriel Field ever bought bread here?' he asked, stepping into the warm, sweet-smelling place.

'Dr Field?' The baker scratched his head, then called to his wife, 'Polly? Know anything about a Dr Field?'

'Was he the one that lanced Susie's carbuncle?' The baker's wife came through into the shop, wiping her hands on her apron.

Just at that moment Simon heard a voice behind him. Tod, having harnessed the mule to his Aunt Poke's milk-float, had wandered along the lane and was spinning a top outside the door and singing in a loud, shrill voice:

> 'Nimmy, nimmy, not,
> My name's Tom Tit Tot.'

Whether this song had any effect on the baker and his wife or whether they had just recollected a piece of urgent business, Simon could not be sure, but the baker said hastily, 'No, there's no doctor of that name round here, young man,' and hurried out of the shop, while his wife cried, 'Mercy! my rolls are burning,' and bustled after him.

Simon walked the length of the row of shops asking at each one, but all his questions, perhaps because of Tod, were equally fruitless, and at length, discouraged, he set off for the Academy, while Tod turned a series of cartwheels along Rose Alley – keeping his trousers on only with the greatest difficulty – and launched a defiant shout of 'My name's Tom Tit Tot' after Simon, which it seemed wisest to ignore.

It was still only half past seven, so there was time to call at the Cobbs' and ask if Caroline might be boarded at the stables there.

The Cobbs were at breakfast and received Simon with great cordiality, offering him marmalade pie, cold fowl, and hot boiled ham. Mrs Cobb, a stout, motherly woman, insisted on his having a mug of her Breakfast Special to see him through the day. This was a nourishing mixture of hot milk and spices, tasting indeed so powerfully of aniseed that Simon thought it would see him through not only that day but several days to come.

'Ah, it's a reg'lar Cockle-Warmer, Flossie's Breakfast Special,' Mr Cobb said fondly and proudly. 'You see, young 'un, my wife was a Fidgett, from Loose Chippings; those Fidgett girls know more about housewifery and the domestic arts by the time they marry than most women learn in a lifetime.'

Simon was very interested to hear that Mrs Cobb came from the same part of the country as himself, while Mrs Cobb was amazed to learn that Simon had passed the early part of his life at Gloober's Poor Farm.

'And you such a stout, sensible lad, too!' she exclaimed. 'I thought they all turned out half-starved and wanting in the head, poor things. O' course we'll keep the donkey here, and gladly, won't we Cobby! The lad won't mind if little Libby has a turn-out on her now and then, I daresay?'

As little Libby Cobb was only two, and looked extremely seraphic, in complete contrast to Miss Dido Twite, Simon had not the least objection to this.

He bade farewell to the Cobbs, hastened down to the Academy, and set to work in the Mausoleum, drawing a bronze figure with a trident. He had not, however, been at this occupation very long when Dr Furneaux appeared and whisked him away to another room where an old lavender-seller had been established with her baskets on a platform to have her portrait painted by a dozen students.

They had been working for a couple of hours and Dr Furneaux was giving a lecture from the platform (largely incomprehensible because he had somehow got his whiskers smothered in charcoal dust and kept breaking off to sneeze) when two people entered the room.

Glancing round his easel Simon recognized the boy

Justin, whom he now knew to be young Lord Bakerloo, the Duke of Battersea's nephew, and his tutor, the pale-eyed Mr Buckle. Justin looked wan but triumphant; his right arm was heavily bandaged and he carried it in a sling.

Buckle addressed Dr Furneaux in low tones. Meanwhile, Justin had caught sight of Simon and nodded to him familiarly.

'Brought it off!' he confided, gesturing with his bandaged arm (which appeared to give him no great pain). 'Done old Fur-nose brown, I have. Can't paint with my dib-dabs in a clout, can I?'

'Did you take a toss?' Simon asked, remembering the headlong way Justin had galloped across the twilit park.

'Walk*er*!' Justin replied, laying the first finger of his left hand alongside his nose. 'That'd be telling.'

'Yes, indeed, *most* regrettable,' Mr Buckle was saying sorrowfully to Dr Furneaux. 'But we must be thankful the accident was no worse. The doctor fears Lord Bakerloo will not be able to use his right hand for at least a month.'

'My dear Justin – my poor Justin!' Dr Furneaux exclaimed warmly, darting to Justin, who winced away nervously. 'Ziss is most tragic news! A painter has no business wiss riding on a horse – it is by far too dangerous.'

'I'm not a painter, I'm a Duke's grandson.' Justin muttered. But he concealed from Dr Furneaux his look of satisfaction at being told not to return until his arm was completely healed.

When evening came, and the students departed to

their homes, Simon returned to Mr Cobb's yard, where he was to meet Sophie, and occupied the interval by blacksmith's work. He had just finished bending an iron rim on to a wheel when she arrived.

'Why!' cried Mr Cobb. 'Is *this* your friend! It's the bonny lass as waits on her Grace. Dang me, but you're a lucky young fellow!'

Sophie had brought a basket of fruit and proposed that she and Simon should walk into Battersea Park and eat their supper sitting on the grass. But the hospitable Mr Cobb would not hear of such a plan.

'Look at the sky!' he admonished them. 'Full to busting! There's enough rain up there for a week of Sundays. You'll just be a-sitting down to your first nibble when it come peltering down on you. No, no, you come upstairs and eat your dinners comfor'ble under a roof; Flossie would never let me hear the last of it if I let two young 'uns go off to catch their deaths of pewmony.'

Sophie protested that it was putting the Cobbs to a deal too much trouble, but as the sky was indeed very threatening they finally accepted, and in return offered to mind Miss Libby Cobb while her mother slipped round the corner to buy two pounds of Best Fresh and a gallon jar of pickled onions.

Young Miss Cobb proved remarkably easy to amuse; she and the kitten chased one another till both were exhausted, and when that happened Simon or Sophie had only to imitate the noise of some animal to put her in fits of laughter. Meanwhile, Sophie told Simon all that had happened to her since he had run away from Gloober's Poor Farm.

'I was lucky,' she said. 'You remember I always liked needlework and Mrs Gloober used to get me to do her mending? Then she began buying fashion magazines and bringing them home for me to make up her dresses. One time I was at work on a blue peau-de-chameau ball-dress with vandykes of lace and plush roses, when her Grace the Duchess came in to inspect the Poor Farm and saw the dress. Next day a pony-trap came over from Chippings Castle: the Duchess's compliments and she'd take the little girl who was so clever with her needle to be a sewing-maid. Mrs Gloober was very angry but she didn't dare refuse because the Duchess was on the Board. But she packed me off without a thing to wear. Since then her Grace has been so kind to me, and now I'm her lady's-maid. When their Graces came up to London for the summer I came with them.'

Then Simon in turn told his story, finishing with the mysterious disappearance of Dr Field and the odd and suspicious behaviour of the Twite family.

Meanwhile, Miss Libby Cobb had again started in pursuit of the kitten. At this moment she caught her foot in a thick rag rug, the pride of Mrs Cobb's heart, tripped and fell against the door opening on to the stair-head. Not firmly latched, it flew open, and there was a thump and a shout. Sophie sprang to catch Libby before she could tumble downstairs, and exclaimed:

'Why, it's Jem! Whatever are you doing there, Jem?'

Jem indeed it was, but in no condition to answer. He must have been just ouside the door when Libby

fell against it, and the unexpected push had sent him down the stairs. He lay groaning at the bottom.

'We'd best get the poor fellow up here,' Simon proposed but before they could do so Mrs Cobb returned from her shopping and let out a shriek of dismay.

'Eh, Jem my man, never tell me you're in the wars again, just when I'd set you right with a tar poultice! What happened?' she asked, as she and Simon between them supported the unlucky Jem up the stairs.

'The door flew open and knocked me down,' he muttered.

'And what was you doing then – listening at the keyhole?' Jem turned pale. 'Nay, only my joke, lad, never heed it. I do believe all the ill-luck in Battersea falls on your poor head. Come you in and lie down on Libby's bed while I put a bit o' vinegar on it.'

While Mrs Cobb ministered to the afflicted Jem, Sophie flew about very capably and set to cooking the Best Fresh, and Simon made a monstrous heap of toast and extracted the stopper of the pickled-onion jar. Soon they sat down to a very cheerful meal with the Cobbs.

Sophie and Mrs Cobb had a fine time exchanging gossip, for Mrs Cobb, it appeared, had been a parlour-maid at Chippings Castle before she got married.

'Ah, you're in clover working for her Grace,' she declared, 'As sweet a lady you'll not find this side of Ticklepenny Corner, poor thing. It's a shame she never had no little ones of her own. If she'd 'a had, I'll be bound they'd be worth twenty of the puny little whey-faced lad they call Lord Bakerloo. He's the Duke's nevvy, you see,' she went on (like all old retainers, she loved talking about the Family). 'The Duke's younger brother, Henry, he married his own cousin, and they had Justin, that was born abroad in Hanoverian parts and sent back to England as a babby when both his parents died. Deary dear, it was a sad end, poor young things, and a sad beginning too – there was a plenty trouble when they married.'

'Why?' asked Sophie.

'Because they were cousins, and she was half French, and a wild one! Her ma was Lady Helen Bayswater – that's the present Duke's aunt. She fell in love with a French painter, escaped from France in the revolution they had, and married him in the teeth of her family, as you might say. Famous, he was, but not grand family.'

'Was the name Marius Rivière?' asked Simon.

'That's it! I never can get my tongue round those Frenchy names! He married Lady Helen and they had the one daugher – what was *her* name? It'll come to me in a minute – and for some time they was at daggers drawn with the old Duke. They say Rivière had been great friends with all the family before, and painted pictures of 'em, but the marriage broke it up. Then Lady Helen's daughter met her cousin, his present Grace's younger brother, and they fell in love, and the trouble began all over again. They ran off to Hanover where his regiment was, and got married. And that was the last that was heard, till word was sent they was dead, and Mr Buckle fetched back the poor babby. By that time the old Duke was dead, and his present Grace had always been fond of his brother, and stood by him, so he brought up Justin.'

'It's rather sad,' Sophie said. 'Poor Justin. You can understand why he always looks so miserable. Specially if he has been looked after by that sour Mr Buckle all his life.'

'Do you know,' exclaimed Mrs Cobb, who had been scrutinizing Simon and Sophie as they sat side by side in the window-seat, 'you two are as alike as two chicks in a nest! I declare, you might be brother and sister. Are you related?'

They stared at one another in astonishment. Such an idea had never occurred to them. How strange it would be if they were!

'We don't know, ma'am,' Sophie said at length. 'We came to the Poor Farm at different times, you see. I was brought up by a kind old man, a charcoal-burner in the forest, till I was seven, and then the Parish Overseer came and took me away and said I must be with the other orphans. But the old man was not my father, I know. I can remember when he first found me.'

'Who looked after you before that, then child?'

'An otter in the forest,' Sophie explained. 'I can still recall how difficult it was to learn human language, and how strange it seemed to eat anything but fish.'

'An *otter*! Merciful gracious!' Mrs Cobb flung up her hands. 'An otter and then a charcoal-burner! It's a wonder you grew up such a beauty, my dear! I'd 'a thought you'd have had webbed feet at the very least!'

'They were both very kind to me,' Sophie said, laughing. 'I was dreadfully sad when the Overseer came and took me to Gloober's.'

'I don't wonder, my dear, from what I've heard of the place.'

'If Simon hadn't taken care of me there I don't know how I'd have got on for the first few years. Later it wasn't so bad, when I learned dressmaking, and Mrs Gloober found I could be useful to her.'

'But you like it better with her Grace?'

'Oh yes, a thousand times! Her Grace is so kind! Sometimes she seems more like an aunt or a godmother than a mistress! Mercy!' Sophie suddenly cried, jumping up as the solemn note of the Chelsea church clock boomed out the hour. 'Ten o'clock already! It's time I was getting back to make her Grace's hot posset. She always likes it soon after ten.'

'I'll see you home,' Simon said. They bade goodbye to the kindly Cobbs, who invited them to come again whenever they had an hour to spare. Halfway down the stairs they were halted by a hoarse shout from above, and turned to see Jem looking through the bedroom doorway, his hair all in spikes and his eyes staring with sleep.

'Soph – please –' he mumbled. 'Could – give – note – Mr Buckle?' He thrust a piece of crumpled paper into Sophie's hand.

'He's half asleep. It's the poppy syrup I gave him,' said Mrs Cobb concernedly, and steered him back to bed.

'I'll deliver your note!' Sophie called, but Jem was already unconscious again. Sophie tried to straighten out the paper which appeared to be a sugar bag. The large sprawling script on it covered both sides:

Mister Bukkle. Sum one cums from u no where. Jem.

'Oh dear,' Sophie said, 'now I've read it – but I didn't mean to. In any case, I haven't the least notion what it means. I hope Mr Buckle will understand it.'

'By the way,' Simon said. 'I had a queer invitation after I saw you last. You remember that odd-spoken old gentleman who was slung up in the top of the tunnel and spoke so sharply to Midwink? When I was on my way back he invited me to go and play chess with him one evening next week. Should I take the invitation seriously, or is he a bit cracked? Who is he, anyway?'

Sophie turned to look at him incredulously.

'Don't you know?'

'Of course I don't know.' Simon gave her a good-humoured pat on the shoulder. 'Don't forget I've only just arrived in London. I'm not such an almanack as you, my bright girl. Who is he, then?'

Sophie burst into a fit of laughter which lasted her as far as the sevants' entrance to Battersea Castle. 'Why,' she gasped, wiping the tears of merriment from her eyes, 'he's the Duke of Battersea, that's all! Certainly you must keep the appointment – his feelings would be hurt if you didn't.'

She gave Simon a quick good-night hug, and he heard her laughing again as she ran down the tunnel and out of sight.

6

When Simon returned to his lodgings the following evening he saw Miss Dido Twite in her night gown looking out rather forlornly from the front window into the twilit street. Her face brightened immediately at sight of him and as he entered the house she put her head round her bedroom door.

'Wotcher, my cully,' she greeted him hoarsely but joyfully.

'Hallo, brat. What's the matter with you?' Simon inquired. She was flushed, and had a long red stocking wound round her throat.

'I have the quinsy,' Dido croaked, 'and Ma and Pa and Penny-lope and Aunt Poke and Aunt Tinty and *everybody* has gone off to Theobalds' Fair and I'm *that* put about and blue-devilled. Mean, hateful things they are – I wish they was all dead!' She stamped her bare foot on the floor and her lip quivered. 'There was to be a Flaming Lady, too, and a Two-headed Sheep and Performing Fleas and a G-giant C-carnivorous Crocodile.'

'Here, don't you think you ought to be in bed?' said Simon, anxious to avert an explosion of tears which seemed imminent. 'I'm sure if you have the quinsy you shouldn't be running about in your nightgown. Come on, I'll tuck you up.'

'Will you stay and play cribbage with me?' asked Dido instantly.

'All right – only jump in quickly.'

She retired through the doorway to a very untidy ground-floor bedchamber evidently shared by the two sisters, for as well as Dido's meagre collection of playthings, it contained curling-tongs, copies of the *Ladies' Magazine,* and a great quantity of frilly garments, which plainly belonged to Penelope, strewn about in a state of disrepair.

'Now you sit *there*,' ordered Dido, jumping into a skimpy dishevelled bed and patting the coverlet. 'Here's the cribbage board. Shall we play for money?'

'No, we certainly shall not,' said Simon reprovingly. 'Besides, I don't for one moment suppose that you have any.'

'No, I haven't a tosser to my kick,' Dido said, bursting out laughing. 'What a hum it would have been if you'd won! Come on – you can start.'

They played for an hour, Dido winning all the time, largely because she was prepared to cheat in the most unabashed manner. Then she began to get restless and peevish, and suggested they change over to loo. Simon, who thought she ought to get some rest, proposed that he should straighten her covers and leave her to try and go to sleep, but she raised vehement objections.

'I don't *want* to go to sleep! I don't *want* to be left alone! There's too many people come into this house at night, walking about and bumping on the stairs.'

'I don't believe there's a soul except us,' said Simon. 'You're not scared of ghosts, are you?'

'I ain't afeared of *anything*,' said Dido with spirit. 'I just don't like people walking about on the stairs and bumping. They clanks, too, sometimes.'

'Shall I get you something to eat or drink?' Simon suggested.

Dido thought she would like a drink of hot milk. 'Ma said she'd leave a mug of milk in the kitchen, but I'd sooner you hotted it. My throat feels like someone's been at it with sandpaper.' She gave him a pitiful grin, looking more than ever like a small, moulting sparrow.

Simon found the Twites' kitchen, a huge gloomy room in the basement. The mug of milk was on the table, but it took some hunting to discover a clean saucepan. The fire in the range was very low and the coal-scuttle empty; he returned to Dido and asked where the coal was kept.

'In the cellar. Door's back o' the pantry. Mind how you go down the steps, they're steep,' she croaked. 'Ma won't let me go down there.'

There were some half-used candles on the kitchen dresser. Simon lit one, took the hod, and went down the steep, narrow cellar stairs. There was another door at the foot, which was locked, but the key was in the lock. He opened this and cautiously entered the darkness beyond, holding his candle high. His foot struck against something metallic which clinked on the stone floor. He lowered the candle and was astonished to see a musket – another – dozens of them, neatly stacked. And beyond the muskets were barrels of a greyish substance which Simon, by feel and sniff, holding the candle at a safe distance, identified as gunpowder. The room was a regular arsenal!

He found a heap of coal in one corner. Thoughtfully he filled his hod and returned to the kitchen, locking the cellar door behind him again. While he mended the fire and waited for the milk to heat he pondered over this discovery. No wonder Dido heard people bumping and clanking on the stairs! No doubt about it, the Twites must be Hanoverian plotters, bent on removing good King James from the throne, and bringing in the Young Pretender, Bonnie Prince Georgie from over the water.

The milk came to the boil and, remembering Mrs Cobb's Special, he shook in some aniseed and took the mug to Dido. She sipped the hot drink gratefully while he beat up her pillows and straightened the blankets with clumsy goodwill.

'Now you must try to sleep,' he ordered, when the mug was empty.

'You've got to stay with me till I go off,' she countered. She looked hot-cheeked and heavy-eyed, ready to fall asleep at any moment.

'Very well,' said Simon. 'I'll blow out the candle.'

'No, don't do that. Put it over on that cupboard where it won't shine in my eyes.'

'Lie down, then.' She curled up, sighing, with her back to him, and he placed the candle on the cupboard. As he did so his attention was caught by a small drawing pinned on the wall. He held the light close and saw that it was a sketch-portrait of Dido, done roughly, but full of life and animation. She was sitting on the front steps, eating a piece of bread and jam. Simon let out an exclamation under his breath and studied the picture intently. The style of drawing was unmistakable: it could be by no other hand than that of Gabriel Field. He looked at the lower right-hand corner where the doctor always signed with his initials, but saw that the whole corner of the paper had been neatly removed by somebody's thumbnail.

He put the candle down and returned to Dido, intending to question her, but she was so drowsy he had not the heart. 'Kind,' she whispered hoarsely. 'Nobody else . . .' Her voice died away. She took a firm hold of Simon's hand and sank into sleep. In any case, what would be the use of questioning her? She would only tell lies about it. Best to mention it to Mr Twite in the morning – it offered complete proof that Dr Field had been in the house and seen Dido.

Had Dr Field stumbled on some evidence of the Hanoverian plot and been put out of the way?

Dido stirred and suddenly opened her eyes.

'Where's your kitty?' she muttered.

'I've lent it to a lady called Mrs Cobb.'

'Why?'

'To catch mice for her.'

Dido lay silent. Presently a large tear rolled out from under her closed eyelid.

'What's the matter?'

'First the donkey went – then the kitty went – next *you'll* go. I don't have anyone nice to play with – they allus leaves.'

'I shan't leave,' Simon soothed her. 'You go back to sleep.' But as the words left him it suddenly occurred to him to wonder what would happen if the Twites realized that he had seen the arms in the cellar. Would he, like Dr Field, mysteriously disappear?

Dido's eyelids flickered open, then shut once more. Her breathing slowly became deep and even, her clutch on his hand loosened. Fifteen minutes went by and then he judged it safe to slip his hand free and stand up. As he did so she moved and muttered in her sleep, 'Can't tell, you see. Pa would larrup me.'

'Never mind,' said Simon softly. 'I think I know.' And he tiptoed from the room.

Simon took a long time to go to sleep. He lay awake worrying, and woke next day with his problem still unsolved. His first impulse had been to inquire the way to the office of the Bow Street constabulary and put the whole matter before them. What would happen then? There would be commotion, uproar, publicity – the Twites would be arrested, no doubt, the guns and ammunition removed, but would he be any nearer discovering what had happened to Dr Field? He doubted it. After much pondering he decided to keep his own counsel a bit longer, and to watch the Twites even more closely.

To this end, when, as he ate his breakfast, he heard a violent quarrel break out on the stairs, he went quietly on to the landing and stood listenting by the banisters out of sight.

'I'll teach you to leave keys in doors!' Mrs Twite

was crying angrily. 'Didn't I tell you to see to the fire and lock the cellar before we set out? Oh, you nasty little minx, you! I'll wager you never fetched the coal. Oh, you hussy, you. All you cared about was prinking and powdering and sticking on beauty-spots!'

Simon heard what sounded like a hearty box on the ear followed by an angry shriek from Penelope:

'Leave me be, Ma! Pa, make her leave me be or I declare I'll leave home. I won't stay here to be abused!'

'Best leave her be, then, Ella, my dove.'

'Hold your tongue, Abednego!'

There followed the sound of a door slamming. Simon waited a moment or two, then ran quietly downstairs.

By the front door he came face to face with Mr Twite.

'Ah, it's our distinguished young Raphael, our Leonardo-to-be,' said Mr Twite with a wide smile which seemed almost to meet round the back of his head while leaving the upper half of his face quite undisturbed. 'I trust you are rejoicing in the pursuit of your studies? Art, art, a hard but rewarding taskmaster!' Evidently rather pleased with the sound of these last words, he repeated them over to himself, shutting his eyes and opening his mouth very wide at each syllable, pronouncing *rewarding* like *guarding*. Meanwhile, Simon waited for an opportunity to ask about the sketch.

'I delay you,' said Mr Twite, opening his eyes and giving Simon a very sharp look.

'No, sir. I was going to ask how Dido does this morning.'

'Poorly, poorly. A delicate sprite,' sighed Mr Twite. 'Dido Twite: a delicate sprite,' he chanted, to the air of Three Blind Mice. 'It is the curse of our family, young man, to be afflicted by spirits too strong for our bodies.'

Simon thought that if Dido were given rather more food, and warmer clothes, and in general more care and attention, her body would be equal to maintaining its spirit, but he did not say so.

'In point of fact,' Mr Twite confided, 'the poor child is quite feverish – my wife has just sent along to the pharmacy for a drop of Tintagel Water.'

'Is that young Thingummy?' called the sharp voice of Mrs Twite, and she came out of the kitchen, attired for the morning in plum-coloured plush. Directing at Simon a smile as glittering as it was insincere, she exclaimed: 'It must have been you, dear boy, who heated up a mug of milk for our little one last night.'

'Yes it was, ma'am. She didn't fancy it cold, so I heated it and put in a pinch of aniseed. I hope I did nothing wrong?'

'Not a bit, dear boy. *Not* a bit. It was a truly Samaritan act.'

> 'The Samaritans came in two by two,
> And paused to bandage the kangaroo –'

sang Mr Twite.

'*Will* you be quiet, Abednego! I do hope, Mr Thingummy,' pursued Mrs Twite, looking at Simon very attentively, 'that you weren't put to too much *trouble* about it. I hope you didn't have to mend the fire, or fetch coals, or anything of *that* kind?'

'No trouble, ma'am,' Simon said. Luckily Mrs Twite took this to mean that he had not had to fetch coal. 'Penny must have told the truth, then,' she murmured, glancing significantly at her husband. 'She forgot to take the key, but no harm's done.'

'She'd better not forget it again, or she'll have a taste of my hoboy.'

Simon seized the chance, when Mrs Twite had retired, of asking who had drawn the little sketch of Dido that hung in her room.

'Sketch of Dido, my boy?' Mr Twite looked vague. 'Is there such a thing? I confess I do not recall it, but, surrounded as we are by talent, it may be by any of a dozen friends.'

'I'll show it to you,' Simon said eagerly.

'Later, later, my dear fellow.' Mr Twite held up a restraining hand. 'This evening, perhaps. For here comes the lad with the Tintagel Water, and Aesculapius must rule supreme.' He gently shoved Simon out of the front door as the boy Tod came up the steps with a large black bottle.

That evening Simon was washing out his shirt in a pail of water when Tod opened his door without knocking and remarked!

'Young Dido's calling for you, and Aunt Twite says, can you sit with her?'

'Very well.' Simon left his shirt soaking. Tod muttered:

'Can't think why she wants *you* . . .'

'Oh, there you are, Mr Thingummy. I declare,' exclaimed Mrs Twite, who looked flushed and irritable, 'I'm clean distracted with that child so feverish as she is; keeps trying to get out of bed, and Penelope gone out to goodness knows where, and a meeting of the Glee Society in half an hour. She's been calling for you, dear boy, so if you would just sit with her till she goes off –'

'Of course I will,' Simon said.

He found Dido in a high fever, throwing herself restlessly about in her bed, muttering random remarks, singing odd snatches of songs. When he took her hand she quieted somewhat and lay back on the pillow.

'Hallo, brat,' said Simon. 'Do you want to play cards?'

'Too hot,' she muttered. 'Tell story.'

Mrs Twite put her head round the door long enough to nod gracious approval, and went quickly back to her Glee Society preparations. Simon racked his brains for a story. Then he hit on the notion of telling his adventures during the years when he had lived in his cave in the forest of Willoughby Chase, playing hide-and-seek with the wolves all winter long. This answered famously. Dido left off her restless fidgeting and settled down, holding on to his finger, listening in languid content.

'I'd like to go there . . .' she whispered.

'I expect you will some day.'

Her eyes opened in a drowsy flicker. 'Will you take me?'

'Yes, very likely, if you are good and go to sleep now.'

'Promise?'

'Very well.'

Her eyes closed and she slept. Simon carefully withdrew his hand and tiptoed across the room to re-examine the little sketch. But it was gone. Annoyed at not having anticipated this and showed it to Mr Twite in the morning, he tried to open the door but found it locked. Since he did not like to knock and risk waking Dido he found himself a prisoner. Having searched the room for some occupation and rejected the chance of reading numerous copies of the *Maids' Wives' and Widows' Penny Magazine,* he went philosophically to sleep, curled up on the floor.

He woke to find Mr Twite shaking him.

'*So* sorry, my dear boy – a most unfortunate oversight. My wife thought you had already retired. No doubt you will wish to do so directly.'

'Thank you,' said Simon yawning. Then he recollected the sketch. 'Mr Twite, that little drawing of Dido – the one that hung just there –'

'No, no, dear boy, no picture hung there. You imagined it, I daresay – yes, yes, your fancy is full of pictures. It is most natural.'

'But I saw –'

'Ah, we artists,' said Mr Twite, waving him out of the door. 'Always at the mercy of our visions. By the way,' he added in quite another tone, 'have you seen my daughter Penelope by any chance?'

'I'm afraid not, sir.'

'Strange – most strange. Where can she have got

to? Doubtless she will turn up, but it is vexatious. Ah well, I'll keep you no longer from the arms of Morpheus.'

Dido was feverish for several days, and Simon sat with her each evening until she was pronounced well enough to get up and lie outside on the patch of thistly grass by the river.

'I shan't be able to sit and tell you stories this evening,' said Simon, finding her so placed one morning as he went off.

'Why not?'

'Because I shan't be home till late.'

'Why? Where are you going? To a circus!' Dido asked with instant suspicion.

'No, no. When I go to a circus I'll take you too. I'm going to play chess with an old gentleman.'

'Stupid stuff,' said Dido, her interest waning. '*I* wouldn't care to do so. Did you know Penny had run off? She left a note saying she wouldn't be put upon. You should have heard Ma create!'

Simon recollected that he had not seen Penelope for several days. He could not feel any sense of loss at her departure.

'P'raps Ma'll make some togs for me, now,' Dido said hopefully, echoing Simon's thoughts. Then she added, 'Where're you playing chess, anyways?'

'At Battersea Castle,' Simon called over his shoulder as he walked off. 'Goodbye, brat. See you tomorrow.'

'Mr Cobb,' Simon said that evening as he mended the springs of a lady's perch-phaeton. 'What would you do if you thought you had discovered a Hanoverian plot?'

Mr Cobb lowered the wash-leather with which he was polishing the panels and regarded Simon with a very shrewd expression.

'Me boy,' he said, 'it's all Lombard Street to a China orange that I'd turn a blind eye and do nothing about it. Yes, yes, I know –' raising a quelling hand – 'I know the Hanoverians are a crew of fire-breathing traitors who want to turn good King James, bless him, off the throne and bring in some flighty German boy. But, I ask you, what do they actually *do*? Nothing. It's all a lot of talk and moonshine, harmless as a kettle on a guinea-pig's tail. Why trouble about them when they trouble nobody?'

Simon wondered whether Mr Cobb would think

them so harmless if he were to see the contents of the Twites' cellar. But just as he was opening his mouth to speak of this the Chelsea church clock boomed out the hour of nine and he had to hurry off to Battersea Castle.

He took the main way, over Chelsea Bridge and through the great gates beyond it. A tree-bordered avenue led to the Castle, which rose like some fabulous pink flower among the encircling gas flares.

'Oo the devil are you and where the devil d'you think you're going?' growled a voice ahead of him. A burly man came out of a porter's lodge halfway along the avenue and halted Simon by pressing a button which caused two crossed lances to rise out of the ground, barring the road.

'The Duke has invited me to play chess with him,' Simon said.

'Play chess with a ragged young tyke like you? A likely story,' the gatekeeper sneered. As a matter of fact it *was* a likely story, since the Duke made friends with all kinds of odd characters, and this the man knew quite well, but he hoped to wring some gate-money out of Simon.

'I'm not ragged and the Duke is expecting me,' Simon said calmly. 'Let me in, please.'

'*Ho,* no! I'm not so green as to let riff-raff and flash coves in, to prig whatever they can mill! I'm not lowering that barricade for you, no, not if you was to go down on your benders to me. Not if you was to offer me so much as half a guinea!'

Simon remained silent and the man said angrily,

'Not if you was to offer me a *whole* guinea, I wouldn't open it.'

'I shan't do that,' Simon said.

'Oh? And why not, my young shaver?'

'Because you'll have to open it anyway. The Duchess's carriage is just behind you.'

The gate-keeper swung round with an oath. True enough, the carriage, which Simon had observed leaving the Castle as he reached the lodge, was pulling up smoothly just behind the man, and the coachman was crying impatiently: 'Jump to it, there, Daggett. D'you think her Grace wants to wait all night?'

Red with suppressed emotion, Daggett hastened to obey.

Sophie, who was sitting in the carriage opposite her Grace, holding a reticule, a telescope, and a mah-jongg set, dimpled a smile at Simon, and the Duchess inquired:

'Is that your young friend, Sophie? He looks a very personable lad.'

'Yes, ma'am,' said Sophie.

The Duchess addressed Simon. 'So you're the young man who is kindly coming to play chess with William and keep him amused while I go to the opera? It is very obliging of you. William detests opera – and I only find it tolerable if I play mah-jongg with Sophie while the singing is going on. But of course one has one's box and must attend regularly.'

'I hope you have a pleasant evening, ma'am,' Simon said politely.

'Thank you, my dear boy. We shall meet again, I

trust. A delightful face,' the Duchess went on, speaking to Sophie as the carriage rolled away. 'You have excellent taste, Sophie dear.'

'Thank you, your Grace.'

The main entrance to the Castle lay up a tremendous flight of curving steps. At the top stood two haughty bewigged footmen in cream-and-gold livery with rose-coloured buttons.

'Good evening,' Simon said civilly. 'I've come to play chess with the Duke.'

Evidently they had been told to expect him. One of them led him in through a lofty hall, up another flight of stairs, and across a great black-and-white tiled anteroom to a pair of doors which he threw open, announcing:

'The young person, your Grace.'

The room Simon entered was a large library with fireplaces on either side. The Duke jumped from a chair by one fireside and came hurrying foward. He was elegantly dressed tonight in satin knee-breeches and a velvet jacket, but still looked absent-minded and untidy – the old – fashioned wig he wore was twisted askew, so was his cravat, and one of his velvet cuffs was covered in ash.

'Ah, this is a pleasure!' he exclaimed. 'I have been greatly looking forward to our game.' He bustled about, pulling forward a comfortable chair and ringing several bells.

'You'll take a little something?' he inquired. 'Blackcurrant brandy? Prune wine? Scrimshaw, bring the chess set. Jabwing, prune wine and biscuits.'

The Duke's chess set was very beautiful. The pieces

were of greenish glass, cunningly twisted and carved. The Duke set them out lovingly on a leather board, polishing each one on his cravat. The white men were clear right through, the black were veined with streaks of darker glass.

They began to play, and it did not take Simon long to discover that his Grace was not a very good player. He tended to start well with some bold moves, but then his attention would wander; he would jump up hastily to search for a quotation in a book, or to examine a patch of lichen on one of the burning logs in the hearth.

'You play very well, my boy,' the Duke said, after Simon had won two out of the three games. 'Who taught you?'

'A friend of mine, sir,' Simon said, sighing. 'A Dr Gabriel Field.'

The Duke's face lit up. 'Ah, Dr Field! He is an excellent player, is he not? And a dear fellow. Where is the good doctor? I have not seen him this age.'

'You know Dr Field?' Simon gazed at him in astonishment.

'Why yes. I met him at the Academy of Art.'

'Rivière's? Where I learn painting?'

'Oh, you learn painting, do you, my boy? I am not surprised to hear it, for you have the face of an artist. Yes, I met Dr Field at Rivière's – I am one of the patrons, you know. Marius Rivière was married to my aunt. I often drop in at the Academy. The good doctor and I have many interests in common: he has advised me on several pieces of scientific research, and helped clean my pictures.'

'Clean pictures, your Grace?' Simon was momentarily puzzled.

'Family pictures, Old Masters, that have become darkened with age.' Simon nodded; Dr Field had given him some instruction in the processes of picture-cleaning on his last visit.

'Indeed,' the Duke went on, 'I wish he would return, for he was halfway through cleaning Rivière's famous painting of a wolf-hunt and I long to have it completed. See, I will show you.'

He led the way to the far end of the library – a good hundred yards off. Here he turned, blowing a shrill blast on a small gold whistle. One of the footmen came running from the door.

'Jabwing, light some more tapers, please, and then bring my gruel.'

Soon half a hundred candles had been kindled and by their clear blaze Simon was able to study a large canvas occupying most of the end wall of the room. The picture represented a hunt in a snowy wood, and he could see that it was by the hand of a master. A group of hunters, richly dressed in costumes of thirty years ago, were galloping to the help of two men and some hounds who were being attacked by a pack of wolves.

Half the picture had been cleaned and restored, the other half was still dark with grease and grime, so that hunters and wolves alike seemed to be plunging into a black chasm.

'It certainly needs cleaning,' Simon remarked. 'It looks very old.'

'In fact the picture is only thirty years old,' the

Duke told him. 'But it was a great favourite of my father, the fourth Duke, and he would always have it hanging by the fireplace where he used to sit in the evenings. With the smoke from the fire, and the great pipe he smoked, the picture became villainously begrimed. The fair-haired lady on the white horse is Lady Helen Bayswater, my aunt, who was married to the painter; he himself is one of the men on foot, and it is thought that his daughter, too, is somewhere in the picture, the part still uncleaned. She was my cousin; they say she was very beautiful but I never met her. She met my younger brother by chance when both were taking the waters at Epsom, they fell in love, and made a runaway match of it. And they both died in the Hanoverian wars.' He sighed deeply. 'Young Justin, their son, is the last of the line, as you can see from the family tree over there.'

Simon looked where he was bidden and saw a chart which meant little to him. Trying to turn the Duke's thoughts in a more cheerful direction – for he looked very melancholy – Simon suggested:

'I could perhaps go on cleaning the picture for you, your Grace, if you like. Dr Field taught me how.'

'Would you, my boy? I should like it of all things! When could you begin?'

'Tomorrow, sir, if you like.'

'Famous!' declared his Grace. 'I will tell my steward to have the glass removed once more. We had it off for Dr Field, but since he's been away so long I told the men to put it back, for fear the picture would get sooted over again and all his work go for nothing. Buckle shall find you the Doctor's cleaning

FAMILY TREE OF THE DUKES OF BATTERSEA

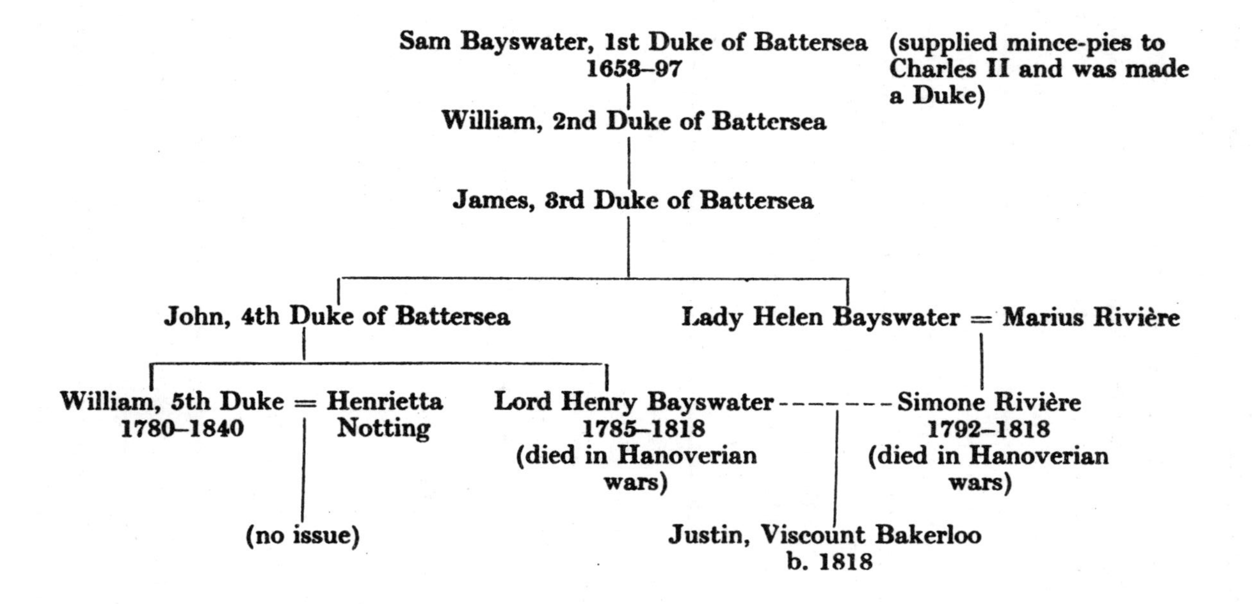

materials. Upon my word, I can't wait to see those poor dirty wolves made neat.'

He began pointing out objects in the murk at the foot of the canvas, and Simon leant forward, intently studying the untouched area. While he was doing so his eye caught a movement reflected in the picture-glass from the opposite end of the room.

Jabwing the footman had brought in a small tray with a basin of gruel which he placed on the chess table. He then stopped and removed something from the Duke's chair; quietly, and looking about to make sure he was unobserved (but he did not see Simon watching him in the glass), he bore this object across the room and slipped it into the pocket of Simon's old frieze jacket which had been left lying on a chair. Then he withdrew silently until, when he was just beside the door, he cleared his throat and said in a loud voice:

'Your Grace's gruel is ready.'

'Thank you, Jabwing, thank you,' the Duke said absently. 'You may go – unless – do you take gruel, my boy? No? You are certain? My Cook had a capital way of making it with white wine and sugar – no? That will be all, then Jabwing.'

The Duke returned to the fireside and swallowed his gruel, meanwhile happily discussing the cleansing operation. Simon, quietly investigated his jacket pocket to discover what the footman had put in it. His fingers encountered a large, round, hard object which, on being withdrawn, proved to be the Duke's gold hunter-watch, set with turquoises, which had been left on the arm of his chair.

Simon stared at the article for a moment, with his brow knitted, and then placed it on a small side-table among a number of crystal ornaments. He was curious to see what would happen.

'I only wish Dr Field would return, he would be so delighted to find that you were helping me,' the Duke was saying. 'He is for ever telling me that my pictures need attention, and his own time is limited, poor fellow.'

'Speaking of time,' Simon said politely, 'I think I should be going, your Grace. It must be late.'

'Should you, my boy? What o'clock is it, then? I'll ring for someone to show you out.'

By the time Jabwing reappeared the Duke had discovered the loss of his watch and was hunting for it fretfully.

'Jabwing, Jabwing, I've lost my watch. What time is it?'

'Eleven past, your Grace.'

'Is it, indeed? I'd no notion it was so late. Jabwing, show the young gentleman out, then come back and find my watch for me.'

Jabwing brought Simon's jacket and, as he did so, contrived to turn it upside down, as if by accident, and give it a smart shake. A round object shot out of the pocket and fell with a loud rap to the marble floor.

'Why!' exclaimed Jabwing in pretended astonishment, 'isn't that your Grace's watch?'

But he spoke a moment too soon, before he had seen what it was.

'No, it isn't, Jabwing,' snapped the Duke testily.

'Where are your eyes? Any dolt can see that it is a hard-boiled egg!'

'My breakfast,' explained Simon, quietly recovering and pocketing the egg.

'And I should like to know,' the Duke went on indignantly still addressing Jabwing, 'what you mean by the outrageous suggestion that my watch would be in the pocket of a visitor, eh? Explain yourself, my man!'

Jabwing was covered with confusion.

'Entirely a mistake, your Grace – very sorry, very sorry indeed. Only on account of the gentleman's being a – a rather *shabby* young gentleman – and the egg's being so – so round, you know – wouldn't for the world give any offence –'

'Well you have given it, blockhead, and it makes it no better to cast aspersions on the young gentleman's clothes. I've a good mind to dismiss you. Don't let such a thing occur again or you'll be sent back to Chippings! Good-night, then, my dear boy. I shall look forward with impatience to our next meeting. Why, there *is* my watch after all,' he continued, catching sight of it on the table. 'I must have laid it there while showing you the Rivière. And, dear me, how late it is!'

Jabwing ushered Simon out and down the great stairway without a word, but his face spoke volumes and if looks could have done it there would have been a banana-skin waiting to trip Simon on every step. As he threw open the hall doors he hissed one word, 'Interloper!' in Simon's ear, and then slammed the door behind him with an insulting crash.

Simon walked down the long drive in a very thoughtful frame of mind. He half wished that he had not suggested coming to clean the picture, but he had taken a liking to the Duke, who seemed a kind old fellow and rather lonely. It was plain, though, that it would be necessary to keep a look-out against such hostile acts as that of Jabwing, who had clearly hoped to get Simon turned out and discredited as a common thief. It was almost, Simon thought, remembering the malevolent gate-keeper and the sour looks of Midwink the valet, as if someone had an interest in keeping him out of Battersea Castle. But why should that be?

Puzzling over this new problem he went home to bed.

7

One morning, several weeks later, Dido waylaid Simon. She had recovered from her fever, but still looked pale, and was shaken from time to time by a dry cough.

'You never plays with me nowadays,' she complained. There was a forlorn droop to her mouth, and Simon took pity on her.

'I'll tell you what, brat, I shall be free on Sunday afternoon, for Mr Cobb's yard is closed then and I'll have finished the other job I'm working on' – he meant the cleaning of the Rivière, which was nearing completion – 'so I'll take you on an outing. What shall it be? A trip down the river on a pleasure-boat? Or shall we go into the country – take our dinners and hunt for highwayman in Blackheath Woods?'

Dido was enchanted at this offer. Her eyes sparkled and she began to jump up and down on the dirty front steps, hanging on to Simon's arm in a very exhausting manner, until a fit of coughing obliged her to desist.

'Clapham Fair! Can we go to Clapham Fair? Pa said he wouldn't take me, he allus has forty winks on Sunday afternoons, and Ma goes to the Lady Triangulists' Social, and Pennylope's gone off . . . They say there's a talking pig that'll answer any question you ask! And there's whirligigs and flying-boats and giddy-go-rounds and Lambeth cakes and treacle sticks!'

'All right, all right, don't deafen me, brat! You shall go to the fair. Only for my sake, will you put on a clean pinafore when we go, and wash your face?'

'Oh, stuff!' Dido put out her tongue at him between the railings. Simon waved a hand to her and went whistling away down the street.

The Duke of Battersea was not at home that evening, having been inveigled, for once, into attending a performance at the opera with his lady. Sophie, who sometimes slipped into the library for a chat when Simon was there, had left a note tucked among his cleaning-tools, informing him that she also would be out, escorting her mistress. For fear of being bored, the Duchess would go nowhere without a supply of amusements, reading-matter, and embroidery things, which it was Sophie's duty to carry. The party would not be home until a late hour.

Simon was disappointed not to see Sophie, but the absence of his Grace's somewhat fidgety companionship made it easier to get on with the job, and he applied himself with a will, whistling gently between his teeth as he uncovered more and more of the large picture until there was only a patch as big as top-hat left to clean.

'Hilloo,' remarked a supercilious voice behind his should after an hour or two had gone by. 'How's the paint-scrubber getting on?' He turned to see young Lord Bakerloo surveying the cleaning operations somewhat scornfully. He seemed disposed to linger, however, rocking to and fro on his heels, picking up first one, then another of the cleaning tools until Simon longed to tell him to leave them be.

'How's old Fur-nose?' he presently inquired.

Simon replied that Dr Furneaux seemed in the best of health, and civilly asked after Lord Bakerloo's arm.

'Can you keep a secret?' said Justin.

'Of course.'

'Well, so can I. Mum's the word.' Justin doubled up with laughter at his own wit and added, 'You won't see me at that old Academy again for a long, long time, I can tell you.'

Simon made no reply to this, but quietly got on with his work, while Justin wandered about behind him, occasionally singing snatches of a ballad which seemed to consist principally of the refrain:

'Hip-hap, habble-dabble-oh,
Shall we go
To Haberdasher's Row?'

until Simon felt there was no place in London that he less wished to visit.

'Devilish dull here, this evening, ain't it?' Justin presently broke off to say. He yawned until his face seemed ready to split. 'I almost wish I'd gone to the opera with the old gudgeons – not that Aunt Hettie asked me,' he added sourly. 'I believe Buckle peached on me; said I hadn't finished my lessons. By the bye, Uncle Bill charged me with a message to you. I was to ask if you was free to play chess with him on Sunday. Getting jumped-up in the world, aren't we? My oh me, playing chess with the gentry and nobil-itee.'

'Do you mean his Grace the Duke invited me?' Simon asked, ignoring the sneer in the last sentence.

'Of course I do. Uncle Bill Battersea, mad as a hatter, see, growing much fatter, see, oh, devilish good. I'm a wit, I am!'

Simon disagreed, but kept his opinion to himself. He said:

'Will you please tell his Grace that I thank him kindly for the invitation but that I shan't be able to accept.'

'Blest if I see why *I* should carry your messages,' Justin said. 'Why can't you write him a note? Or can't you write?' he added rudely.

Simon checked an irritable retort, calmly wrote a note on a page of his sketchbook, folded it into a cocked hat, and laid it on his Grace's fireside table.

'Fancy that! We *can* write!' said Justin with heavy sarcasm. Plainly he was spoiling for a quarrel, and longed to provoke Simon into setting about him. Simon, instead, began to feel rather sorry for him; he seemed lonely and bored, disappointed at not being taken to the opera, and very much at a loose end.

'Anyway, why *can't* you come on Sunday?' Justin inquired with the persistence of a buzz-fly. 'It ain't very polite to turn down Uncle Bill's invitation.'

'I'm taking Dido Twite to Clapham Fair.'

'*That* little bag of bones? What the dickens do you

want to do that for?' Justin exclaimed, truly astonished. 'She's as dirty as a gutter-perch, and got no more manners or gratitude than a hedge-fish.'

Simon remarked mildly that he had promised Dido a treat long since, and she had chosen to go to the fair.

'Well, I wish I was coming instead of Dido,' Justin remarked frankly. 'It's a prime good fair, I can tell you. I sneaked out last year and went with Jem the stable boy, but now old Buckle-and-Thong's living in the Castle, keeping such a tight eye on me, I daresay I shan't be allowed.'

'You're welcome to come with me if you can get permission,' Simon said.

Justin's face lit up. '*Could* I? Oh, that'd be spanking. But,' he added gloomily, 'it's no use asking, for if Buckle heard I was going with you and Dido Twite he'd never allow it. It'd be the monkey's allowance, sure as you're alive. He don't permit me to associate with *low-born* persons. He's a sight stricter than Uncle Bill! I'd slip off anyways, but they keep me so devilish short of blunt that I've hardly two groats to rub together. I suppose you couldn't lend me a cartwheel, could you?'

'Yes, all right,' Simon said calmly. 'But I shall tell your uncle that I am taking you, you know. I daresay he'll have no objection, but I don't want you to do anything behind his Grace's back.' He handed over the coin.

'If you *tell* him, we're making the whole arrangement for Habakkuk,' Justin said discontentedly. 'Surly old Buckle will find some way to stop my going, I'll bet you a borde. How I hate him, the cheese-faced old screw!'

'Lord Bakerloo!' said an acidly angry voice just behind his back. He whirled round. Mr Buckle stood there.

'What are you doing in the library, pray?' Buckle said. 'You know that his Grace left strict instructions you were not to consort with the cleaning boy and hinder him from his work. Back to your studies, my lord, if you please.'

'Oh, very well,' replied Justin sulkily, and began to slouch away, making a grimace at Simon. Mr Buckle, who had hitherto ignored Simon, now cast one sharply penetrating and strangely malignant glance at him. His eyes moved on from Simon to the picture, completely clean at last. Something about it suddenly seemed to attract his very particular attention; he stared at it fixedly for a moment or two, then glanced at Simon again, with eyes dilated, then back at the picture. 'Good God!' he exclaimed under his breath, gave Simon a last hard scrutiny, and hurried after his charge.

Simon, very much surprised, inspected the picture attentively himself to try and discover what had fixed the tutor's interest. The last section to be cleaned was the portrait of a dark-haired boy on a pony. There seemed nothing odd about him that Simon could see; in the end he gave up the puzzle and began putting his tools together, preparatory to departure. At this moment he heard a confusion of voices outside the door and a group of persons burst into the room, all talking at once.

The Duke was in front, with her Grace the Duchess, followed by Midwink, the sour-faced valet, and Sophie, besides a couple of footmen and an elderly lady's-maid, who was alternately wringing her hands, examining a hole in a large opera-cloak she carried, and lamenting at the top of her voice:

'Oh, my lady, my lady! Cloth of copper tissue embroidered with fire-opals! Fourteen guineas the inch! Ruined! And lucky you was not to be all burnt in your seats! Oh, why wasn't I there?'

'Nonsense, Fibbins, we did quite well without you,' the Duchess replied briskly. 'Now, Scrimshaw, don't stand about gaping, but bring refreshment! We have all had an unpleasant experience and our spirits need sustaining. His Grace wants prune brandy and Stilton, while I will take a glass of black-currant wine and a slice of angel-cake. So will Sophie, I'm sure, won't you, my dear? Indeed, without your cool head

I don't know where we should all have been. We should certainly not be here now.'

'No indeed!' interjected his Grace. 'Gal's got a head on her shoulders worth two of any of those dunder-headed ushers at Drury Lane. Very much obliged to ye, my dear; shan't forget it in a hurry.'

'Oh, truly, my lady, and thank you, your Grace; it was nothing.'

Hearing this praise of Sophie, Simon could not resist lingering.

'Hallo, you there, my boy?' his Grace cried, discovering him. 'You work while we play, eh? And better it would have been if we'd all stayed at home minding our own business. Here's such an adventure we've been through; only just escaped with our lives, thanks to clever little Miss Sophie here.'

'What happened?' Simon asked, no longer attempting to conceal his lively interest.

'Why, my lady wife drags us all off to the opera (and miserable plaguy slow it was, too, I don't mind telling you; I can never make head nor tail of these fellers warbling away about their troubles – pack o' nonsense, if you ask me, when anyone can see they've never wanted for a good dinner in their lives). All of a sudden in the first act we all smell smoke, and next thing you know, the whole of our blessed box is afire – curtains, carpets, and all! And can we get out? No, we cannot! Why, do you ask?' The Duke, in his excitement, had quite thrown off his usual vague air. 'Why, because the box door is locked, and though we shout and call, nobody can find the key! So we should all three have been nicely frizzled for anything anyone could do, if it hadn't been for little miss, here.'

'What *did* Sophie do?' Simon asked, absently accepting a slice of cake a glass of blackcurrant wine from Scrimshaw.

'Why, she outs with Madam's embroidery, which as you may know, is a piece of tapestry big enough to cover the end wall of this room, rolls it into a rope, hangs it over the front of the box, and tells me to slide down it!'

'And did you, your Grace?'

'To be sure I did! Haven't had such a famous time since I was a little feller in nankeen snufflers sliding down the stair-rail at Chippings Castle!'

'And did her Grace slide down the rope too?' Simon inquired, much astonished.

'Bless you, no! Took a fit of the vapours at the very idea! So we was all in a flim-flam, if Sophie hadn't thrown the tapestry down and called out, 'Hold it tightly by the corners!' So I and half a dozen other gentlemen held it out tight, while her Grace and Sophie jumped into it – one at a time, of course; as it was, her Grace's weight nearly pulled my arms out o' the sockets, didn't it, my dear?'

'Such an indecorous thing to be obliged to do!' sighed her Grace, fanning herself with a piece of cake.

'Yes, and it's my belief that you'd hardly have done it then if little Miss Sophie hadn't given you a smart push from behind, eh, miss? I saw you,' said the Duke, grinning at Sophie, who blushed, but defended herself.

'Her Grace was – was hesitating a little, and really there was no time to be lost. The flames were already catching her cloak.'

'Ruined! Ten thousand guineas' worth of copper brocade,' wailed the lady's-maid.

'Oh, be quiet, Fibbins! You should be grateful her Grace herself isn't burnt to a crisp, instead of that miserable cloak I've never liked above half. Yes, and two minutes after they'd jumped, the whole box crashed down into the stalls. What do you think of that, eh?'

Simon then recollected his manners and took his leave, sure that the ducal family would not wish the presence of a stranger after such an alarming adventure.

The Duke clapped him kindly on the back. 'Off, are you? How's the picture getting on? What, done already? Come, that's famous. I'd no notion you'd do it so quickly. See, Hettie, doesn't it look better?'

'Indeed, it is a great, great improvement,' her Grace said warmly. 'I'd no idea that dingy old painting could be made so bright and handsome. Why, good gracious! William, look at this, only look!'

'What, my love? What has surprised you?'

'Look at this girl on the pony!'

'That *girl*, my dove, is a boy, observe his breeches!'

'Girl or boy, what does it matter?' said the Duchess impatiently. 'But whichever it is, he or she is the very spit image of Sophie!'

8

It was late that night before Simon returned to his lodgings. The Twites' part of the house was all in darkness, and he had to feel his way up the steep stairs by the light of the moon which shone in at the landing window. He did not trouble to light a candle in his room, but was about to undress and jump into bed when an unexpected sound made him pause.

The sound, which came from the bed, was a muffled and broken gulping, somewhat resembling the grunts of a small pig.

'Who's there?' Simon said cautiously.

The only reply was a dejected sniff. Beginning to guess what he should see, Simon found and lit his stump of candle. It displayed a small miserable figure curled up on his bed with its face hidden in the pillow.

'Dido! What are you doing up here? What's the matter?'

She raised a tear-stained face and said woefully, 'Ma won't let me go to the fair!'

'Why not? Have you been naughty?'

'No, I never. But she was in a fair tweak about summat Pa said – they was at it hammer and tongs.

I heard him shouting that she was under the thumb of her havey-cavey kin and would have us all in the Pongo – and then when I asked about the fair she just glammered at me and said no.'

'Well, you were a dunderhead to ask her when she was cross, weren't you?' Simon said, but not unkindly. He sat down on the bed, put his arm round her, and gave her a consoling pat on the back. 'Why don't you be extra good for a day or two and then ask her again; it's odds but she'll have forgotten she forbade you.'

'N-no,' said Dido forlornly. 'Acos when I said *why* couldn't I go, she said acos I'd got no warm dresses that were fit to wear outdoors.'

'Lord bless us! Can't she buy you something, or make you something? You don't have to keep indoors all winter, surely?'

'She said she couldn't get anything till Friday fortnit when Pa gives her the housekeeping. It's not *fair*!' said Dido passionately. 'She was allus favouring Penny – only just afore Penny run off she had a candyfloss shawl and three pair of Manila gloves and a blue-and-white striped ticking over-mantle! Ma jist don't like me, she never buys me *anything*!'

This was true; Simon saw no point in disputing it.

'And that's another reason why Pa was cagging at her,' Dido went on, 'Acos she'd spent all the housekeeping on Penny's duds and a load of Pictclobbers.'

'What are Pictclobbers?' Simon asked, pricking up his ears.

'*I* dunno.' Dido was not interested. 'They put 'em

in the cellar. And now there won't be nothing to eat but lentil-bread and fish-porridge till Friday fortnit and I can't go to the fair.'

'Would your Ma let you go if you had something to wear?'

'She said yes. But she knew I hadn't got nothing, so it was a lot of Habakkuk.'

'Oh,' said Simon. He reflected. 'Well, look, don't be too miserable – I've a friend who might be able to help. She's very clever at making dresses, and perhaps she'd have something of hers that she could alter. I'll ask her tomorrow. So cheer up.'

Dido's skinny arms came round his neck in a throttling hug. '*Would* she? Simon, you're a proper Nob. I'm sorry I ever put jam in your hair. I think you're a bang up – *slumdinger*!'

'All right, well, don't get your hopes up too high,' he said hastily. 'Your ma may not agree, even if I can get something.'

'Oh, it's dibs to dumplings she will, if she gets summat for nix,' said Dido shrewdly.

'Now you'd better nip back to bed before you get a dusting for being out of your room.'

'It's all rug. They're out: Pa's playing his hoboy at Drury Lane and he got tickets for Ma and Aunt Tinty to go tonight.'

'Still, I expect they'll be in soon; anyway *I* want my sleep.'

'Oh, all right, toll-loll,' said Dido, whose spirits had risen amazingly. 'But I'm nibblish hungry. I'm *fed* up with fish-porridge – hateful stuff.'

'There's a bit of cheese on the table.'

'I've et it.'

'Oh, you have, have you? Well, here, take this sausage, and be off, brat, and don't take things that don't belong to you another time.'

'Slumguzzle,' said Dido impertinently, but she gave him another hug (thereby anointing his hair with sausage) and condescended to leave him in peace.

Just before he went to sleep a drowsy thought flickered through his mind. Dido had said that Mr Twite was playing his hoboy at Drury Lane. *Drury Lane*. Was not that where the Duke and Duchess and Sophie had met with their misadventure? Was there any connection between the two events?

Next morning, as he ran down the front steps, he saw a small pale face at the downstairs window directing at him a look full of silent appeal. He waved reassuringly but did not stop to speak as he was late, and, moreover, saw Mrs Twite approaching with a basket of herrings, presumably for the fish-porridge. She gave him a chilly nod, scowled reprovingly at Dido, and passed within. Simon wondered what she would say if she knew Dido had told him that the housekeeping money had been spent on Pictclobbers. What were Pictclobbers, anyway? He was pretty sure they were not coal. Pistols or muskets seemed more likely.

It was a cold, grey November morning, but presently the sun rose, dispersing the river mists and gilding the last leaves on the trees. Dr Furneaux ordered his students outside to 'paint hay while ze sun shines", as he put it.

Simon was sitting on the river-bank not far from

the Academy, hard at work on a water-colour sketch of Chelsea Bridge with the dreamlike pink towers of Battersea Castle behind it, when a handsome pleasure-barge swept under the bridge, travelling upstream with the tide. It passed close to Simon so that he was able to see the Battersea Arms (two squirrels respecting each other, vert, and az., eating mince-pies or) embroidered on the sail.

'Good morning, Simon!' a voice called, and he noticed Sophie leaning over the forward rail. She wore a white dress with red ribbons and carried the usual assortment of needments for the Duchess – a basket of shrimps to feed the gulls, a book, a parasol, a battledore and shuttlecock, and a large bundle of embroidery.

Simon waved back and called, 'What time shall you be home? Can I see you this evening?'

'We shan't be late,' Sophie answered. 'His Grace and my lady are off to Hampton Court to take luncheon with His Majesty, but we shall return directly afterwards because my lady is still tired from last night's adventure. I'll come round to Mr Cobb's at nine – will you be there?'

'That will do famously,' Simon called. The Duke, who, dressed in full Court regalia, was steering in the stern, saw him and waved so enthusiastically that he nearly dropped his pocket handkerchief overboard.

The day passed pleasantly in the warm autumn sunshine. At noon the students lit a fire and brewed acorn-coffee; later, Dr Furneaux came out and criticized their work. He discussed Simon's picture with ferocity, going into every point, often seizing the brush to alter some detail, until his whiskers were covered with paint.

Gus winked at Simon behind the Principal's back and whispered, 'Bear up, cully! The more old Furnose thinks of you, the more he's into you.' Then his eyes widened, looking past Simon, and he exclaimed, 'Stap and roast me! What the deuce is the matter with that boat?'

Simon turned to look at the river. A boat was coming from the direction of Hampton Court, but, for a moment, he did not recognize the ducal barge, so strange an appearance did it present. It was creeping along low in the water with hardly any of the hull visible, and the whole craft was curiously wrapped about in folds of material, so that it looked more like a floating parcel than a boat. Somebody had just jumped off it, and as they watched there were three more splashes, and they saw the heads of swimmers making for the shore.

'It's sinking!' exclaimed Gus.

'And the rowers have jumped clear,' said Simon, recognizing the cream-and-gold livery of the swimmers. 'But where's the Duke and Duchess and Sophie?'

In a moment he saw them as the barge, carried along by the outgoing tide, slowly wallowed past. They were all in the stern, the Duke and Sophie trying to persuade the Duchess to jump for it.

'Indeed you must, ma'am!' implored Sophie. 'When the ship sinks – and she will at any minute! – we shall all be sucked under.'

'But I can't swim!' lamented the Duchess. 'I shall

certainly be drowned, and in my best Court dress too – murray velvet with gold sequins – it will be ruined and it cost over twenty thousand—'

'Hettie, you *must* jump! Never mind the perditioned dress!'

'But it weighs twenty-three pounds – it will sink me like a stone. Oh, help, help, will nobody help us?'

'All right, your Grace!' shouted Simon pulling off his shirt. 'We're coming!'

Half the students of the Academy dived joyfully off the bank and swam to the rescue, delighted at such a diversion, and this was just as well for the next minute the barge filled up completely, turned on its side, and precipitated the three passengers into the water. The Duchess would undoubtedly have sunk had not, by great good fortune, her voluminous skirts and petticoats filled with air for a few moments so that she floated on the surface like a bubble while Sophie supported her.

'Dammit!' gasped the Duke. 'I can't swim either, come to think! I never – aaaargh!' He disappeared in a whelter of bubbles, but luckily Gus and Fothers, forging through the water like porpoises, both reached the spot at that instant and were able to dive and grab him. Meanwhile, Simon, Sophie, and half a dozen other students managed to land the Duchess while others swam after the barge and steered it to a sandspit on the far side of Chelsea Bridge.

Dr Furneaux, meanwhile, after wringing his hands and whiskers alternately, when he saw that the rescue was safely under way, had very sensibly organized some more students into the building up a fine blaze from the embers of the noon fire so that the victims of the wreck could warm themselves immediately. The setting sun and the huge bonfire threw a red light over the strange scene; steam rose in clouds from those who had been immersed, while others ran to and fro fetching more branches.

'By Jove!' said the Duke, as he stood steaming and emptying water out of his diamond-buckled shoes. 'What a scrape, eh? I fancied my number was up that time – so it would have been too, if it weren't for your plucky lads, Furneaux! Much obliged to 'ee all!'

'Indeed, yes!' The Duchess smiled round warmly upon the dripping assembled students. She looked much less bedraggled than anybody, as the upper part of her body had never been submerged, thanks to the speed with which she had been towed to land. 'You are a set of brave, good souls. You must all come to dinner at the Castle as soon as possible.'

Dr Furneaux beamed with pride and affection for his students. 'Yes, yes,' he said, 'zey are a set of brave garçons when it comes to a tight pinch – it is only ze hard work zey do not always enjoy!'

'What happened to the barge?' Simon asked Sophie as they stood drying themselves. 'How did it come to sink?'

'Nobody knows exactly,' she answered. 'It was certainly all right when we reached Hampton Court. But on the way home it seemed to move heavily in the water, and when we had gone a certain way – I do not know where we were –'

'Mortlake, or thereabouts,' the Duke put in.

'It seemed to be sinking lower and lower, and

suddenly her Grace gave a scream – we were all on deck, but she looked down the companionway and saw there was nearly a foot of water in the cabin, and more coming in. There was a hole in the side! So I had the notion of passing her Grace's tapestry under the hull, over the hole, and pulling it up tight against both sides, to stop the leak. We did so, and it worked tolerably well for quite a long way –'

'Ay, my child, it was a brainwave,' the Duke said. 'Had it not been for your clever wits 'tis a herring to a ha'penny we'd ha' been shipwrecked at Putney or some such godforsaken spot where we would undoubtedly have perished with not a soul to hear our cries. For you could not have rescued both of us, Sophie

my dear, and as for those cowardly jobberknolls of rowers, they were no more use than a fishskin fowling-piece – I'll turn every last one of them out of my service, so I will. Where are they?'

The rowers, however, when they reached land, had prudently made off and did not even wait for their dismissal; they were seen at Battersea Castle no more.

'Alas for my tapestry, though,' the Duchess sighed. 'I fear it will be quite ruined.'

'Nonsense, my dear,' her husband exclaimed. 'We'll have it dried and cleaned, and you'll see it will be as good as new. And even if it ain't *quite* the same, I'd as leif keep it – do you realize that tapestry has

saved our lives twice? And each time thanks to adroit little Miss Sophie here? We are much in your debt, my dear.'

'Where did you learn to swim so well?' the Duchess inquired.

'Oh, it was nothing, your Grace,' Sophie said shyly. 'I learnt to swim at the Poor Farm; indeed we were obliged to, with the canal so close by – someone was for ever falling in. But please think no more about it, my lady. Look, here comes the carriage and I am persuaded your Graces should be taken home *immediately* and be put to bed with three hot bricks each to avoid all danger of an inflammation.'

'Quite right, my child, quite right! Hettie, let us be off. Dr Furneaux, will you bring all your students along to take pot luck with us tomorrow night? Ay, and I've something famous to show you all – my big Rivière canvas which this good boy has cleaned.'

Dr Furneaux gladly accepted on behalf of his students and expressed his eagerness to see the restored painting. Amid hurrahs and waving caps the carriage drove away towards Battersea Castle, and as night was now falling fast the students decided to abandon work and make a party of it. More acorn-coffee was brewed, those who had money went and bought potatoes in Chelsea Market to roast in the embers, while those who had none fetched chestnuts from Battersea Park or merely danced minuets and quadrilles by the light of the moon.

When the chimes of Chelsea church clock boomed out the hour of nine Simon recollected his appointment to meet Sophie. He set off at a run, though wondering if the task of caring for her rescued mistress might have prevented Sophie coming out again.

She had not failed him, however. He found her sitting with the Cobb family helping Mrs Cobb hem pinafores for Libby while she regaled them all with a lively account of the shipwreck.

Simon asked how the Duke and Duchess did.

'Famously snug,' said Sophie. 'They both went to bed with hot bricks, and I gave them a dose of the poppy syrup that I made according to Mrs Cobb's recipe.'

'Ay, you can't beat my poppy syrup,' said Mrs Cobb complacently.

'And they were both very kind to me,' Sophie went on. 'The Duke gave me five guineas and this gold enamelled watch – see, Libby, how pretty it is with the blue flowers – and her Grace gave me a week's holiday, besides two beautiful dresses and five lengths of stuff to make things for myself. But what was it you wanted to ask me, Simon?'

Simon explained the troubles of poor Dido Twite: an unfeeling mother, a diet of fish-porridge, and no dress to wear to the Clapham Fair. Sophie's kind eyes misted in sympathy as she listened, and Mrs Cobb cried:

'Well, I declare! Fancy treating a child so! She could have some of Libby's clothes, but they'd be too small, I daresay.'

'It's the simplest thing in the world,' Sophie said. 'I can use some of the stuff her Grace gave me to make the child a dress. It will take no time at all to whip it together if you can give me some idea of her size, Simon.'

'Oh, no, that's a great deal too good of you,' he objected. 'I wondered if you'd have some old dress put by that you could cut up for her, Soph.'

Sophie however declared that the Duchess had given her so many things she could easily spare some material. 'The poor little thing, let her have something really pretty and new for once. There is a blue merino that might be just the thing. Is she dark or fair?'

'She is always so grubby that it is hard to tell,' Simon said doubtfully. However, he thought blue merino would do very well.

'I'll make it tomorrow,' Sophie promised. 'As I've the day off, it's odds but I'll have it finished by the evening.'

'Come and do it here,' offered Mrs Cobb. 'You'll be company for me, my dear; Cobby's off to Hackney to look at some carriages.

'Soph, you are a Trojan,' Simon said. 'I made sure you'd be able to help.' A bright idea struck him. 'If you have the week off you could come to the fair, couldn't you? We could make a regular junket of it. It's on Sunday – the day after tomorrow.'

'Why, I should love to!' Sophie said, her eyes sparkling at the thought.

They agreed to fix a meeting-time and place next evening, when Simon came to fetch the dress.

Dido's problem was now solved, but as Simon walked home after having escorted Sophie to the gates of Battersea tunnel, he reflected that the cloud of mystery in which he moved seemed to be thickening daily. He wondered if he ought to warn the Duke that danger threatened – if it did – or would that merely raise unnecessary alarm in the kindly old gentleman's breast? But the sinking of the barge seemed highly suspicious, following, as it did, so soon after the fire in the opera-box. Not for the first time Simon wished that Dr Field were at hand to advise him. It seemed more and more plain that the doctor must have stumbled on some piece of the Hanoverian plot and been put out of the way.

As Simon climbed the steps of 8 Rose Alley, he saw Dido's wan face pressed to the window-pane. He wondered if she had been there all day, and gave her a reassuring smile and wave. She darted out to intercept him in the hall.

'Have you got the mish? Come in here – Ma's got a gentleman visitor in the kitchen and Pa's asleep.' She pulled him into her untidy bedroom.

'It's all right,' Simon said. 'My friend's making you a dress and she'll have it finished by tomorrow night. So all you have to do is get cleaned up – you can't wear a new blue merino dress looking like that.'

'New blue merino!' breathed Dido, round-eyed. 'Coo, I'll wash and wash and *wash*! But what about the mint-sauce? Wasn't it dear?'

'No, because my friend had the stuff given her as a present.'

'New stuff and she give it away to someone she didn't even know. She must be loose in the basket!' Such generosity seemed hardly conceivable to Dido.

'Shall I tell your ma about the dress?'

'Best, not jist now. She's been out all day visiting Aunt Minbo at Hampton Court and come home as cross as brimstone! She said I wasn't to disturb her while the gentleman visitor was there or she'd clobber me.'

'All right, I'll tell her in the morning. Good night, brat,' said Simon. Hampton Court! he thought. Could there be some connection between this visit and the wreck of the barge?

On his way upstairs he happened to glance back just in time to see Mrs Twite's visitor come quietly out of the kitchen.

It was Mr Buckle, the tutor.

'There must be a connection between Battersea Castle and this house,' Simon said to himself positively as he got into bed. 'And it's time something was done about that load of Pictclobbers in the cellar. I'll go to Bow Street and inform the constables tomorrow.'

He wondered what would happen to the Twite family then. Presumably Mr and Mrs Twite would be haled off to jail. What would become of Dido? Surely children did not get imprisoned for the misdoings of their parents? Would the poor little thing have to go and live with one of her disagreeable aunts?

Recalling the new dress and the fair he resolved to put off his visit to Bow Street until Monday. Let Dido have her one day of pleasure. After all, he thought, a day's delay can't make much odds.

He went to sleep.

9

The dinner that the Duke of Battersea gave Dr Furneaux's students was long remembered at the Academy of Art. As the Duke explained apologetically, the menu was put together at such short notice that the guests could only expect pot luck; just a neatish meal. There were but three courses: the first consisted of oysters, lobsters, salmon, turtle-soup, and some haunches of turbot; this was followed by turkeys, chickens, a side of beef, and a whole roast pig; the last course consisted of veal-and-ham pies, venison pasties, salads, vegetables, jellies, creams and fruit. 'Just a pic-nic,' as the Duke observed. 'But as we are all such near neighbours, I hope you won't take offence that we haven't been able to do better in the time.'

Neither Dr Furneaux nor his students showed any tendency to take offence. The students, many of whom had never seen so much food in their lives before, ate like famished wolves. Gus, sitting by Simon, and surrounded by high ramparts of oyster shells, had eaten steadily and in silence for an hour when at last he broke off to announce with a sigh:

'It's no use: I couldn't cram in another crumb, not

if you was to pay me. It *does* seem a waste with all that's left! Ah well, this dinner ought to do me for a week, then it's back to apple-peel and Mrs Gropp's parsley. I must say, his Grace is a prime host, ain't he, Fothers? Nothing behindhand about this set-out, is there?'

Fothers could not reply; he had eaten nineteen jellies and was leaning back in his chair with a glazed expression.

The Duke stood up and cleared his throat rather shyly, amid shouts of 'Three cheers for his Grace!' 'Silence for the Dook!' 'Pray hush for old Batters!'

'Gentlemen,' the Duke said. 'My wife and I are very happy to welcome you here tonight. You saved our lives yesterday and we shan't forget it. There has always been a bond between my family and the Academy of Art ever since it was founded by Marius Rivière, who, as you may know, married my aunt, Lady Helen Bayswater. From now on the bond will be even closer. I should like to make this dinner an annual event—' ('Hooroar for Battersea!' 'Good health to old Strawberry Leaves!') – 'and I am also

going to endow the Academy with five scholarships for needy and deserving students. They will be known as the Thames Rescue Bursaries. The first two have already been awarded by myself and Dr Furneaux in consultation to Mr Augustus Smallacombe and to Mr Simon – I'm afraid I don't know your last name,' the Duke ended, breaking off and looking apologetically at Simon, who was so astonished that he stammered:

'M-mine, your G-grace? – I don't know it either.'

'Were you never christened?' asked his Grace, much interested, 'or had your parents no surname?'

'Why, you see, sir, I was an orphan,' Simon explained. 'I never knew my parents.'

'Then where –' The Duke's further question was interrupted by Jabwing the footman, who chanced to drop a very large silver tureen full of oyster shells with a resounding crash just behind his Grace's chair. Then the students began cheering Gus and Simon so vociferously that no more could be said. The Duke smilingly nodded to Simon and indicating that he would very much like to hear his history on a later occasion, stood up and invited his guests to come and view the restored Rivière canvas.

They all trooped up the great flight of stairs from the banqueting-hall to the library. Here the end wall had been curtained off by a large piece of material – was it the Duchess's tapestry turned back to front? Simon rather thought so – and when everybody had been marshalled in, and Dr Furneaux shoved to a position of honour at the front, the Duchess pulled a string to unveil the picture.

The material fell to the ground and there followed a silence of astonishment.

'Devil take it!' exclaimed his Grace. 'What's become of the picture? Scrimshaw, Jabwing, Midwink – where's the Rivière gone?'

Nobody knew.

'It was there this morning, your Grace,' Jabwing said.

'Well, I know that, stupid! You didn't take it out for a last clean-up, did you, my boy?' the Duke asked Simon, who shook his head.

The Duchess, feeling that the spirits of the party might be sadly lowered by this mishap, cried, 'Oh, do not regard it, William! 'Tis odds but it's merely been mislaid and will turn up directly if we do but keep our heads. Let us think no more about it, but, instead, amuse ourselves and our guests with dancing or diversions which I'm sure the young people would much prefer.'

'Let's play Hunt the Picture!' exclaimed Gus.

'Capital notion!' shouted somebody else.

'Huzza for Gus!'

'We'll find the picture for your Graces, never fear!'

In a trice the high-spirited students had scattered from the library and were darting upstairs and downstairs, along galleries, through suites, in and out of closets, saloons, antechambers, armouries, falconries, heronries, butleries, and pantries all over Battersea Castle in search of the missing picture. They turned the whole place topsy-turvey in their enthusiasm, but the Rivière canvas was not forthcoming, though innumerable other pictures were whisked down from the walls and submitted for the Duke's inspection.

'Is this it, your Grace?'

'Is this?'

'Is this?'

Pictures were soon piled high in the library. But the Duke shook his head to all of them.

'Dear me,' sighed the Duchess, 'I could wish that these *delightful* young people were a little less *volatile*.'

At that moment a chandelier, on which Fothers had been swinging from side to side as he examined some pictures that hung rather high up, fell to the floor with a loud crash. The chandelier was shattered but Fothers was unhurt, though he looked rather green.

'Dashed uneasy motion,' he murmured. 'Like on board ship. Shan't try *that* again.'

He picked himself up and went off to search in the muniment rooms.

'Oh, fol-de-rol, my dove,' said the Duke, 'I don't know when I've enjoyed myself so much. Never seen the old place looking so lively. Anyway, we won't trouble our heads any longer about the picture – of a certainty some poor half-witted niddlenoll must have gone off with it – one of those whatd'ye-callems with a mad craving for pictures. I'll tell the magistrates about it tomorrow and ten to one the feller will be laid by the heels in a couple of days if he doesn't walk in with it saying he's Henry the Eighth.'

Soon after this Simon took his leave, expressing

warm gratitude to the Duke and Duchess for their hospitality and for the unexpected and most welcome Thames Rescue Bursary. It was nearly time for his appointment with Sophie.

As he ran down the stairs – matters were in such chaos all over the Castle, with students dashing hither and thither, that no footman attempted to see him out – he thought he heard somebody trying to attract his notice.

'Hey there, you! Hillo! Psst!'

He looked round the hallway and saw Justin waving to him from behind a suit of armour.

'What is it?' Simon said.

'I'm coming to the fair with you tomorrow.'

'Famous,' said Simon. 'I told his Grace about it and he doesn't mind.'

'That ain't to the purpose,' Justin said. 'I tell you, Uncle Bill's always agreeable. It's Buckle who'd put a spoke in the wheel – sour old cheesebox – but it's the luckiest thing in the world, he's been called away to Deptford on two days' urgent private business – rich aunt dying or some such humdudgeon – and won't be back till tomorrow evening. Where shall I meet you?'

'On Chelsea Bridge, an hour after noon,' Simon suggested.

'Tooralooral,' Justin said conspiratorially, and disappeared back behind the suit of armour as if he expected that the very walls would report on his plans to Mr Buckle.

Sophie, true to her word, had finished the blue dress.

'Soph, you're the kindest good girl in the world,' Simon said, and gave her a hug. 'I'll buy you some fairings tomorrow, see if I don't. Now, shall I take you back to the Castle?'

'No, for Mrs Cobb's invited me to stop the night here, thank you.'

As Simon had half expected, Dido was lurking up in his room, on tenterhooks with anticipation.

'Have you got it? Have you got it?' she demanded in a whisper before he was through the door. When he lit a candle and showed her the dress she was absolutely dumbstruck with admiration.

'Oh!' she breathed. She took it reverently from him, laid it out on the bed, and stroked it as if it had been a living thing. '*Oh!* Ain't it *naffy*! Shall I put it on now?' She held it up against her.

'Certainly not,' said Simon firmly. 'If you did, it's odds but you'd go to bed in it and come out tomorrow looking like a piece of mousetrap. You'd best leave it here, where it won't get dropped and trampled on – *I* know how you treat your things.'

'I *never* would with *this*! Oh, wouldn't Penny be green if she could see it! I wish I could see her face.'

'Well, run along now, cully,' Simon said. 'The sooner you go to sleep, the sooner morning will come.'

She started towards the door, then turned and, coming back, pulled his head down to her level. 'Thank you,' she whispered gruffly in his ear, then bolted from the room.

But Simon, getting into bed, felt a pang of dismay. Did Dido but know it, she had little cause to thank him for what he was going to do soon.

They set off for the fair next day in high fettle, met Justin on the bridge, as arranged, and went on to collect Sophie from the Cobbs. Dido was delighted to meet the kitten again there and begged that it might be allowed to accompany them to the fair, but Simon felt that this would be too much of an anxiety; he had enough responsibility as it was. At first Justin and Dido were inclined to regard one another with jealous suspicion and hostility: Justin looked down on Dido as a gutter-brat, and she sneered at him as a high-nosed counter-coxcomb. But Simon and Sophie were so cheerful and good-natured that no one could be long in their company without succumbing to their influence, and soon the whole party were in charity with one another and marched off towards Clapham in good spirits. Dido thanked Sophie very prettily for the blue dress, while Justin went so far as to say that she looked quite well in it and he wouldn't have recognized her.

The fair was already in full swing when they reached Clapham Common. Hucksters were shouting their wares, shrill music from the trumpets and hurdy-gurdies competed with them, and the roar of the happy crowds could be heard above that of the giddy-go-round.

'What shall we do first?' said Simon, surveying the colourful booths. 'Shooting Gallery, Imperial Theatre showing Panoramas from History, Fat Lady, Snake-Charmer, Living Skeleton, Mermaid, Flying-Boats, Wise Pig, Drury Lane Drama, Swan-Boats on the Long Pond, Whirligigs?'

'Oh!' cried Dido. 'Everything! *Everything!*'

Simon looked at Sophie. Her cheeks were pink and her eyes shone bright with excitement. 'Isn't this famous!' she said. 'Who'd have thought, a year ago, that we'd ever be having such a gay time?'

They did everything. They won coconuts at the coconut-shies, looked at the Fat Lady and the Living Skeleton (very poor show for a penny, Dido considered), flew on the flying-boats (Justin turned very pale, but recovered himself after partaking of seven ginger-nuts and a glass of lemonade) and sampled the Drury Lane Drama and the Imperial Theatre. They interviewed the Talking Pig, which would answer any question put to it – and found that the answers consisted of grunts. They ate oysters and plum cake and ginger-wine at Barney's Restaurant. Justin treated Dido to two rides on the giddy-go-round (the Duke had given him half a guinea and he had forgotten to return Simon's half crown); they whirled off, riding on a golden goose and a scarlet camel respectively. Simon took Sophie sailing in a swan-boat, and the whole party met again at the shooting-gallery, where Simon, whose marksmanship was excellent after several years of hunting for his dinner with a bow-and-arrow, knocked down ten bottles with ten shots.

'First prize, sir,' said the man glumly, and handed Simon a huge china vase. It was so big that Dido could have climbed inside it.

'He doesn't want to carry that about,' said the quick-witted Sophie. 'Give him what it's worth instead.'

The showman gave Simon ten shillings ('I daresay it's worth three times as much,' muttered Justin) and he spent it on doughnuts for the whole party and a visit to the Fire-Breathing Dragon (where Dido disgraced them by tiptoeing round to the back and discovering a little man in the dragon's stomach producing jets of steam by means of a boiling kettle).

Then they listened to a lady singing Cherry Ripe, and inspected the Mysterious Minnikins, who proved to be puppets.

Then, feeling somewhat tired and hungry, they ate mutton-pies and drank pineapple punch at a chop-stall by the Amazing Arcade, where there were little tables set out on the grass.

By now evening had come and fireworks from the Spectacular Pyrotechnical Display were making wonderful swoops and sparkles and whirls of colour against the darkening sky.

'I suppose we should be going soon,' Simon said. 'Mrs Twite said be back by ten, and so did the Duke.'

Justin and Dido immediately broke into pleading for 'just one more show'. 'Look, there's a fortune-teller, Madam Lolla,' said Dido. 'We ain't been to her yet. Oh, *please*, Simon!'

Simon counted his money and reckoned that he had just enough for the fortune-teller and the journey home, so they entered Madam Lolla's booth.

She was a fat, dark gypsy-woman with black eyes and a pronounced moustache, impressively dressed in a quantity of purple draperies.

'Cross my hand with silver, young ladies and gentlemen,' she said affably, and told them that Simon would have a long journey over water, that Justin would soon meet a long-lost relative, and that

Sophie would be lucky all her life 'because of your pretty face and taking ways, my dearie'.

'Pho, what dull, mingy fortunes,' cried Dido. 'Tell mine! I'll lay there's something more exciting than *that* in it!'

She stuck out her grubby hand to the gypsy who pored over it for a minute and then looked at her oddly.

'What's the score, then missis?' Dido said. 'Doesn't I get a fortune?'

'Yes, of course, dearie,' the gypsy said quickly. 'You'll meet a tall dark stranger and have a surprise and go on a journey.'

'Oh, what stuff.' Dido was impatient. 'Nothing else?'

'Only one other thing,' the gypsy said. 'You had a present today, didn't you, missy?'

'Yes I did.' Dido glanced down proudly at her dress, which, contrary to her usual habit, she had contrived to keep clean and unspotted through all the hurly-burly of the fair.

'Well, soon you'll be *giving* a present,' said the gypsy. 'You'll be giving it to the two people as gave you yours, and it'll be a gift as costs all you've got to give, and is worth more than they know. And there'll be sorrow in the gift as well as happiness, but they'll be grateful to you for it as long as they live.'

'Is that all? Pooh, what a capsy, weevilly fortune. Give a present, indeed! I'd like to know how, when I ain't got any mint-sauce. Nothing more?'

'No,' snapped the gypsy, suddenly and unaccountably angry. 'You've tired me out, the lot of you. Be off, and leave me in peace.'

They were all tired, they realized now. Justin stayed with the two girls under a tree at the common's edge, watching the fireworks, while Simon ran off and found a hackney carriage. They drove home in the silence of exhaustion, first to the Cobbs, to drop Sophie who was staying there for her week's holiday, and then on to Battersea Castle. Justin wanted to be left at the entrance to the tunnel, but Simon, who had promised the Duke to look after his nephew carefully, thought it best to take him to the main door.

'Ain't this swish?' Dido kept murmuring as they bowled up the long drive between the gas flares.

'Oh, odds boddikins,' muttered Justin uneasily as they pulled up. A tall figure stood on the Castle steps awaiting them with folded arms.

'It's Uncle Buckle!' exclaimed Dido. She put down the window on her side and called out. 'Hillo, Uncle Buckle! Look at me! Ain't I the dandy? We've been to the fair!'

'*Dido!*' exclaimed Mr Buckle, thunderstruck. He then turned to Justin, who was just alighting, and said terribly, 'My Lord Bakerloo! What is the meaning of this – this *escapade*?'

'Uncle Bill said I might go,' Justin mumbled sulkily.

'I am sure he had no idea you would be consorting with such *low* – *vulgar* – companions as these.'

'I ain't low!' Dido called out indignantly, but Mr Buckle took no further notice of her, and went on rating Justin in a harsh, carrying voice. As there was nothing they could do for the unfortunate boy, and it seemed unkind to listen to his set-down, Simon asked the jarvey to drive on to Southwark, the coach turned, and they continued their journey.

'Poor Justin,' said Dido, giggling, as they rumbled through the dark streets. 'I wonder if Uncle Buckle will dust his jacket for him? D'you reckon Ma will give me a trimming for going on the spree with a Dook's nevvy?'

Simon thought it unlikely.

'Anyways,' said Dido with a sigh, 'I wouldn't care if she did! It's been the best bang-up day of my whole life and I'll never forget it, *never*! Wasn't the Punch and Judy a ripsmasher!' She fell into a silence of recollection.

'I never knew Mr Buckle was your uncle,' Simon remarked presently.

'Lor, yes, he's Ma's brother, but we ain't gentility enough for him, so he don't visit us above once in a blue moon. I'll tell you what, Simon,' said Dido, looking carefully around as if to make sure that Mr Buckle was not riding with them in the hack, 'I can't give you a present, like Madam Lolla said, but there's one thing I *can* do for you – and I'd *like* to, as you've give me such a prime good time – I can tell you what happened to Dr Field!'

Simon was silent with astonishment for a moment or two.

At last he said cautiously:

'I *should* like to know that, Dido.'

'Well, it was like this,' she told him. 'Pa said I was

never to mention it to a living soul, or he'd beat me and shut me up in the boot-hole, but I don't care! You see Dr Field used to lodge in our house –'

At this moment the hack turned into Rose Alley and stopped outside No. 8.

'Why, there's Ma!' cried Dido. 'Wait till I tell her what a famous time I've had. Ma, Ma, we saw the Drury Lane Drama!' She opened the door and tumbled out on to the pavement, eager to relate her day's doings. Mrs Twite, however, only said:

'It's long past your bedtime, child. Come along in at once.'

Simon paid off the driver and turned to follow Mrs Twite. But she seemed to have locked the door behind her, and, as he rattled the latch unavailingly and then rapped the knocker, something dark and soft and suffocating was forced down over his head, and a pair of hands gripped his throat. He struggled and struck out, but other hands pinioned his arms and legs, while the clutch on his throat tightened. A rocket seemed to explode on the back of his head, he crumpled forward on to the steps, and was conscious of nothing more.

10

Simon came to by slow degrees. Once, long ago, he had lain ill of a fever at Gloober's Poor Farm, and had been left, sweating and shivering and delirious, in the granary, where he would probably have died had not Sophie sometimes stolen away from her duties to bring him food and keep him covered with horse blankets.

For some time he thought he was back in the granary. It was dark, but he could smell the same smell of meal and canvas and timber. Only one thing puzzled him: a strange regular creak and groaning which seemed to come from all round him; he finally concluded it must be the blood pounding in his feverish head. When he tried to move he found he was quite unable to do so.

I must be very ill, he thought. I wish Sophie would come.

But Sophie did not come and soon the fever, or nightmare, whichever it was, had him completely at its mercy. Although he could not move of his own will, yet he found himself rolled from side to side as if by a giant invisible hand, and was soon bruised and aching from head to foot.

Could I be in a cart? he wondered. But no; if I were I should hear the wheels and the horse's hoofs. I must be in the granary and I think I must be going to die. He rolled again, this time over and over; it was as if the floor of the place heaved up, up, up, in a long, tilting swing, and then down, down, down, in the other direction; he rolled and slid, helpless and dizzy. How much of this rolling and battering he endured he did not know; it seemed to go on for an eternity of misery, but at last fever and exhaustion and rough treatment overcame his bruised body and he fainted again.

When next he came to it was because somebody was shining a light very close to his face. He moved his head dazedly, opened his eyes, and quickly shut them again. He could hear low voices close to him.

'Hold the glim nearer this way, sapskull! How can I see what I'm doing?' 'Sapskull yourself! It's not as easy as all that. Here, let me do that and *you* hold the light.' 'Not on your Jemima! You'd probably slice his dabs off.'

Simon became aware that something was being done to his numb, cramped hands. They had seemed immovably jammed against his sides but now, suddenly, he heard a snap and they were free. He realized that he had been tied up all this time, and struggled feebly to hoist himself on to his elbows.

'Wait a minute, don't be in such a pelter, we ain't unfastened your trotters yet,' somebody whispered sharply in his ear. Obediently he relaxed and lay back, curling and uncurling his fingers which tingled as the blood ran into them.

Now he was shoved into a reclining position and found the neck of a bottle tilted against his mouth. He gulped and choked and spat, as liquid ran down his gullet and over his chin.

'Enough – ' he muttered weakly, pushing the bottle away. 'No more now – later.'

The drink – it was prune wine – soon did him good; he opened his eyes and looked about. Close to him, illuminated by the flickering light of a candle, were two familiar faces. After a few seconds he identified them as those of Justin and Dido.

'What the deuce?' He raised himself feebly and looked into the gloom beyond them, where he saw ramparts of piled sacks and timber. 'Where am I? What are you two doing here?'

'*Hush!* Don't make a row. We're in the *Dark Dew*.'

'Here, give him another drink,' Justin whispered.

Simon accepted another swig. Meanwhile, Dido's

words had penetrated his mind and connected with something he remembered hearing Mr Twite say.

'The dark dew? What do you mean? What is the dark dew?'

'It's a ship, o'course,' Dido whispered impatiently. 'We're all at sea. Ain't it a spree?'

'A *ship*?'

'Uncle Buckle had you shanghaied and taken on board her at Deptford because you was getting to be such a nuisance, always poking and asking questions.'

'Where are we now?'

'*I* dunno,' said Dido, giggling. 'The *Dark Dew* is bound for Hanover – Bremen, Pa said (that's where they pick up the Pictclobbers, you know) – but they don't take you there. You get dropped off on an island on the way. Inchmore, it's called. Fubsy sort o' name, ain't it?'

'But what about you and Justin – what are *you* doing here?'

'That's the cream of it.' Dido giggled again. 'O' course I didn't know you was going to be kidnapped, though I been suspicioning that Pa would do summat o' the sort. I jist luckily happened to be looking out o' the window arter we got home from the fair, to see if you was coming in, and I saw Pa and Captain Dark put a bag over your head. Coo, you didn't half struggle! Pa had to clobber you with the butt of his barker, and then they carried you off feet first. I thought I'd follow after; I've never liked it at home above half. Anyways, I was jist going to hop it when His Royal Nibs here came along.'

'Justin, you mean? But why? We left you at Battersea.'

'Yes, well, I wouldn't stand it,' said Justin sulkily. 'You heard what a set-down the old grinder was giving me, a body couldn't bear any more of it! He said you was a danger to me and he'd see to it I'd never have a chance to meet you again. After the prime time we'd had, too! So after he'd left me with a lot of Latin lines I thought I'd just show him and I went down to the stables and made one of the grooms saddle me a horse (lucky Waters wasn't about) and rode to Southwark. I thought I'd call for you and we'd go to Drury Lane, just to show old Buckle-and-Thong who was master. But when I got to Rose Alley, there was Dido just smitching off to go to Deptford, and she told me you'd been scrobbled. So we thought we'd come along for the lark. Dido knew where the ship lay –'

'Captain Dark allus comes to us when he's got a ship in,' Dido put in knowledgeably. 'There's three of 'em – *Dark Dew, Dark Dimity,* and *Dark Diamond*. He runs mixed cargoes to Holland, and brings back arms from Hanover – for the Cause, you know. But, Croopus, we had such a time finding you! We sneaked on board in the dark and hid in the forecastle – Justin nipped into a chest and I squeezed behind the grog-barrel – and then when we was out to sea we thought we'd look for you but there was such a storm! All we did was fall over! Justin nearly lobbed his groats – didn't you, Nibs? – and I didn't like it above half.'

'Oh, that was a storm, was it?' said Simon,

remembering the hours of rolling misery. 'I thought I was feverish. How long did it last?'

'Matter o' two days. And then it took us for ever to find you, on account you was stowed away down here in the hold.'

'I'd have been in a bad way, but for you,' Simon said gratefully. 'But what's to be done now? Does nobody know you're on board?'

'Not a soul. Ain't it famous? We've been having such a game of hide-and-seek! When Captain Dark comes out o' his cabin, Justin nips in and nobbles his bottle of mountain dew (that's what we been giving you). Then the cook comes out o' the galley – I nips in and grabs a black pudding and a hunk of tack. Fast as the sailors coils up the ropes, we uncoils 'em again. We've been undoing things and unwinding things till they think the ship's betwaddled.' Dido was laughing so much that here she was obliged to stop and stick the candle in a crevice between two planks because she was spilling hot wax over Simon's legs.

'Are you better, Simon?' she asked presently. 'If you are, I've got a bang-up plan.'

'What's that, brat?'

'We'll *all* play hide-and-seek with the sailors. We'll turn everything in the ship upsy-down, till they're so set-about and dumbflustered they don't know which way they're going, and then we'll watch our chance and lock 'em in the roundhouse, and sail the ship back to Deptford ourselves.'

While Simon admitted that this was a pleasing plan, he saw snags.

'Can you sail a ship, Dido?'

'I knows the ropes,' she said confidently. 'Habbut you?'

'Never been in one in my life before,' Simon had to admit, which evidently somewhat dashed Dido's high opinion of him. Justin's acquaintance with ships had been limited to trips up the Thames in his uncle's barge, and it was plain he was not a keen sailor; throughout the conversation he had remained pale and silent, swallowing frequently.

'I don't really believe we can sail the ship ourselves,' Simon said.

'Well then –' Dido refused to be cast down – 'we'll smidge some barkers – I knows where they keeps the guns and balls – and hold 'em up, make *them* sail us back.'

'That's a likelier plan. How many are there in the crew?'

'Matter o' fourteen or fifteen, and most of 'em tipple-topped or right down half-seas-over all the time. Captain Dark's the wust of 'em – you never see him but he's got a bottle in his hand and one in his pocket.'

'That's what we'll do, then,' said Simon. 'Where do they keep the guns?'

'Up on deck, in the roundhouse. We could snibble up now, it's night-time and there'a only a couple of coves on peep-go.'

Unfortunately, Simon discovered when he tried to move that he was still a great deal too weak to stand. His legs gave way and he fell back groaning against the meal-sacks.

'It's no good, brat,' he gasped. 'I'll have to wait till

I get my strength back. Lying tied up all this time without food has left me as limp as a herring.'

Dido knit her brows. 'I'll lay you'd do better in the air,' she said. 'This here hold's got a breath in it like a mouldy coffin. Let's put him on a sack and haul him out, Justin.'

Justin looked doubtful, but when she ordered him not to squat there gaping like a jobberknoll but to find an empty sack he nodded palely and obeyed. They laid the sack by Simon and he dragged himself on to it.

The whole project seemed utterly impossible but somehow, thanks to Dido's indomitable spirit, it succeeded. Simon was drawn along on the sack to the foot of the ladder that led up from the hold; then, with Dido pulling from above and Justin pushing from below, he contrived to hoist himself up through the hatchway.

'All rug now?' said Dido after a period of rest. 'Come on, we'd best bustle or it'll be morning before we're up top.'

Once more they set to hauling Simon along a dark gallery. While they were resting in the shadows at the foot of the next ladder, a man came down it, but he never saw them; he reeled as he walked and a strong flavour of spirits wafted from him.

'He's bosky,' Dido said calmly. 'Drunk as a wheelbarrow. They're all like that – slacking the cables after the storm.'

With a fearful effort, Simon was hoisted up the last ladder. Dido's shrimp-like frame seemed to possess amazing strength, both in muscle and willpower: she hauled like a horsebreaker and exhorted her two companions in a wild flow of whispered gutter-language that had a most stimulating effect. Even so, they were all collapsing from exhaustion by the time they reached the deck, and had to lie down helplessly for many minutes. Luckily, as Dido had said, the crew had all been drinking freely after the storm; most of them were asleep and the two on watch were in no state to notice anything unusual.

'Brush on, cullies,' whispered Dido presently. 'There's a fire in the galley; we might as well have a warm-up, and we're out o' view there.'

The galley was a warm and cluttered place; it seemed to serve the purpose of a handy storehouse, for it contained chests and bales and piles of clothes. A fire glowed red in an iron stove, and a snoring man lay sprawled on the floor in front of it.

Simon's last recollection was of being thrust into a sort of cocoon composed of rope-yarn and old rags behind some chests. Then Dido dropped a duffel-cloak over him and he slept.

He was roused by a violent blow on the head and opened his eyes with a gasp, thinking they were discovered. He saw the scared faces of Dido and Justin, who were wedged with him behind the chests; then he realized that they were not under attack; a heavy iron hook, hanging from a coil of rope on the wall had swung out and struck him. The ship was plunging violently. The hook flew out again, and Simon reached up dizzily and pulled it down.

'We must be running into another storm,' he whispered.

The ship echoed and re-echoed with noises – the confused shouts of half-tipsy men, the hum, sometimes rising to a wail, of wind in the rigging, and the roar and crash of the sea itself. They could feel the *Dark Dew* shudder, shrink, and then plunge on as each wave struck her. Feet pattered across the deck and someone shouted an order to reef all sails; the sleeper in front of the galley fire groaned, pulled himself together, and staggered out.

'I might as well prig some peck while the going's good.' Dido said, and crawled out from their hiding-place. She came back in a moment with two large handfuls of raisins. 'There you are, cullies. Keep swallowing – it's much the best in this sort o' toss-up.'

'I can't *stand* it,' moaned Justin. Dido eyed him scornfully. A dim grey morning light was filtering in through the open door and Simon could see that Dido was as white as a sheet, but she seemed to be alert and cocky, thoroughly enjoying the adventure.

'You *are* a loblolly,' she told Justin. '*I* think it's prime – I've never had such a bang-up lark, except for the fair. I'd sooner be here than at home any day.'

'If only the ship wouldn't lurch about so!' whimpered Justin, as a weight of water struck the roof above them with a thunderous crash. 'There's water coming in now.'

'Pooh,' said Dido, pale but game. 'That's only a bit of sea hitting the deck.'

'But I've got a pain in my bread-basket.'

'So've I, but I don't make such a song-and-dance about it.'

'Hush – listen,' said Simon, who had been straining

his ears. He caught a long-drawn-out call, repeated twice, and was trying to make it out, as it echoed again over the sound of the wind.

'. . . Ay-ay-ay-ay . . . ire . . . ire . . . *Fire!*'

'Fire in the hold! Fire!'

'*Fire?*' breathed Dido, staring at Simon with dilated eyes. Now she did seem a little scared. 'Fire in the hold? But that's where *you* were, Simon! Croopus, it's lucky we got you away from there!'

'That candle, Dido – that candle you stuck between two planks. Did you ever go back and fetch it – or put it out?'

'I – I don't reckon as how I did,' she whispered. 'D'you think that's what started the fire?'

'It might be.'

'Oh, they'll easily put it out,' Justin said hopefully. 'Won't they? *Won't* they?'

The other two did not answer. They were listening. A sudden puff of smoke blew through the galley door. The clamour on deck increased, and above the sound of wind and waves Simon now thought he could detect a different noise – could it be the crackle of fire?

'What'll happen?' whispered Dido, very subdued.

'Oh, there must be some boats – if they can't put the fire out – ' His words were interrupted by a sudden extraordinary noise, so loud that it seemed to reduce all the sounds that had preceded it to mere taps and whispers. It was a rending, grinding roar that lasted for as long as Simon could draw five breaths – then the ship seemed to stop dead in her course and there was an awesome silence.

'What is it? What's that noise?' cried Dido. None of them could bear to stay in hiding any longer, they all leapt from their nook and ran to the galley door. Simon almost fell from weakness, but grabbed the doorpost and hung on, looking out. Dido clutched hold of his hand.

The scene before them made even Simon gasp. The *Dark Dew*, burning like a torch, had literally broken in half, and the forward part of the ship was already drifting away, carried by the fierce wind and waves. They saw two or three men on it trying to launch a boat; then the whole hulk fell over sideways, swamping boat, crew, and all; in a few minutes it had disappeared from view.

The after half of the ship, containing the galley, remained motionless but continued to burn; great detached fragments of smoke and flame flew past on the wind.

'Wh-what's h-happ-pened? Why aren't we moving?' said Dido with chattering teeth. 'D-do you think we've run ag-g-ground?'

'On a rock, maybe—' Simon stepped out on to the dangerously canted deck and grabbed at a shroud to steady himself. 'Look, there are rocks over there, you can see the waves breaking on them.'

'Are we near land?' Dido asked hopefully. 'Can we get ashore?'

'Heavens knows. Look, they're trying to get another boat free.'

A knot of men at the stern were struggling to drag loose a dinghy that had become wedged beneath a fallen spar. They were in a panic; each cursing his mates and getting in the way of the rest. A wild-eyed man with a black beard rushed past the galley and began knocking the men aside with a wooden spike so as to come at the boat himself, shouting orders meanwhile.

'That's Captain Dark,' Dido said. 'I'd best go and speak to him, I reckon; we don't want to get left here in the nitch, if they're shoving off.'

The boat was free now, and she darted across the deck and grabbed Captain Dark's arm. He gave a tremendous start at sight of her, and the rest of the men gaped, thunderstruck at this apparition.

'How do, Captain Dark. Ain't this a turn-up, then?' said Dido, pale but perky.

'Where in the name of Judas did you come from, you devil's brat?'

'I ain't a devil's brat! You know me – I'm Dido Twite. I stowed on your ship, with Justin there, acos you was taking my cully away.'

Captain Dark turned and saw Justin and Simon. He gave them an ugly glance, and the men by the boat began to mutter, 'No wonder we come to this, with a brood of Jonahs aboard. Everybody knows childer bring ill-luck at sea.'

Suddenly a great piece of the deck fell in, and flames burst out of the galley window.

'Never mind talking now, skipper! For God's sake let's get the boat launched,' someone shouted urgently. Captain Dark shook off Dido and rapped out an order; the boat shot off the deck into the sea. Instantly the whole group of men tumbled off the *Dark Dew* into her, higgledy-piggledy, fighting each other like furies. Captain Dark was among them, wielding an oar vigorously. It was plain there was not going to be room in the boat for everybody. Several men were knocked into the sea but did their best to clamber in again, dragging out their mates as they did so.

'Wait, wait!' Dido called frantically. 'Wait for us! You've left us behind!'

'You weren't asked on board, were you?' someone shouted. 'Save yourselves – we don't want you.'

The boat drifted away. Its crew were too busy struggling for places to worry about pulling at the oars or steering. Simon saw a huge green hill of sea rise beneath its keel and tip the boat sideways like a walnut shell. He could not bear to look any longer and turned his eyes away.

'*Save us!*' whispered Dido in horror, staring past him. 'They've *gone*! *Simon!* They've gone! What'll we do?'

'We'll have to manage for ourselves, that's all,' Simon said, pulling himself together, trying to sound more hopeful than he felt.

They clambered down to the stern, which the fire had not yet reached, and then realized what had happened to the ship. Her rudder had caught and jammed between two rocks, so that she was held fast and battered until her forward part had broken away.

'She won't last here long,' Simon said. 'We'd best shift off as soon as we can. I believe that might be an island over there.'

Day had now fully broken and a wild yellow light shone fitfully between squalls of rain. They glimpsed a long, craggy ridge of land about half a mile ahead; then black cloud came down and blotted out the view.

'H-how c-can we g-get there?' asked Justin.

Simon cast his eyes round what remained of the deck. There was a large water-cask lashed to the mast; he dragged it free.

'Here you are,' he said to Justin. 'This'll do for you, neat as ninepence. Pass this bit of rope round your middle and through the bung-hole – so – now the cask can't float away from you. Here's an oar; hang on to the end of it and we'll let you down; you can go first as you're a Duke's nevvy.'

He rolled the barrel into the sea and Justin, whimpering a little, was let down into it and pushed off with the oar, which Simon then passed to him.

'Fend yourself off from the rocks!' he shouted as the cask bobbed away.

'What about us?' asked Dido, doggedly clenching her teeth. 'I can't swim.'

Simon looked round once more. There were no other barrels, and the flames were coming uncomfortably close.

'It'll have to be this for you and me,' he said, and laid hold of the broken spar which had hindered the men from launching the boat. Ropes were still made fast to it, and he passed a couple of these round Dido and tied her on as securely as he could.

'I d-don't like this above half,' she said, shivering.

'Never mind. I'm going to push you in and then jump after you. Hold tight to the pole! Now jump!'

'Oh, my lovely new dress! It'll get ru –'

A wave closed over Dido, but she reappeared next minute, gamely clinging to the spar. Simon dived in and managed to grab the other end of it.

'That's the ticket! Now all we have to do is swim to shore.'

'Can you see Justin?'

'Yes, he's floating on ahead of us. We'll be all right – you'll see,' Simon said as reassuringly as he could. He gave Dido an encouraging smile and she smiled wanly back. She looked a piteous sight with her wet hair hanging in rats' tails over her face.

Simon swam with his legs, pushing the cumbersome spar ahead of him with his arms. It was an exhausting struggle. His heart grew so heavy in his chest, and beat so hard, that he began to feel as if it would work loose and sink from him like a stone.

'Are you all right, brat?' he gasped.

She made some indistinguishable reply. Presently he heard her say, 'Are we nearly there?'

'Just keep going. Kick with your legs.'

They laboured on. Dido, looking back, cried out that the *Dark Dew* had gone. She had crumbled together like a burning ember and slipped under the waves.

'Lucky for us we weren't on board then,' panted Simon. 'And I should have been, Dido, if you hadn't come and set me loose. I owe you my life.'

'But s'posing it was us that set fire to the ship?' Dido gulped miserably.

'Oh – as to that – very likely it wasn't. With all those drunk men on board, it's a wonder the ship lasted as long as she did.'

A wave slopped against Simon's chin and he closed his mouth. He was beginning to feel very strange: his legs were numb from the waist down and hung heavily in the water.

'I – I'll have to stop for a minute, Dido,' he said hoarsely. One of his hands slipped off the spar and he only just succeeded in grabbing it again.

'There's a rock, let's make for it,' she said. 'We can rest for a bit.'

With a last effort Simon swam towards the rock. They managed to drag themselves up its slope, getting badly scraped by limpets, and lay side by side on the narrow tip, shivering and exhausted.

'Can you see Justin – or the land?' Dido asked after a while. She huddled closer to Simon. He opened his eyes with an effort, and moved his head, but could see nothing save cloud and driving rain. His eyelids flickered and closed again; he sank into a sort of dream, only half aware of Dido, who occasionally moved or coughed beside him.

Once or twice he realized that she was pushing food into his mouth – damp and salty raisins or crumbs of cheese.

'Keep some for yourself, brat,' he muttered weakly.

'I ain't hungry . . .'

In Simon's feverish fancy the rock seemed to sway up and down as the *Dark Dew* had done – tilting, tilting, now this way, now that . . . Or was he on the branch of a tree, back at home in the forest of Willoughby? Was that sound not the howl of the sea but the howl of wolves? No, it was the sea, but Dido was talking about wolves in the forest; her words came dreamily, in disjointed snatches:

'Climbing from one tree to the next . . . I'd have liked that . . . Shying sticks and stones at the wolves down below . . . you could laugh at 'em . . . it must have been prime. *I* wouldn't 'a wanted to go to London, dunno why you did. You *will* take me there some day, won't you? To the forest? You said you would. And I'll throw stones at the wolves . . . I'm glad you came to London, Simon. Nobody ever told me such tales afore . . . and you took me to the fair . . . Coo, that dragon was a proper take-in, though, wasn't it? . . . I liked the Talking Pig best . . .'

She coughed and crept closer still against Simon. For some time there was silence, except for the harsh screams of gulls. Simon drifted further and further away towards the frontiers of unconsciousness.

'Simon,' Dido said presently in a small voice. His only response was a faint movement of his head.

'Simon, I think the tide's coming in. It's coming higher up the rock. I – I don't think there's going to be room here for both of us. Maybe – maybe I'd better try and float to the shore to get help?'

Simon did not answer. His eyes were closed, and he lay limp, white, and motionless, with the waves breaking not three feet below him.

11

Sophie was puzzled. She had been staying at the Cobbs' for five days now, during which time Simon had not once come to see her or to work in Mr Cobb's yard. Mr Cobb was puzzled too.

'Simon's sich a reglar-working cove in the usual way. I hope there's nowt amiss,' he muttered, looking with knit brows at the panel of a barouche which Simon had been in process of adorning with a viscount's coat-of-arms. 'Here's thisyer job promised to Lord Thingumbob for Toosday, and looks like I'll be obleeged to cry rope, which ain't my way. I hope the boy's all right. Hey, Sophie, lass! How about your taking a hack – here's a crown for the fare – and tooling round to Southwark to see if he's sick abed?'

Sophie agreed with alacrity and was about to fetch her bonnet when a small grubby boy sidled into Mr Cobb's yard and made his way towards her.

'Is you Miss Sophie?' he asked, fixing her with a piercing eye.

'Yes I am,' she replied. 'What can I do for you?'

'You're sure as how you're Miss Sophie? Cos I wasn't to give it to no one else, and, Croopus, I've had sich a time finding you. Fust I axes at the Castle – nobody gammons – nearly gets chucked in a horse-trough for me trouble. Then a gaffer says to come here. *Is* she Miss Sophie?' he demanded of Mr Cobb.

'Miss Sophie she be,' Mr Cobb answered heartily.

'Then I can give it you.' He handed her a very dirty folded bit of paper, and added hopefully, 'She says as you was very kind and 'ud likely give me a farden. And, please, I cooden come afore today, my gammy's *that* strict I cooden give her the slip, but today she's laid up with a proud toe.'

Sophie laughed at this and gave him sixpence, saying, 'Thank you, my dear. Here you are, then – buy yourself some Banbury cakes. But who told you to come?'

He looked conspiratorially round the yard, sank his voice to a whisper, and said, 'Why, *she* done. Young Dido Twite. But she's gorn now – along o' the others.' Then he bolted off between the carriages and vanished out of the gate.

Sophie opened the note which was addressed, in staggering capitals, to MIZ SOPHY.

Dere Miz Sophy. i thankx yu onst agin fer the dress. its reel Prime. Fust nue dress i iver wuz giv. Simon as bin kid naped in a Shipp. Me an Justin is goin 2 for the Lark. i like Simon an it isn Fare he shd be All Alone. the Shipp is the dark due. Yrs respeckfly Dido Twite

'Good gracious!' exclaimed Sophie, when she had

read this letter twice. 'He has been kidnapped! And Justin too! Can this be true? I must inform her Grace!'

'*Kidnapped?* Young Simon?' Mr Cobb fairly gaped at her.

'Yes, on board a ship called the *Dark Due*. Do you know of such a vessel?'

'The *Dark Dew*? By Ringo, yes! She and a couple of others belong to that shifty, havey-cavey Nathaniel Dark, the one who ran off with Buckle's wife.'

'Mr Buckle? Justin's tutor? I didn't know he'd ever been married,' said Sophie, momentarily diverted from her worry.

'It was years ago. Buckle was glad to be rid of the woman. By all I hear she never stopped talking. Dear knows what Nat Dark did with her, for he didn't marry her. Left her in furrin parts, I daresay. He's a dicey cove; up to the teeth with the Hanoverians, too. That settles it,' said Mr Cobb, grabbing his hat from a mounting-block and cramming it on his head. 'I'm for Bow Street. Young Simon said summat once about Hanoverians –'

'The Twites, in Rose Alley,' said Sophie, nodding.

'Ah, and I said, "Leave well alone". But when it comes to kidnapping . . . It's as plain as a pike what's happened: he's twigged their lay and been put away.'

'But where will they have taken him?'

'Ah, there, lass, now you're asking. Those Dark ships goes coasting all the way up to Newcassel and then across to Hanover – they might put him anywhere that's awkud to get at. Only thing is to nobble the bunch – at Rose Alley, you say? – and winch 'em tight till they lets on where he's to.'

Mr Cobb started for the gate, then paused to ask, 'Was you wishful to see me, Jem?'

'Only to ask was his Grace's curricle ready yet, Mr Cobb?' said Jem, coming out from behind a pile of wheels.

'Ready this evening, tell Mr Waters.' Jem nodded and followed Mr Cobb into the street, where he set off at a run towards the Castle.

Sophie was not long in following him. Inquiring for their Graces, however, she learnt that they were calling on His Majesty. Not surprisingly, the Castle was in an uproar over the disappearance of Lord Bakerloo, and the Duke had gone to ask that a national proclamation be made offering a reward for information as to the whereabouts of the Battersea heir.

Sophie found the Duchess's embroidery (which was suffering from a week's neglect) and sat putting it to rights in the library, waiting for their Graces to return.

The whole chamber was still stacked high with the piles of pictures which the Academy students had taken down during their vain hunt for the Rivière. There had been no time to rehang them in the more urgent search for Justin. Sophie, established with her embroidery on a footstool by the fire, was screened by a pile of canvases from the view of anybody entering the room.

Presently she heard two people speaking in low tones.

'This has put a pretty crimp in our plan,' a voice said angrily. 'What was that fool, Dark, about not to notice he'd two other brats on board? And *Justin*, of all people – it couldn't be worse.'

Sophie recognized Midwink's tones.

'What I'll do to that boy when I catch him!' The other speaker was Mr Buckle. 'The whole thing nearly in our hands and he has to run off like a – like a guttersnipe! If those students hadn't been on the river-bank the other day – or if that meddlesome girl hadn't gone to the opera – Justin would have been Duke of Battersea by now and we'd be in clover.'

'Well, as things are, he's not,' said Midwink sourly. 'And the old boy's still alive, and till we get Justin back we'd best *keep* him alive; we don't want some cousin stepping in and claiming the dukedom. I've got the poison but I won't use it till Dark brings back the boy.'

'I only hope Dark has the sense to do so,' Buckle said with a curse. 'It drives me wild having to rely on such a nabble-head. And now we've got to shift the ken from Rose Alley – and if Jem doesn't warn Ella before the Bow Street runners get there – '

'Jem's trusty enough,' Midwink said. 'He took the Duke's fastest chaser – he'll be there by now. Where did you tell Ella to take the stuff?'

Buckle sank his voice to a murmur and Sophie could only catch the words 'vegetable cart'. Midwink gave a cackle of laughter and said, 'They'll never think of looking *there*. But are you sure no one will blab?'

'I don't believe there's a soul in the Castle that's not a Hanoverian to the hilt,' Buckle replied. 'Barring the girl. Now as to my plan. Soon as we hear from Dark that he has Justin safe – If we hear before the mince-pie ceremony – '

'Aha you mean to poison the Christmas mince-pies?'

'No, better than that.' Buckle dropped his voice again and Sophie missed the next words. He ended – 'all sky-high togoether – and the wench as well. My heart's in my mouth, now, every time the Duchess looks at her. Why did she have to pick *that* one, out of all the paupers at Gloober's . . . I thought she'd died in the woods but it must be – '

'Hush!' said Midwink. 'Is that the carriage? Best not be found here.'

The two men left the room.

Sophie remained where she was, almost paralysed by fear and astonishment. So *Buçkle* was at the bottom of the plot – Buckle and Midwink! And Jem was with them, and had galloped off to warn the Twites to leave Rose Alley. And every servant in the Castle – almost everybody – was a Hanoverian to the hilt. Moreover, it was plain that the Duke and Duchess were in grave danger – two attempts at murder had only accidentally failed and a third, somehow connected with mince-pies, was merely postponed until Justin's return. Why Justin? Sophie wondered, and then realized that if Justin became the sixth Duke of Battersea, following the murder of his uncle, he would still be so much under his tutor's thumb that Buckle would in fact control all the ducal power and money. Perhaps it was a blessing, then, that Justin had run away.

But meantime how to protect the helpless, elderly Duke and Duchess? The Duke had the greatest respect for Buckle, and would be most unlikely to believe in any accusation against him unless it were backed by positive proof. Perhaps the raid on Rose Alley would provide this. If not, it seemed to Sophie that the best plan would be to get the Duke and Duchess away from Battersea. But how was this to be achieved?

Her thoughts were interrupted by the Duchess, who arrived in a great bustle.

'Ah, there you are, Sophie, dear child! I am so delighted to see you again. We are to depart instantly for Chippings – His Majesty very sensibly suggested that that naughty Justin might have run off there for a bit of wolf-hunting. Pack me up a few odds and ends, will you, my dear, just for a night or two – warm things, it will be cold in the North – Don't forget the croquet and my water-colours . . . Ah, you have the tapestry, that's right. You are to come, too, of course, so pack for yourself as well. We start as soon as the train is ready.'

'The train, ma'am? Won't his Grace be using the coach?'

'No, he thinks a train will be quicker. He has gone to charter it now.'

Sophie was thunderstruck. She had never travelled on a train in her life – indeed the nearest station to Chippings was at York, over thirty miles away, for the Duke, who considered trains to be dirty, noisy things, flatly refused to have them running over his land.

Sophie struggled with her conscience. This seemed a heaven-sent opportunity to get their Graces away from trouble, and she was excited at the prospect of the journey, but still it was her duty to mention Dido's letter. She showed it to the Duchess, who read it with astonishment.

'Dido Twite? Who is Dido Twite, my child?'

'Oh, she is a poor little thing that Simon has befriended, the daughter of his landlady.'

'But why should Simon have been kidnapped? And why should Justin have gone with him? Depend upon it,' said the Duchess, 'this will turn out to be nothing but a Banbury Story. Is this Dido Twite a truthful little child?'

Sophie was bound to admit that she hardly thought it likely.

'I have it!' declared her Grace. 'You say this *Dark Dew* belongs to Captain Nathaniel Dark? Yes, and I remember him – a shifty rogue who tried to sell his Grace a shipment of abominable smuggled prune brandy, watered, my dear, and tasting of tar. His ships put in regularly at the port of Chipping Fishbury – be sure, those naughty boys have begged a sea-passage in order to get to Chippings, and if we travel by train, like as not we shall be there before them. Yes, yes, my dear, I will show the note to his Grace, but, depend upon it, that is the solution. Now, run and pack the croquet things, and do not forget the billiard-balls and my small harpsichord.'

With a clear conscience Sophie ran off to carry out

her Grace's wishes. Packing the water-colours neatly into a crate with the harpsichord, she remembered that curious remark of Buckle's concerning herself – 'Why she had to pick *that* one, out of all the paupers at Gloober's – my heart's in my mouth, now, every time the Duchess looks at her – ' What could he have meant? Sophie's heart began to beat rather fast. Might it be possible that, all the time, she had relations somewhere? But why should Buckle know anything about it? Pray, Sophie, do not be nonsensical, she admonished herself, and knelt to fasten the croquet mallets into their case.

An hour later they set off. The Duke, not very well-informed about trains, was indignant to discover that even when he chartered a special one it would not come to his door, but had to be boarded at the station. However, a pair of carriages transported the party across London with their baggage to the terminus, where a strip of red carpet running the length of the platform, a bowing station-master, and porters bearing bouquets and baskets of fruit restored his Grace to good humour.

Sophie learnt with joy that neither Buckle nor Midwink were to be of the party. The first six hours of the journey passed peacefully. After a light luncheon they played billiards in the billiard car until the increasing motion of the train, as they entered more hilly country, rendered this occupation too hazardous. The Duke, having nearly spitted his lady with a cue, returned to the saloon coach, sighing that he wished they had Simon with them, for there was nothing in the world he would like so much as a game of chess.

'I can play a little, your Grace,' Sophie said. 'Simon has been teaching me. But I fear I am only a beginner.'

His Grace was delighted, declaring that any opponent was better than none. 'For her Grace can't be bothered to learn the moves.' Sophie unpacked the glass set from his valise and they played two or three games with great enjoyment, the more so as his Grace won them all. Then, unfortunately, a lurch of the train threw the black glass Queen to the floor and broke off her crown.

The Duke was greatly vexed by this, but the Duchess said placidly:

'Do not put yourself in a pucker, my dear. If you recall, I had this set made for your birthday by the old glass-burner in the forest and, depend upon it, he will be able to put Her Majesty to rights again. We can call at his hut on the way to Chippings.'

'Ay, so we can, my dear,' said the Duke. 'What a head you have on your shoulders. Old Turveytop can do the business in a twinkling, I daresay.'

Sophie became very excited. 'Is that old Turveytop the charcoal-burner, your Grace? Why, it was he who brought me up! I should dearly like to see the old man again – he was always so kind to me.'

'Old Turveytop brought you up, did he? But you are not related to him, child?'

'No, ma'am. He found me in the forest when I was little more than a baby.'

'But you had no clothes, child – nothing to indicate where you had come from?'

'Nothing, ma'am, except a little silver chain-bracelet with my name, Sophie, on a shield, and on the other side a kind of picture with tiny writing that was too small for my foster-father to read.'

'Have you the bracelet yet, my dear?' said the Duchess, showing the liveliest curiosity. 'I should so like to see it. Since we looked at the Rivière picture I have had the strangest feeling –'

Sophie's face had clouded at a sad recollection. 'When I grew, and the bracelet would not meet round my wrist, my foster-father put it away for me, your Grace. I am sure he will have it still –'

'Why did he not give it to you when they took you to the Poor Farm, my child?'

'He was not there at the time,' Sophie said miserably. 'He was away on the wolds cutting peat when the overseer came and took me away. I have so often wondered if he knew what had become of me.'

'Could you not write to him?'

'Mrs Gloober would not allow it.'

'Never mind, child, soon you will be able to tell him yourself.'

Poor Sophie was to be disappointed, however. Night had come when they reached York, and they were obliged to rack up at an inn rather than undertake the dangerous journey across the wolf-infested wolds in the dark. They set out early next day in a pair of hired carriages, and, after several hours' brisk driving, had reached the outskirts of Chipping Wold, a huge, wild, and desolate tract of country, moorland and forest, which must be traversed before they reached the village of Loose Chippings. Sophie was on her home ground, here; her eyes brightened and she gazed eagerly about, recognizing every tree, rock, and tumbling stream

'There! There it is,' she presently exclaimed. 'There is the track leading to my foster-father's hut.'

The Duke ordered the baggage-coach to wait on the turnpike while the party jolted along the rocky track in the smaller open carriage. Soon they were passing among dark trees growing steeply up the sides of a narrow glen, and the driver whipped up his team and laid his musket ready on the box. After about half a mile the track widened, however, and they reached an open, sunny space where stood a small log-and-turf hut.

Sophie could restrain herself no longer. She tumbled out of the carriage, crying, 'Turvey, Turvey! Are you there? It's me – Sophie! I've come back!'

The door of the hut opened and a young man came out. Sophie halted in dismay.

'Who – who are you?' she stammered. 'Where's Turvey?'

'He's dead, miss.'

'*Dead?* But – but he can't be! Who are you – how do you know?'

'I'm his nephew, miss. Yes, they found my uncle dead – it's ten days ago now – lying spitted with an arrow at his own front door.'

By this time their Graces had alighted and crossed the clearing. Sophie turned, speechlessly, to the Duchess with tears streaming down her face, and was enfolded in a warm and comforting embrace.

'There, there, poor child,' said her Grace. 'There, there, my poor dear.'

'Oh, ma'am! Who could have done it?'

'Eh, it's a puzzle, isn't it?' exclaimed the Duke. 'D'you reckon it could have been thieves?'

'It seems a random rummy thing,' said young Turveytop, 'for every soul knew Uncle hadn't two bits to rub together. But thieves it must ha' been. The whole hut was ransacked and rummaged clear – every mortal stick and rag the old man possessed had been dragged out and either stolen or burnt. There wasn't a crumb or a button left in the place. Yon's where the bonfire must ha' been.'

And he stepped back, revealing a huge, blackened patch of grass behind the hut.

12

Simon opened his eyes with difficulty. He was aware, first of racking pains in all his joints; then that his head hurt. He moved and groaned.

'Hush up, then, your Grace, my dearie,' a voice exclaimed, just above his head. 'Hush up a moment while Nursie changes the bandage and then you'll be all right and tight.'

Simon hushed – indeed it was all he could do – and a pair of hands skilfully anointed his head with cool ointment and wound it in bandages. '*That's* better,' the voice said. 'Isn't it now, your Grace? Now old Nursie's going to rub you with oil of lavender to keep off the rheumatics – lucky those jobberknolls brought some on the last shipment or it would have had to be codliver oil which, say what you like, is *not* so pleasant.'

Without waiting for any reply the hands set to work, pummelling and massaging his aching body until he was ready to gasp with pain. But after a little he became used to the treatment, even found it lulling, and drifted asleep again. When he next woke he felt a great deal better. He raised himself on a elbow and looked about.

He was in a small, wooden, cabin-like room, one wall of which was almost enitrely window. The room was neatly and simply furnished and the floor was covered with rush matting. A wood fire in a stone fireplace hissed and gave off green flames from sea-wrack; the bunk in which Simon lay was covered with a patchwork quilt.

'I must be dreaming,' he muttered.

'Dreaming? Certainly not. Nobody dreams in my nurseries. Get this down you, now, my precious Grace.'

A firm arm hoisted him up and a cup was held to his lips. He choked over the drink, which was hot and had a strange, sweet, medicinal taste.

'What is it?'

' "What is it?" he asks. Doesn't know Nursie's own Saloop when he gets it! Best goat's milk, best Barbadoes (since those robbers won't bring me cane), best orris. You'll sleep easy after that, your Grace, lovey.'

While she straightened his pillows Simon for the first time succeeded in getting a look at the person who called herself Nursie. She was a plump, elderly woman, enveloped in a white starched apron. She had a cheerful, rather silly face, and a quantity of grey-brown hair which she wore in an untidy bun on top of her head.

'Where's Dido?' Simon suddenly asked.

"Di-do-diddely-oh. "Where's Dido?" he asks, and well he may. Where indeed, for there's nobody of that name on *this* island, to my certain knowledge.'

Simon's heart sank. 'It is an island, then? Are there others?'

'No, my duck diamond.'

'Where did you find me?'

'Out there,' she said, and lifted him so that he could see the sea. 'We had a tiddely breath of a blow, yesterday, and when the clouds lifted a bit Nursie looks out and what does she see? A lump of seaweed on a rock, she sees – only the seaweed has arms and legs and there never was seaweed on that rock before – so Nursie gets out the rowing-boat and rows across to have a look. And there's his blessed Grace lying up to the knees in water – another half-hour with the tide coming in and you'd ha' been gulls' meat.'

'Indeed I am very grateful,' said Simon faintly, 'but wasn't there also a little girl called Dido, wearing a blue dress?'

'No dearie,' she said quietly.

'I must go out and look for her – and Justin too – ' Simon exclaimed, struggling up. A spell of giddiness took him. With a disapproving cluck, Nursie laid him down again.

'Don't you worry your gracious head, my dearie. If the little girl's come to land, Nursie will know soon enough. The island's not so big. Why, there's only – '

Her words were interrupted by a timid knock at the door. She started.

'Well, there! Perhaps the boy *wasn't* dreaming. Unless it's the Hermit.'

The door opened and a damp, miserable figure tottered in: Justin, with his soaked clothes in rags and his draggled hair dripping over a cut on his forehead.

'Fancy!' said Nursie. 'If it isn't another of 'em. Well you *are* a drowned pickle, to be sure!'

'Justin!' said Simon eagerly. 'Have you seen Dido?'

'Oh, hilloo, Simon, are you there?'

Justin sank limply on to a wooden settle by the fire. 'Dido? No, I've not seen her.' He added listlessly, 'I dareseay she's drowned, if she hasn't turned up. *I* was, nearly. That wretched barrel broke on a rock. I think you might have found me something better.'

His words were muffled, for Nursie had seized a large towel, enveloped his head in it, and was rubbing his hair dry. No sooner had she finished, and combed the hair back from his face, then she let out a shriek.

'Justin! My own precious poppet! My little long-lost lamb! My bonny little bouncing blue-eyed babby!

She hugged Justin again and again.

'Hey!' protested Justin. 'Who do you think you are? *I* ain't your blue-eyed babby – I'm Lord Bakerloo!'

'Oh no, you ain't, my bubsy! You can't fool someone as has dandled you on her knee a thousand times. Why, I'd know that scar on your chin anywhere – that was where your pa dropped you in the fender – Eustace was always clumsy-handed – let alone you're as like him when he was young as two peas in a pod. And there's the mole on your neck and the bump on your nose – You're my own little Justin that I haven't seen since you was two years old.'

'I'm not, I tell you! I'm Lord Bakerloo!'

'Dearie, you can't be,' she said calmly. '*He's* Lord Bakerloo – him over there on the bunk – or the Dook o' Battersea if his uncle ain't living yet. How do I know? Because o' the Battersea Tuft – I found it on the back of his head, plain as plain, when I was bandaging that nasty great cut he's got.'

Battersea Tuft? What did the woman mean? Was she mad! Simon put his hand up to his bandaged head in perplexity, and winced as he touched a tender spot. What tuft?

'You must be dicked in the nob,' Justin persisted. 'Who are you, anyway?'

'Who am I, my precious? Why, I'm your own ma, Dolly Buckle, that's who I am, and you're my precious little Justin Sebastian Buckle! Where's your pa, then, all these years, what's he a-doing now? I'll lay *he's* feathered his nest. Always a cold, cunning schemer was Eustace Buckle, planning on next Sunday's joint before this one was fairly into the oven.'

'B-B-Buckle?' stammered Justin. 'You're trying

to tell me he's my *father*? Oh, what a piece of stuff! I *won't* believe it! My father was Lord Henry Bayswater.'

'Oh, no, he wasn't, dearie. And don't speak like that of Eustace. A good husband he may not have been, but a careful father he *was*. It was on account of that that I felt free to go off with Nat Dark (ah, and a snake-in-the-grass *he* turned out to be, dumping me on this island because he said I talked too much). Oh, no, Master Henry Bayswater wasn't your father – who should know better than I, as dandled his lordship on my knee? He had two children, Master Henry did, or so I did hear, off in them Hanoverian parts, two children, a boy and a girl. You,' she said to Simon, 'you must be the boy, my precious lordship. What's your name?'

'Simon,' he told her weakly.

'Simon? O' course it would be – after your dear ma. Simone, she was, Simone Rivière, Lady Helen Bayswater's daughter, and own cousin to her husband.'

'*What?* You mean I'm – But why should I – Oh, no, it can't be true,' said Simon, sinking back on his pillow.

'Of course it isn't true!' exclaimed Justin angrily.

Nursie, or Mrs Buckle, gave them a placid smile. 'You'll allow I ought to know,' she said. 'I as is ma to one of you, and was nurserymaid in the Castle when t'other one's pa was a boy, until the black day I married Eustace Buckle.'

'But I don't understand,' Simon said. 'If this mix-up happened – which I still can't believe – how did it come about?'

'Why, dearie, it's plain as plain. It's all along o' that scheming, artful Buckle. Always off on some plot or ploy, he was, leaving me lonesome with the babby. One time he goes off to Hanover. Well, my lad, thinks I, *I'm* off this time, too, so I goes on a cruise with Nat Dark.'

'Leaving *me*?' exclaimed Justin in a voice squeaky with indignation. 'Your own *child?*'

'Well, I couldn't take you on a ship, dearie. Puny little thing you were in those days. I left you in good care – with your pa's sister Twite. Ah, I never did care for that shovel-faced Ella Twite,' she added reflectively.

'So what happened?' Simon asked.

'Why, Nat Dark took a sudden dislike to me, dropped me on this island, and here I've been ever since. But what I'd guess happened to you is that Buckle got charge of Master Henry's children somehow –'

'Lord Henry died,' Simon put in. 'He and his wife both died in the Hanoverian wars.' It seemed strange to think he might be speaking of his own parents.

'Eh, the poor young things! That'll be it, then. Buckle took the children, managed to cast 'em off somewhere – the hard-hearted villain, *I'd* tell him what I thought of him – and handed his own babby over to his Grace at Chippings Castle. But what happened to your sister, I wonder?' she said to Simon.

'I think I can guess.'

'That Buckle, he's a deep one,' she pursued. 'Didn't he ever *tell* you he was your own father?' she asked Justin.

'No.' Justin looked sick, as if, against his own wishes, he found himself forced to believe the story.

'I'll lay he would have when you got to be Duke. *Then* he'd have been in the driver's seat. Eh, would you ever believe such wickedness? Now I daresay you can do with a bite to eat, and you too, your lordship.'

She bustled about, and presently fed them on ham and eggs.

'Mrs Buckle,' said Simon presently.

'Yes, my lovey? Call me Nursie, do, it sounds so comfortable.'

'Nursie, if Captain Dark left you on this island, what, fourteen years ago, how have you managed to live?'

'Eh, bless you, love, Nat Dark calls by from time to time on his way to Hanover with a load of flour, or a pig, or a couple of pullets. I'll say this for him, he's a considerate rogue. But he always lies half a mile offshore and floats the things in on a raft for fear I'd scratch his eyes out if I caught him.'

'I see,' Simon said. He guessed that, once the conspiracy was under way, both Mr Buckle and Captain Dark would have an interest in keeping the talkative Mrs Buckle marooned for fear she should spill the beans.

'Is there nobody else on the island?'

'Only one other.' Mrs Buckle began to laugh. 'Eh, he's a rum chap, if you like. I call him the Hermit. Captain Dark dropped him with the groceries last summer. I thought he'd be company, but, bless you! he's not one for a chat. Always painting he is. "Mrs Buckle," he says to me, "forgive me, but you're interrupting my train of thought." Eh, well, it takes all sorts to make a world.'

Simon was on his feet with excitement. After the meal of ham and eggs he felt much stronger, almost his own self again.

'Where is he? Is he far from here?'

'Bless the lad, no, nobbut up at top of hill. But mind those legs, now, lovey, you're full weak yet – '

Clucking distractedly Mrs Buckle followed Simon to the door, trying to fling a pea-jacket round his shoulders. He hardly noticed. Behind the cabin was a heathery slope, grazed by a few sheep and goats. He ran up it, found it led to another, and that to a third, which ended in a high crag. At the foot of the crag someone had built a small shack – someone was sitting outside it, wrapped in a cloak, sketching.

'Dr Field!' Simon shouted. 'Dr Field! Dr Field! It's me – Simon! Oh, Dr Field, I'm so glad to see you again! I thought I'd never, never find you!'

13

'Bless me,' said the Duke, 'you mean there was nothing left at all?'

He stepped into the charcoal-burner's hut. The door was half off its hinges. Inside, the place was bare; as the man had said, completely ransacked.

'But what about the little gal's bracelet, eh? Have you noticed a small silver bracelet anywhere, my man?'

'No, sir. Most likely the thieves'll have taken it,' said young Turveytop gloomily, but Sophie noticed him dart a sharp glance round the log walls, as if looking for possible hiding-places.

'I believe – ' she began, and then checked herself.

'Hark – what was that sound?' exclaimed the Duke.

Sophie turned her head, listening, and became very pale. Young Turveytop rushed to the door. The Duke, following, saw him dart across the clearing to where the open carriage stood, with the driver still in the box.

'Mizzle, you fool! Don't you know what that is?' Turveytop shouted at him, and threw himself on to one of the two carriage-horses, slashing at the traces with a knife. In a moment he had galloped off down the track; an instant later the driver had followed him on the other horse.

'Hey! Come back! Stop!' shouted the Duke.

'Good gracious! What very extraordinary behaviour! Sophie, what can be the meaning of it? Why have they taken our horses?'

Sophie cast a desperate glance round the open clearing. It was in a coign of the valley: on three sides the forest climbed steeply up an almost perpendicular slope. The fourth side, from which the baleful cry proceeded, was the way they had come.

'Sophie, child, why are you looking so anxious? What is the matter?'

'It is wolves, ma'am, and coming this way. We must take refuge in the hut until they are gone by,' Sophie said, trying to maintain a calm voice and appearance.

'Wolves? But . . . *Oh,* those craven wretches!' exclaimed the Duchess.

' 'Pon my soul! Have the men just made off and left us in the lurch? I shall write to *The Times* about this!'

'Please, ma'am – your Grace – *please* go into the hut!' Sophie was almost dancing with impatience; she practically pushed their Graces through the narrow doorway. The threatening, eager cry swelled louder and louder.

Sophie cast about for a weapon. The driver had gone off with his musket, but luckily some luggage had been fastened at the rear of the carriage. She seized a bunch of croquet mallets, a bag of billiard balls, and, as an afterthought, the Duchess's embroidery.

'Sophie! Make haste!' the Duchess called anxiously.

Sophie ran back to the hut, where the Duke was vainly trying to adjust the broken door.

'Infernal thing!' he muttered. 'Dangles kitty-cornerwise – any wolf could nip through the gap. Have you a notion how we could fix it, Sophie, my lass? Ah, croquet mallets, that was well thought of – those should keep the brutes at arms' length.'

'I think we can block the doorway – if your Grace would not object to my using your embroidery once again?'

'No, no, take it, take it by all means!' the Duchess cried distractedly.

Sophie quickly folded the massive piece of material into three and hung it over the door-hole, pegging it with slivers of wood into chinks in the log walls.

'What about the windows, my child?'

'My foster-father made them small and high on purpose,' Sophie said. 'Ah! Here come the wolves – you can hear the patter of their feet on the dead leaves – '

In spite of her calm and confident manner Sophie's heart beat frantically as the terrible howling swelled around the hut; it sounded like a hurricane of wolves. Soon the hut began to shake as wolves dashed themselves against the wooden walls. Sophie trembled for the precariously fastened tapestry, but the Duke, showing unwonted courage and resource, seized a pair of croquet mallets and stood guard behind it. Sometimes a shaggy head or a pair of glaring eyes appeared at the windows, but the Duchess and Sophie pelted these attackers with a vigorous rain of billiard balls until they dropped back again. Once a corner of the tapestry came loose as a wolf hurtled against it, and the front half of its body thrust into the room, with fangs bared and slavering tongue, but the Duke and Duchess fell upon it simultaneously and belaboured it with croquet mallets until it retreated, yelping, and Sophie with desperate haste pegged the tapestry back in position.

How long the battle continued it would be hard to say; it seemed an eternity to Sophie – an eternity of darting from point to point, hurling a ball at one window, reaching up with a mallet to thrust back an attacker at another or strike at a paw that had found foothold on the sill. There was never an instant's rest. But at last the wolves, many of them hurt, evidently decided that this quarry was not to be easily captured. The whole pack ran limping off into the forest; Sophie, on tiptoe at the window, saw them disappear down the track the way they had come.

For many minutes longer none of the three in the hut dared to hope that the wolves had gone for good, but they took advantage of the lull to rest; Sophie and the Duke leaned panting against the walls, while the Duchess sat plump down on the floor and fanned herself with the *Instructions for the Game of Billiards*.

'Sophie! Sophie!' she sighed. 'I do not know how it can be, but when we are with you we always contrive to run into such adventures!'

'Come, come, Hettie,' his Grace said gruffly. 'Admit that the lass always rescues us, too. It's thanks to Sophie we aren't vanishing down the gullets of twenty wolves at this instant. By Jehoshaphat, my child, you're a well-plucked 'un, and with your wits about you, too; you should ha' been a boy! I'd a thousand times sooner have you at my side in a pinch than that whey-faced Justin.'

'Thank you, your Grace.' Sophie curtsied absently, but her expression was worried. She knew they must not remain in the hut much longer, for the wolves might return, and night was not far distant.

Regardless of the Duchess's little shriek of dismay, she put aside the corner of the tapestry and slipped out of the hut. Many billiard balls were lying on the grass round about, and she hastily gathered up as many as would go into her skirt and passed them in to the Duke.

'Now, your Graces, I am going to run to the main road for help so do you, pray, peg up the tapestry again, and do not take it down until you hear me call.'

'But supposing you meet with a wolf, my child?'

'I'll make him regret the day he was born,' Sophie said grimly, taking another croquet mallet from the carriage. She picked up her skirts and ran like the wind. She met with no wolves along the path, but to her dismay, as she neared the turnpike, she began to hear a sound of howling and snarling, mixed with terrified whinnies. She collected a number of small rocks into her skirt and went on cautiously.

Coming round a thicket she saw that, although the main body of the wolf pack had evidently gone elsewhere, half a dozen stragglers remined and were attacking the baggage-coach which still stood in the road. The coachman and one of the horses was missing – it was plain that he had followed the example of his cowardly companion and made off.

The other three horses, half mad with fright, were rearing and striking out at the wolves with their hoofs. Sophie lost no time in coming to their aid.

'Shoo! You brutes!' she shouted in a loud angry voice. 'For shame! Leave the poor defenceless horses alone or it will be the worse for you! Attacking them when they are harnessed, indeed!' and she followed this up with a hail of rocks, several of which, at such close quarters, found their targets and effectually startled and scattered the wolves. Before they could recover, Sophie rushed among them, whirling the croquet mallet round and round, striking first one, then another, until she won her way through to the coach and jumped up on the box. There, to her delight, she

found the driver's blunderbuss, which in his fright he had forgotten to take. She discharged it among the wolves, and this completed their rout entirely; they made off at top speed. Sophie was so much amused at the doleful spectacle they presented as they fled that she burst out laughing, and then applied herself to soothing and making much of the three horses, who were sweating and trembling with fear.

After waiting a few moments to make sure the wolves did not return, Sophie mounted the leading horse, unfastened the traces, and made him gallop back along the track. Arriving at the clearing she harnessed him to the light carriage and called to their Graces to come quickly, for the way was clear.

When the Duchess saw that the wolves were indeed gone she embraced Sophie and allowed herself to be assisted into the carriage. The Duke followed, first taking down the tapestry from the doorway. 'For,' said he, 'it's odds but it will be needed to save our lives some other time.'

'Now, your Grace,' said Sophie, 'if you will but sit on the box with the blunderbuss, I've an errand that won't take a moment –'

'Oh, Sophie! *Pray* be careful!'

'It's quite all right, ma'am, I shan't be gone from your view.' And indeed, Sophie merely crossed the clearing to a huge hollow oak on the far side, and put her hand into a small cavity halfway up the trunk. She felt about carefully inside, and her face broke into a smile.

'Ah!' she said. 'I thought it was possible the thieves might not know about Turvey's hiding-place. He never kept his treasures in the hut, for fear of fire.'

She drew out a small bundle, wrapped in leather and tightly fastened. Handing it up to the Duchess, she jumped into the carriage and took the blunderbuss from the Duke, who shook up the reins. The affrighted horse needed no urging to leave the clearing, where the odour of wolf was still strong.

The Duchess, meanwhile, was exclaiming over Sophie's find, as she tried to undo the leather fastenings. 'Only imagine its still being there. How clever of you to have remembered the place, Sophie dear! And how strange that Turveytop's nephew was not aware of it!'

'*That* wasn't his nephew!' Sophie said scornfully. 'Turvey never had a nephew.'

'That man was not his nephew? Who was he, then?'

'One of the thieves, I daresay, come back to have another hunt round. That was probably why he was so quick to make off.'

'The wretch!' exclaimed his Grace in strong indignation.

As they had now reached the turnpike again, Sophie busied herself with unharnessing the horse and setting him back in the shafts of the baggage-coach. This, being enclosed, would be the safer conveyance in which to complete their journey.

Sophie offered to drive, but the Duke, who had been a famous whipster in his youth, pooh-poohed this suggestion, telling her that she had done quite enough fire-eating for the time, and must now sit inside, rest, and prevent her Grace from falling into a fit of the vapours which might afflict her when she reflected on the perils they had passed through.

Her Grace at the moment was far from thinking of vapours; she was still eagerly tugging at the knotted leather thongs of the little packet. 'How provokingly tight they are fastened! I am so impatient to see what is inside this little bundle, Sophie dear!'

Sophie, remembering the old man's treasures, watched with rather a sad smile. At last the knots were undone and the contents poured into the Duchess's lap. Her Grace stared at them, somewhat dismayed: instead of gold or jewels, they consisted of a knotted root, shaped like a fist, some quartz pebbles, a few dried-up flowers and berries, a stone with a hole in it, and a sprig of white heather.

'But the bracelet?' exclaimed her Grace.

'Here it is, ma'am.' And Sophie, with gentle fingers, delved to the bottom of the little heap and brought out something so black and tarnished that it might easily have been thrown away as rubbish.

'Mercy! Is that silver? It does not look like the second-best dinner service,' the Duchess said, eyeing it doubtfully.

'Indeed it is silver, ma'am, and when I have polished it with hartshorn and spirits of wine you will be surprised at the difference,' Sophie replied briskly, to cover the slight catch in her voice at the thought of the kind old man who had kept her treasure so carefully.

Fortunately both hartshorn and spirits of wine were at hand, since the Duchess never travelled without them for fear of a faint, so for the next twenty minutes, while the Duke drove them along at a fast canter, Sophie occupied herself with vigorous polishing.

'Now, ma'am, tell me if it is not much improved,' she said at last, and held up a slender shining chain, at the end of which dangled a little shield. The Duchess took it with trembling hands. On one side of the shield the name SOPHIE was engraved; on the other side was a coat-of-arms between two names so tiny that it was impossible to read them.

'My quizzing-glass – where is it? Quickly, child! Why, that is the Battersea coat-of-arms!'

'Can you read the names, ma'am?' said Sophie, trembling.

'Wait a minute, wait – I can nearly see – this coach rocks about so – H – E – N – Hen – what is that next letter, can it be an R? Why yes, Henry! *Henry Bayswater!*' the Duchess read out in an astonished voice. 'And *Simone Rivière!* Sophie! My child! My own dear husband's dead brother's long-lost child!'

And she enfolded Sophie in a suffocating embrace.

'But ma'am,' Sophie said in a dazed voice. 'Do you mean to say – How can this be?'

'Oh,' said the Duchess impatiently, 'depend upon it, it is somehow the fault of that wretched, careless Buckle. I *thought* it had been said that Henry and Simone had two children, but Buckle, when he came back from Hanover with the baby, swore the girl had died. In reality, I suppose, he lost you in the forest on the way to Chippings and was ashamed to confess. Only fancy, so you are Justin's sister! I declare, you look a thousand times more like the family than he does. No wonder you resemble the girl in the picture – she was your mother, Simone.'

'Simone?' said Sophie, thinking hard. 'That was my mother's name? And she had two children, a boy and a girl? Do you know, ma'am, I believe that Justin is *not* my brother – I believe I know who my brother is –'

The two of them had been so absorbed by their discoveries that they had not noticed the coach draw to a halt.

'Well, my lady,' the Duke said, putting his head in at the window, 'do you mean to stay chattering all day, or had you not observed that we've reached Chippings and our good Mrs Gossidge is waiting to welcome us?'

'But I'm *that* put about, your Graces,' declared Mrs Gossidge, a pleasant, rosy-faced woman, dropping a whole series of curtseys, 'for, the weather being so bad, and not knowing your Graces was on the way, I've nothing fit to put on the table, bar a singed sheep's head and a dish of chitterlings – but there! I see you've brought Sophie with you, so I daresay she'll turn to and help me, having a light hand with the paste, if she hasn't learnt too many grand London ways.'

'Put anything before us that you've got,' said his Grace good-humouredly, 'for we are devilish sharp-set – your singed sheep's head will do famously. Is Master Justin here?'

'No, your Grace, why, should he be?' Mrs Gossidge looked bewildered. 'Isn't he with your Grace, then? Mogg! Hold the horse still, do! And Sophie, bustle about then, girl! Take up her ladyship's things and then come and help me in the kitchen!'

'Wait a minute, Gossidge, wait –' the Duchess called. 'Miss Sophie isn't – William! Only think what we have discovered –'

But Sophie, twinkling at her Grace, had jumped down and run upstairs with a load of knitting-wools, while the Duke had hurried off to the stables, and Mrs Gossidge had vanished to re-singe the sheep's head and get out all her jars of preserved whortleberries.

14

After three days on the island of Inchmore, Justin was a changed boy. He declared that he had never had such prime fun before, that he would like to stay on an island for the rest of his life 'out of reach of old Buckle, with his prosings and preachings about the duties of Dukes'. He added:'I'd sooner have my ma, any day. She's a one-er, ain't she, Simon? And as for being a lord, now I've thought it over I reckon it's a mug's lay; I never liked it above half, and that's the truth. You're welcome to the life, Simon – Buckle and all. I'm only sorry Buckle's my pa. I'd as lief there was no connection.'

Simon thanked Justin absently for his good wishes. The island air did not appear to have done Simon so much good as it had Justin; he was thin and pale, and Mrs Buckle clucked over him concernedly. He had, in fact, spent most of the three days in a vain search of the island for Dido, assisted by Dr Field.

'Oh, she'll be as right as a trivet somewhere, I dare-say,' Justin asserted, and Mrs Buckle said comfortably:

'Now, don't you worry, my dearie. Depend on it, any child of that tight-fisted, stony-hearted Ella

Twite will be all right – she'll fall on her feet, you may lay.'

But on the afternoon of the fourth day, when Simon was once again scouring the rocky, cliff-fringed beach, he found, washed ashore, the very broken spar with ropes tied to it which he and Dido had used to help them swim to the rock.

Now hope was dead indeed. Simon stood staring at the spar for a long time, as if he expected it to speak and tell him what had happened. Justin, who had come running up to exclaim over it, checked himself, and Dr Field quietly drew him away. Simon turned and walked off along the shore at top speed as if he hardly knew where he was going.

'Eh, dearie dear!' said Mrs Buckle distressfully. 'Young folks allus takes things so hard. Poor lad. Poor lad. I daresay the little lass was nothing much, wi' those parents — Still, I'm sorry I said what I did about Ella Twite. Shouldn't you go after him, Dr Field?'

'Best leave him to get over it by himself,' Dr Field said, looking after Simon with concern on his kind face.

Simon was gone a long time; he made the complete circuit of the island, and did not return to Mrs Buckle's until the rising tide and gathering dark warned him that he must delay no longer. It was bitterly cold; a few flakes of snow stung against his face, and the foam-wreaths on the sand were beginning to be crisp with frost.

As he approached Mrs Buckle's hut, crunching over the shingle, Justin ran out and caught hold of his arm.

'Hurry, Simon! There's another ship in! Mrs Buckle says it's *Dark Dimity* – putting in beyond the headland. They've lowered a boat!'

'Ah, there you are, Simon, my boy!' Dr Field was as excited as Justin. 'I was about to come in search of you. It's best we all stay together. I daresay the scoundrels want to ask for news of *Dark Dew*. Maybe we can somehow turn this to our advantage. Do you boys hide behind a rock, for they don't know you're here. Mrs Buckle, come with me.'

He strode down to the landing-place – a natural rock jetty shelving into deep water – and the boys crouched down in the dusk, listening to the splash of oars.

While they searched for Dido, Dr Field and Simon had exchanged their stories. Simon learned that, as he had guessed, Dr Field had overheard the conspirators in Rose Alley discussing a scheme to murder the Duke of Battersea by setting fire to his opera-box. Full of indignation, he had rushed impetuously into their midst, shouting, 'Traitors! Assassins! Miserable wretches!' and had been outnumbered, overpowered, and haled off to the *Dark Dew*, which happened to be in port at the time.

'I suppose I was lucky to be marooned on Inchmore and not tied into a parcel and dropped into the river off Wapping Stairs,' he remarked. 'But I should soon have become devilish bored here – the light in winter isn't good for painting. And Mrs Buckle, kind soul though she is, I find beyond anything tedious. I've been longing for a chat with old Furneaux or a game of chess with the Duke. Only fancy your being his nephew, Simon – though I thought all along you must be related, as soon as I had a sharp look at that Rivière painting. I'm glad to hear you've cleaned it, by the way. Bless me – ' he burst out laughing – 'bless me, what a shock it must have been to Buckle and the Twites when, no sooner had they got rid of me, than you turned up – an orphan from the Poor Farm at Loose Chippings, spit image of Simone Rivière, *and* with a gift for painting. Of course they knew I was expecting a boy, but they couldn't have known who you'd turn out to be.'

'There's Sophie, too,' Simon said. 'I hope she's not in dreadful danger. If Buckle realizes . . . We must get back as soon as we possibly can. Who knows what may be happening while we are here?'

Now the boys could hear the creak of oars in rowlocks, and there came a hail from the boat.

'Is that you, Field? Stand where we can see you and keep your arms raised above your head, or you'll get a dose of medicine you don't like and it'll take the form of lead! You too, Mrs Buckle! We want you to answer some questions.'

'Oh, Elijah Murgatroyd!' quavered Mrs Buckle. 'How can you be so wicked, threatening a poor defenceless woman with one o' them horrid guns. Put it away, now, do! Guns are never allowed in my nurs – '

'Stow your gab, Dolly Buckle!' the voice said, sounding more human. 'Now then, Dr Field, speak up, Has the *Dark Dew* put in here this week?'

'If we tell you, will you give us a passage to the mainland?'

'Not on your Oliphant! Captain Dark would have my guts for garters if I did.'

'No he wouldn't,' Dr Field said calmly 'The *Dark Dew* went down with all hands in the storm four days ago. Burnt out – the crew were drunk at the time – split on a rock, and broke up.'

'Is that the truth?' The voice sounded incredulous.

'True as I stand here.'

Simon heard a muttered discussion in the dinghy: 'Reckon it *could* be the truth, Cap'n Murgatroyd?' '*Could* be – dear knows there's enough liquor and loose-screws aboard *Dark Dew* – if it ain't, where in tarnation *is* the brig!' 'Dolly Buckle may have thought up this tale.' 'Maybe. I'm not taking any chances yet, that's suttin. Dr Field!' the voice went on.

'Well?'

'Have you any remedies for quinsy?'

'Quinsy? I ususally give ipecac – ' Then the doctor checked himself and asked instead: 'Who has quinsy?'

'Two of my men on board have it, mortal bad.'

'You'd best let me look at them,' Dr Field said, while in the same breath Mrs Buckle cried, 'Beef tea, beaten egg in hot milk, and cocoa! Oh, the poor fellows, lying sick on that nasty ship without a woman's care! Let me aboard to nurse 'em, Elijah, do!'

Captain Murgatroyd and his mate conferred in low tones. Presently Murgatroyd said, 'No harm if you come aboard for the night, I suppose. We was going to heave-to till tomorrow anyway. But no nonsense, mind! You're not coming away with us. Dolly Buckle can make a quart or so o' beef tea and cocoa, and that'll last the men till they're better.'

'I'd best dose you all while I'm at it,' Dr Field said. 'Quinsy is highly infectious. I'll have to get my medicines.'

One of the men accompanied Dr Field, the other assisted Mrs Buckle to carry eggs, goats' milk, and spirits of rhubarb to the dinghy. Presently it pulled away with its cargo and the two boys stole back to Mrs Buckle's hut and settled down for the night; Justin to sleep peacefully, Simon to toss and turn in wakeful misery, thinking of Sophie and Dido.

Early next morning he rose and looked out. A thin snow was falling and beginning to lie on heather and rocks. *Dark Dimity* was still anchored in the bay, and a dinghy was pulling towards the shore. Unsurprised, he saw that its sole occupant was Dr Field. Simon woke Justin and the two boys ran to the jetty.

'Doped the lot of 'em,' said Dr Field, grinning cheerfully as he shipped his oars and indicated two men sprawled on the bottom boards. 'They're all sleeping like babies. Help me get these beauties ashore and then we'll go back for some more.'

'How did you do it?' Simon asked.

'A species of seaweed that's common on the rock here is a powerful soporific. I ate some myself one month, when Dark was a bit slow bringing the groceries; put me into a deep sleep for two days; Mrs Buckle thought I'd stuck my spoon in the wall. Woke up feeling fit as a fiddle, though. So I dried and powdered a lot; thought it would come in useful if ever I got back into practice. Yes, that's right, drag them into the hut.'

'Won't they be surprised to wake up and find we've

gone off and left 'em!' giggled Justin, delighted at the neatness and simplicity of the plan. He helped Simon ferry over the rest of *Dark Dimity's* crew, two by two, with a few supplies. 'We must be humane, after all,' Dr Field said. 'We'll tell the Preventives about them when we land, and they can come and fetch 'em to jail.'

Mrs Buckle, meanwhile scandalized at the disreputable condition of the ship, had been scrubbing decks and polishing brasswork; she would even have attempted to wash and mend the dirty, ragged sails had there been any soap, and had not Dr Field dissuaded her.

'There'll be work enough sailing the ship to land,' he warned her. 'I've kept the two men with quinsy, they're still too weak to give trouble. They can take it in turns steering while the boys and I handle the sails, if you'll keep guard over them with a gun, Mrs Buckle.'

'What, me touch one o' them nasty things? I'd as lief blow my head off!'

But when she found it was not loaded and was to be used merely as a threat, Mrs Buckle agreed. The *Dark Dimity,* being on the return journey from Hanover, was loaded down to her marks with pistols, Pictclobbers, gunpowder, and bullets.

The two sufferers from quinsy quailed at the sight of Mrs Buckle nervously waving a blunderbuss, and were only too anxious to obey Dr Field's orders, the more so when he told them they should go free if the *Dark Dimity* arrived safely at the port of Chipping Fishbury.

Shortly after noon the *Dark Dimity* weighed anchor, with one of the two invalids steering while Dr Field and the boys worked the capstan. As the brig left the shelter of the island her sails slowly filled with wind. They had all been too busy to notice the weather, but now Simon realized that it was snowing fast; the flakes streamed past him in ribbons of white, blown by a knife-edged wind from the north-east. When he looked back, presently, from his perch in the rigging, for they had already found it necessary to reef some sails, he saw that Inchmore was no more than a white bump amid the threatening waves.

'It's a good thing we built up the fire before we left,' Dr Field said. 'Those men are going to be feeling cold by the time they wake up. This wind is exactly what we need; we can run before it all the way to Chipping Fishbury.'

He rubbed his hands in satisfaction, stamping his feet on the snow-covered deck to warm them. 'Mrs Buckle! I don't think those two men will give any trouble now. How about putting your blunderbuss away and going to the galley to make us all some of your excellent hot beef tea?'

15

A huge fire blazed cheerfully in the nobly-proportioned fireplace of Chippings Castle Great Hall. Beside it the Duchess dozed in an oak settle, surrounded by her embroidery. Occasionally she woke and put a stitch or two into the tapestry.

Upstairs, in an attic leading on to the Castle battlements, the Duke was happily occupied with one of his experiments – something to do with air-balloons. After the last few weeks of excitement – rescues by land and water, peril of fire, drowning, and wolves, not to mention the loss of a nephew and the discovery of an unexpected niece – his Grace was badly in need of peace and solitude.

Sophie, seated at the fireside opposite the Duchess, also appeared to be peacefully engaged, in mending the Duke's socks, but her thoughts were not peaceful. She was anxious and miserable, longing to be back in London. The party had now been at Chippings for three weeks, but still Justin had not turned up. Everybody here was kind and faithful, she was sure, and the Duke and Duchess were safe, but Sophie felt dreadfully isolated. She wanted to know what had happened in Rose Alley. What had become of Simon, Justin, and Dido?

It had been snowing now for two days, there were reports that the wolves on the wolds were becoming very bold, and Sophie feared greatly that the Castle might be cut off from all news for weeks and weeks – perhaps until spring.

As if to give emphasis to her thoughts, a baleful howling arose outside, and the stabled horses neighed and stamped in fear. Sophie shivered, threw a log on the fire, and went to look out of the window, but although it was hardly more than mid-afternoon the day was so dim with whirling snow that she could see nothing.

The Duchess nodded, yawned, and opened her eyes. 'What was that noise, Sophie dear?'

'I'm afraid it was wolves, ma'am.'

'Oh dear me, wolves so early? I suppose that means we shall not be getting the evening paper from York,' her Grace said dolefully. But just then they heard a fusillade of shots, a tremendous jingling of sleigh-bells, and, almost immediately, an urgent tattoo of knocks upon the great door of the Castle.

Sophie ran to the door, but old Mogg the steward was before her.

'All right, all right,' he grumbled, letting down the massive bars. 'Leave a bit of t'door standing, cansta? We doosn't want t'wolves taborin' in and setting by her Grace's fire – '

'And we don't want the wolves biting off our breeches pockets while you fiddle with the bolt!' shouted an impatient voice.

'Naay, that's nivver t'paper boy?'muttered Mogg, scratching his head. 'Happen t'wolves got him and yon's t'replacement? Or could it be woon o' they doddy travellin' salesmen? Ye can coom in, but coom in slow and careful, for if ye're a highwayman I'll shoot ye full o' gravel chips,' he warned, and pulled an ancient pistol out of his green baize apron pocket. He stepped back from the door, which burst open, allowing four people and a wolf to surge into the hall. The wolf was chased out again, with kicks and curses. Sophie let out a joyful shriek:

'*Simon!* You're *safe*! Oh, how glad I am to see you. And Justin too – their Graces will be so relieved. Ma'am, ma'am, see who's here!'

'What about the evening paper?' grumbled Mogg, but nobody heeded him amid the cries of wonder, relief, and joy. Sophie was hugging Simon, the Duchess was simultaneously patting Justin's head and shaking hands with Dr Field, though rather puzzled as to how he came to be with the party.

'Why, if that beant Dolly Buckle!' old Mogg suddenly ejaculated. 'Eh, Dolly, ma lass, 'tis a rare long year since we've seen thee here! Wheer's 'a bin, lass?' Then his jaw dropped and he gaped at Simon, whom he had only just noticed. 'And who's *thon?* Why, t'lad's the dead spit of Mester Henry as died in Hanover!'

'Who is he?' shrilled Mrs Buckle.

'Who is he? Why, use your wits, Matthew Mogg. Who should he be but his young lordship?'

'Nay,' said Mogg obstinaely, '*yon's* his young lordship, Mester Justin there. Nobbut skin and gristle, granted, but he's bahn to be lordship for all that.'

'Him? He's my Justin that I never thought I'd rear, aren't you my lovey?'

Justin looked slightly embarrassed and sidled away from his mother's embrace. 'But as for Master Simon,' she went on, 'he's Family, not a doubt of it, for he's got the Battersea Tuft.'

'Tuft, sitha? Let's see, then, lad. Kneel down on t'flagstones, tha be's such a beanpole.' Rather puzzled Simon submitted to the old man's parting the thick black locks on the back of his head, where Mogg evidently found what he expected, for he cried, 'Eh, tha's reet, Dolly, my woman! To think that I should see the day! Eh, your Grace, tak' a look at this!'

'Why, what a curious thing!' the Duchess

remarked. 'A little tuft of white hair among the black, precisely like the one my husband had before all his hair turned white. Is that the Battersea Tuft?'

'Indeed it is, ma'am,' Mrs Buckle cried. 'All the Battersea babies have had it.'

'Then Sophie must have it too – Sophie, child, kneel down!'

Sophie, laughing, allowed Mrs Buckle to uncoil the plaits of her long dark hair and discover the little white tuft on the back of her head. 'I never knew it was there myself!' she said.

The Duchess was looking from Simon to Sophie and back, declaring in wonder:

'I do not believe I have any eyes at all! Why did I never notice the likeness before? Of course they are brother and sister! Why, they are as like as one

guinea to another. We must tell his Grace the news at once!'

'He's in the attic,' Sophie said, and she ran from the room. As she darted up the winding stair she wondered what troubles Simon had been through to make him look so pale and haggard. She had asked where Dido was, and he had answered: 'I can't tell you here,' in an undertone, and with a look that went to her heart. Poor Simon! Poor Dido! What could have become of her?

Sophie knocked on the attic door and ran into his grace's workroom, which was full of a general mess of scientific apparatus lying strewn over several large tables. The Duke was not there, but the outer door on to the battlements was open and gusts of snow were blowing in.

'Your Grace! Uncle William?' Sophie called. 'Are you there?' She peered through the open door into the snowy dark. A lighted lantern stood on the leads and there were footprints in the snow, but she did not see the Duke until she looked up.

'Mercy!' she exclaimed.

A pair of legs was dangling just above her. Peering past through the fluttering snowflakes, Sophie could just see the outline of an extremely large air-balloon above her head; it was rising and tugging his Grace upward as he clung to it with one hand, while with the other he held on to the guttering of the attic roof.

'*Your Grace!* Oh, pray take care!' Sophie gasped. She pulled at his legs with all her strength, and then, discovering a dangling rope, ran it through a staple evidently intended for mooring, and dragged the balloon and its passenger back to safety.

'Ah, thank you, Sophie, my child,' said the Duke, wiping off the snowflakes which had settled on his hair and eyebrows. 'I was just wondering how much longer I could hang on. The mooring-rope slipped out of my fingers after I had pumped in the air. Have you made it fast? Capital. Is it not an excellent balloon? I am delighted with my work; quite delighted. It surpasses all my expectations as to buoyancy.'

'Yes, indeed, it's beautiful,' Sophie said, dragging his Grace indoors as if she feared that he, too, might take off into the night air. 'Only think, Uncle William, Simon is here – and Justin, and Dr Field, and Mrs Buckle! Simon has the Battersea Tuft, which proves he is my brother and your nephew, and Justin is Mrs Buckle's son – oh, it is all most complicated.

And I am sure they have had *such* adventures. Do, pray, come and hear all about it!'

The Duke looked quite bewildered by this stream of news, all delivered at top speed, but he permitted Sophie to pull him down the winding stairs and into the Great hall.

In no time the whole party were sitting down to crimped fish, pickled cockles, venison and whortleberry pies, and a huge platter of spiced parkin. While they ate, Sophie and the Duchess bombarded Simon and Dr Field with questions, and each told his tale; Mrs Buckle put in explanations until the whole story of Buckle's plot and the Hanoverian conspiracy was made plain. Sophie then recounted how she had heard Buckle disclose his intentions to poison the Duke as soon as Justin returned.

Justin, who had been looking more and more miserable and apprehensive as the tales were told, revealing him as the unwitting tool of all this villainy, now broke down altogether and fairly boo-hooed.

'None of it's my fault,' he howled. 'I never asked to be swapped as a babby, and prosed and preached at and made into a Duke! Oh, boo-hoo, n-nobody likes me and I shall be t-turned out into the snow to starve! I wish I was back on Inchmore with my ma, I do!'

The Duchess exclaimed warmly:

'*Nonsense,* Justin dear. Nobody thinks of putting you out in the snow. Nobody blames you for what you didn't know about – I am sure we all pity you for having such a thoroughly unpleasant father. You can go back to Inchmore if you wish, next summer

– in winter I am sure it must be most disagreeable and you had best stay here at Chippings with your mother, who has kindly agreed to help Mrs Gossidge with the housekeeping. Now, stop crying and do not be such a great gaby! Mrs Buckle, perhaps he is over-tired and should be put to bed.'

'Indeed he should, your Grace. I declare I'm ashamed of him,' exclaimed his mother, and whisked him away, crying, 'Come along, my ducky, do, and don't make such a show of yourself, my precious lambkin, or Ma will be obliged to give you two Gregory's powders and a spoonful of calomel. Look at Simon. *He's* not crying!'

Simon looked pale and heavy-eyed, however, as the Duchess noticed with kindly concern. Dr Field quickly finished the tale of their adventures: they had turned *Dark Dimity* over to the Preventives at Chipping Fishbury, the two recovered sufferers from quinsy had been allowed to ship as deck-hands on a collier going south, and, learning that the Duke was at Chippings, the rest of the party had come straight there in a hired sleigh, only slightly hindered by wolves on the way.

The Duke looked quite bewildered at this tale – he always found it hard to take in many new ideas all at once – and as everybody was fatigued with emotion and excitement they decided to go to bed and leave the discussion of plans till the next day.

All night the snow fell steadily, and by the morning it lay five feet deep in the Castle court, and the drifts were three times the height of a man. From the embrazured windows nothing could be seen but a white wilderness in which the trees seemed to be standing waist-deep. But at dawn a pale sun rose, drawing brilliant sparkles from the icicles on the branches.

'Now,' said Dr Field, who was sitting with the Duke and Duchess at a late breakfast, 'we have only two problems.'

'What are they?' asked Sophie, pouring his chocolate. She already felt a great confidence in his practical sense.

'You say that Cobb sent the Bow Street Runners round to Rose Alley?'

'Yes, but I fear they will have found nothing. The Twits had been warned by Jem.'

'There has been nothing about it in the papers,' the Duchess put in.

'Neither Mr Cobb nor the Bow Street Officers knew that Buckle was involved?'

'No, for I overhead him plotting with Midwink *after* Mr Cobb went to Bow Street.'

'So Buckle at present thinks himself secure, and knows nothing of the loss of *Dark Dew* and *Dark Dimity*. Our two problems are to discover where the Hanoverians now keep their arms, and to reach London fast enough to take them by surprise.'

'I have a very good notion of where the Hanoverians now put their arms,' the Duke said. 'Just before we left, Buckle asked me if he might house his fossil collection in the Battersea Castle vaults. I said I had no objection, and gave him the key.'

'Of course!' exclaimed Sophie. 'That's why Midwink said, "They'll never think of looking there."

You can enter the vaults from the tunnel, can you not? They could move the things in with very little risk of being seen.'

'And as for travelling to London,' pursued the Duke. 'I have the most suitable equipage upstairs that could be devised – a strong, commodious, elegant air-balloon, capable of carrying at least eight persons and their luggage for hundreds of miles. Simon, my boy, which way does the wind blow?'

Simon, who had been gazing out of the window, deep in sorrowful reverie, jumped at being addressed, but replied readily enough, 'It still blows from the north, your Grace.'

'Nothing could be more convenient. I have been working on a steering-device for the balloon, but I am not yet fully satisfied with it. A north wind, however, should blow us straight to London.'

'Travel in a balloon!' exclaimed the Duchess, aghast. 'William! Are you out of your mind? We should all be killed – blow away to the South Pole – starve – freeze to death – crash to the ground – stick in a tree – *oh*, the very idea gives me the vapours!'

'Nonsense, Hettie,' said the Duke impatiently, as Sophie administered hartshorn and fanned the palpitating Duchess, 'we shall be famously snug. We can take up a brazier to keep us warm, besides fur rugs and such gear, food, amusements, knitting, and so forth; then, if we want to descend, why, we merely pull the cord, let out the air, and slowly deflate the balloon. It's as simple as kiss your hand!'

Dr Field was delighted at this plan.

'Besides,' the Duke pursued, 'have you forgotten

the mince-pie ceremony on Christmas Eve? It is our loyal duty to be back for that.'

'What is the mince-pie ceremony, your Grace?' inquired Dr Field. 'And where does it take place?'

'Why, you see,' explained the Duke, 'it is the hereditary duty of our family to furnish the King with mince-pies, and the presentation takes place at Battersea Castle on Christmas Eve. In fact we have the King to dinner, serve some mince-pies at table, and give him a wash-basket of 'em to take away afterwards, while the trumpeters blow a special tune called the Battersea Fanfare. If we start today – it's five days to Christmas – we ought to arrive in nice time for the ceremony.'

Sophie, Simon, and Dr Field looked at one another in dismay. With such a nest of vipers hiding under its roof, Battersea Castle seemed the most dangerous place in the world to invite King James III for a mince-pie dinner. Would there be time to clear out the Hanoverian conspirators beforehand?

'I daresay Buckle knows nothing about this ceremony?' Dr Field said at last, hopefully.

'Pshaw, my dear fellow, he has made all the arrangements for years. Besides which, I wrote him by carrier pigeon last week, reminding him to have the mince-pies baked in good time.'

'This complicates matters,' said Dr Field, scratching his head. 'As your Grace has pointed out, we must get going at once. We shall need plenty of food, charcoal, telescopes, a weapon or two – '

'Dominoes, playing-cards, spillikins, billard-balls,' noted Sophie, ticking them off on her fingers. 'Thank goodness, at least we need not fear wolves in a balloon – '

'But suppose there should be eagles!' cried the Duchess fearfully. 'Oh, William! Need we really travel in this dreadful apparatus? I shall be unwell. I *know* I shall be unwell!'

'Smelling-salts, hartshorn, spirits of wine,' Sophie noted down.

'And, Sophie, my dear, whatever else you put in, pray do not forget your Aunt Henrietta's embroidery!'

16

Four days later, on Christmas Eve, the great rose-coloured balloon was drifting over the wooded heights of Hampstead.

Sophie, paying little attention to the snow-covered landscape as it passed slowly by beneath, was busily engaged with making a Court dress for the Duchess to wear at the mince-pie ceremony; she sat in a whirlpool of apricot-coloured velvet, which she was embroidering with topazes. Sometimes the Duke raised his head from the chessboard to say with a chuckle:

'Bless me, Sophie, m'dear, it's fortunate that I built the car as big as I did; any smaller and, with all that stuff of yours some of the passengers would have had to hang over the side!'

In fact, the wicker, galleon-shaped car, with its high-decked ends and low waist, was excellently adapted to their needs. Dr Field and the Duke played chess at the forecastle end, Simon steered on the poop, directing the balloon's progress, when necessary, by means of a pair of dangling ropes, while Sophie with her dressmaking and the Duchess with her Patience occupied the central portion.

One night, when all the others were sleeping, snug under furs and sheepskin rugs, Simon had told Sophie the whole sad story of Dido's end, and his own grief and remorse that he had not been awake to stop her from trying to swim to shore.

'For I am sure that is what happened, and I should have saved her, Sophie.'

'You must not think in that way, Simon dear, for it is wrong,' Sophie said, affectionately clasping his hands. 'You could do no more than you did – Mrs

Buckle has told me how ill you were. And – do you know? – somehow I cannot be sure that Dido is drowned. Somehow I believe that she is not.'

'Why, Sophie, what else could have happened?'

'Oh, I do not know – perhaps a ship could have rescued her. I feel in my bones that we shall hear of her again. So do not grieve too much. You did all you could for her and were a deal kinder to her, I am sure, than any of her miserable family.'

This talk with Sophie cheered Simon a great deal.

It was decided that when they reached London Simon should instantly repair to Chelsea Barracks, to enlist the help of the Yeomanry against the conspirators, while Dr Field escorted the Duke and Duchess to Battersea Castle.

'For Buckle will scarcely try any of his villainy so long as he remains uncertain of Justin's whereabouts,' he pointed out.

Justin had been offered a ride to London in the balloon, but had refused with horror; a sea-voyage was quite bad enough, he declared. He was to remain at Loose Chippings with his mother, who would only come to London if it was needful to give evidene against her infamous husband.

'I will tell Dr Furneaux and the students that we are back, also,' Simon suggested. 'They are all good fellows who enjoy a fight and, being so close to the Castle, they will be handy in case of trouble.'

'You could arm them,' Sophie observed, biting off a thread. She had completed the Duchess's gown and was now finishing one for herself: white tissue with gold ribbons. 'If Uncle William has a spare key to the

Castle vaults on him, they could let themselves in and take some of the Hanoverians' Pictclobbers.'

This sensible plan won instant approval and the spare key was handed to Simon.

The travellers were fortunate in the timing of their arrival over London. Snow had been falling all day, but towards dusk the clouds dispersed, drawing away westwards in great high-piled crimson masses across which the balloon drifted south, inconspicuous against such a flaming background.

'We shall be able to take Buckle by surprise,' Dr Field said with satisfaction. 'Good heavens,' he added, looking down at the snow-covered city of London sprawling beneath them, pink in the sunset glow, 'wolves in Hyde Park already – before Christmas! I fear it is going to be a hard winter. Best prime your pistols, Simon; if they have reached Hyde Park they may have reached Battersea Park; you may have to dash for it.'

Soon they saw the Thames: a shining ribbon of ice that curled its way between Chelsea and Lambeth.

'There's Chelsea Hospital,' Sophie said.

'Dear me! I had best reduce the pressure.' The Duke gave a tug to the string which released the valve; some air escaped, and the balloon's silken globe sank, crinkling and quivering, until they were barely above the rooftops.

'Oh, William! Pray take care!'

'I know what I am about, my dear,' his Grace said testily.

In fact the Duke had misjudged his landing a little, but this turned out to be just as well, for he had proposed to alight in Battersea Park, which was full of wolves. Instead, the balloon came to rest in Mr Cobb's yard, where the proprietor was alone, greasing the runners of a high-perch phaeton sleigh.

'Weel I'll be drawed sideways!' he exclaimed. 'If that ain't the neatest rig I ever did see! Simon, me boy! Well I *am* pleased to see you! We'd given you up for lost, indeed we had – thought the wolves must 'a got you. And his Grace! And her Grace! And little Miss Sophie! Floss!' he bawled up the stairs, 'here's our boy Simon back, safe and stout, wi' all the Castle gentry! It be a proud day when your Graces sets foot in my yard!'

He helped the Duke and Duchess down, while Mrs Cobb and Libby with the kitten in her arms came marvelling out to gaze at the great rose-coloured bubble that had settled by their front steps.

'Thank'ee, thank'ee, Cobb, my man,' the Duke said. 'We should be greatly obliged if you could let us have a conveyance to take us to the Castle.'

'Why, your Graces can have thisyer phaeton sleigh. It's as sweet a little goer as ever slid, and I've a beautiful pair o' match greys, won't take but a moment to put them to. But that balloon! Dang me if that don't beat cock-fighting, that do! I'll soon be in a new line o' business if sich things gets to be all the crack!'

He fetched a pair of horses and harnessed them to the sleigh, while Dr Field helped the Duke and Duchess to their high-perched seats.

'Mr Cobb,' asked Sophie, climbing up behind them, 'did the Bow Street Runners find anything when they raided Rose Alley?'

'Nay, lass, the birds had flown. Someone must 'a peached, for never a soul was there, not so much as a grain of gunpowder. There, your Grace, that's all right and tight. Watch for the wolves in the park, sir, they be fair audacious. But these horses can show them a clean pair of heels. Is this gentleman a-going to drive?'

He handed the reins to Dr Field.

'Much obliged, Cobb, thank'ee. Now, can you do us one more kindness? Can you ride like the wind to Bow Street and ask them to send some brisk, stout officers to the Castle – we are expecting trouble, and His Majesty may arrive at any moment. Dear me, yes,' the Duke said, inspecting his timepiece, 'we must hasten. I hope Buckle has everything in readiness; it was unfortunate that we were blown off course for two days. However, I daresay all will be well – Buckle is such a capable fellow – in his way. Simon, my dear boy, we shall hope to see you at the Castle directly you have informed Dr Furneaux and the Yeomanry.'

With a creak and a jingle the sleigh sped away.

Mr Cobb offered Simon a horse, or his own donkey, but he said that he could go faster on foot. He raced down to the Academy where, most fortunately, Dr Furneaux was outside, superintending a snow-fight between a dozen of his students on the frozen river, while the rest of them sat on the bank attempting with numb fingers to sketch the scene.

Dr Furneaux let out a cry of joy at sight of Simon, which, to anybody who did not know him, would have sounded more like a roar of fury.

'Ah, scélérat, coquin, misérable! Méchant gars! Espèce d'espèce! How do you dare to show your face, after being absent so many days and giving your poor old teacher so much worry! I will bastinado you, I will escallope you, I will use your head for a doorknob!' He hugged Simon and shook him with equal ferocity.

'It was not my fault, sir, I promise you!' Simon exclaimed, half laughing and half choking as he tried to escape from these signs of affection. 'I have had such adventures. And, sir, I have found Dr Field! He is back in London. He will come to see you very soon! But I must not stop to tell you now. Sir, his Grace the Duke asks a favour of you. He has just returned to Battersea Castle, where there is a nest of Hanoverians. I am going for the Yeomanry, but meanwhile could some of the students station themselves near the Castle – just to look out for trouble, you know?'

'Entendu, why certainly, nossing could be simpler. Étudiants!' roared Dr Furneaux, 'away, all, to Battersea Park, to sketch ze Castle against ze sunset!'

'I say, though, dear old sir,' pointed out Gus, who stood near by, 'what about the wolves in the park? Know how it is when you're sketching – get absorbed – wolf sneaks up behind – poof, snip, snap, swallow! – and all your paint-water's spilt.'

'Vraiment, zat is a difficulty. Aha! I have it. One student will paint, ze ozzer fight wiss ze wolves.'

'Famous notion! But what does he fight with?'

'We know where there are some weapons,' Simon interposed, and gave Gus the key to the Castle vaults, explaining that the door led to them from the tunnel. 'Watch out for Hanoverians, though; they may have somebody on guard.'

'We'll clobber 'em if they do,' said Gus joyfully.

Simon ran off to Chelsea Barracks with a lighter heart; plainly the students would be prompt to the rescue, should trouble arise in the Castle.

Unfortunately, he encountered great difficulty in carrying out his mission at the Barracks; they appeared to be deserted, and when at length he did discover an officer – engaged in taking a Turkish bath – he was told that half the regiment had been put to sweeping the snow off Parliament Square, while the rest were away on Christmas leave. However, the officer promised that he would try to get fifty men on to Chelsea Bridge in an hour's time, and with this unsatisfactory arrangement Simon had to be content.

He himself hurried back towards the Castle, hoping that Mr Cobb had been more successful at Bow Street.

As he reached the corner of the King's Road, his ears were assailed by a mournfully familiar music – a sad and breathy tooting which could come, surely, from only one player and one instrument. He looked about, and saw a tall thin man with a luxuriant black beard and moustache standing in the gutter and playing on a hoboy. In front of the man lay a cap, with a few coins in it.

'Mr Twite!' Simon exclaimed.

The man started. 'No, no, my dear young feller,' he said quickly. 'Must be mistaken. Somebody else, not that name, Twite? No, no, quite another person.'

But the tones were unmistakable in spite of the disguising beard.

'What are you doing here, Mr Twite?'

The musician glanced quickly up and down the street.

'Well, my dear boy, since you *have* plumbed my incognito – I'll avail myself of the chance of a word with you. Delighted to see you back, by the way – missed you.'

Mr Twite spoke in the most amiable, carefree manner, as if his had not been the hand which, at their last meeting, had dealt Simon such a stunning blow. He led Simon into a doorway and went on confidentially:

'A tombstone for my wife I will not ask, for between you and me she was a Thorn – '

'Tombstone? But – I don't understand.' Simon was mystified. 'Is Mrs Twite dead?"

'No,' replied her husband cryptically. 'Not *yet*. But dear little Dido – the last of the House of Twite – the flower of the flock – I should wish that some suitable memorial be erected to her on the island of Inchmore. A simple stone with a simple legend – perhaps *Dido Twite, A Delicate Sprite*?'

'Yes – yes of course,' said Simon, somewhat shaken. 'But – you heard, then?'

'Those two sailors from *Dark Dimity* whom you so kindly liberated reached London yesterday and told my brother-in-law the whole tale. I'm delighted to hear that my dear young nephew Justin is still in good health.'

'But – good heavens – if Buckle knows *that* – then the Duke and Duchess are in deadly danger. I must be off to the Castle at once!'

'I most strongly advise you *not* to.' Mr Twite laid a detaining hand on his arm. 'No, indeed, that is the *last* place I should visit at present. But perhaps you were not aware that Mr Buckle proposed to blow up their Graces and His Majesty shortly by means of dynamite?'

'*What?*'

'Buckle's somewhat *wholesale* arrangement is that, at nine o'clock, when he himself, and his followers, will have left the place, a lighted fuse will reach the charge in the vaults. The Duke and Duchess and His Majesty, peacefully unaware of their solitude, will be alone in the Castle preparing to watch from the library a display of fireworks which they have been told will take place as the clock strikes nine. Fireworks! My brother-in-law is seldom humorous, but that strikes me as a neat touch.'

'But if that is so – let me go! I must run. I must warn them! Thank heaven it is only a quarter to five,' Simon said, as the church clock's chimes rang out not far away.

'Wait, wait a moment, my rash young friend. To tell the truth,' said Mr Twite, again looking round cautiously, 'I have of late become somewhat wearied of my dear wife and her family and their burning political ambitions. I resolved to rid myself of the whole boiling and start afresh, overseas, in a land where musicians are treated with respect. So – in short – I altered the fuse – *curtailed* it – timing it to explode at *five*, when my dear wife, brother-in-law, sisters-in-law, and the rest of them will still be inside the Castle. Was not that an ingenious notion? I flatter myself it was,' he said, rubbing his hands. 'Dear Ella, her sisters, Eustace Buckle, Midwink, Jem, Fibbins, Scrimshaw, and that disagreeable fellow who calls himself young Turveytop – yes, indeed, the world will be a more peaceful place without them. Dear me, the boy has not waited! Think, think, my impetuous young friend!' he called after Simon. 'Reflect on what you are doing!'

But Simon, his heart pounding in his chest, was racing at top speed towards Mr Cobb's yard.

17

'Is my coronet on straight, Sophie? Are my gloves properly buttoned? The diamond buttons stick so – '

'Come on, come on, Hettie, there's no time to waste. I can hear the cheers! His Majesty will be here at any moment!'

The Duke took his wife's arm and fairly ran her down the stairs. Sophie and Dr Field followed, protectively near. As yet, nobody had noticed them. The Castle servants appeared to be in a state of disorganization, all milling about downstairs; neither Midwink nor Fibbins had appeared to help their Graces.

As they descended, Buckle's voice could be heard below, giving orders to a large number of people.

'You all know what you have to do – every soul to be out at half past eight. After the fanfare and the dinner – disperse! Each carry something – Midwink take charge of the jewels – Scrimshaw the plate – '

'Good evening, Mr Buckle,' the Duke said. 'Are the arrangements for His Majesty's reception all complete?'

Buckle whipped round. For an instant an ugly expression came over his face, but this was rapidly replaced by his usual pale-eyed, impassive stare.

'Quite ready, your Graces,' he replied smoothly. 'I am glad to welcome your Graces back to Battersea.'

'Well you won't be when you hear our news!' the Duke snapped. 'We know that you're a damned scoundrel, who palmed off your own whey-faced brat in place of my nephew and niece, and tried to murder me three times! But your crimes have caught up with you, and I shall be surprised if you don't end your days in the Tower, you rogue! The Bow Street men and the Yeomanry are on their way now; we

don't want any unpleasant scenes at present, but as soon as His Majesty has left you'll be arrested.'

Mr Buckle's eyes flashed, but he replied in a low, even tone:

'Your Grace is mistaken. I intend to amend my ways. I see my faults – I am truly sorry – and in future your Grace will have nothing to complain of.'

'Well,' said the Duke, a little mollified, 'if you are *truly* sorry – '

'William!' exclaimed the scandalized Duchess.

'Don't believe a word the hypocrite says! I am sure he has not the least intention—'

'Hark!' interposed Sophie. 'Here is His Majesty! I can hear the fanfare, and the students cheering.'

Indeed, as the Royal sleigh left the frozen Thames, along which it had sped from Hampton Court, and crossed the short snowy stretch of park to the Castle, the assembled students burst into loyal shouts:

'Hooray for Jamie Three!'

'Long live King Jim, good luck to him!'

'Yoicks, your Majesty!'

The Duke and Duchess, with Sophie behind them, ran down the red-carpeted front steps of the Castle to greet His Majesty, while the students formed a ring and, with snowballs and horse-chestnuts, kept the inquisitive wolves from coming too close.

'Sire, this is a happy day. We are pleased to welcome you to our humble roof – '

'Och, weel, noo, Battersea, it's nice to hear that. And how's your gude lady?'

The king was a little, dapper, elderly Scottish gentleman, plainly dressed in black, with a shovel hat on top of his snuff-coloured wig. He carried a slender hooked cane, and a large black bird perched on his wrist which, at sight of the Duchess, opened its beak and gravely remarked:

'What's your wull, my bonny hinny?'

'Mercy on us!' exclaimed her Grace. 'Where did your Majesty get that heathen bird?'

'Why, ma'am, the Sultan of Zanzibar gave her to me for a Christmas present. And I find her a great convenience – don't I, Jeannie, my lass? – for there's a wheen Hanoverians aye trying to slip a wee drop of poison into my victuals, so I e'en employ Jeannie as a taster. She takes a nip of brose and a nibble of parritch, and soon has the poisoned meat sorted. Not that I mean to decry your hospitality, ma'am, but one must be careful.'

'Why yes, yes, indeed one must!' The flustered Duchess then pulled herself together and graciously invited His Majesty to do himself the trouble of stepping into the banqueting-hall. Sophie, following, noticed a pale gleam in Buckle's eyes, and thought he looked as if he meant mischief. She wished the Bow Street Runners would come, or the Yeomanry – surely it must be nearly an hour since they parted from Simon? What could have happened? She could see that Dr Field shared her worry, for he kept glancing at his watch.

'What time is it?' she whispered to him when a dour-faced female (Aunt Tinty, had she but known it) brought in the mince-pies, with flaming prune brandy poured all over them.

'Twenty minutes to five,' he whispered back. 'Where the devil can that boy have got to with the Yeomanry?'

'Will you have a mince-pie, Your Majesty?'

'Na, na, thank you, Duchess. They play the very deuce with my digestion. But Jeannie will, won't you, lass?'

Jeannie ate several mince-pies with every appearance of satisfaction, smacking her beak over the prune brandy.

'Are they safe?' Dr Field whispered to Sophie.

'I brought them from Chippings,' she whispered back. 'I wouldn't trust the mince-pies Mr Buckle had provided.'

Even so, none of the party save Jeannie felt inclined to sample the mince-pies. She, after her fourth, perhaps because of the prune brandy, suddenly became over-excited, flew round the banqueting-hall twice, pecked Mr Buckle on the ear, and disappeared through a small open window.

'Jeannie – come back, lass!' cried her master, starting up. 'A gold guinea to the man who catches her!'

None of the footmen seemed moved by this appeal; they stood motionless, and one or two of them sniggered. Sophie felt ready to sink with shame, but Dr Field went to the window and shouted to the students outside:

'His Majesty offers a gold guinea to the person who brings back his pet bird.'

A tremendous cheer went up, and the sound of many running feet could be heard, accompanied by cries of hope and disappointment.

'Shall we adjourn to the library for coffee?' the Duke suggested. 'I believe later on we are to see some fireworks.' The party began moving up the stairs. 'I daresay one of the students will soon bring back your bird – ' the Duke was going on comfortably, when suddenly the most astonishing hubbub – shouts, shots, and crashes – broke out downstairs by the main doors.

'Gracious heavens!' cried the Duchess in alarm. 'What can be going on?'

A somewhat bedraggled Gus burst through the Castle doors and came charging up the stairs. His hair stood on end, one eye was blacked, and his face was covered by what looked like peck-marks, but he held the squawking Jeannie triumphantly in both hands.

'Here you are, Your Majesty!' he panted. 'And I wish you joy of her! She's a Tartar! But sir and ma'am, and Your Majesty, I don't think you should stay here, I don't indeed. Those villains downstairs are up to tricks, I believe. I had the devil's own job to get in, they were all massed about the hall with pikes and Pictclobbers. The sooner you are all out of the Castle, the better it will be, in my opinion.'

'Oh dear, oh, William!' lamented the Duchess. 'We should never have let His Majesty come here – '

'Nonsense, Hettie. The Yeomanry will be here directly. All we need do is keep calm and retire to the library till it all blows over.'

'Let us go higher up! That noise terrifies me – it sounds as if they are all fighting each other before coming up to murder us.'

'What does His Majesty say?'

His Majesty had been busy settling Jeannie's ruffled plumes and politely affecting to be unaware of his hosts' problems. Appealed to, he said amiably:

'Och, let us go higher up, by all means. Did ye not say there were to be fireworks? The higher up, the better the view.'

'I winna say nay to a wee dram,' remarked Jeannie unexpectedly.

'Hush, ye ill-mannered bird. Lead the way upstairs, then, Battersea.'

The Duke had the key to a small privy staircase leading to the battlements, and up this he led the King, while the rest of the party followed.

It was now almost dark, except for a fiery pink streak lying across the western sky; down below in the park the obscurity was broken by flashes as the students skirmished with the wolves and aimed a shot from time to time at Hanoverians in the Castle doorway.

'Brave boys! They're keeping the scoundrels boxed in!' exclaimed the Duke. 'When the Yeomanry come – oh, why *don't* they come?'

'But look – look who *is* coming!' Sophie pointed, almost stammering in her excitement. 'The balloon! It must be Simon!'

'Why does he come in the balloon? Because of the Wolves?'

'It is certainly Simon!'

An applauding shout went up from the students as the balloon drifted over them, shining in the light of the gas flambeaux which were now beginning to illuminate the park. Simon leaned over the side and shouted down urgently:

'Keep away from the Castle! Away, for your lives!'

Then he threw out some ballast, and the balloon soared up to the level of the battlements. Grasping the hooked end of the King's cane, he was drawn close to the Castle walls.

'Please, your Graces and Your Majesty – don't waste a minute!' he begged. 'Climb on board, quick! You are in the most deadly danger – there is not an instant to be lost! Sophie – Gus – Dr Field – jump in as quick as you can!'

He sprang on to the battlements and helped the Duke lift his wife into the car.

'I say, ain't this a famous balloon, though?' said Gus, helping Sophie. 'Will it hold us all, Simon, me boy?'

'Yes, yes – only hurry!' Simon was frantic with impatience as the King somewhat stiffly and gingerly clambered into the waist of the car, assisted by Dr Field and the Duke.

At this moment Buckle rushed out of the attic door on to the roof, followed by Mrs Twite.

'I told you they were escaping!' she shrieked, her face distorted with rage. 'I told you I saw a balloon! After them, Eustace, quickly!'

Buckle started towards Gus, who felled him with a large snowball and leapt nimbly on board. Mrs Twite threw herself at Simon and grabbed him round the middle.

'Oh, you wretch!' she exclaimed, pummelling him. 'I'll teach you to come meddling, asking questions, helping them to escape just when the Cause is about to triumph!'

'Who the deuce is that harpy?' the Duke asked in bewilderment.

'Simon, quick – dodge her!' Sophie cried anxiously. Everyone else was now on board and the balloon was already moving away from the Castle walls in the evening wind. Simon wriggled out of Mrs Twite's grip, dodged her round some chimney-stacks, tripped Buckle, who tried to intercept him, ran for the battlements, and, with a tremendous effort, hurled himself across the rapidly widening gap. He fell sprawling over the gunwale, half in and half out, but Sophie and Gus grabbed him and hauled him to safety. Meanwhile, the car tipped and lurched terrifyingly, then sank a few feet. The Duke and Duchess with desperate haste flung overboard all the loose articles of baggage they could lay hands on to lighten the load: braziers, rugs, provision hampers all went tumbling into the park, and the balloon rose higher.

Mrs Twite let out a fearful shriek of disappointed rage, but Buckle, with an oath, pulled out a pistol and fired at them.

'Mercy, mercy, he's hit the balloon! Oh, what shall we do?' cried the Duchess.

Sophie bit her lip. They could all hear the hiss as air rushed out of the puncture. The balloon started to sag.

'Dear me! Hadn't reckoned on anything like that,' muttered the Duke.

'I have it!' cried Sophie suddenly. 'The tapestry! Aunt Hettie's embroidery! Simon, can you climb up and lay it over the hole?'

She handed him the bundle of material and he swarmed up a guy-rope and flung an end of the cloth over the top of the globe. Gus caught and held it tight on the other side, and the air-escape was checked. Dr Field scrambled to the tiller to steady their progress, and the balloon glided, swayingly, down and away from the Castle.

'Oh, oh, he's going to shoot again!' cried the Duchess.

Buckle, with deadly intent, was aiming at the balloon once more.

But as they watched, frozen in suspense, the thing that Simon had been expecting came to pass. With a noise so loud that it seemed no noise at all, the whole Castle suddenly lifted up, burst outwards, and disintegrated in one huge flash of orange-coloured light. The balloon rocked and staggered. Fragments of stone showered about them.

The Duchess fainted. Fortunately the hartshorn had not been flung out; Sophie was able to find it and minister to her Grace.

'Dod!' said King James. 'Nae wonder ye were in sic a hurry, my lad! We're obleeged to ye – very. Aweel, aweel, that rids the world of a muckle nest of Hanoverians – but I'm afeered there's no' much left of your Castle, Battersea.'

'No matter, no matter!' said the Duke somewhat distractedly. 'To tell truth, I never greatly cared for it. I should much prefer to live at Chippings. We'll lay out a pleasure garden on the site – yes, that will be much better. Simon, my dear boy, I can't thank you sufficiently. We are indebted to you for all our lives. Sire, may I present to you my nephew Simon, Lord Bakerloo. As for those miserable Yeomanry and Bow Street Runners, we might as well never have applied to them for all the help the have been.'

But as they sank slowly towards the snowy grounds of the Academy, a sound of martial music was heard: the banging of drums and squealing of fifes heralded the arrival of the Chelsea Yeomanry who came marching in brave array down the Chelsea Bridge Road, while along the bank of the river twenty Bow Street Officers galloped at full speed, led by Mr Cobb. Meanwhile, the students, having observed the balloon's escape, had come running across the park, and all these forces converged to welcome the rescue party as they reached the ground.

Dr Furneaux was in the forefront.

'Ah, my poor sir, my dear friend!' he exclaimed, giving the Duke a bristly hug. 'How I commiserate wiss you. Your home lost – destructuated by zese brigands! Not zat I ever admired it – indeed, a most hideous building. But still, ze saying goes, dos it not, ze Englishman's castle is his home? And poor madame, helas! But nevaire mind, you shall live in ze Académie, bose of you, if you wish. I make you most welcome, and my students shall design you a new castle, moderne, confortable, épouvantable! Ziss we shall do directly!'

'Oh, thank you, dear Dr Furneaux, but we think we shall retire to Chippings, and turn the Castle grounds into a pleasure-garden for you and your students. Meanwhile, His Majesty has kindly offered beds at Hampton Court to myself and my wife and niece and nephew here, and Dr Field.'

'Niece and nephew?' Dr Furneaux stared in bewilderment first at Simon and Sophie, then at the Duke. 'What is ziss? What of ze ozzer one – ze little Justin?'

'It was a case of mistaken identity,' the Duchess explained kindly. 'Simon is our real nephew and heir; he will be the sixth Duke of Battersea.'

Dr Furneaux was aghast. 'Ah, non, non, non, non, non, *non,* NON! Ziss I will not bear! Ziss I cannot endure! I get me a boy a good boy, a painter, a real artiste, a genius! And what do you do? You make of him a Duke! Every time it is ze same! I say, pouaaah to all Dukes!'

'Oh, come now, my dear Furneaux –'

Luckily, perhaps, at this moment the Royal sleigh, which had been summoned post-haste by the colonel of the Yeomanry, arrived at the river-bank with its attendant outriders. The King and his guests were all packed in, under layers of swansdown rugs. Good-byes were shouted, whips were cracked.

'I'll be back in the morning early, Dr Furneaux!' Simon shouted. 'For a long day's painting! And we'll mend the balloon.'

'And collect Aunt Henrietta's tapestry!' Sophie called.

'And give a Christmas dinner to thank everybody for their help!' shouted the Duke.

Simon thought of another, sadder task, which he would hasten to perform: the small white stone on Inchmore's heathery slope with the name DIDO. And Sophie thought of the orphans at Gloober's Poor Farm to be rescued and given happy homes.

The sleigh-bells jingled, the horses began to move away in their felt slippers.

'Good-night! Merry Christmas! God Save King James!'

'Merry Christmas!'

'And a Happy New Year!'

Faster and faster the procession glided off into the dark, a long trail of brilliant lights, red and gold and blue, winding along the frozen Thames to Hampton Court, until at last the glitter and the music of the bells died away, and the students went home to bed, and the mysterious peace of Christmas night descended once again upon Battersea Park.

NIGHT BIRDS ON NANTUCKET

Part One

1

On board the Sarah Casket *– the sleeper wakes – tale of the pink whale – half a world from home*

Late in the middle watch of a calm winter's night, many years ago, a square-rigged, three-masted ship, the *Sarah Casket*, was making her way slowly through northern seas, under a blaze of stars. A bitter, teasing cold lurked in the air; frost glimmered on the ship's white decks and tinselled her shrouds; long icicles sometimes fell chiming from the spars to the planks beneath. No other sound could be heard in the silent night, save, from far away, the faint barking of seals.

On the deck a child lay sleeping in a wooden box filled with straw. Sheepskins covered her warmly. Had it not been for her breath, ascending threadlike into the Arctic air, she would have seemed more like a wax doll than a human being, so still and pale did she lie. Near by squatted a boy, hunched up, his arms round his knees, gravely watching over her. It was his turn below, and by rights he should have been in his bunk, but whenever he had any time to spare he chose to spend it by the sleeping child.

She had been asleep for more than ten months.

Presently a bell rang and the watches changed. Bearded sailors came yawning on deck, others went below; one, as he passed the boy, called out:

'Hey, there, Nate! No sign of life yet, then?'

The boy shook his head without replying.

One or two of the men said:

'Why don't you give over, boy? She'll never wake in this world.'

And one, a narrow-faced character with close-set eyes and a crafty, foxy look to him, said sourly:

'Why waste your time, you young fool? If it weren't for you and our sainted captain she'd have been food for the barracootas long ago.'

'Nay, don't say that, Mr Slighcarp,' somebody protested. 'She've brought us greasy luck so far, hain't she? We're nigh as full with whale-oil as we can hold.'

'Hah!' sneered the man called Slighcarp. 'What's *she* to do with the luck? We'd have had it whether we picked her up or no. I say she'd be best overboard before it changes. I've allus hated serving on a chick frigate.'

He went below, muttering angrily. Meanwhile the boy, Nate, calmly and taking no notice of these remarks, addressed himself to the sleeping child.

'Come on now, young 'un,' he said. 'It's your supper-time.'

One or two of the men lingered to watch him as he carefully raised the child with one arm and then, tilting a tin coffee-pot which he held in the other hand, poured down her throat a thick black mixture of whale-oil and molasses. She swallowed it in her sleep. Her eyelids never even fluttered. When the pot was empty Nate laid her down again in her straw nest and replaced the sheepskins.

'Blest if *I'd* care to live on such stuff,' one of the men muttered. 'Still and all, I guess you've kept her alive with it, Nate, eh? She'd have been skinny enough by now, but for you.'

'Guess I like looking after live creatures,' Nate said mildly. 'I'd been a-wanting summat to care for ever since my bird Mr Jenkins flew away in the streets of New Bedford. And Cap'n Casket says there's no more nourishing food in this world than whale-oil and m'lasses. Ye can see the young 'un thrives on it, anyways; six inches she's grown since I had the feeding of her.'

'And for what?' snarled the first mate, the foxy Mr Slighcarp, reappearing from the after-hatchway. 'What pleasure is it for us to see our vittles vanishing down that brat's throat when, so far as anyone can see, it's all for Habakkuk? Break it up, now, men! Those that's going below, *get* below!'

The men were dispersing quickly when a cry from aloft galvanized them in a different way.

'Blo-o-ows! Thar she *blows*!'

The lookout in the crosstrees was dancing up and down, dislodging, in his excitement, about a hundredweight of icicles which came clanking and tinkling to the deck. His arm was extended straight forward.

'Whale-o! Dead ahead, not more'n a mile!'

And indeed on the horizon a pale silvery spout of water could just be seen.

Like ants the men scurried about the ship while Mr Slighcarp shouted orders.

'Set royals and t'gallants! Bend on stuns'ls! Lower the boats!'

Light as leaves, three long cedarwood whaleboats glided down from the davits on to the calm sea. But just before the boats were manned a startling thing occurred. As if roused by all the commotion, the child lying in her straw-filled box turned, stretched, and yawned, drawing thin hands from under the sheepskin to knuckle her still-shut eyes. The boy Nate had gone below, but one of the sailors running by noticed her and exclaimed:

'Land sakes to glory! Look at the supercargo! She's stirring! She's waking!'

'Devil's teeth, man! Never mind the scrawny brat now! See to the boats!'

Thus urged, the men swung nimbly to their places in the boats, but they went with many a backward look at the child who was moving restlessly now under the pile of sheepskins, still with her eyes tight shut. Waves of colour passed over her pale face.

But the boats had sped away, hissing in white parallels over the dark sea that was like a great rumpled black-and-silver patchwork quilt, before the child finally opened her eyes and struggled to a sitting position.

She looked about her blankly. All was still now on board the whaler. Even with the added canvas the ship made but slow headway in that light air and the boats had long drawn ahead. Only a few shipkeepers remained on board and they were occupied elsewhere.

The child stared vaguely about her until at length her eyes began to fix, with puzzled intelligence, on the few things visible in the dim light from a lantern hanging over her head. She could see white-frosted planking, a massive tangle of rigging between her and the stars, a dark bulk, the try-works, amidships, and, above, the gleam of spare tools lodged on the skids.

'This ain't the *Dark Dew*,' she murmured, half to herself. 'Where can I be?'

The boy, Nate, was passing at that moment. When he heard her voice he started, nearly dropping the mug he carried. Then he turned and cautiously approached her.

'Well I'll be gallied!' he breathed in amazement. 'If it isn't the Sleeping Beauty woke up at last!'

The child stared him him wonderingly and he stared back at her. He saw a girl who might have been nine or ten, with a pointed face and long tangled brown hair hanging over her shoulders. She saw a thin boy of about sixteen, hollow-cheeked and with eyes set so deep that it was imposible to guess their colour.

'*You* aren't Simon,' she said wonderingly. 'Where's Simon?'

'Human language, too! Who's Simon?'

'My friend.'

'There's no Simon on board this hooker,' the boy said, squatting down beside her. 'Here, want a mug o'chowder? It's hot, I was just taking it to the steersman – he's my uncle 'Lije. But you might as well have it.'

'Thank you,' she said. She seemed dreamy, still only half awake, but the hot soup roused her. 'What's your name?' she asked.

'Nathaniel Pardon. Nate, they call me. What's yours?

'Dido Twite.'

'Dido – that's a funny name. I've heard of Dionis – never Dido. You're British, ain't you?'

'O' course I am,' she said, puzzled. 'Ain't you?'

'Not me. I'm a Nantucketer.' And he sang softly:

'Oh, blue blows the lilac and green grows the corn
And the isle of Nantucket is where I was born,
Sweet isle of Nantucket! where the plums are so red,
Ten hours and twelve minutes south-east of Gay Head.'

'Never heard of it,' Dido said. 'What ship's this, then?'

'The *Sarah Casket*, out of Nantucket.'

'Did you pick me up?' she asked, knitting her brows together painfully in an effort to recall what had happened.

'Sure we picked you up, floating like a bit o' brit. And from that day to this you've lain on the deck snoring louder'n a grampus; *I* never thought you'd trouble to wake up. You seemed all set to sleep till Judgment. Cap'n Casket allowed as how you musta had a bang on the head, maybe from a floating spar, to knock you into such an everlasting snooze. You musta had considerable dreams all that time, didn't you?'

'Dreams?' she murmured, rubbing her forehead. 'I can't remember . . . The ship caught fire and me and Simon was in the sea, hanging on to a spar. Then we was on a rock . . . You're sure you didn't pick up a boy called Simon?'

'No, honey,' he said gently.

'Maybe some other ship did.' Dido was still hopeful. 'When'll we get to port?'

''Bout eight months from now. Maybe nine.'

'Eight *months*? Are you crazy? There ain't that much sea atwixt England and Hanover.'

'That's not where we're bound, chick. Back to Nantucket, that's where we'll be heading, soon's our casks are all full. That'll set you a step on your way, anyhows. Guess you can find some packet out o' New Bedford that'll take you to England.'

Plainly these names meant nothing to Dido.

'Where are we now, then?' she asked.

'Somewhere north o' Cape East. Just got to raise another whale or two and we'll be homeward bound. Then all the casks'll be full.'

'Full of what?'

'Spermaceti o' course – whale-oil. What d'you think you've been living on for the last ten months?'

'Ten months? I've been aboard this ship for *ten months*?'

'Guess so. And pretty scrawny you'da been by now if I hadn't kept pouring whale-oil and sulphur and m'lasses down your gullet.'

Dido looked quite dazed. 'Ten months,' she repeated, half to herself. 'How did you come to pick me up, then? Where was it?'

For the first time the boy Nate appeared slightly embarrassed. 'Well,' he explained hesitantly, 'we was a mite off course. It was thishow, you see. Cap'n had fixed to go after sperm-whales in the western grounds, so we was a-cruisin' off Madeira. And then the Old Man – he's a fine captain, just old pie on knowing where they're running, could raise you a whale in a plate o' sand, but he's funny in one way, awful peculiar–'

He stopped, his mouth open.

'Go on,' said Dido. 'How's he funny?'

A voice from behind made her start.

'What is thee doing up on deck, Nate?' it said sternly. 'Thee should be in thy bunk at this hour.'

Dido turned and saw a tall man, dressed all in black. He had a long black beard almost covering his white shirt-front; his face was severe but two great mournful eyes in it seemed as if they paid little attention to the words he spoke; they were fixed elsewhere, on vacancy.

'I – I'm sorry, sir, Cap'n Casket,' Nate said, stammering a little. 'I was taking a hot drink to Uncle 'Lije when I saw the little girl had wakened up.'

'So she has. So she has. How strange,' murmured Captain Casket, bending his eyes on Dido for the first time. 'Does thee feel better for thy long sleep, my dear?'

'Yes, thank you, mister,' Dido answered bashfully.

'Nate, since the little one has woken, thee had better fetch her some slops.'

'Yes, sir, cap'n. Shall I fetch some o' Miss Du–'

'Don't be a fool, boy!' Captain Casket said sharply. 'Thee knows it is impossible. They – they would be too small. There must be some boys' gear in one of the slop chests, fetch out a bundle. And shears: that long hair won't do aboard a whaler.'

'Yes, sir.' Nate ran off in a hurry. Captain Casket fixed his sad wandering eyes on Dido but they soon moved back to the horizon and, heaving a deep sigh, he seemed to forget her. She was in too much awe of him to speak.

At length, turning to her again, he said:

'Has thee family and friends in England, my child?'

'Y-yes, sir!'

'Poor souls. This will have been a sorrowful time for them. No matter, the joy when thee is restored to them will be all the greater.'

'Yes, sir. Thank you for picking me up,' Dido said bravely.

'Providence must have ordered that we should be sailing by. His ways are strange.' Captain Casket's grave face lightened in a smile of rare sweetness and simplicity; he added, 'Now thee has wakened up, my child, thee can be of considerable help to me in thy turn.'

'Yes, sir. H-how?'

'Tomorrow will be soon enough to explain the task I have in mind for thee. I will not burden thee tonight. Here comes Nate now, with the clothes. When thee has put them on, thee had better sleep again.'

He moved away silently over the deck.

Nate came running with an armful of clothes and a great pair of shears. He proceeded to chop off most of Dido's hair.

'That feels better,' she said, shaking her head. 'Can't think how it come to be so long, it never used. It musta growed while I was sleeping. Why won't long hair do aboard a whaler?'

'Why? Because o' the gurry,' Nate said grinning. 'Now, can you fix yourself up in them things?'

'What's gurry?'

'Slime. You'll see at cutting-in time, if the men have had greasy luck.'

Nate had brought nankeen breeches, a shirt, a monkey-jacket, red drawers, Falmouth stockings, and a pair of leather brogans.

'These'll be too big for me,' Dido said. But she soon found they were not. 'Great snakes! I ain't half growed since I been a-laying here.'

'Guess that'll be all the whale-oil. We could see it was doin' you good. You used to cough considerable, at first, but you haven't done so for months.'

Dido looked round to make sure they were not overheard. 'What were you going to tell me about Captain Casket? And why does he talk in that queer way?'

'He's a Friend – a Quaker – that's why. And what I was going to tell you –' Nate in his turn glanced behind him and, seeing the deck was clear, went on, 'He's allus had a kind of an uncommon fancy, you see – ever since he was a boy, Uncle 'Lije says. First-off on this trip it warn't so noticeable. His old lady, Mrs Casket, she sailed along with us because she warn't well and they reckoned sea air would do her good. But it didn't. She took sick and died, poor soul, afore we ever sighted Santa Cruz. When she was on board he kept to plain whaling. But when she died and –' Nate came to a halt and started again. 'She was a mite solemn-like and fussy in her ways, and scared to death of the sea, but there warn't no real harm in her. She used to make gingerbread and molasses cookies sometimes, afore she was took ill. Can you bake cookies?' he asked Dido.

'No.'

'Oh. Well, after she died Cap'n Casket got quieter and quieter. Never smiled – not that he was ever much of a one for a joke – never spoke. One day he said he saw the pink whale.'

'What's queer about that?' asked the ignorant Dido.

'What's queer? Well, they don't *come* pink whales, that's all! But Uncle 'Lije says Cap'n Casket for ever had this notion that one day he *would* see one. No one liked to say anything, but they thought he was a bit touched. Anyway, he swore he'd seen it and it was making north'ards and we was bound to follow it. Then Mr Slighcarp, he's the first mate, he allowed as *he'd* seen it too. Some thought he was just humouring the Old Man but anyways we chased it, up past Finisterre and Finistère and Ushant and Land's End, and next thing we was squeezing through the North Sea past London River. Clean lost the pink whale but that's where we picked *you* up. Only you was fast asleep and wouldn't wake to tell us where your home port was. For all we knew you mighta been a Fiji Islander. So I adopted you, kind of like a mascot because I'd lost my pet mynah bird. Then Cap'n Casket he sees the pink whale again, off John o' Groats, and she leads us a fair dance first south right round the Horn and then north again up past the Galapagos and Alaska to where we are now.'

'Did you ever catch her?'

'Not likely! No one's ever seed her but Mr Slighcarp and the Old Man. Still, we had good luck, we caught plenty other whales after that first little dummy run. But some o' the men was a bit ashamed of getting so far off the whaling grounds as we was when we picked you up.'

Suddenly Dido's lip quivered.

'I wish you hadn't! I wish some English ship had picked me up!'

'Well, there's ingratitude!' Nate said indignantly. He added in a gentler tone, 'We couldn't leave you to drown, now, could we? You'll get home soon enough.'

But, for Dido, the dreamlike strangeness of her surroundings, the huge dark frosted ship, the blazing Arctic sky across which mysterious arches and curtains and streamers of red and green now flickered – most of all the fact, only half understood, that she was an immense distance, half a world away, from home – all this was suddenly too much to be borne. She flung herself down on the pile of sheepskins and cried as if her heart would break.

'There, there!' said Nate uncomfortably. 'Come now, don't take on so, don't! Supposin' somebody was to see you?'

'I don't care!' wept Dido. 'I wish I was at home. Oh, I wish I was at home *now*!'

2

The captured whale – the mysterious weeper – Captain Casket's task

When Dido woke once more dawn had broken, wild and red and dim. The ice-covered ship gleamed like a Christmas tree. What had roused her was the shouts of the men, who had returned towing a large sperm-whale; their three boats spread around it like tugs. Dido was astonished at the sight of this huge, mouse-coloured monster, almost as big as the ship, it seemed, with its steep face, flat and featureless as the side of a house. At first, in alarm, thinking it was still alive, she scrambled out of her straw bed and retreated to the far side of the deck. But then she realized that it was dead and the men were making it fast to the ship.

'What are they going to do with it?' she asked Nate, who ran along the deck with five mugs of hot coffee in each hand. By day he was revealed as a long, lanky redhead, with friendly grey eyes and a great many freckles.

'Cut-in, o' course. I can't stop now, chick. Why don't you step down to the camboose and get some breakfast? Doctor'll be astonished to see you.'

Dido guessed that the camboose must be the kitchen, but she was too interested in what the men were doing to leave the deck for a while. Several men had gone over the side and now stood on stagings like painters' cradles slung from ropes between the ship and the whale. They were armed with long-handled, sharp-edged spades. Meanwhile a huge hook, lowered from the rigging, had been sunk into the whale's side. At this point the rest of the crew all combined their strength to turn a massive windlass, while they encouraged each other by singing:

'Oh, whaling is my only failing,
Sailing whaling's done for me!
Life's all bible-leaves and bailing –
Never ask me in when there's decent folk to tea!'

Now, to Dido's amazement, while every timber of the ship seemed to strain and strive, the body of the whale slowly began turning over in the water as the men wound the windlass-handle and pulled on the rope attached to the hook. While the whale turned, the cutters on the hanging planks skilfully sliced round its body so that the blubber, or skin, was peeled off in a spiral like orange-peel. When a considerable length of this great blubber-strip had been drawn up on the hook, sections of it as large as blankets were cut clear by the men on deck and lowered through a forward hatchway.

'Hush your weeping and your wailing
Six-and-thirty months I'll be at sea,

Tears and grumbles are unavailing –
And never ask me in when there's decent folk to tea!'

'What do they do with it down there?' Dido asked a passing man. He scowled at her. It was Mr Slighcarp, the first mate.

'Ho! *You've* woken up to plague us, have you? Don't you go near the try-works or I'll spank you with a deck spade.'

'They mince it up, ready to be boiled down for oil,' another more good-natured man told her. 'There's a blubber-room down there, I dessay Cap'n Casket'll let you have a look some time. Mr Pardon, the second mate, will maybe show you; he's right pleased to know you've woken up at last; he's down below cutting-in now.'

'Keep your sturgeon, salmon, grayling,
Shark, bonito's not for me.
Whales are all I'll be impaling –
And never ask me in when there's decent folk to
tea!'

Dido wondered what the angry-looking Mr Slighcarp had meant by the try-works. Then she saw that an iron door had been opened at one side of the square brick structure in the middle of the deck; a fire roared inside it and men ran to and fro feeding the flames with bits of tarred rope and frizzled scraps of whale, poking the blaze with long-handled fire pikes. Two huge metal pots were built in above and into these were being tossed chunks of blubber, sliced most of the way through into paper-thin slices so that they looked like books. The brew in the try-pots began to melt and bubble; thick, black, greasy smoke rolled over the deck.

'Cor, love a lily-white *duck*!' gasped Dido, as a murky bank of the smoke surged towards her and almost smothered her. 'I never in all my born days smelt such a smell, *never*! It's enough to make a bad egg burst out crying and go home to mother.'

Nate, who was passing with the empty mugs, laughed. 'You'd better get used to it,' he said. 'There's going to be plenty more afore we're through.'

At noon a little old bow-legged Negro whom everybody addressed affectionately as Doctor came on deck with a steaming cauldron of something that smelt very appetizing, and the men helped themselves from it when they could snatch a moment from their labours.

'Go and help yourself!' Nate called to Dido – he was sharpening tools on a grindstone.

Rather timidly she approached the cook who gave her a flashing white grin and handed her a tin pannikin of hash.

'You like lobscouse, eh? Best lobscouse from here to Christmas Island, eh Mr Pardon? Make a change from whale-oil, I b'lieve?'

Mr Pardon, the white-haired, kindly-faced second mate, who was also gulping down a bowlful of food, had his mouth full and couldn't speak. But he smiled at Dido and as soon as he could, said:

'Bless me! Who'da taken you for the poor little shrivelled poke we hauled on board ten months ago? Why you're as chipper and lively as any lass in Nantucket. I reckon that ten months' rest did you a sight o' good.

Eat up the lobscouse, dearie, I'll lay you can do with some solid vittles.'

'What's it made of?' Dido asked, looking suspiciously at the mixture in her pan.

'Why, corned beef and hardtack and good salt water, eat it up! You can still do wi' a bit more flesh on your bones.'

Mr Pardon hurried back to his post over the side, adjuring her as he went to 'keep clear of the gurry'.

Dido could see what he meant; by this time the whole deck was covered with an unbelievable mess of oil and slime and bits of the whale's thin outer skin. It seemed impossible that the planks should ever be clean and white again. The sails were blackened by smoke and the rigging was all furred up with greasy soot.

'When I'm old and weak and ailing
Sailing whaling still I'll be;
Lash me standing to the lash-railing –
And never speak my name when there's decent folk to tea –'

came the voices from the windlass.

Dido picked up a cutting-spade and moved cautiously over the littered deck, but she had the ill-fortune to tread on a particularly slippery patch of oil, lost her footing and slid, entangling the cutting-spade between the legs of Mr Slighcarp as he stretched up to pull down a blanket of blubber from the hook. He fell sprawling with the blubber on top of him, and when he rose cursed Dido most evilly. Matters were not helped by the shouts of laughter from the crew.

'I – I'm sorry, mister,' Dido gulped. 'I couldn't help it, honest!'

'Git below!' snarled Mr Slighcarp. 'I'll have no frog-spawn like you littering the deck while I'm in charge. Git!'

Terrified, Dido picked herself up and scurried away. Guided by a gesture and a wink from Nate, she slipped down a hatchway and found herself suddenly out of the noise and stink and bustle, on a neat little winding stair, white-painted and silent. Where did it lead? On she went, cautiously exploring, and presently entered a good-sized stateroom, also white-painted, and very tidy. A rocking-chair stood by a glowing stove; a swinging bed was made up with a patchwork quilt; over this hung a compass, upside down. Dido studied the compass for a moment but it meant nothing to her; nor did the charts spread on the table. A huge book held them down; she opened it; it was the Bible. While sniffing the petals of a blooming pink geranium on a shelf she was startled by a small sound from somewhere close at hand. It sounded like a sob.

Arrested, Dido stood motionless, listening. Yes! There again! More sobs, half stifled at first, then breaking into a low, wailing cry, '*Mamma! Oh, Mamma!*'

Dido thought she had never in her life heard a sound so lonely and desolate.

The cabin was empty; where, then, did the voice come from? There were two doors, one on each side, in the white panelling. Trying them, she found that both were locked, but the sound seemed to come from behind the right-hand one. When she tried it a frightened voice whispered, 'Who's there?'

'It's me. Dido Twite. Who are you?'

No reply. Dead silence from beyond the door. Dido tried again.

'Come on! Do say summat! I ain't a-going to bite you! Why are you shut in?'

No answer.

'Croopus,' Dido sighed to herself. 'This is a rum brig and no mistake. Pink whales and spooky voices. Don't I jist wish I was at home with Simon!'

A whisper hit her ear like a small cold draught. She leaned to catch what it said.

'I believe you're Aunt Tribulation. *Go away!*'

'I'm Dido Twite, I tell you!'

'Go away!'

'Pooh,' said Dido, hurt. 'All right, I just will. And you can holler for me next time.' She made her way back on deck, greatly puzzled. Whose could the voice be? No one she had seen or heard of yet, that was certain. It had sounded like a child – but nobody had mentioned a child.

This time, keeping well clear of the try-works and the fierce Mr Slighcarp, she made her way to the quarter-deck. There she found Captain Casket, silent, withdrawn, and stern-looking. He had his back to her and was studying the compass in the binnacle, so she tiptoed to the rail and stood watching two gulls on an ice-floe as they quarrelled over a scrap of blubber.

Presently she felt a chilly sensation in her shoulder-blades and turned to find that Captain Casket had his strange sad eyes fixed on her.

He cleared his throat once or twice, as if speaking were not a very common activity with him, and said:

'What is thy name, child?'

'D-Dido, sir. Dido Twite.'

'A heathen name,' the captain murmured. 'No matter. There may be godliness within.' He scrutinized her with an intent, close regard, as if measuring her for some purpose he had in mind. Dido looked back wonderingly.

At last he said:

'Thee has a firm chin, my child, and a philanthropic brow.'

'Has – have I?' Dido said, surprised. 'Coo, I never knew. Maybe I got some o' the gurry on it when I fell down.' She rubbed her forehead with her sleeve.

'I need thy help,' Captain Casket went on. 'Thee looks like a strong, brave character.'

Am I? Dido wondered. She realized with surprise that she did feel strong, far stronger than she had been before she fell into her ten-month sleep.

'Does thee think thee can be kind but firm with somebody not so blessed in courage and strength?'

Suddenly Dido began to guess what he was leading up to. Forgetting her slight awe of him she blurted out, 'Well, mister, if it's anything to do with that poor little thing that you got locked up downstairs I can tell you straight I think it's a wicked shame. How would *you* like to be locked up?'

Captain Casket looked at her sadly. 'Child, thee doesn't understand,' he said. 'I am not her jailer. She did it herself. She bolted herself in when her Mamma died. No words of mine avail to draw her forth.'

'Ohhhh!' Dido breathed, round-eyed. 'Mercy gracious, why ever'd she do that? Is she your little girl, then?'

'Yes,' he said, sighing.

'What's her name? How old is she?' Dido was all curiosity. What a queer thing, to shut oneself in a cabin!

'She's nine,' he said heavily. 'Her name is Dutiful Penitence Casket.'

'Croopus,' Dido murmured.

'Her Mamma, my dear wife, though endowed with every Christian virtue, had one foolish failing,' he went on, half to himself. 'This was her incurable fear of the sea. I thought that if I took her with me on a voyage it would allay her fear and improve her delicate health. Fool! Fool that I was.' He paused and added in a lower tone, 'But the ways of Providence are strange to us.'

'And so the poor lady took and died?' Dido said compassionately as he seemed to have come to a stop.

'Yes, my child. And Penitence, who had imbibed her mother's fears, believed the sea had caused her death.'

'So she shut herself up.'

'From that day to this,' he agreed, sighing. 'I believe she thinks the sea will kill her too, if she ventures out.'

'Coo,' said Dido. 'What a jobberknoll. But what does she do for prog – for vittles?'

'The little cabin where she slept next to my wife is also the store where my dear Sarah kept preserves and spices and medicines. I believe Penitence has been living on beach-plum jelly and sassafras all this time.'

'What a do, eh? Don't she never *wash*?' said Dido with the liveliest interest.

'There is a little hatch through which I can sometimes

get a glimpse of her and through which a basin of water may be passed.'

'Well, my Ma would soon clobber me if I went on in such a way,' said Dido frankly. 'And if you was to ask me, *I* think she sounds touched in the upper works. But I can see what you wants. You wants me to put the wheedle on her and make her come out, ain't that so?'

'Yes, my child. Thee has guessed right. I have a hatred of violence or trickery; I would not force her to come out. But if thee can somehow *persuade* her . . .'

He looked at Dido hopefully, and added: 'After all, we did pull thee out of the sea. We saved thy life.'

'Yes,' muttered Dido ungratefully, 'and if you hadn't I might a bin picked up by an English ship and safe home now, instead o' freezing at the fishy back end o' nowhere. Anyways, why didn't you ask Nate or Mr Pardon to have a go with the little girl?'

Captain Casket appeared slightly embarrassed. At last he said, 'My child, I tell thee this in confidence. The crew are not aware that Penitence has locked herself up in this way. They – they believe that she is ailing. To have it known that she defies me would be bad for discipline. Thee –' he gazed at her anxiously – 'thee will not divulge what I have told thee, my dear?'

'Oh, *now* I twig your lay,' Dido said. He looked bewildered. 'I see why you been so havey-cavey about her. All right, I'll keep mum. And I don't mind having a try.'

'Thee is a good child. I am truly grateful,' Captain Casket said almost humbly. 'I feel thee may succeed where I have failed.'

Dido gave him a sharp look. 'Ain't trying to butter

me up, are you? If I manage to wheedle her out in the fresh air, so you ain't shamed when we gets to port and she won't come out, will you see I gets a passage on the fust ship that'll take me back to England?'

'Anything in my power I shall do,' he assured her quickly. 'As soon as we return to New Bedford I shall inquire about sailings.'

'What'll happen to Dutiful Penitence – glad *I* wasn't saddled with such a handle – then?'

'Oh, my sister Tribulation will look after her,' Captain Casket said, avoiding her eyes. 'Now I must leave thee to oversee the cutting-in. Goodbye, my child. Thee may have the use of my stateroom. I will move into Mr Slighcarp's cabin.'

As he walked aft, rather fast, Dido stared after him thoughtfully. Why had he been so anxious to get away? Somehow she felt that, although he seemed a good man, she could not entirely trust Captain Casket. He had more in his mind than he had told her. And she thought poorly of him for allowing his daughter to get the upper hand in so decided a way. Weak, she thought. He means well but he's weak. That's the sort that allus lets you down in the end.

Still, she thought, I can look after meself. I'm a big girl now, near as big as Simon. And she surveyed her extra six inches with pride before squatting down, chin on fists, to consider the problem of how Dutiful Penitence Casket was to be persuaded out of her shell.

3

Talking to Penitence – the veiled lady – hopscotch – Dido makes a promise

Long after dark had fallen Dido was still squatting on the quarter-deck, her brow wrinkled in thought. Twice since her talk with Captain Casket she had gone below, tapped on the panel in the captain's stateroom and tried to persuade the hidden occupant of the little room beyond to come out. Her first attempt had met with no response; next time the only reaction had been a fierce, miserable whisper from behind the panel:

'Go away. Go *away*! Whoever you are I shan't come out. I know you're only trying to trick me to go up on deck and be drowned!'

Dido saw that she would have to be clever.

'What do you do all day long in there?' she asked, the beginnings of a plan sprouting in her mind. There was no answer. She had not really expected one. She went on, half to herself: 'Well, I don't wonder you gets blue-devilled if you does nothing but sit and think o' drowning all the time. Cheesy, *I* calls it!'

She left the cabin, shutting the door behind her with a loud annoying slam.

After more than sixteen hours of frantic, continuous work the captured whale had been all cut up and melted down; Mr Slighcarp's watch staggered below, blind and speechless with fatigue. At last the moment arrived that Dido had been waiting for. She stretched, rose, left the quarter-deck, and went along to the try-works, which were simmering down, now, to a dull red glow. Half-a-dozen weary men were scrubbing the deck with ashes; their shadows flitted to and fro under a towering Arctic moon. From time to time they paused in their labours, dipped bits of hardtack in the still molten blubber and chewed them. The good-natured Mr Pardon was supervising the work.

'Why, dearie,' he said in surprise, 'you shoulda been in your bunk hours agone. Cap'n Casket tells me he's given you his stateroom for to be company for little Miss Penitence. Mr Slighcarp's not best pleased at having to move in with me, but 'tis more fitting for you than lying here on a donkey's breakfast. And I guess you'll be better able than a man to look after that poor little ailing lass.'

Dido nodded soberly. 'Mr Pardon,' she said.

'Well, dearie?'

'What's Captain Casket's little girl like?'

'Like?' Mr Pardon scratched his white head, puzzled. 'Why, I guess she's like all little gals. Sews her sampler, reads her lesson – Mrs Casket allus used to hear her lessons when she was alive, poor lady.'

'But what's she like?' Dido persisted. 'What kind o' games does she like to play?'

'Play? Why, I dunno as how she plays any *games*.

But my nephew Nate here'd know better'n I do; his home's not too far from the Casket place.'

'Games?' said Nate when appealed to. 'Don't reckon she ever played any. Very quiet little thing, sorta peaky. Her ma allus kept her pretty much at her stitching and so forth.'

'Blimey,' muttered Dido, 'what a set-out. No wonder she's such a misery. Mr Pardon, d'you reckon as how you could make me a shuttlecock for her? Out o' whalebone or summat? I could stick it with gulls' feathers.'

'I don't see why not,' Mr Pardon said doubtfully. 'Guess it would be simple enough. But what would Cap'n Casket think? Mrs Casket allus used to say that toys were inventions of the Devil.'

'I guess he'd have to put up with it,' Dido said. 'He asked me if I'd try to take Dutiful Penitence outa herself. She's pining for her ma.'

Nate was interested in the scheme. 'I could make a whalebone bat,' he offered. 'And some checkers or spillikins.'

'Could you? That'd be bang-up!'

Dido went below, well pleased with the way matters were shaping.

The big cabin was lit up by a hanging whale-oil lamp. Dido turned the wick up to its brightest. Then she listened. No sound came from Dutiful Penitence, so Dido banged the cabin door, opened and shut some drawers several times as loudly as she could, and overturned a chair with a tremendous clatter.

She heard a sleepy stir from beyond the panel. 'Papa, what's the matter?' said a scared voice. 'Is it a storm?'

Dido made no answer. She climbed up on to the

chart table and then, after carefully judging the distance, jumped four feet to a wall shelf, where she clung like a squirrel. From there, making use of the hanging compass, she swung to the bed, landing with a thud. Then she crawled to the bed-foot, put her knee on an open drawer, and clawed herself across to another shelf, aware, as she did so, though without showing it, that the panel had opened a crack and that she was being watched. She balanced on the shelf, gauging the distance to a chair.

'Who are you?' asked an astonished voice. 'And what *do* you think you're doing? Where is Papa?'

'I told you already,' Dido said without looking round. 'I'm Dido Twite. Your pa's given me his cabin.' She steadied herself and sprang. The chair fell, and threw her to the ground. 'Drat it,' Dido said coldly, getting up and rubbing her knee. 'Now I shall have to start again.'

'Start *what* again?'

Taking no notice of the question, Dido climbed back on to the chart table. This time she chose a different route, throwing herself like a flying-fox on to a large sea-chest, which seemed full of bottles, to judge from the loud clatter when she landed on it.

She scowled in concentration, considering a sideways clamber across the door as against an awkward diagonal jump to the bed. She chose the former.

'What are you doing?' the voice repeated.

Dido dragged herself up with difficulty and turned round. She was now perching like a gargoyle on a sort of dresser. 'Why!' she said exasperatedly. 'What d'you think I'm doing? What does it *look* as if I'm doing?

Making cheese? I'm getting round the room without touching the floor, o' course. I shoulda thought any ninny coulda seen *that*. You must be a slow-top. Now, don't interrupt again, you put me off.' She knit her brows and pressed her lips together, then with a mighty spring succeeded in launching herself from the dresser to the fallen chair, which slid conveniently across to the bed.

'Now I'm going to sleep,' Dido announced. 'Mind you don't make a noise and wake me.' She turned out the light. All this time she had never looked towards the open hatchway. Yawning loudly she snuggled down under the blankets. Silence fell.

After a longish pause the voice asked:

'Why didn't you want to touch the floor?'

Dido made no answer, but, instead, let out a slight snore.

Very early next morning Dido, who needed little sleep after her ten-month nap, woke and scurried up on deck before any sound came from Dutiful Penitence.

The *Sarah Casket*, all her barrels now filled with whale-oil, was speeding south under a clear sky. Already the icy mountains of Alaska were out of sight. Some of the men were hard at work hammering in the lids of the great hogsheads, twice the height of Dido, before these were lowered into the hold; others were scrubbing every inch of the deck and bulwarks with ashes and bits of blubber, even climbing into the rigging to wipe the shrouds. Soot and ashes flew away on the fresh breeze, and the ship by degrees began to look so tidy and clean that Dido could hardly believe it was the same in which, only the day before, whale-oil had run like greasy dark ink over the deck.

The kindly Mr Pardon had contrived time out of his duties to make a shuttlecock. He gave it to Dido. 'It ain't very grand; I made a bit of a mux of it,' he apologized. 'But I reckoned you'd ruther have it *soon* than *fancy*. I'll make a better one now I got the hang – I'm real pleased to do it. Young 'uns should have playthings. And Nate, he's fixing ye a right handsome battledore but 'twon't be finished yet a piece because Mr Slighcarp's sent him up to scrub the crow's nest.'

Dido looked up and saw a tiny figure, miles up it seemed in the clear piercing air. Nate waved a scrubbing-brush cheerfully and she waved back.

'This here's a fust-rate shuttlecock,' she told Mr Pardon. 'Just what I wanted. Cap'n Casket's little girl will be astonished, I reckon.'

'Don't forget your breakfast, dearie,' Mr Pardon said as she turned to go below.

'That's a notion,' Dido said. She added to herself: 'I dessay Dutiful Pen has had enough o' plum jelly to last a lifetime; let's see what a sight o' summat else does for her.' She skipped along to the camboose by the wheelhouse. 'What's for breakfast?' she asked briskly.

'Ah! Is little chick passenger!' The black cook gave her his beaming grin. 'I have nice fu-fu, also nice plum-duff.'

'Can I have two helps o' plum-duff? I'll take some down for Dutiful P. She might fancy it.'

'Is picky and choosy, that one,' the cook said, shaking his head. 'Is not fancy my cooking.' However, he dealt out two large portions of delicious raisin pudding, made with dripping and potash.

'You like some coffee?'

'Thanks, mister. Any milk?'

'Not yet, honey. Goat she took and died. In some month we make Galapagos Island. Then maybe coconut milk.'

Dido ran down the companionway with the food and sat down at the chart table, where she began to eat one portion of plum-duff with smacking sounds of enjoyment.

'Nibblish good prog,' she remarked loudly. 'Better'n my ma makes, anyhows.'

When she had finished her plateful she got up, leaving the second portion untouched and well in view, took the shuttlecock out of her pocket, and began to kick it into the air. As Mr Pardon had said, it was not a very well-made one, being slightly unbalanced, and at first Dido found difficulty in keeping it up for more than two or three kicks. She persevered, however, bounding about the room until she was breathless and bruised from collisions with the furniture. She noticed that the panel had opened an inch and an eye was peering at her with silent, astonished attention.

'This room ain't big enough,' Dido complained presently, when she was becoming more experienced with the shuttlecock and had worked her score up to twenty-three. 'I'm a-going on deck, I am, where there's plenty of room.'

She departed, slamming the door behind her. Although strongly tempted to linger and look through the keyhole, she knew this would be foolish. Instead she clattered up the companion stair and went out to the quarter-deck.

However she soon found that there was little room, even here, to practise her game, for the men were tidying out the hold, to make room for the last casks of whale-oil, and had brought all the stores up on deck: bundles of hoops and staves, great sides of salt beef, sacks of hardtack, and a whole mass of other gear lay heaped in disorder. The casks of oil in the hold were being hosed, to keep them watertight, and there was such a general hubbub of to-and-fro activity that Dido seemed to be constantly underfoot and in everybody's way. Nate, playing on a sort of zither made of whalebone, helped the men keep time.

They were singing:

> 'Strong to Pleasant, Wake to Guam
> Winds are favouring, seas are calm,
> Midway down to Pokaaku
> Typhoon cuts our mainmast through.
>
> 'Easter, Disappointment, Nome,
> Through the watery world we roam,
> Tristan, Fogo, Trinidad,
> Winds contrary, weather bad,
> Christmas, East, Kwajalein –
> When shall we see Brant Point again?'

The zither gave Dido an idea. There were bundles of whalebone pieces lying about the deck, of assorted sizes and shapes. 'I reckon they can spare me a bit,' she said to herself. 'I won't bother to ask Cap'n Casket, he looks a mite cagged.'

The captain was taking no part in the bustle; he leaned against the mainmast with his eyes fixed on the far horizon.

Dido picked up a piece of bone about the size of a walking-stick and quietly made off with it.

'Now all I want's a tool; land's sakes, they must have plenty on a ship this size if I could find out where they keeps 'em.'

There was a smith's forge by the foremast and a carpenter's bench aft of the try-works but both these were too much under observation at present; hoping to find other stores Dido nipped down the forward hatchway into the blubber-room. This was unoccupied, now, and silent; a sort of tidemark on the wall showed where yesterday the blubber had been stacked kneedeep. At the moment the room was being used for the temporary storage of things taken from the hold; a pile of oakum and sail-canvas occupied most of the floor. Dido turned to leave, seeing nothing she could use, but then stopped, arrested by the unexpected sight of a boot protruding from under the canvas.

It was bottle-green, elastic sided, quite unlike the brogans worn by the sailors. It looked like an English lady's boot. Where could it have come from? Puzzled and inquisitive, Dido gave it a tug, and then jumped back with a yelp of alarm as the boot disappeared swiftly beneath the canvas. There was a foot inside it!

Curiosity overcoming her caution, Dido approached the heap once more and pulled aside some folds of canvas. A sort of writhing motion went on in the middle of the heap, the sailcloth was displaced, and suddenly, rather as a serpent darts out of its lair, the figure of a tall, veiled lady uncoiled and shot from under the pile of stuff. She towered over the quailing Dido, who would have run for it had she not been held fast by the ear.

'What do you think you are doing here?' the lady said in a low, grating tone.

'P-p-please, ma'am, I d-didn't mean no harm!' gulped Dido. 'I was only looking for a c-c-corkscrew!'

'A likely story! Prying and meddling where you'd no business to be! Repulsive child! You deserve to be severely punished. Now, listen here, miss!'

'Y-y-yes, ma'am?'

'If you so much as mention that you have seen me to anyone – anyone at all – I shall learn of it. And it will be the worse for you. You wish to return to England, do you not?'

'Yes, ma'am,' Dido whispered, very much astonished.

'Then you had better keep a still tongue in your head! Otherwise your chances of ever seeing London River again are very, very small. Do you understand? Now – *go!*'

Dido needed no encouragement – something in the veiled lady's aspect had struck her with mortal terror – but she received a final warning in the form of a box on the ear, that shot her out of the doorway.

Numb and chattering with fright she scurried up the companionway and back on deck. Luckily nobody had noticed her come out. The whole crew were trying to manhandle a spare anchor out of its usual resting-place so as to cram a few casks of oil underneath it. Frightened though she was, Dido kept her wits about her; she

grabbed a handful of tools from the carpenter's bench and then, still gasping for breath, ran down to the captain's cabin.

She was too discomposed to notice that the hatchway shut with a click as she entered the room, but she did observe, when a little more recovered, that the plum-duff on the second plate had been eaten. She grinned to herself and, sitting up, inspected the tools she had taken. Choosing a drill, she set to work on her whale-bone rod.

It proved a long, fiddling task, which occupied most of the day. Though aware that she was often watched, Dido pretended not to notice. She found it impossible to work all the time, for her fingers became stiff. Twice she broke off to make a tour of the room without touching the deck, each time attempting a new route. She also played several games of shuttlecock, and chalked herself out a hopscotch square on the chart table. Here she encountered a difficulty, however.

'I wisht as how I had a pebble,' she remarked aloud. 'Or a marble, or a penny, or even a button would do. Oh well,' heaving a deep sigh, 'can't play hopscotch, that's all. Funny how I has a *fancy* to play hopscotch. Anyway I reckon it's dinner-time; I'll nip up to the camboose and see what's cooking.'

She took the empty plates and left the room.

All the time she had been working and playing part of her mind was occupied with the puzzle of the mysterious veiled lady in the blubber-room. Could she be a stowaway? Dido wondered. She might have been hidden in the hold and obliged to take refuge elsewhere because of the general turnout. But where could she have come on board? What did she live on? Did none of the crew know about her presence?

'Somebody must know,' Dido said to herself as she absently accepted two bowls of porpoise chowder from the cook, '*somebody* must know, and musta told her about me. Else how did she twig I was English? I wonder who told her?'

She returned to the cabin, ate her meal, and flung herself on the bed for a nap, burying her face in the pillow and letting out snores. For a long time there was silence; then she heard a cautious clink. She redoubled her snores, shutting her eyes so tightly that she saw red and green stars. Presently the hatch was heard to close with a gentle click. For good measure Dido lay five minutes longer, then, yawning loudly, she opened her eyes. The second chowder bowl was empty. Beside it lay a large leather button.

'Well I never!' Dido exclaimed in astonishment. 'Fancy my not noticing that there button afore! Jist what I needed for hopscotch! Now, can I remember the rules, I wonder?'

Having dumped the chowder bowls on the floor she climbed on to the table. Addressing herself as if she were a slow-witted pupil she proceeded to rehearse the rules of hopscotch. She was thus occupied when the door opened unexpectedly and she met Captain Casket's startled eyes.

'Is – is thee all right, my child?' he asked.

'Now look here,' said Dido crossly. 'Let's get this straight from the fust. You gives me your cabin, right, then it's *mine*. See? I don't expect no monnicking and chissicking – no *interference*,' she explained impatiently as she met his questioning gaze. 'You keep outa here. Ain't you got the ship to look arter? You go watch for that pink whale o' yourn. *I'll* tell you if you're wanted here.'

She gave him such a fierce scowl that he retreated, gingerly shutting the door. 'That's got rid o' *him*,' Dido said with satisfaction. 'Now maybe we can tend to business.'

She practised hopscotch very enjoyably for an hour or so, then worked on her piece of whalebone. When this was completely hollowed out into a tube she made a mouthpiece at one end and a series of holes along it. If blown on hard enough it produced a plaintive sound, like the call of a hungry bird. After much labour Dido had several notes adjusted to her satisfaction, and was able to play 'God Save King Jim' and 'Who'll Buy My Sweet Lavender?' This was received with awestruck and flattering silence from the watcher behind the panel.

'I wisht I knowed a few more tunes,' Dido said at length. 'Seems as how while I'd been asleep I forgot most o' the ones I used to know. Ah well – maybe I'll remember some more tomorrow. I'll jist step out for a breath o' fresh air now, and then go to kip.'

She went in search of Nate, and found him sprawled on the main deck, weaving a rope mat in a rather inattentive and dreamy fashion while he tried over the words of a chanty.

'Oh it's gally and roll, me boys, ripple and run,
So hold to your hand-lance, the chase has begun,
Tally-ho! till she breaches, come, join in the fun
We're off on a Nantucket sleigh-ride.

'It's flurry and scurry, she bolts and she sounds
And something and something tum tiddle tum
grounds
And something else ending in bounds or in rounds
Hey ho! for a Nantucket sleigh-ride.

'Oh, hallo, chick,' he broke off, on seeing Dido. 'I've got summat for you. Finished it as soon as old man Slighcarp went below.' And he brought out a beautiful little battledore, ingeniously made from woven strips of bone.

'Coo!' said Dido. 'It's naffy! Ain't you clever? I'll lay Dutiful Pen won't be able to hold off when she sees this! Could you make another one, d'you reckon?'

'Guess so,' Nate said agreeably. He started singing again:

'Tum tiddle tum tiddle tum tiddle tum grounds
Pull on! head to head as his noddle he rounds . . .

'Can you think of a rhyme for sounds, chick?'

Dido could not. 'Does you make 'em up, then?' she asked, much impressed.

'Sure.'

Finding Nate such a kindred spirit Dido showed him her whalebone pipe.

'That's cunning,' he said, blowing on it. 'Mighty smart work for a liddle 'un. Who learned you to do that?'

'My pa,' Dido said proudly. 'He plays on the hoboy, so he learned me how to make a tootlepipe.'

'Say, we'll be able to have some fine concerts now when old Slighcarp's under hatches.'

'It's time I was under hatches too,' Dido remarked, looking up at the moon. ''Night, Nate.' And she added to herself, 'I've a kind of a notion that Dutiful P might surface tonight, so I'd best be there.'

It had been an energetic day, with the hopscotch, the shuttlecock, the climbing, and hard work on the pipe; Dido turned out the lamp as soon as she reached the cabin, flung herself on the bed, and went straight to sleep.

About two hours later she found herself suddenly broad awake. The *Sarah Casket* was still speeding south before a following wind; Dido could feel the rush of the great seas as they lifted and drove past the ship's sides. Every timber creaked, and even down here the hum of wind in the rigging could be heard. Moonlight came through the ports; a patch of it on the floor hardly shifted, so steady was the ship on her course.

Dido wondered what had woken her.

The she felt the clutch of little cold hands on her arm.

'Who is it?' she whispered.

'It's me. Dutiful Penitence.'

'Ain't you cold, jist? Best come under the quilt, hadn't you?' Dido said matter-of-factly. She felt a small shape huddle up against her under the patchwork. Just at this moment the steersman evidently altered course a point or so, and the oblong of moonshine slid round, revealing the visitor.

She was a thin little creature, frail-looking as a cobweb (and no wonder, if she's been living on plum jelly ever since Santa Cruz, thought Dido), with long silvery hair, not very well brushed. She stared gravely at Dido.

'Are you really a girl?' she asked after a while.

'Yes, what d'you think? A mermaid?'

'But where did you come from?'

'Your pa picked me up, off the coast of England. I was in a ship what caught fire and sank. And I've been asleep for ten months – so Nate says – all the time you was in storage.'

'You were *in the sea*? Didn't you get scared?'

'It wasn't bad. I hung on to a spar.'

'You must be brave! Are you English?'

'Yus. And don't I jist wish I was back in England,' Dido remarked with feeling. 'But your pa says he'll put me on a boat from New Bedford, wherever that is.'

'Near Nantucket. We may unload there before going home. But I don't suppose I *shall* be going home now,' Dutiful Penitence said drearily. 'There'd be nobody to look after me except Aunt Tribulation, Papa says, and I won't stay with *her*. Maybe Cousin Ann Allerton will have me in New Bedford.'

'Who's Aunt Tribulation?' Dido asked. She had heard the name before. Could this be the lady in the blubber-room?

'Papa's sister. She's dreadfully sharp and unkind. She lives in Vine Rapids now but she came to stay once and upset me and Mamma. Oh, she did upset us! She told dear Mamma that she was a fool, bringing me up to be a cry-baby. Papa wanted to leave me with her when he took Mamma to sea, but I heard Mamma say she wouldn't dream of allowing it; she said Aunt Tribulation was a real dragon, and it was lucky she'd no children of her own, for her rough, slapdash ways would probably be the death of any child she had charge of. Mamma wouldn't want me to stay with a dragon.'

'What does she look like?'

'I can't remember – quite. I was only five when she came. I remember her scolding me, and saying I was a little wet-goose, because I was afraid of her dog.'

'Hum,' said Dido. 'For a sea-captain's daughter you certainly are a rum 'un, Dutiful. And, look here, whoever tied that handle to you musta been dicked in the nob and *I'm* not going to lay my tongue round it every time. I'll call you Pen. Agreeable?'

'Yes, thank you,' Penitence said shyly. 'No one ever gave me a short name before. How old are you, Dido?'

'I've sorta lost count,' Dido admitted. 'With the long nap and all. Round about eleven, I reckon. What did you do all the time shut in that cupboard, Pen?'

'Oh, it wasn't bad. Come and see.'

They lit the lamp and Penitence showed Dido her little room. It was really a store-cupboard with shelves all round, but one of them had been turned into a bunk. There were a few lesson-books, writing materials, sewing-things, and rows and rows of empty jelly bottles.

'I did lots of lessons,' Penitence explained, 'and I read the Bible and learned a hymn every day. Shall I say one?'

'Not jist now, thanks,' Dido answered promptly. 'Croopus, ain't you *good*, though? Didn't you never get fed up?'

'Oh no. I kept a journal – but it wasn't very interesting,' Penitence confessed. 'And I worked on my sampler.' She held up an extremely large square, embroidered in cross-stitch with a ship and whales and gulls and a long piece of poetry beginning, 'Myfterious Magnet! Ere thy ufe was known, Fear clad the Deep in horrors not its own.' It was nearly finished.

'I'd sooner have done roses and doves,' Penitence went on, 'but dear M-Mamma thought it would please Papa if it had sea things. I began it when I was six.'

'Well!' said Dido. 'I'd ha' been blue-devilled in here. Specially when it's such prime fun on deck.'

Penitence shivered. 'I couldn't *bear* to go on deck. That dreadful sea! I know I'd fall in! And all the cross, rough men, and the horrid smells and dirt. Mamma always said it was dangerous up there. You won't try to make me go, will you?'

'Bless you, no. It ain't my affair. Anyhows we can have a bang-up time in the cabin now you've decided to come out and be civil.'

'Will you teach me that game with the feathered thing? And play tunes on your pipe?'

'Course I will. Us'll have rare fun.'

'You don't think Mamma would mind?' Penitence said hesitantly. 'She said playing games was a sin.'

'*Croo*–' Dido began, but bit the words back.

Her own parents, as she recalled, had never seemed particularly kind or fond of her, but at least they were quite *sensible*; all that was said of Mrs Casket, however, seemed to suggest that the woman had been an utter fool. Musta been queer in her attic, Dido thought. 'Reckon she knows better now?' she suggested gruffly. 'Lawks, if you never played, what *did* you do at home?'

'Helped with the housework.'

'Well I done that too. But I played arterwards.'

'After I'd done my tasks Mamma used to let me sit on her lap while she read the Bible,' said Penitence. Her composure faltered. 'If – if I'd been extra good, she used – she used to sing a h-hymn –'

Here, breaking down altogether, Penitence threw herself on the bed, buried her head in the quilt and cried. She cried very much indeed.

Dido looked at her worriedly. There was little consolation to offer. Foolish, Mrs Casket may have been, but her daughter had plainly thought the world of her.

'Don't take on so,' Dido said after a while, with awkward sympathy. 'Want a hankersniff? I've got one.'

But as Penitence made no reply, just went on crying and shivering and choking, Dido sat down on the floor by her, feeling oddly grown-up and capable and protective, and put an arm round her.

'Cheer up,' she muttered. 'I'll keep an eye on you. It won't work out so bad. You'll see.'

The small silvery head rubbed against her.

'Will you? Will you really?'

'That I will.'

'And when we get home to Nantucket? Will you stay with me then? So's Papa don't leave me all alone with Aunt Tribulation? I'd die if I was to be looked after by a dragon. Please? *Please!*'

The thin arms came round Dido's neck in a tight hug, so that she could hardly breathe.

'Well – maybe,' Dido said reluctantly. 'Just for a little while. You know, I dessay your Auntie Trib ain't so dragonish really. But till your pa gets you fixed up with somebody else –'

'Oh, you are kind! You're so much braver than I am.

I'm scared of *everything*. But you've even been in the *sea*! If you'll – if you'll stay with me it will be much better. Will you promise?'

'All right,' Dido said, sighing.

'Would you – would you sing something now? That song you were singing before?'

'All right,' said Dido again. She began to sing in a small gruff voice:

> 'Who'll buy my sweet lavender?
> Three bunches a penny!
> Fresh picked in Sevenoaks this morning,
> Three bunches a penny!'

She stroked the tousled head. It lay heavily on her shoulder, and before long drooped in sleep.

Dido sat and stared at the lamp, which they had forgotten to turn out. Presently its yellow flame swelled and wavered in a blur of tears. Resolutely she blinked them away. It was stupid to be homesick when she knew her family wouldn't be missing her much anyway, if at all.

4

Encouraging Pen – the Galapagos – gamming with the Martha –
Mr Slighcarp's strange behaviour –
round the Horn and back to New Bedford

'Psst! Hey! Cap'n – Cap'n Casket! Will you step this-away?'

Captain casket started, as Dido's voice roused him from his usual sad reverie; he turned and saw her standing behind him.

Making sure that no one could overhear she came close to him and hissed conspiratorially:

'I've done it! She's out!'

Captain Casket appeared thunderstruck.

'On deck?'

'No, no, no, gaffer. Not yet. Give us time. But she's out in the cabin eatin' of plum-duff and a-playin' hop-scotch. I'll have her on deck one o' these days, though, s'long as you don't come creating and badgering.'

'Thee is a remarkable child,' Captain Casket said solemnly.

'I say though,' Dido went on, 'what 'bout this Auntie Trib, then? She fair gives young Pen the horrors. Pen thinks she's a dragon. It'll be all my work for Habakkuk if Pen finds Auntie Trib's going to have charge of her in Nantucket; she'll snib herself up in the pantry again before you can say whale-o!'

Captain Casket looked harassed. 'Sister Tribulation is really a most estimable character,' he murmured. 'She is endowed with every Christian virtue.'

'You allus says that,' Dido interjected.

'My poor Sarah – my poor wife never understood her. But I am sure that *thee* could persuade Dutiful Penitence to like her aunt, my child.'

'That's as maybe,' Dido said drily. 'Anyhows, you better consider if there ain't somebody else as could do the job. I'm a-warning you, see? Blimey, on an island the size of Nantucket' – Dido had found it on the map by now – 'there must be somebody else as could have charge of her. Now, I'm a-going to teach Dutiful P to play shuttlecock; lor, I don't wonder the poor little tyke's so mopish. She ain't had no upbringing at all!'

It took several weeks of Dido's company and encouragement before Penitence could be persuaded on deck. Dido was too shrewd to hurry her. They played endless games in the cabin, sang songs, asked riddles, and talked, each telling the other the whole story of her life. Penitence was quite amazed by Dido's tales of the London streets and could never hear enough about the fairs and the fights, the street markets, Punch and Judy shows, glimpses of grand people in their carriages, and the little Scottish King James III, against whom the Hanoverians were always plotting.

'Fancy living in such a great city!' Penitence said

dreamily. 'Why, where we lived in Nantucket it's almost five miles to the next *house*.'

'Wouldn't suit me,' Dido said. 'I likes a bit o' life and company.'

'My mamma didn't like it either. She came from Boston. When Papa went to sea,' Pen confessed, 'she used to take me for long visits to Cousin Ann in New Bedford. We didn't stay in Nantucket much.'

Dido had become quite fond of Pen by now – there was more in the funny little thing than met the eye – but none the less it was a relief to run up on deck now and then, to talk to Nate and joke with the sailors; after a few hours of Pen's company she felt she wanted to shout and jump and climb into the rigging. Pen had grown absolutely devoted to her and, Dido considered, was coming out of her mopey ways very well.

Pen still kept her quiet tastes, though; she liked to spend several hours a day doing lessons and sewing; she offered to read the Bible or hymns to Dido but this, for the most part, Dido politely refused.

'Tell you what, though,' she suggested. 'How 'bout asking your pa if we can invite Nate to come down and sing you some o' his songs? He knows a rare lot, and on top o' that he's allus rattling off new ones. Wouldn't you like it, eh?'

Penitence looked doubtful. 'Is he very big? He isn't rough? He wouldn't tease me or hurt me?'

'Now, *Pen*! Don't you know me better'n that by now? Would I ask him if he was liable to do such blame-fool things? I'm *surprised* at you!'

Pen apologized, Captain Casket's permission was obtained, and Nate, rather bashfully, came down to the stateroom with his zither. At first Penitence trembled a good deal at the close presence of such a tall, lanky, red-headed creature, and was quite speechless with shyness. But when Nate sang:

> 'Oh, fierce is the Ocean and wild is the Sound
> But the isle of Nantucket is where I am bound,
> Sweet isle of Nantucket! where the grapes are so red,
> And the light flashes nightly on Sankaty Head!'*

she was quite delighted, clapped her hands, and exclaimed, 'Oh that *is* pretty! Sing it again!'

Nate sang it again, and many others. Dido, curled up under the chart table, hugged her knees and congratulated herself. From that day, Nate was a welcome visitor in the cabin; in fact he was with them, singing a song about the high-rolling breakers on the south shore of Nantucket, and the brave fishermen who launched their dories through the foam, when a sudden shout from the deck startled them.

'Land! Land-ho!'

'Must have sighted the Galapagos!' said Nate, scrambling to his feet. 'Blame it, why wasn't I up aloft? Cap'n Casket allus gives half a dollar to the first one that sights land. See you later, gals!' And he bolted out.

'How about it, Pen?' Dido said carelessly. 'Coming up for a look-see? Nate says there are giant tortoises on the Galapagos, as big as tea tables.'

* Actually Sankaty Light was not built till 1850, but for the purpose of this book I have brought it into existence thirty years earlier.

Pen hesitated, in an agony of indecision; at last she agreed.

Dido was quite glad of the chance to bring Pen on deck when Mr Slighcarp would be ashore, buying fresh fruit and vegetables; the rest of the men were kind and friendly to her but the first mate always had a scowl and a harsh word; she had been rather anxious about the effect of this on Penitence. Luckily the deck was quite empty when, clutching Dido's hand in a tight grip, Penitence timidly followed her up the companionway and came blinking into the sunshine.

'Oh,' she breathed in astonishment. 'Isn't it *bright*? And warm! I thought we were in the Arctic.'

'We left that behind weeks ago,' Dido said kindly. 'Sit down on a coil o' rope, you're all of a tremble.'

Penitence sank down obediently. In the bright sunshine her face seemed as pale as a primrose, and contrasted strangely with Dido's healthy tan. At first she was pitiably nervous, her great blue eyes widened and she clasped Dido's hand violently whenever a wavecrest broke near the ship.

Unfortunately the land was too far away for much to be visible except a low-lying mass with some scrubby trees on it. But they were excited to see another ship, the *Martha*, anchored not far off.

Presently Captain Casket wandered along towards them. He started uncontrollably when he saw Penitence, but Dido gave him such a fierce scowl of warning that he tried to conceal his astonishment and only said:

'I am glad to see thee out in the fresh air at last, Daughter. Thee must get some roses into thy cheeks like those of thy little friend.'

Penitence made an awkward bob, and answered, 'Yes Papa,' in such a subdued tone that it was hardly audible; she seemed greatly relieved when he walked away along the deck.

Soon there came a hail from the *Martha*, and a boat was lowered and rowed towards them; a cheerful red-faced man called: 'Jabez! Cap'n Jabez Casket! Are you there? Can I come aboard for a gam? I've some mail for you, only eight months out o' New Bedford.'

'Come aboard and welcome, Cap'n Bilger,' Captain Casket called, and the skipper of the *Martha* was swung aboard. He handed over a batch of letters for the *Sarah Casket*'s captain and crew, and asked if they could spare any ship's biscuit as most of his had been spoiled by a leak; he offered coffee and Lemon Syrup in exchange (which the cook was glad to accept since Pen had eaten all the jelly).

'Concern it!' exclaimed Captain Bilger, slapping his leg in annoyance. 'If I haven't forgotten to bring over that blame bird!'

'Bird? What bird?' Captain Casket inquired.

'Why, a bird belonging to that boy of yours, Nate Pardon. One of my men caught it flapping about the streets of New Bedford before we sailed and recognized it as his; we've had it aboard ever since. I'll be thankful to see the last of it, I can tell you. That bird would talk the ears off a brass monkey. Now I come to think, I've another letter for you, as well. It got a mite damp, came unstuck, and I put it aside from the others. My memory's fuller of holes'n a dip-net.'

'No matter,' said Captain Casket. 'My men can call round by the *Martha* when they come back from provisioning and pick up the bird and the letter. Young Nate will be glad to see his pet.'

The two captains went below to gossip and, an early tropical dusk falling soon after, Dido and Penitence also retired to their cabin to play hunt the thimble and speculate as to what sort of things Nate's bird would be able to say.

Pen was quite tired out by the fresh air and the excitement of being on deck; she soon went to bed and to sleep. Dido, however, was not sleepy; she returned to lean on the rail and gaze wistfully at the lights on shore. Presently she heard Captain Bilger taking his leave, and later still the men returned. Having been instructed by signals with a lantern they rowed round by the *Martha* and picked up Nate's bird, but Dido heard Mr Slighcarp telling Captain Casket that Captain Bilger found he had been mistaken about the extra letter; it was after all not for him but for the captain of some other ship.

Nate was overjoyed to recover his bird, which he had never expected to see again, and showed it off proudly to Dido.

'His name's Mr Jenkins. Ain't he beautiful?'

Dido admired the bird's glossy black plumage and brilliant yellow bill.

'What does he say?'

The bird gave her a haughty glance and remarked:

'Dinner is served in the small ballroom, your grace.'

'Ain't he a stunner?' Nate said. 'He goes on like that all the time. We reckoned as how he musta belonged to some lord or duke once.'

'Order the perch phaeton,' croaked Mr Jenkins. 'A

young person has called, your lordship. Tea is served in her grace's boudoir. Ho, there, a chair for Lady Fothergill!'

'You silly old sausage,' said Nate, giving his pet a loving hug. 'There aren't any lords or dukes here.'

Affronted and on his dignity, Mr Jenkins clambered out of Nate's arms and ascended to the top of his head, where he suddenly shouted in a stentorian voice, 'God save the King! Hooray for Jamie Three! God save our sovereign lord King James and DOWN WITH THE GEORGIANS!'

Mr Slighcarp happened to be passing at that moment. He gave a violent start and dropped the telescope he was carrying. It fell with a crash.

'Who said that?' he cried.

'It was the bird, Mr Slighcarp, old Jenkins.'

'Well don't let him do it again or I'll wring his neck!' the mate said with an oath. 'Plague take the creature, you'd best keep him under hatches if he's liable to go on like that. I won't have it, see?'

Much abashed, Nate hurried his pet below. Dido, who was still feeling wakeful, retreated to a patch of shadow against the bulwarks and curled up there, listening longingly to cheerful sounds of music and singing from the *Martha*.

Presently Captain Casket approached her. He was a changed man; his eyes glittered feverishly and he walked with a rapid, excited step.

'Ah, my child,' he said cordially. 'Is not this stirring news?'

Dido thought he was referring to the mail he had received.

'You fixed up what you're going to do about young Pen, then, when you gets back to Nantucket?' she said hopefully. 'Someone offered to look arter her?'

'Oh, that. No, no, Captain Bilger tells me that the pink whale has been sighted off the Peruvian coast. We shall see her! I feel certain that we shall see her soon!'

'Oh, bother the pink whale,' Dido said testily. 'What about Pen?'

'Ah yes. Dear Tribulation writes with true sisterly feeling, having just heard of my poor wife's death. She will move to Nantucket and look after Dutiful Penitence and the house for me.'

'But, blame it!' Dido said in exasperation. 'Pen don't *want* to live with her Auntie Tribulation! On account of summat her ma said she's scared to death of the notion; it won't answer at *all*! Can't you get that into your seaweedy noddle?'

'She suggests further,' Captain Casket went on, dreamily looking out over the water and ignoring Dido, 'that a companion, some other girl of her age, would be an advantage for Penitence, since my farm, Soul's Hill, is situated in a somewhat lonely location. So if thee will accept the charge, my child, not for very long, of course, that will solve all our problems, will it not? Thy quick wit will soon smooth over any little difficulties between my daughter and her good aunt. And when Penitence is settled and happy, my sister Tribulation will no doubt see that thee is found a passage to England. Remember, too, that we rescued thee from the sea, my child, and that thee owes us a debt of gratitude.'

Silenced for the moment, Dido scowled after him as he walked away. An hour or so went by and she was

about to retire when she noticed the figure of Mr Slighcarp standing not far away. Something furtive and cautious about his manner attracted her interest and she watched him sharply as he made his way to the rail. Unaware of Dido, squatting motionless in the shadows, Mr Slighcarp looked quickly all round him and then proceeded to tear in tiny pieces some sheets of paper which he had carried hidden in the breast of his jacket, and drop them over the side.

'What's he doing that for?' wondered Dido. 'What's so tarnation private about a letter?'

Then she recalled that Mr Slighcarp had been asked to collect a letter for the captain, and that he had not done so. He had said Captain Bilger had made a mistake, the letter was for somebody else. Was it possible that he had lied? Could the letter really have been for Captain Casket after all? Suppose this was it? But why should he be destroying it?

There seemed no answer to this puzzle, or none that Dido could supply. She continued to watch Mr Slighcarp attentively, however, and was somewhat astonished by what he did next. Making sure, as he thought, that he was unobserved, he produced a pair of boots from under his jacket, and brushed them long and carefully.

Dido's heart beat fast and she nodded to herself grimly.

A brilliant tropical moon swam overhead and by its light, and that of a pewter lantern not far away, every detail of the scene was clearly visible. The boots that Mr Slighcarp brushed were no sailors' brogans, but a pair of English ladies' buttoned travelling-boots in dull bottle-green.

At last, satisfied, apparently, with the appearance of the boots, Mr Slighcarp retired once more, in the same prudent and furtive manner.

Dido remained on deck for a considerable time longer. At first she had half a mind to tell Captain Casket about the incident. But then she decided not to. After all, what had she to go on but suspicion; who could say that the letter was not Mr Slighcarp's own? He had every right to tear up his own letter. Furthermore, if Mr Slighcarp realized that Dido had seen him tear it up, he would know that she had also seen him brushing the boots. He would be revealed as the accomplice of the stowaway lady in the blubber-room. Dido had not forgotten this lady's fiercely whispered threat, 'Keep a still tongue in your head. Otherwise your chances of ever seeing London River again are very, very small!'

'I'll keep mum,' she finally decided. 'After all, if I did tell Captain Casket, like as not he'd only gaze at me in that moon-faced way o' his and start to talk about his everlasting pink whale. I dessay it wasn't his letter. And I don't want an up-and-a-downer with old man Slighcarp. I'll keep a still tongue. But I'll watch.'

Nate, whose turn it was on the middle watch, came on deck at this moment, and passed the time of night with Dido. Mr Jenkins, sitting on his shoulder, gave a polite croak, and remarked:

'Your lordship's bath is ready in the tapestry room. I have warmed the morning paper, Sir Henry. Pray bring his grace's bath-chair this way. Down with the scurvy Hanoverians!'

'Best watch out for Mr Slighcarp,' Dido said grinning.

'No danger, it's his watch below,' Nate said. 'That's why I brought old Jenkins up for a breath of air.'

'I wonder why he riles Mr Slighcarp so,' Dido said yawning.

'Don't you know? Because Mr Slighcarp's English too, but he was a Hanoverian, on the other side. He wanted to get rid of that king you got. So he don't like it when the old bird says "Down with the Hanoverians". He had to run abroad in a hurry or he'd a been clapped in prison, the militia was after him. Leastways, that's what Uncle 'Lije said. Mr Slighcarp hasn't shipped with Cap'n Casket very long, but he stayed in Nantucket a piece before that.'

'He's English? Mr Slighcarp?'

'Sure. You'd think he'd a taken a bit more of a shine to you,' Nate said, 'seeing you both come from the same part.'

It was a long time, almost dawn, before Dido fell asleep, and when she did so her slumbers were soon broken short by a sudden and violent disturbance.

The whole ship seemed to give a tremendous bound, like a startled horse; there were loud and prolonged cries overhead; feet thudded on the deck and Dido heard the crash and rattle as sails were shaken out and the anchor was dragged bodily from the bottom.

'What's the matter, what's happened?' Pen cried fearfully – she had been jerked out of bed by the ship's unexpected movement and was whimpering on the floor. 'Is it a hurricane?'

Dido held up a hand for silence. She was listening attentively to the shouts overhead.

'No,' she said drily after a minute. 'It ain't a hurricane; a little thing like that wouldn't get your pa so stirred-up. Oh, well, one thing, it'll help us on our way home at a rattling good pace. That is, allus supposing the old gal plays her part and don't go skedaddling off to Timbuctoo or Tobago.'

'How do you mean? What old gal?'

'Why,' Dido said, 'the pink 'un. Rosie Lee. Hear what they shouted? We're a-chasin' after that there sweet-pea-coloured whale of his'n.'

The days and weeks that followed were fierce and rugged. Careering after her quarry through the South Pacific Trades, the *Sarah Casket* flew along under every sail that she would take. Main-tops, top-gallants, and stunsails were set, the rigging thrummed like a banjo, and often, as they drove through the southern seas, their mainmast was bent over so far that Nate declared they might as well use it for a bow, if they ever got close enough to the pink whale, and fire off a harpoon from the mainstay.

Nothing would persuade Penitence on deck now, and even Dido, when they reached the wild easterlies and heavy squalls in the straits of Magellan, was glad enough to stay in the cabin playing pachisi.

At first Dido was inclined, like the others, to believe that Captain Casket had merely imagined his glimpse of the pink whale at Galapagos, until one evening, south of Cape Horn, she saw something between two wildly blowing williwaws that she at first took to be a momentary view of the setting sun – except that it lay to the east. It was like a rosy, iridescent bubble balanced amid the black, leaping seas. Then the storm came down again and they saw it no more. But Captain Casket, with a frantic, exultant light in his eye, kept the ship under a full press of canvas, heedless of danger, clapping on new sails as the old ones ripped away. Without regard to tempest, tidal wave, or terremoto, he fought his way round the Horn, making a record passage of it, while his men served four hours on and four off, becoming haggard and thin from wear and tear and lack of sleep. The captain himself never seemed to sleep at all and his eyes were red from scanning the horizon.

There were few chances for Nate to come down to the cabin now; he was kept busy all the time as a lookout, or taking soundings, or mending the tattered sails. Sometimes he could be heard singing as he sewed, with Mr Jenkins (who had acquired a wholesome respect for Mr Slighcarp) supplying the chorus in a subdued croak:

'Stow your line-tubs, belay tail-feathers,
It's rough, it's rugged, it's blowy weather.
Make your passage and follow the moon –
Dinner is served in the blue saloon.

'Slush the spars and splice the rigging
Leave your scrimshaw and grab your piggin
Bail, boys, bail! for your wage and lay –
Her ladyship's carriage blocks the way.'

Mr Jenkins spent a good deal of this time with the

girls in the cabin; Nate was glad to know that his pet was in a safe spot, and the girls were glad of the company, particularly as Mr Jenkins made an extremely civil guest. He would play tiddlywinks (if ever they struck a long enough patch of calm weather), flipping scrimshaw counters into a cup with great dexterity and enjoyment; while his grave observations about life in high society kept Pen and Dido amused for hours.

Past Trinidad they chased, past the Brazilian coast, through the Sargasso Sea (which slowed down the pink whale a little, for she got weeds caught in her flukes), past Bermuda, past Cape Hatteras, and so home. But the pink whale, unfortunately, seemed disinclined to stop, and mutterings were to be heard among the men that at this rate they'd likely be skating past Newfoundland before they discharged cargo and had their pay.

A deputation waited on Captain Casket and pointed out to him that they were low on stores and water, that there wasn't a single unmended sail on board and that what hardtack was left would walk away from you along the deck if you let go of your ration for a moment. With great difficulty he was persuaded to put in to New Bedford.

And so it was that, almost seven months to the day after she had first opened her eyes on board the *Sarah Casket*, Dido had a chance to set foot on solid ground.

'New Bedford!' she said ungratefully. 'Where's that, I ask you? Land sakes, Cap'n Casket mighta just as well nipped across to Dover, it wouldn't a taken him but a few more weeks.'

She glared with disfavour at the trim roofs of the town climbing its hill above the harbour. 'Still,' she admitted in acknowledgment of the forest of masts, 'I will say there's a-plenty o' shipping here; maybe I'll find some bark as'll take me on to England.'

'You promised you'd come home with me first, you *promised*,' Pen reminded her anxiously.

'All right, all right, I ain't forgotten,' Dido growled. 'I've said I'll see you right and I will – if we can only get your pa to tend to your affairs for two minutes together. You know you had a notion your cousin Ann Allerton might put you up.'

Captain Casket hardly even attended to the business of getting his ship safely docked. His eyes were constantly turned back towards the open sea, and his thoughts were all with the pink whale, who had unfairly taken the chance to nip off round Cape Cod and into the Gulf of Maine. Would he ever catch up with her again?

It was dark before the *Sarah Casket* was alongide the wharf and made fast. Penitence begged to go ashore then and there, but Captain Casket wouldn't hear of disturbing Cousin Ann Allerton so late in the evening, and left them to spend one more night on board. Dido stayed awake for hours, sniffing the land-smells, listening to the shouts and the splash of oars in the harbour and the cry of gulls, and the music coming from the sailors' taverns. She dragged a chair to the port and squatted there looking out at the lights as they gradually dimmed and died along the wharfside and in the streets above the warehouses.

Strangely enough, although she was now nearer home than she had been for the last year, she felt more lonely and homesick than ever before.

'Pen!' she whispered after a while. 'Hey, Dutiful! Are you awake?'

The only answer was soft, even breathing. Dido sighed, and was about to climb down from her perch and go to bed, when she heard a faint splash, close to, and the creak of oars. Turning back, she was just in time to see Mr Slighcarp, his foxy features visible in the light of a lantern, help a tall, veiled woman over the *Sarah Casket*'s side into a dory, and row quietly away across the harbour.

Part Two

5

Trouble with Cousin Ann – Captain Casket slips his cable – arrival in Nantucket – the Casket farm

'We can't stay with your cousin Allerton,' Dido said glumly, 'and *that*'s for sure.'

It had taken her less than ten minutes to reach this conclusion. After ten days she was of the same mind.

Cousin Ann Allerton was a frail, erect old lady dressed in black silk with a white bib and cap. She almost fainted when her snapping black eyes first took in the untidy appearance of the two girls – even Pen's dress was fairly bedraggled by this time with oil and tar on its frills. And as for Dido – !

'Don't stand on the clean doormat!' Cousin Ann said frantically. 'Keziah! Keziah! Fetch an old sheet directly and put on a pail of water to heat. Mercy! Just look at that child's feet! And her *hair*! Bring some towels, every stitch they have on will have to be burned. Get out the tallow and kerosene, gracious knows how we are going to get that grease off. Fetch the sulphur and calomel, I don't doubt they need a good dose after eating dear knows what foreign truck on board ship. And when you've done that, run down the road and ask Miss Alsop to step up, they'll have to have everything new, I can see that – furs, flannels, merinos, poplins, and tarlatans. Bonnets, of course, and boots; mercy on us what a pair of little savages.'

'I'd ruther keep my britches,' Dido said scowling.

'Quiet, child! The idea! Pass me the bath-brick, Keziah, till I give them a good scrubbing.'

Dido had never been treated so in her life before and was almost too thunderstruck to protest; in no time they were put to bed in a spotlessly neat bedroom with white chintz curtains and fringed white dimity bed-covers, a braided rug exactly in the middle of the floor and a square of oilcloth in front of the wash-stand.

'Why've we got to go to bed in daytime?' grumbled Dido. 'We ain't done nothing wrong!'

'Oh, for the land's sake, will you hold your hush. You must stay out of sight of the neighbours till you've something fit to wear.'

Miss Alsop the dressmaker soon arrived, and with Cousin Ann's help two brown calico dresses trimmed with white tape were hastily run up so that the children might put them on, get out of bed, and help to hem some more garments.

'I won't stand for it,' Dido muttered again and again, wriggling her neck furiously in her starched collar as she sewed under Cousin Ann's gimlet-eyed supervision. The only respite they had from sewing was when the gaunt and gloomy maid Keziah compelled them to swallow another dose of rhubarb or senna or sassafras tea; Cousin Ann seemed quite certain that they had brought the plague with them from abroad and must be physicked at frequent intervals to prevent it from spreading through the town.

Even Captain Casket was mildly surprised at the transformation in the two children when he came to call. Dido badly wanted to tackle him about the possibility of finding a home for Pen other than with Aunt Tribulation, and about her own passage to England, but he paid only a brief visit and never came near Cousin Ann's house again, so busy was he with refitting and reprovisioning the ship, and asking all newcomers for news of the pink whale. Meanwhile the children were kept under strict supervision; only allowed out for a short walk once a day, to the end of the road and back.

However, on the ninth day while Keziah was at a missionary meeting, Cousin Ann found herself obliged to lie down with a headache brought on, she said, by the trampling of children's feet upstairs in the bedroom. No sooner had she retired than Dido was out of the house like a bullet.

'*You* can stay, Pen, if you're scared to come,' she said, 'but I wants to see your pa and get things fixed up shipshape.'

Pen said she would remain at home in case Cousin Ann needed anything, so Dido flew down the hill to the wharfside. What was her horror, when she reached the berth that had been the *Sarah Casket*'s, to find it empty!

'Hey,' she said to a boy who was fishing near by, 'where's the ship that was here?'

'Sailed this morning on the early tide.'

'She didn't! You're bamming!'

He shrugged. 'What d'you think she did, then?

Walked away up the hill? The old skipper was raring to go – someone telled him they'd seen a pink whale off Gay Head. He was missing his first mate when he sailed but he said he couldn't wait, so he up anchor and off; guess he's halfway to the Grand Banks b'now.'

'Oh, croopus,' groaned Dido, She turned and walked wearily back up the steep hill; her legs felt as heavy as lead. 'Now we are in the basket! What an old chiseller Cap'n Casket is; I mighta knowed he'd play us a trick like that – sneaking off on the quiet so's Pen couldn't make a fuss, I'll lay! One thing's certain, though – I ain't a-goin to stop any longer with Cousin Ann.'

Luckily Cousin Ann was of the same mind. She had had the forethought to collect money for their fares to Nantucket from Captain Casket when he called, and the very next day they were dispatched, with their new clothes, on the packet *Adelaide*, a small schooner loaded up to her eyebrows with coal, cordwood, and water-melons.

A rising gale delayed the crossing considerably, and dusk had fallen by the time the ship rounded Brant Point and came safe into Nantucket harbour. Salty, soaked, and shivering, the girls clambered on to the wharf with their bundles. 'Hey!' the captain called into the gloom.

'Anyone here from the Casket place?'

Nobody answered. The two children waited for some time, until most of the other passengers, or people unloading goods from the packet, had left.

'Well, it ain't no manner of use standing here all night,' Dido said, clenching her teeth to prevent their chattering. 'And it ain't half a-going to rain in a minute.

What'll us do, Pen? Can we walk to your pa's farm? Is it far?'

'N-nine miles,' shivered Pen. 'It's much too far to walk with our bundles.'

'Had us better put up at an inn?'

'Oh, no! They're sure to be full of horrid rough sailors.'

'Well I ain't stopping here,' Dido said, and led the way into Nantucket town with Pen following irresolutely. 'Maybe we'll see somebody you know if we wander a bit; maybe your Auntie Trib reckoned the packet warn't coming and went shopping or started home again. I can tell you one thing, I'm crabbish hungry,' she added, as they passed a chowder parlour and a heart-breaking smell of food drifted out to them.

'Oh, so am I!'

'Got any money?'

'Why, no,' faltered Penitence. 'Cousin Ann only gave me the boat tickets.'

'Hum,' Dido said. She hefted her bundle thoughtfully. Just ahead of them, on the corner of Main and Union streets, was a store with windows still brightly lit up and a sign that said: 'Bracy and Starbuck, Ships' Outfitters and General Soft Goods'.

'I'm a-going in here,' Dido said, and did so, ignoring Pen's apprehensive squeak. She addressed herself to a man behind the counter.

'Hey, mister, I've got a load of clobber here that I don't want, will you buy it off me?'

To Pen's horror the man was quite prepared to buy the carefully-made dresses and frilly underwear considered suitable by Cousin Ann. 'What do I want with 'em?' Dido said. 'I'd sooner have a pair of britches any day.' She bought herself a red flannel shirt and a pair of denim trousers for one dollar sixty-two cents, and still had two dollars left. 'Come on, Pen,' she said, 'we'll go get us some prog. By the way,' she asked the outfitter, 'you don't know if there's anybody in town a-waiting for Miss Pen Casket, does you?'

'Little Miss Casket for the Casket farm?' he said. 'Why yes, the old mule's been in every day this week. Guess he's still around; Mr Hussey at the Grampus Inn knows not to loose him till the packet's been in an hour. Are you little Miss Casket then? My, how you have growed!'

Dido didn't wait to chat. 'Which way's the Grampus Inn?' she asked. 'Come on, Pen, hurry!' Slipping and stumbling, they ran along the cobbled streets, scaring a number of sheep which appeared to have come into the town to take shelter, and reached a building with a wildly swinging sign that showed a grampus in full spout. Below the sign was tethered a mule-cart; the dejected mule, his coat sleek with rain, seemed to be trying to keep his head dry by hiding it between his forelegs.

'Is that your pa's cart?' asked Dido.

'I – I'm not sure,' Penitence confessed. 'It's such a long time since I was at home. There *was* a mule – I think he was called Mungo – but I used to be scared of him, I never noticed what he was like.'

'Oy,' said Dido, going round to the mule's front end. 'Psst, you! Hey! Is your name Mungo?'

The mule made no response, except to give her a

despising glance from one white-rimmed eye, backwards, between his legs.

'I'm going in to ask,' Dido said.

'Oh dear, I'm sure you shouldn't go into an inn!' Pen lamented. 'There will be dreadful people. It isn't ladylike behaviour!'

'Oh, *scrape* ladylike behaviour!' Dido snapped impatiently. 'If you want to get soaked and starved, *I* don't!'

She marched into the inn. Having ascertained that it was indeed Captain Casket's mule and cart standing outside, she said: 'Well, if he's waited for us every day this week it won't kill him to wait another twenty minutes,' and to Pen's fright she ordered three bowls of clam chowder. However, the chowder was so welcome when it came, savoury and hot, full of tender little clams, that Pen at length overcame her qualms and consented to eat it.

'Who's the third bowl for?' she asked.

'Why, poor old Mungo, o' course,' Dido said reprovingly. 'If he's got nine miles to go through the wet he ought to have summat to stay his stomach.'

'Will he like it?' Pen quavered.

'We'll soon see, won't us? If he don't, I dessay you can do with a second help.'

However, the mule seemed quite willing to accept a helping of chowder and appeared to improve greatly in his spirits once he had snuffled it down. The dish was returned to the inn, Dido helped Pen into the cart and wrapped her in a quantity of sheepskins which were found under the seat. Then she untied Mungo's head, slapped him with the reins, and they were off.

'Whizzo!' she said, as they rattled through the dimly lit streets. 'This is something like, ain't it? I loves drivin' – if only it didn't rain and blow *quite* so hard. I say, Pen, does you know the way?'

'Mungo knows it, I dare say,' said Pen faintly – she had soon left the box and was huddled down in the bottom of the cart trying to keep herself from slipping about. 'Mamma used to send him in to market on his own with the eggs and stuff. Just give him his head, he'll find his way home.'

In no time they were out of the little town and making their way along a high and exposed sandy track in open

country. The wind and rain buffeted them and it was too dark to see anything except some low-growing shrubs by the roadside. A distant, continuous roar could be heard to their right, and from ahead of them came louder, but intermittent booming.

'What's all that row?' Dido said.

'It's the waves.'

'But we've just come from the sea.'

'Nantucket's an island, don't forget,' Pen sighed drearily. 'What you can hear is the breakers on the south and east shores. Oh, how I hate it!'

'Now, *Pen*, cheer up, do!' Dido said. 'How about a

song to keep ourselves cheerful, one o' Nate's?' And she began to sing in a hoarse but tuneful voice:

'Oh, fierce is the Ocean and wild is the Sound,
But the isle of Nantucket is where I am bound,
Sweet isle of Nantucket! where the grapes are so red,
And the light flashes nightly on Sankaty Head!'

Inspired by this, Mungo the mule actually broke into a canter and so they went briskly on their way through the storm.

'Hey,' said Dido, at last, 'Pen, here's a gate. Croopus, did you ever see sich a peculiar one? Is this your pa's place?'

'I think so,' Pen sighed faintly, peering forward in the gloom. 'Yes, he put up the gate; it is made of a spermwhale's jawbone. Oh, I am so cold and wet and miserable.'

'Ne'mind, in ten minutes you'll be tucked in bed with a warming-pan. There's a barn, anyhows; Mungo seems to think he lives here.'

In fact, after they had passed the gate, which was like an enormous wish-bone, Mungo trotted into the big barn without worrying any further about his human passengers; Penitence was rather impatient when Dido insisted on unharnessing him and giving him a rub with a wisp of hay, 'Just in case,' she said, 'your Auntie Trib don't fancy stepping out into the wet. All right, come on now, bring your traps.'

There appeared to be quite a group of farm buildings set in a hollow of the hillside with a few trees round about. Not a light showed anywhere and it was hard to be sure which was the dwelling-house.

At last they found what seemed to be a house door and Pen, a sudden memory returning from earlier childhood, stood on tiptoe and discovered a key hanging on a nail.

'Hooroar,' Dido said as they stepped inside. 'Ain't I glad to get in out o' the wet. Know where the candles is kept, Pen?'

'N-no, I forget,' Pen said dolefully. 'Oh, isn't it dark and cold!'

Luckily, feeling about, Dido chanced to knock over a candle; when it was restored and lit they saw that they were in a large, old-fashioned kitchen which, given warmth and light, would have been a cheerful place enough. There was a big potbellied stove, black, unlit, and unwelcoming; a brightly-coloured braided rug, and a dresser covered with dishes. An enormous grandfather clock ticked solemnly against the wall. The place was clean and tidy but silent, empty, and deathly cold.

'Oh,' whispered Pen. 'What shall we do now?'

'Do? Why, go to bed. Things'll be better in the morning,' Dido said stoutly. 'Where's the stairs?'

Pen opened a door disclosing a steep narrow flight, and Dido went ahead with the candle.

'Hey,' she said, checking to let Pen catch up, 'look, there's a light under that door at the end o' the passage. Must be your Auntie Trib's room. We'd better go and tell her we've come.'

'B-b-but,' whispered Pen tremulously, 'supposing it *isn't* her?'

She clutched Dido's arm.

'Why, you sapskull! Who else could it be? Come on!'

Dido marched boldly along the passage and rapped on the door.

'Miss Casket?' she called. 'It's us – Penitence and Dido, just arrived.'

From the room beyond a voice replied, 'And about time, too! Wipe your feet on the mat before you come in.'

Even Dido quailed momentarily at the sound of this voice. It was low, harsh, and grating; there was something very forbidding, and something strangely familiar about it. Her hand trembled slightly and she spilled a drop of hot wax from the candle which went out; then, summoning resolution, she pushed open the door and went in.

By the light of one dim candle on the bedside table they could see a woman in the bed, propped against many pillows, regarding them fixedly.

6

Aunt Tribulation – pigs and sheep –
green boots in the attic – Aunt Tribulation is hungry –
Pen meets a stranger

'Light another candle,' ordered the woman in the bed, 'and let's have a look at you. Hum,' she said to Dido, 'you don't favour my side of the family. Must take after that poor sickly Sarah.'

'You got it wrong, ma'am,' Dido said hastily. 'That's Pen there. I'm Dido Twite.'

Although she stared at the girls pretty sharply, it was hard for them to see much of Pen's aunt, for she held the bedclothes up to her chin, and had on a nightcap with a wide frill that left most of her face in shadow. They could just make out a gaunt, nutcracker chin, and a thin nose, so like a ship's rudder that Dido half expected it to move from side to side. A pair of tinted glasses hid Aunt Tribulation's eyes from view. Dido grinned, thinking of the wolf, and subdued an urge to exclaim: 'Why, Auntie Trib, what big eyes you have!'

'*You're* a pasty-faced little bag of bones,' Aunt Tribulation commented, looking at Pen. 'Haven't filled out as you grew, have you? Well, I hope you're both used to hard work, that's all. You'll get no lounging and pampering here.' She thumped on the floor with a rubber-shod stick to emphasize her words. 'There's all the house chores and the farm work; *I* can't help you, as I've been sick abed ever since I got here; this damp island air turns a body's bones to corkscrews. So you'd best get to bed now.'

'Where shall we sleep, Aunt Trib?' Dido asked.

'In the chamber at the other end of the passage. Sheets and blankets are in the cedarwood box. Mrs Pardon's been coming over to tend the animals, but you'll have to do them now. Feed the hens and pigs at four, groom the mule. Light the stove – you'll need to chop some kindling if there's none in the cellar; and the peat's in the peat-house – and you can bring me a pot of coffee and a bowl of gruel at seven. Look sharp now.'

Too dazed by the length of this list of tasks to make any protest, the girls retreated, and found their room, which was as bleak and clean as at Cousin Ann's, but lacking the washstand, square of oilcloth, and braid rug. Shivering and yawning they dragged comforters and sheets from the cedar box, made up the bed, and tumbled into it, huddling against one another for warmth.

'I'm that tired I could sleep for a week o' Thursdays,' Dido murmured drowsily. 'Dear knows how we'll ever wake at four.'

Pen was asleep already, but Dido lay for a moment trying to think why Aunt Tribulation's voice had sounded so familiar. Then she too fell deep asleep.

She need not have worried about how they were to wake; there were three roosters on the farm whose lusty crowing had the girls roused long before any touch of dawn had crossed the sky. Dressing themselves hastily in warm things – Dido put on the denims and red shirt she had bought – they groped their way downstairs.

They lit the potbellied stove, staggered in from the pump with a bucket of water between them, fed the animals, and were just making the gruel when a loud thumping on the floor overhead proclaimed that Aunt Tribulation was awake. Pen went up to see what she wanted and was greeted with the words:

'Where's my breakfast? You're ten minutes late.'

'I – I'm very sorry, Aunt Tribulation.'

'Sorry! Sorry's not good enough. Don't forget to scald the coffee pot. And clear the coffee with eggshells. And when you've brought me my breakfast and washed the dishes and towels, you can scrub the kitchen floor and dust the parlour. Then you'll have to make some bread. And that other girl can hoe the potato field.'

'Huh,' Dido said when this programme was unfolded to her. 'Don't she want us to cut down no trees? Or slap a few bricks together and put up a new barn? Anyhows I'm a-going to have some breakfast before I start on that lot. Here, I'll take up the old girl's prog, Pen; I've fried you some eggs; sit down and get 'em inside you, you look like a bit o' cheesecloth.'

Aunt Tribulation received her breakfast tray without enthusiasm. 'Wash your face before you come up another time, girl,' she said harshly. 'And where's my napkin? You should have used the pink china, this is kitchen stuff.'

'Lookahere, you ungrateful old cuss,' burst out Dido, her patience at an end, 'you oughta be thankful I didn't bring it up in a baking-pan! Lord bless us, am I glad you ain't *my* Aunt Trib.'

She ran out of the room, slamming the door behind her.

To Dido's great surprise and relief, Pen proved a handy little creature with the indoor tasks; she had been taught by her mother to wash and bake and cook and polish; 'which it's as well,' Dido admitted, 'for I never could abide housework and I don't know a waffle-iron from a skillet; if I'd a had to make the bread it'd turn out tougher'n old boots. It beats all how you get it to rise so, Pen. You'll have to teach me; one thing, housework ain't so bad when it's just us on our own. In fact it's quite a lark. Pity the old gal couldn't go back to wherever she came from.'

'Oh Dido,' confessed Pen – they were out of earshot of Aunt Tribulation now, sociably hoeing the enormous potato field together, 'she frightens me *dreadfully*! Her eyes glare so – at least I'm sure they do behind her glasses! And her voice is so angry and scolding. I'm sure I shall never get used to her.'

'Now, now, Pen,' Dido admonished. 'Remember as how you're learning to be brave? Every morning when you get up you must say twenty times, "I am not scared of Auntie Trib." You'd best start now.'

'I am not scared of Auntie Trib,' Pen said obediently. But then she broke out, 'It's no use, Dido, I *am* scared of her!'

'Well, we'll have to get you out o' the habit,' Dido said stoutly. 'You watch me, see how I stand up to the old sulphur-bottom.'

Pen gulped, nodding, but she looked apprehensive.

'Do you remember her now you see her again, Penny?' Dido asked. 'Is she like she was when you was small?'

'Just as frightening,' Pen said. 'But I don't really remember her much. It was Mamma, saying she was a dragon that I remembered. She looks older than I expected. And even crosser!'

Dido pondered over Pen's words. Really, she thought, there's nothing to prove that this lady is Aunt Tribulation at all. This is a mouldy lookout for me getting back to England; I don't see leaving Pen with old Gruff-and-Grumble.

She thought this again when the noon hour came and they entered the house to the accompaniment of a regular hurricane of thumps from upstairs. Pen ran up to inquire her aunt's wishes and returned trembling and in tears, so fierce had been the request for 'gingerbread and apple sauce and look sharp about it, miss! What have you been doing all morning, I'd like to know? Idling and playing and picking flowers, I suppose!'

'Oh, pray don't scold, Aunt Tribulation, pray don't. Indeed, indeed, we haven't been idling; we have hoed more that half the potato field.'

'Old harridan. I wonder how she knew you'd made some gingerbread?' Dido said. 'She must have a nose on her like a bloodhound. There's some apples down cellar, Penny, I saw them when I was getting the kindling for the stove. And there's hams and onions and molasses and bushels of beans, so we shan't starve and nor will old Mortification upstairs.'

As Pen hurried to get the apples Dido, stoking the stove, muttered, 'Ill, my eye! If she's so ill, what's her nightcap ribbon doing on the kitchen floor? You've been poking and snooping and spying, you old madam, you, to see whether we did the housework, you horrid old hypocrite!'

When the apple sauce was made she took a saucerful up to Aunt Tribulation with the cap ribbon ostentatiously stuck like an ornament at the side of the dish. 'I guess this is yours, Auntie Trib,' she remarked innocently. 'I can't *think* how it come to be lying on the floor downstairs. Acos you haven't been down, have you?'

Aunt Tribulation took this very much amiss. 'Impertinent girl! Don't speak to me in that way. Apologize immediately!'

'Why should I?' Dido said reasonably. 'You ain't been extra polite to us.'

'You shall be shut up in the attic till you learn better manners.'

'Tally-ho! I'm agreeable,' said Dido. 'I can jistabout do with a nap arter all that hoeing.'

'Not now,' said Aunt Tribulation, who appeared suddenly to recollect that she had other plans for the girls. 'I want you and Penitence to shift the sheep up to the high pasture. And mind you count them! Do that as soon as you've washed the dishes. And don't forget to make up the stove. And feed the hens and pigs.'

'Sure that's all?' inquired Dido. 'Nothing else as how you can lay your mind to? Sartin? Tooralooral, then.'

'Now, how the mischief are we to count these here blame sheep?' Dido said, as the girls walked down the sandy lane to the pasture where the sheep were grazing.

'There's a gate in those railings over there,' Pen said. 'If you could get behind them and drive them, I could count them as they came through.'

'Clever girl, Pen. You've got a right smart head on your shoulders when you doesn't get all of a-pucker and a-fluster.'

Dido ran off across the rough pasture which was not grass but low-growing scraggy shrubs and bushes. Pen waited by the gate, and, conquering a slight tendency to shrink in alarm as the sheep streamed towards her, manfully counted them.

'Two hundred and twenty-three,' she said when they were all through and being driven up towards the high pasture. 'I wonder if that is the right number?'

'Well if it ain't you may lay Auntie Trib will tell us fast enough. Croopus, don't the wind blow up here, and can't we see a long way!'

'All over the island,' Pen said wanly, looking across the rolling, shrubby moorlands to the line of the ocean. On the south shore white, mushrooming clouds of spray from breakers could be seen dimly through a belt of haze.

'What's that white tower to the east?'

'Sankaty Head lighthouse. There's a forest between us and it,' Pen said with a faint glimmer of pride, 'but you can't see it. It's called the Hidden Forest. That's uncommon, isn't it?'

'Rummy,' agreed Dido, 'So's your pa's house. Why's it got a balcony on the roof? And why's it standing on legs?'

'I don't know about the legs. The balcony was for Mamma so she could look out to sea and see if Papa's ship was in sight. Look, isn't that a man coming to call at the house? We'd better go home.'

'Race you down the hill,' Dido said, and was astonished when Pen nodded, picked up her skirts, and darted away down the sandy track.

But when they reached the house, panting and laughing, nobody seemed to be about. The man had vanished. They ran into the kitchen, and Dido went up to Aunt Tribulation's room.

'Is somebody called here?' she asked, knocking and entering. There was a sort of flurry from the bed, as Aunt Tribulation huddled down in her pillows. Two spots of crimson showed on her thin cheeks.

'Do not come in until I give you leave, miss!' she croaked.

'Sorry, I'm sure! We were feared you mighta had to get up and answer the door.'

'I have done no such thing! Be off to your work!'

'Good land, don't be in such a pelter. I'm just a-going,' Dido said, injured. But in the passage outside she paused, remembering that the door next to Aunt Tribulation's opened on an upward flight of stairs. Must lead to that fancy balcony, she thought. I've a good mind to step up, won't take but a moment. She tried the door. Strangely enough it was locked now, though she was sure it had been open before.

'Why are you loitering out there, girl?' Aunt Tribulation called angrily from her room.

Dido shrugged and ran downstairs.

'Does that door by Aunt Trib's room lead up to the roof, Penny?' she asked.

'Yes, and to the attic.'

'Where's the key kept?'

'In the door, mostly,' Pen said in surprise. 'But there's a spare, because once when I was little I locked myself in there. Oh, I was scared, and so was Mamma!'

'Where's the spare live, then?'

'On a hook at the back of the china closet. Why?'

'Just I've a fancy to go up there sometime,' Dido replied calmly. She did not add that she was also curious to know what Aunt Tribulation was up to: it seemed clear that while the girls were out she had locked the attic door and taken the key. Why had she done so?

'What'll us do now, Penny?' she inquired.

'I suppose we're free,' Pen said doubtfully. 'I'd like to do some lessons. And write my journal and sew my sampler.'

'Not on your Oliphant. There's the old gal a-thumping again.'

Aunt Tribulation called imperiously for Pen to bring her more gingerbread and apple sauce.

'How many sheep did you count?' she demanded.

'Two hundred and twenty-three, Aunt Tribulation,' Pen quavered.

'One missing! That one must be found, miss.'

'Y-y-yes, Aunt!'

'Make haste and set about it, then.'

Pen bore up till she was downstairs, but then she burst into tears.

'Oh, I'm so tired! And look, it's nearly dark outside. Do you think we really need go tonight, Dido? I'm sure we'd never find it. And I don't believe I can walk another step.'

'Nor you shall,' said Dido sturdily. 'Be blowed to the

old faggot. How does she expect us to find one sheep in the dark in umpty miles o' wild country? That's a crazy notion. It'll look after itself till morning, I reckon; we'll find it then. Run along to bed, Pen, while I stoke the stove and lock the back door.'

Pen was already half asleep by the time Dido tiptoed up and snuggled in beside her under the quilted comforters.

'I brought the back and front door keys,' she whispered, tucking them under the pillow. 'Just so's to be on the safe side. 'Night, Dutiful. You'll have to write a letter to your pa about all this.'

'Good night, Dido. Yes, I will write a letter.'

Halfway through the night Dido woke up and lay listening sharply. This ain't half a creaky old house, she thought. Every pine board seemed to have its own separate voice, and when the wind blew it was almost like being on the ship. But no wind was blowing now, and yet a board had creaked. Burglars? Dido slid a hand under the pillow and satisfied herself that both keys were still there. Pen slept peacefully. The creak was not repeated and, after a while, Dido too drifted back into sleep and dreamed that she was asking Aunt Tribulation to lend her the fare to England, while Pen weepingly begged her not to go, and Aunt Tribulation made no reply except to shake her red wattles, wink a black, beady eye, and croak, 'Certainly not! Certainly not! Get up, you lazy girl! Cock-a-doodle-doo!'

'Wake up, Pen, it's morning.'

'Oh, no, it can't be!' moaned Pen. 'I could sleep for hours longer.'

'Never mind. At least we shan't have to light the

stove this morning. I can jistabout do with some bacon and coffee.'

They dressed in the warm kitchen. While Dido was brushing Pen's long hair, Pen said, 'That's odd. I thought we left the window fastened. Look, it's only pushed to.'

Dido considered the window in frowning silence for a moment before going out to the pigs. But she only said: 'Oh well, lucky nobody noticed it and got in.'

After breakfast Dido found the spare attic key and ran softly upstairs. She slipped the key into the keyhole – it fitted, the door opened; and she tiptoed on up the next flight. She found herself in a huge room with a sloping roof and low dormer windows. It stretched the length of the house and was filled with all sorts of odds and ends – old trunks, old boots, boxes, bales of sacking, flour-bags, two stuffed birds under a glass cover, some wooden stub-toe skates, an old fowling-gun, and so forth. Dido looked around sharply. She did not quite know what she was searching for, but almost at once she found it: faint, sandy footprints on the floor.

Those weren't made long ago, Dido said to herself. If they had been, they'd a soon dried up and blowed away.

A ship's ladder and a trapdoor led out on to the roof; looking down from the widow's-walk balcony Dido saw Penitence hanging clothes on the line. I'd best be getting back to work, she thought, before the old gal finds I'm up here, and she closed the trapdoor and tiptoed down the ladder. At its foot she stopped short, riveted by the sight of something that she had missed on her first hasty survey of the attic. Behind one of the chests, as if it had been hurriedly thrust out of sight, was a bundle of ladies' clothes: bonnet, gloves, a black silk dress and a cloak of grey twill. On top of the bundle was a pair of bottle-green boots.

Dido tiptoed over and inspected these. They had white stains on them.

Salt water, she said to herself. *Those* haven't been here long.

I'd best get outa here.

After giving another quick, darting look round the attic she slipped down the stairs and softly closed and locked the door behind her. None too soon, it seemed; she could hear terrified wails coming from Aunt Tribulation's room.

'Dido said I might go to bed!' Penitence was saying through her tears. 'Dido said we'd never find it in the dark. And indeed, Aunt Tribulation, we were dreadfully tired. Dido said th-that looking at night-time was a crazy notion.'

'She did, did she? She shall be punished for that. And you, miss, had better go out now, and I don't wish to see you again until the sheep is found! I am going to make myself obeyed from now on, do you understand?' Aunt Tribulation rapped on the floor with her stick.

Frowning, Dido walked into the room.

'So, girl!' Aunt Tribulation addressed her fiercely. 'You countermand my instructions, do you?'

'Yes,' Dido agreed. 'They was downright addlepated. And you didn't oughta shout at Pen that way, you'll scare her into historics. Pen,' she added, more in sorrow than anger, 'haven't I told you about not putting the blame on someone else? Stick up for yourself, girl!'

Pen gave her a miserable glance.

'Still, we mustn't be too hard on the old gal,' Dido added, with a sudden seraphic smile at Aunt Tribulation. 'When she shouts at you, Pen, remember her rheumaticks is hurting her cruel bad.'

Plainly Aunt Tribulation did not quite know how to deal with this.

'Penitence!' she snapped. 'Be off!'

Pen hesitated, then ran from the room.

'As for *you*,' Aunt Tribulation went on, 'you can miss your dinner. Go out, finish hoeing the potato field, then do the cornfield, and don't come back till it's finished.'

'Blister your potato field,' Dido replied calmly. 'I'm a-going to help Pen find that sheep. And if I miss my dinner, so will you, acos there won't be no one to bring it up to you.'

With which parting shot she ran downstairs to the kitchen. Pen had already started down the track. For several hours they searched unsuccessfully. There were plenty of sheep to be seen grazing the rough pasture as they went farther afield, but not one with the red C which was Captain Casket's mark. At last, when they were about halfway to Polpis and the sun was high in the sky, Dido suddenly cried: 'Oh, look, Pen! I do believe that there's a sheep with a red mark. Look, by the bushes. Quick, let's go arter him. Brrr! though; ain't it turned cold all of a sudden!'

While they were searching, the children had not noticed that a fine white sea-mist had come creeping over the island. Just as they started after the wandering sheep the mist caught up with and engulfed them.

'Hey, where are you, Pen?' Dido called anxiously.

'Here! I'm here!'

'Blame it, it's like walking through porridge! Where in thunderation is your voice coming from? Stand still, till I find you,' Dido said, feeling her way forward. But Pen suddenly shouted excitedly:

'Oh, I see it, I see the sheep! I believe I can catch it, too!'

There came the sound of running footsteps, which faded into the distance, then a disappointed cry, 'Oh, drat!'

Missed it, diagnosed Dido. Seconds later a damp, dew-spangled sheep bolted past her, nearly knocking her down, and disappeared into the dimness before she could grab it.

Blazes, Dido thought. Now I've lost 'em both, Pen *and* the sheep. Which'd I better go after? Pen, I reckon. The sheep can look after itself.

'Penitence!' she called lustily. 'Du-oo-tiful! Penitence! Where are you?'

No answer – only a plaintive, faraway bleat. Not *you*, woollyknob, Dido thought crossly. She floundered on into the smoky whiteness, tripping over wet, tangling shrubs, getting caught in thornbushes and low-growing holly, stumbling into holes and out of them again.

At last she struck a track which led uphill. Night was falling by now. Dispirited, weary, and very worried about Pen, she turned along it. Maybe I'll come to a house or a farm, she thought, where I can ask somebody to give me a hand hunting. At this rate the poor little brat stands a chance of being out all night and that'd just about *do* for Pen; she'd be seeing ghosts and boggarts for the rest of her life.

She hurried along the track, which sloped more and more steeply uphill and suddenly brought her out into a familiar barnyard. Why, curse it, Dido thought angrily, I'm *home*, what's the good o' that? No hopes Auntie Trib will give a hand. I'd best turn right round and go back the other way.

She was just turning wearily down the dusky track when a lantern light showed in the barn door.

'Dido!' called Pen's eager voice. 'Is that you?'

'Penny!' Dido exclaimed joyfully. 'You're back, then!'

'Yes, and, what do you think? I found the sheep

again! Wasn't that a bit of luck? And, Dido, I have had such a curious adventure, listen –'

'You found the sheep? You brought it back all on your own?' Dido was amazed. 'I'd never a thought you had it in you, Pen! How ever did you manage to fetch it along? Where is it now?'

'In the barn. I led it,' Pen said.

'How, for gracious' sakes?'

'Well,' Pen said rather shyly, 'I thought, how would Dido set about it? So as I hadn't got a rope I took off my stockings and tied them together. It was the sheep that found the way home, not me. But I was dreadfully worried about where you'd got to, Dido. I'm ever so glad to see you.'

'Well, us'd better turn to and do the evening jobs while there's still a glim of daylight,' Dido said. 'You can tell me about your adventure when we're indoors making supper, Pen.'

They made haste with their tasks. Both were tired, wet, and hungry – though Dido grinned to herself as she thought how much hungrier Aunt Tribulation would be.

'Done the fowls? Good. That's the lot, then,' she said to Pen as they met at the back door.

'Oh, Dido,' breathed Pen fearfully. 'There's a light in the kitchen. Do you suppose –?'

'Ssh!' Dido laid a finger on her lips and opened the kitchen door.

The kitchen was warm and bright but had lost some of its cheerful atmosphere. For Aunt Tribulation, fully dressed, was sitting in the rocking-chair by the stove. She was no less formidable up than she had been in bed; although she had taken off her tinted glasses the grey eyes they had concealed were cold and singularly unwelcoming. She wore a brown-and-white checked gingham dress, and a brown shawl; an enormous brown brooch with enough hair in it to stuff a pincushion fastened her white fichu. Her grey hair was strained back into a tight knot behind her head. She looked hungry.

'We found the sheep, Aunt Tribulation!' Pen announced proudly, after a momentary check in the doorway.

'So I should hope! You've taken long enough about it. Is the feeding done? Then hurry up and make my supper.'

'Pen must change first,' Dido said firmly. 'Her dress is sopping and she's got no stockings on.'

'Make haste, then. And, pray, why were the larder and cellar doors locked, and what have you done with the keys?'

'Oh dear, did you want them?' Dido exclaimed innocently, drawing the keys out of her breeches pocket. 'I locked the doors acos we found the kitchen window open this morning and I was feared that burglars or wild animals might get in and steal our vittles or frighten you, Auntie Trib! O' course I never thought you'd be coming down for summat. I thought you was much too ill.'

Supper was taken in baleful silence and as soon as the children had washed up the dishes they escaped to bed, Dido almost bursting with suppressed laughter.

'Now tell me your adventures, Dutiful,' she said when

they were snug under the quilt and the candle blown out.

'It was the strangest thing! After we lost each other I hunted for you, and I ran towards where I thought you had been standing, but I must have gone astray, for I ran on and on, a long way, and suddenly I found myself among high trees.'

'Trees? Why, there ain't but bushes and bits of scrub for miles.'

'I must have been in the Hidden Forest, you see,' Pen explained. 'It seemed so mysterious in the mist! When I called to you, as I had been doing on and off all the time, my voice echoed back so boomingly that I was afraid and dared not do it any more. I became confused in the wood and, trying to return the way I had come, went on, I think, in quite the wrong direction. Then all of a sudden I found myself up against a strange kind of barrier.'

'A fence, like?'

'No, not a fence, nor yet a wall . . . It was about as high as my head and very thick, and round like a great iron pipe; yes, like an iron pipe as big as a great tree-trunk.'

'That's rum,' Dido said. 'What held it up, then?'

'It was mounted all along its length – and it was *very* long, I never saw either end – on pairs of cartwheels.'

'Sounds as if maybe someone gets their water through it,' Dido suggested.

'But there are no farms anywhere near the Hidden Forest! And that's not the end of the story.'

'No? Hurry up, then, Dutiful, my eyes is closing in spite of themselves.'

'I thought I would feel my way along the pipe and so get out of the wood. But I had not gone very far when I bumped into a man.'

'What sort o' man? What was he doing?'

'Oh, Dido, he was strange! He was tapping on the pipe with a hammer. He gave a great start when I bumped into him – I would have screamed, but that *he* seemed even more frightened! I said I was lost, and which way to Soul's Hill? And he said, "Whisper", laying his finger on his lips and looking all round, and then he pointed which way I should go and led me to the edge of the wood. Then he whispered something, and it took me *such* a long time to make out what he was asking – he spoke in such a strange, foreign way! At last I realized that it was *boots* he wanted – he showed me his feet in thin, foreign-looking shoes, all wet and torn and muddy. So I promised I would see, there might be an old pair of Papa's sea-boots, and was that all he wanted? And he said – I *think* – that he had a great longing for something sweet, could I bring him any cakes or sugar or jam? To keep out the cold and damp. He said he would wait by the fork in the track every night from seven till nine.'

'Was he a beggar?'

'No indeed I am sure he was not! For he gave me money to pay for the boots – three English gold coins.'

'*English* coins? How d'you know they were English?'

'Because there is a picture of a king and the words *Carolus II Rex Br.*'

'Good cats alive!' Dido said. 'An old guinea piece! There's still quite a lot on 'em about, my pa used to get them for playing on his hoboy. D'you think the man was English, Pen?'

'He certainly was not American. But he didn't speak like you – his language was very queer. He was a sad-looking man with a face like a monkey, and big ears, and nearly bald. He said not to tell anyone that I had seen him, and if I came with the boots I was to croak like a night-heron. I *think* that was what he meant. And he said how glad he was that he would soon be back in Europe.'

'*Did* he?' Dido was more and more interested. If this man is really going back to Europe soon, she thought, and if I could make friends with him, and if I could get Pen fixed up somehow . . . Who can the man be?

'We must look him out a pair o' boots tomorrow, Pen,' she said. 'I don't mind taking 'em to him if you're scared to go back. There's a deal of old boots up in the attic.'

And one pair of salt-stained, bottle-green ones that ought not to be there, she remembered, just before she went to sleep. Was it possible that Aunt Tribulation and the veiled stowaway of the *Sarah Casket* were one and the same person?

7

Aunt Tribulation gets up – second trip to the attic – Dido's in the well – return of Captain Casket – trip to the forest – the conspirators – the gun

Aunt Tribulation had evidently decided that it was easier to keep an eye on the girls if she got up, for the next day, and all the days following, she was downstairs by seven conducting a close scrutiny into all that went on. Indeed, as Dido said, it was hard to believe that anything had ever been the matter with her at all, so active and vigilant was she now in pursuit of the children and in keeping them hard at work.

'What does she take us for, perishing slaves?' grumbled Dido.

It was by no means so easy to circumvent Aunt Tribulation now she had come downstairs. She was large and strong, much larger than Dido, who remained small for her age, though wiry and healthy. After Dido had been rapped with a thimble numerous times, shut up in the grandfather clock, deprived of meals, and made to sit on the whale's jawbone for two hours, she saw that cunning and strategy would be needed.

'As well as learning you to stand up to her, Pen,

we've someway got to make her *humble*, so she's real sorry for her nasty nature and won't never bother you no more,' Dido said one morning when they were out hoeing the cornfield.

'Do you think that would *ever* be possible?' sighed Penitence.

'Have you written the letter to your Pa yet?'

'Yes, I have it in my chemise pocket.'

'Now, the mischief is, how're we going to get it to Nantucket to post it? No use to give it to old Mungo and ask *him* to take it to the mail office.'

Market days had come and gone, but Aunt Tribulation had sternly vetoed any idea that Dido or Pen might go in with the farm produce and do some shopping. Mungo, as usual, was sent on his own with a written list of groceries needed, which the owner of the main store would check and supply.

'If we could give the boots to your monkey-faced friend, *he* might post the letter for us,' Dido presently reflected. 'The trouble is how to wheedle Aunt Trib outa the house so's I can slip up to the attic and grab a pair. She never stirs except just into the yard.'

'I could tell her one of the sheep was sick and ask her to come up to the pasture.'

'She wouldn't care,' said Dido, who privately suspected that Aunt Tribulation knew little more about farming than the girls themselves. 'No, I have it, Penny, you must pretend you think I've fallen down the well. She wouldn't like that; no water, for one thing, and who'd do the work? She'd come out to help you grapple for me with a rope, and I could nip round to the back and climb up the willow tree and in our window.'

'But if she found out?' breathed Pen in horror.

'We could say you made a mistake. I'll drop my red shirt down, so's it looks like me down there,' said Dido. 'Pity we couldn't drop Auntie Trib herself down.'

In pursuit of this plan Dido contrived that evening to smuggle out her red shirt hidden in a pile of cheese-cloths, and dangle it down the well on a loop of thread until it caught on a projection about thirty feet below. The weather favoured them; it was misty again, and dusk was falling. Dido beckoned to Pen, who was in the hen-house, and whispered:

'Now, *screech*!'

'Oh,' faltered Pen, 'I don't believe I can!'

'Consarn it, Pen, you'd screech fast enough if a wild bull was rushing at you! Let on that one is!'

Pen gave a faint wail.

'Louder than that!' hissed Dido. 'Here, I'll do it!' She let out a fearful scream and then quickly slipped away round the corner of the house. The back door flew open and she heard Aunt Tribulation's voice.

'What's the matter?'

'Oh, Aunt T-Tribulation,' Pen stammered, 'I'm – I'm afraid Dido's in the well.'

'Blimey, *she'd* never get to Drury Lane,' Dido groaned to herself as she rapidly shinned up the willow tree. 'I never heard sich a rabbity bit of acting.' She scrambled in at their chamber window and pulled the spare attic key out of her pocket.

In a moment she had darted up to the attic and seized the largest and least worn pair of sea-boots; then, on a sudden thought, she tiptoed to the bundle of clothes behind the chest, pulled out a bonnet, and looked inside.

It bore a London dressmaker's label and a name: Letitia M. Slighcarp. So did the cloak. Dido did not dare wait to examine the rest of the clothes; she fled silently down the stairs again, relocked the door, and was out and dropping from the willow tree all in the space of half a dozen heartbeats. She could still hear voices and splashings from the direction of the well so she thrust the boots into a clump of fern, strolled nonchalantly round the corner, and remarked:

'Hilloo? Dropped summat in the water?'

It was as well she arrived when she did for Aunt Tribulation had tied a rope round Pen, who had a perfectly ashen face and was shaking like a leaf, and was apparently on the point of lowering her to the assistance of her companion.

'You abominable girl! Where have you been?' Aunt Tribulation exclaimed, dashing at Dido and boxing her ears.

'Down the orchard, hanging up the cheese-cloths. Why, whatever's the matter?'

'Didn't you hear us shouting? Penitence thought you were in the well.'

'No, did she?' Dido replied, and burst out laughing. 'You *are* a one, Pen! You musta seen my shirt, that blew down when I was taking it to hang out. What a sell!' And she began to sing:

'Oh, what a sell,
Dido's in the well.
Who'll save her bacon?
Auntie Tribulation!'

Aunt Tribulation, perfectly enraged, exclaimed, 'So you thought you'd make a fool of me, did you? Oh, you wicked little hussies, you shall have nothing but bread and water till the end of the week!' and she flew at Pen, who was the nearer, and shook her till she whimpered:

'It was Dido's idea, Aunt Tribulation, not mine! P-p-please stop! It was Dido's idea!'

'Oh-oh,' Dido said to herself. 'Here we go again. Now we *shall* be in the suds.'

But just at this critical moment an interruption occurred.

By now it was thick dusk and they could see only a few yards. Sounds, however, carried clearly in the mist, and they suddenly became aware of voices and footsteps approaching up the lane.

'Someone's coming!' breathed Penitence.

Aunt Tribulation turned her head sharply, heard the voices, and hissed, 'Go indoors, you girls! Make haste!'

Astonished, the girls did as they were bid, but went no farther than the deep porch. They were too curious to know who the visitors might be, for no callers had come to the farm since their arrival. Was Aunt Tribulation expecting somebody?

A voice – a boy's voice – said, 'Here we are, I b'lieve. Ain't this the Casket place?' Then, apparently seeing Aunt Tribulation, 'Evening, ma'am. Would you be Miss Casket?'

'Yes I am,' she snapped, 'and I don't allow tramps and beggars on this land, so be off with you both!'

'But ma'am –' the boy began to protest, and then Pen gasped as a man's voice said slowly and wonderingly:

'Why, isn't this Soul's Hill? We're home! However did we come to be here?'

'Be off!' Aunt Tribulation repeated.

'But ma'am! He's your brother! He's Cap'n Casket, don't you *know* him?' the boy blurted out and at the same moment Pen cried, '*Papa!* It's Papa come home!' and Dido shouted, 'Nate! Nate Pardon! What in mercy's name are you doing here?'

Both girls rushed forward joyfully, but checked a little as they came in view of Captain Casket. He looked thin and dazed, older than when they had seen him last; in a few weeks his hair seemed to have become a great deal greyer. But he smiled dreamily at Pen and said, 'Ah, Daughter, I am glad to see thee well.'

'Nate, what's happened?' Dido said quickly in a low tone. 'It's not the ship – the *Sarah Casket* –?'

'We don't know,' Nate replied in the same tone. 'Let's get him indoors, shall we, before I tell you about it? He's still not himself.'

'Come in where it's warm and dry, Papa,' said Pen protectively, and took Captain Casket's hand to lead him in. He looked about him, still with the same bewildered expression, and said:

'So thee is living at home now, Penitence? I am glad of that. But who is this?' pointing to Dido.

'Why, Dido Twite, Papa. Don't you remember her?'

'Perhaps,' he said, passing a hand across his brow. 'I am tired. I become confused. Then who is looking after thee?'

'Papa, don't you remember Aunt Tribulation? Here she is! She has been – has been looking after us.'

'Ah yes, Sister Tribulation. She said she would come,' he murmured.

At this moment Aunt Tribulation, who had remained in the rear while these exchanges were going on, stepped forward, firmly took Captain Casket's other arm, and said:

'Well, Brother! Fancy seeing you home so soon! Deceived by the mist, and never thinking but that you were several thousand miles off, I almost took you for a tramp! This is a surprise, to be sure! What has become of your ship? Not a wreck, I trust?'

She seemed less than pleased at seeing her brother; indeed, thought Dido, she seemed decidedly put out.

Captain Casket looked at her in his wondering manner and murmured, 'Can it really be Sister Tribulation?'

'Of course it is I, Brother! Who else should it be?' she exclaimed impatiently, leading him in.

'Thee has aged – thee has aged amazingly.' He sat down in the rocker, shaking his head.

'We're none of us getting any younger!' snapped Aunt Tribulation.

'He is still a bit wandering in his wits, ma'am,' Nate explained in a low voice. 'What he's been through fair shook him up.'

'What happened?' Penitence inquired anxiously.

'It was the pink whale, you see.'

Nate glanced towards the captain, who seemed to have gone off into a dream, rocking back and forth, soothed by his chair's familiar creak and the homely things about him.

'We sighted her about ten days outa New Bedford,'

Nate went on, 'and, my stars, did she lead us a dance! Round and round about, first north, then south, in the end we was nearer Nantucket than when we first started. At last we came right close to her, closer'n we'd ever been before; lots of the men hadn't rightly believed in her till then, but there she was, sure enough, just about like a great big strawberry ice. Well, Cap'n Casket, he says, "No man goes after her but me," he says, and he wouldn't let any o' the harpooners go in the boats. Just the one boat was lowered. He said I could be one of the rowers, because I had an eye for detail and a gift for language, and would be able to record the scene.'

'Well, and so? What happened?'

'She acted must uncommon,' Nate said. '*I* never see a whale carry on so. Soon's she laid eyes on Cap'n Casket she commenced finning and fluking and bellowing, she breached clean out of the water, she whistled, she dove down and broke up agin, she brung to dead ahead of us, facing us with her noddle end, and kind of *smiled* at the cap'n, then she lobtailed with her flukes as if – as if she was wagging her tail like a pup, she rolled and she rounded, she thrashed and tossed her head like a colt, she acted justabout like a crazy dolphin. By and by she settled and started in swimming to and forth under the boat, rubbing her hump on the keel, and that busted the boat right in half.'

'She didn't know her own strength,' murmured Captain Casket as if to himself. 'She meant no harm. It was only in play.'

'What happened then?' breathed Dido, round-eyed.

'I don't know what happened to the other rowers in

the boat,' Nate said. 'We was all tossed out a considerable way. I just about hope they got picked up by the ship. I was swimming near Cap'n Casket in the water when we was both heaved up as if a volcano had busted out under us, and blest if it wasn't old Rosie hoisting us up on her back! And you'll never believe it, but she started to run, then, and she never stopped till she brung to and dumped us off Sankaty beach. Then she sounded and we never saw her no more. So we waded ashore and walked here – I reckon the cap'n had best be put to bed, ma'am.'

Indeed Pen, who found this tale almost too frightening to contemplate, had already busied herself with heating some bricks in the oven for the captain's bed, and warming one of his spare nightshirts before the fire.

'Oh, Papa,' she paused by him to say, 'I am so *thankful* you were spared.'

He patted her head absently. 'Is that thee, Daughter? What is thee doing on board? I thought I left thee in New Bedford.'

'He must certainly go to bed,' pronounced Aunt Tribulation.

'I'll be off home, ma'am, now I've seen him safe here,' Nate said. 'My folks live over to Polpis.'

'But have a bite to eat first – have a hot drink!' Dido exclaimed. 'Try some o' Pen's herb tea and her pumpkin pie – it's first-rate. And you haven't told us what happened to the ship – did they see you thrown into the sea and picked up by the pink 'un?'

'I guess not,' Nate said. 'There was considerable fog come up. Like as not if the other men gets picked up, they'll reckon me and Cap'n Casket musta been drowned.'

'Well you ain't, that's the main thing,' Dido said. 'Oh, Nate, your bird! Poor Mr Jenkins! Was he with you in the boat?'

'No, no, chick, he'll be all right,' Nate said, laughing. 'Reckon Uncle 'Lije'll look after him for me till they puts back into port.'

Aunt Tribulation now bustled Captain Casket upstairs while Pen started heating a posset for him. 'Oh, Dido!' she whispered. 'I'm so happy Papa has come home! For Aunt Tribulation will hardly – will hardly like to be so unkind to us while he is here.'

Dido nodded sympathetically. In fact she was by no means so easy in her mind about the situation. For a moment at first she had hoped that, if Aunt Tribulation really was an imposter, she would be exposed by Captain Casket's failure to recognize her as his sister, but it was soon plain that he was too wandering in his wits for this to be likely. And if he continued so, Dido feared that he would have small effect on Aunt Tribulation's sharp and bullying ways. And what would become of his promise to secure Dido a passage to England? In any case she could hardly go off and leave Pen while matters were in such a train. Her heart sank. There seemed less and less chance of her ever reaching home again.

Nate wiped his mouth and rose. 'Thanks for the pie, it was real good,' he said. 'I'll be on my way.'

'Oh, Nate,' Pen said earnestly, 'I'm so *grateful* to you for bringing Papa safe home!'

It was the first time she had ever plucked up courage

to address him directly, and Dido gave her an approving look. Nate smiled down at her.

'That's all right, little 'un,' he answered awkwardly. 'Hope he's soon better.'

'I'll come out with you,' Dido said. 'I hain't shut up the hens yet.' And she muttered to Pen, 'I'll take the boots along to you-know-who while I'm out. If *she* asks where I am, say the black sow got loose and I'm chasing her. Needn't bother about getting your letter posted now, that's one thing.'

'Nor we need!' Pen said, recollecting. 'Oh, Dido, take the poor man this sassafras candy too!'

'I'm coming a piece of the way with you,' Dido explained to Nate when they were outside. 'I've an errand in the forest. Lucky there's a moon behind the clouds.'

The sandy track showed up white ahead of them.

'The forest?' Nate said, surprised. 'That's a mighty queer place to have an errand.'

'Oh, Nate!' Dido exclaimed. '*Everything*'s queer altogether! I'm right down glad to see you, I don't mind saying. I reckon there's some regular havey-cavey business going on.'

'What sort o' business?'

'Well,' Dido said, 'I don't reckon as how things can be wuss'n they are now, so I might as well tell you the whole story.'

Which she proceeded to do, omitting nothing: the veiled lady on the ship, Mr Slighcarp and the boots, the torn-up letter, the night departure in New Bedford harbour, the mysterious visitor at the farm who had so inexplicably vanished, the footprints in the attic, the sounds in the night and the open window, and the green boots and clothes marked Letitia Slighcarp.

'Whatever do you make of it all?' she asked.

'Seems as if old Slighcarp's muxed up in it somehow, dunnit?' Nate said. 'He never sailed this trip, so he must be ashore somewhere.'

'Yes, I know. Do you suppose he's maybe lurking in these parts? But then who's *she*, if she's not Aunt Tribulation? And where's the real Aunt Tribulation? Oh, Nate, d'you think they could have *murdered* her?'

'Easy now,' said Nate. 'One thing at a time. You say there was a letter at Galapagos saying Auntie Trib could come to Nantucket. Maybe there was another letter, written later, saying she's changed her mind. Maybe Mr Slighcarp read that one and tore it up.'

'Yes, but why?'

'Why, you chucklehead, so's he could put the stow-away lady in Aunt Trib's place. She must be some kin of his, his wife or sister.'

'The second letter had sprung open with the damp, I remember now,' Dido said. 'That could be it. Croopus, Nate, ain't you clever! She must be Letitia M. Slighcarp, and old foxy-face is skulking somewheres round about, coming to see her when we're outa the way.' She chuckled. 'He musta got locked in that night when I put the keys under my pillow, and had to climb out the window. He musta been in the house the whole time. No wonder the old gal wasn't over-and-above pleased to see Cap'n Casket come home! No wonder she thought he was a tramp at fust! She'd never met him before. Mr Slighcarp musta brought her here while we was still in New Bedford with Cousin Ann. But what's the point o' lodging her here? Someone'd be sure to rumble her in the end.'

'It surely is a puzzle,' Nate said. 'But wait a minute, wait! Old Slighcarp had to leave England and skedaddle abroad in a hurry because he'd been plotting against the king, and the militia was after him. Maybe it's the same with her. Maybe she had to skip quick, and when he saw this chance he grabbed it. We was several days off the English coast. That would explain why old man Slighcarp was so powerful keen to follow the pink whale round thataway, if he knew Miss Slighcarp wanted picking up.'

'Of course! That must be it! But what'll us do now?'

'Well,' Nate said, 'I s'pose the best would be to get holt o' the real Aunt Tribulation. But you still haven't told me why you're going to the forest.'

'That's summat quite different. Pen met a rummy little cove there, camping beside a big iron pipe, and he asked her to get him some boots and candy. He gave her three English guineas and said he was soon going back to Europe. I was curious about him; I reckoned I'd go along to see was there a chance of my getting a berth on his ship. Reckon this changes things, though; I can't lope off till it's settled about Auntie Trib.' She gave a deep sigh.

'It seems to me,' Nate said, 'as how this man must be connected with old Slighcarp. Else what is he doing, camped in the middle o' Nantucket?'

'Maybe so. Pen said he was scared stiff o' summat. He told her to whisper, and to croak like a night-heron when she came to meet him.' Dido chuckled at the thought of Pen trying to imitate a night-heron. 'Maybe he's scared of old Slighcarp?'

'I dunno what to make of it,' said Nate. 'Hadn't I better stay with you while you give him the boots? Sounds a mite chancy to me.'

'Done,' said Dido promptly. 'Maybe you'll be able to smoke his lay. But you better glide along kind of cagey in case he sheers off when he sees there's two of us.'

'Where was you meeting him?'

'At the fork in the track.'

'That's only half a mile now.' Nate sank his voice to a whisper. 'You keep on the track and I'll slide alongside in the brishes.'

Dido nodded. He slipped into shelter and she went on at a good pace, but walking as silently as she could on the sandy path.

When she reached the fork, easily visible in the cloud-filtered moonlight, she squatted down by a wild plum thicket, cupped her hands round her mouth, and let out a gentle croak. This was answered almost at once, and somebody moved out of the thicket. It was not possible to see him very clearly, but Dido recognized the small, bald man of Pen's description.

'Is it little kindgirl?' he whispered. 'You boots with?'

'Yus,' Dido whispered back. 'I brung 'em.'

'But you are unsame child!' Alarm and suspicion could be heard in his voice.

'I'm her friend, guvnor,' Dido reassured him. 'She was a-seeing to her pa and couldn't come out. Sorry we ain't been before – it warn't so easy to get aholt o' the boots. This here's candy.'

'Ah, miracle, nobleness! All the time is only to eat

fish, fish, fish! You are a heaven-sentness,' he whispered. His language was both guttural and hissing; Dido found it very hard to follow. He was already sitting in a bayberry bush and pulling on the boots with little grunts of satisfaction. 'Gumskruttz! Forvandel! Zey are of a fittingness! I am all obligation.'

He fervently kissed Dido's hand, much to her astonishment, dropped his old shoes in the bush, then, whispering, 'Plotslakk! Momentness – I bring you –' vanished back into the thicket. Almost at once he reappeared, thrust a prickly, wriggling bundle into Dido's arms, tried to kiss her hand again, thought better of it, said urgently, 'Each nat will be a bringness. Hommens. For you. If you bring kaken?'

'Kaken?'

'Pankaken. Appelskaken. Siggerkaken.'

'Cakes,' Dido guessed. 'I'll try,' she whispered.

'Is good, noblechild! Wunderboots! Blisscandy! I say good nat.'

Before she could stop him, he faded into the bush as if something had startled him. 'Hey!' Dido whispered as loud as she dared. 'Mister! Come back!'

But he was gone.

After a few moments Nate rose soundlessly out of the shrubs where he had been lying, almost at Dido's feet.

'Well,' she whispered. 'What did you make of *that* lot? And what in tarnation's he given me?'

'Lobsters.' Nate identified the wriggling mass. 'Big 'uns too. He was a rum job, wasn't he?'

'One thing's for certain –' Dido was disappointed –

'he ain't English. Pen was right. Dear knows what peg-legged lingo that was he spoke.'

'I'd sure like to know what he's doing in Nantucket,' Nate muttered. 'Up to no good, I bet. I've a good mind to nip into the forest and scout around.'

'Oh, yes, Nate, let's!'

'Not you, chick. It wants smart scout-work. One's enough.'

'I can snibble along jist as quiet as you!' Dido said, hurt. They argued about it in whispers; Dido was so insistent on coming that in the end Nate was obliged to give way.

Proceeding with the utmost caution they crept towards the forest. The ground began to slope steeply downhill and presently they were in the shelter of the trees where, as it was much darker, they had to go forward very slowly, one step at a time.

Nate, who was a couple of paces ahead, suddenly let out a stifled grunt.

'What's up?' breathed Dido, coming alongside.

'Nearly busted my nose on the tarnal thing. Must be the pipe,' he muttered. 'We'd best follow it.'

They turned at right angles and stole along beside the pipe, slowly and carefully, Nate still in the lead. Presently he paused. A faint light showed ahead and voices could be heard. Dido moved up as close behind Nate as she could and peered past him. The lobsters which she still carried nipped the hand that Nate had put out to check her and he let out a hiss of protest.

'Mind, stoopid!'

'Sorry!'

They could dimly see a small log hut. A fire burnt in

front of it and three or four men were gathered round talking in low voices.

'Where's the old professor gone?' one of them said.

'Oh, he likes to mooch about the wood on his own in the evening. He's everlasting on the lookout for the black-crowned night-heron or some sich foolishness. He's all right, don't fret about him, he won't go far.'

'I'd rather he stayed in camp, just the same.'

With a start, Dido recognized this voice as Mr Sligh-carp's. She gave Nate's shin a gentle kick. He nodded.

'When's the *Dark Diamond* due?' another voice asked.

'Any day now.'

'Thank the lord. I can justabout do with a decent smoke. I'm *cheesed-off* with smoking peat and eating shellfish. Will the ship wait and take us off at the same time's she leaves the charge and shot?'

'Depends on how the professor makes out. If he can

finish before she gets here, fine; we can blast off and then clear out.'

'What about your sister?'

'Take her too, o' course.'

'But ain't she *wanted* over there?'

'Well, so are most of us wanted, aren't we?' Mr Slighcarp said impatiently. 'But don't you see, things'll be different in England by the time we get back?'

'Oh, ah, so they will. O' course. I'd forgot. But, say, how'll we *know*? Suppos'n old Breadno makes a mistake? We don't want to go sailing over and put our heads into a hank-noose and end up on Tyburn!'

'We'll sail to Hanover first, dunderhead! The news will have reached them by then.'

'Aye, that would be best,' the other voice agreed gloomily. 'I does so *long* to get my chops round a bit o' British bubble-and-squeak.'

'Bubble-and-squeak! It'll be roast goose and champagne when you get it, cully!'

'I'm going to look for the professor,' Mr Slighcarp said uneasily. He rose to his feet.

At this moment one of the lobsters Dido carried, which had been squirming more and more vigorously, escaped from her grip and fell into a bush. She grabbed it.

'Hark! What was that?' Mr Slighcarp said, turning sharply.

'It's only the professor, guvnor, here he comes.'

By a great piece of good fortune the man to whom Dido had given the boots – apparently the professor referred to – stepped into the clearing at this moment.

'Hey there, Professor Breadno, see some good night birds?'

'We're all justabout night birds if you ask me,' yawned one of the men. 'I'm going to turn in.'

Dido kicked at Nate's shin again and began to step delicately backwards. She was apprehensive of another accident with the lobsters. Nate waited for a few more minutes before following, but presently joined her on the edge of the forest.

'Did you hear any more?' she breathed.

'Nope. They were asking the prof where he got his boots and he said he found 'em in a bog.'

'I wonder if they'll believe him. What a parcel of peevy coves, eh? Regular mill-kens.'

'I still can't make out what they're at,' Nate said, as they hurried silently back to the path. 'They seem to be Hanoverians, that's plain, but what the mischief are they doing in Nantucket? We ain't got none o' your fancy kings over here, a plain president's good enough for us.'

'It's plumb mysterious,' Dido agreed. 'Tell you what, though, I'll take the little professor cove some cakes – if I can slip past old Mortification – and try to get a bit more outa him. Supposin' I can make out what he means.'

'I'm glad I came back home,' Nate said. 'I think it's downright rusty the way these lowdown deadbeats make themselves at home in our island, and whatever deviltry they're plotting, I think they ought to be rousted out someway.'

'I'm agreeable,' Dido said. 'Specially if Aunt Tribulation's one of 'em. I allus thought she was a no-good. What d'you think we ought to do, Nate?'

'I'll think, and let you know. I'll stay home for a piece, anyhow. My Ma'll be quite glad to have me minding the sheep and helping with the chores. I won't try to get another ship till the *Sarah Casket* comes back. I'd sooner ship with Cap'n Casket, when he's better, I'm used to him.'

'If he *gets* better,' Dido said doubtfully. 'If he don't I reckon I'm stuck here for life.'

'Well there's plenty wuss places than Nantucket you could be stuck in.'

As they were by now a good way from the forest, Nate burst into song:

'I'll tend to my lambkins in pasture and grove
A shepherd I'll be and daylong will I rove;
In the isle of Nantucket I'll finish my days
A-following my sheep and a-watching them graze.'

'I do wonder what those scallions is up to,' Dido speculated.

'Well, whatever it is, it's bad business. I'll tell you one thing, chick.'

'What's that?'

'That there pipe of Pen's ain't no pipe but a *gun* – and it's the longest gun I ever laid eyes on!'

'Croopus!' said Dido. 'That's why the ship's coming with powder and shot. But who're they going to shoot, d'you reckon?'

'Search me. But whoever it is, they've gotter be stopped.'

8

Captain Casket's illness – Dido sees the doctor – the professor in the bog – an abominable plot – Aunt Tribulation overhears

To Dido's surprise and concern there were still lights burning in the farm as she approached. Surely it was long past the usual hour for bedtime? Did this mean that Aunt Tribulation had seen through Pen's story of the straying sow and was waiting up to conduct an inquiry? Prudently, she hid the pair of lobsters in a bush lest they should lead to questions.

When Dido walked into the kitchen, however, she saw at once that the unusual wakefulness was not on her account. The stove was roaring, a large black kettle steamed, Pen was anxiously heating a poultice, while Aunt Tribulation, with a grim expression, aired blankets, nightcaps, and chest-protectors before the fire.

'Oh, Dido!' Pen exclaimed. 'Papa is dreadfully unwell, he is in a fever! I have tried him with everything, balsam and cordial and rheumatic pills, but none of them did him any good. He tosses and turns so, and throws off the bedclothes; he seems to think he is in a boat.'

'Did you find the sow, miss?' Aunt Tribulation snapped at Dido.

'She's in the barn,' Dido replied. 'D'you think we should get a doctor?' she said to Pen.

'Oh, I do! Would you go for one, Dido?'

'A doctor will hardly thank you for fetching him out at this hour,' Aunt Tribulation remarked sourly. 'Here, child, take these warm things up to your father, *I'm* going to bed. I've done all that can be expected in my delicate state of health.'

'Isn't she perfectly hateful,' Pen whispered when Aunt Tribulation had departed. 'She doesn't seem to care a *bit* about poor Papa. As for her "delicate state of health" I don't believe there was ever a thing wrong with her.' Pen was distractedly looking through the store cupboard in search of more remedies. 'What's in this jar?' Can you read the label, Dido? It's dear Mamma's tiniest writing. I can't make it out.' Impatiently she rubbed the tears from her eyes. 'Oh, Dido, supposing Papa were to *die*?'

'We shan't suppose any such nonsense,' Dido said firmly. 'Huckleberries in gin, this is, smells like stingo stuff. Try them on him, Penny, see if he likes 'em.'

They hurried upstairs with the warm clothes and the poultice, the pot of huckleberries, and a stone jar full of boiling water for the captain's feet.

It was very difficult to get him wrapped up and poulticed. As Pen had said, he kept throwing himself about, crying, 'Towno! Towno! Alow from aloft! I'm all beset, bring to! Give it to her, she's pitching. Her spiracle's under . . . Stern all, we're stove!'

He sprang up in bed, and the poultice flew across the room.

'Never mind the dratted poultice,' Dido said at last in exasperation. 'It's all cold and dusty by now anyways. Here, you hold his hands a moment while I try to slip some o' these huckleberries down him. Hold tight!'

Pen held on manfully. 'Papa! Don't you know me?' she pleaded. 'It's Penitence!'

'Thar she blows!' shouted Captain Casket. But as he kept his mouth open to prolong the bellow, Dido neatly popped in a spoonful of the huckleberries. The captain immediately shut his mouth. He swallowed. A surprised expression came over his face.

'Quick! Another spoonful!' whispered Pen.

When Dido raised the spoon again he opened his mouth eagerly, and she was able to feed him the rest of the potful without difficulty. He murmured to himself,

'Truly it has been a wonderful summer for the fruit, wonderful! We must all –'

His eyelids fluttered down and he suddenly fell back on the pillow, fast asleep.

'*That's* a mussy,' Dido said. 'Now let's snug him up warm and then as soon as it's light, Pen, I'll go for the doctor. D'you know his name?'

'No, but anyone in Nantucket town would be able to tell you.'

They wedged the captain about with hot bottles and laid several comforters on him. Pen sat down by him, anxiously holding his hand. Since her father had come home, needing her help, Pen was a changed creature. She seemed to have thrown aside her needless fears and become quite practical and self-reliant. But just the same, Dido could see that this was no time to burden her with the tale of the conspirators in the wood; Captain Casket's illness was enough to worry about.

It did not seem worth trying to sleep as there wanted but an hour to daylight; instead Dido fed the animals and harnessed Mungo to the cart.

'I'm off, now, Dutiful,' she called softly up the stairs. 'I'll be as quick as I can.'

Jumping into the cart, she shook up the reins, and started Mungo at a rattling pace towards Nantucket town. One thing, she thought, it's nice to get away from Auntie Trib for a bit. I hope she don't give poor Pen the runaround while I'm gone; likely she'll sleep a good while yet as she was up so late.

The day was a fine one and her spirits rose. Dawn had flooded the upland commons with ruddy light and crimsoned the distant line of the sea. Old Rosie would look just the thing out there now, Dido said to herself. For the first time she recalled Nate's strange tale of how the pink whale had seemed to welcome Captain Casket. A rummy business altogether, Dido reflected. Sounded as if old Rosie had taken a fancy to him somewhere and remembered him, but why? He wasn't so handsome, why should she go out of her way to put down the red carpet for him?

Mungo was suffering from several days' lack of exercise and bolted along so fast that when they descended the gentle incline into Nantucket town it was still quite early. Not many people were about in the cobbled streets. Dido bore right towards the waterfront and left Mungo tethered to a post in Whale Street while she asked her way on foot.

'Old Doc Mayhew?' said a fisherman on the wharf. 'He lives on Orange Street. That ain't but a few minutes from here.'

The doctor lived in a handsome white house, Quaker style, with a fanlight and three windows on each floor. Dido banged loudly on the door and told the housekeeper that Doctor Mayhew was wanted urgently.

'He ain't taken but a mouthful of breakfast. Could you wait ten minutes?'

'Oh well, I guess Cap'n Casket won't die in that time,' Dido agreed. She was dying for some breakfast herself and strolled back, looking for a baker's shop, but was soon startled by a familiar voice, calling in the next street:

> 'In the spring of the year when the blood is too
>   thick

There is nothing so good as a sassafras stick!
Who'll buy my stick candy
So nice and so dandy?
Pickled limes, jelly doughnuts, come snap 'em up
quick!"

'Nate!' Dido exclaimed, and ran into Main Street, where she found Nate making his way slowly along in a small pony cart laden with trays of delicacies, presumably made by Mrs Pardon.

'Hallo, chick!' he said when he saw her, and then filled his lungs again and shouted:

'I've several different kinds
Of pickled tamarinds!
Try my pickled bananas, walk up, take your pick!
Try my liquorice roots, worth a dollar a lick!'

A number of housewives came to their doors and bought his wares, which included doughnuts, biscuits, and waffles.

'Try my
lemony
wintergreen
sassafras
peppermint
superfine candy, a penny a stick!'

Children came running for the dazzlingly coloured candy sticks.

He called:

'Popcorn and peanuts and pecans and popovers
Wintergreen wafers and hermits and jumbles
Gingersnaps, crullers, marshmallows and turnovers
Sample a cookie and see how it crumbles!'

Dido bought some popovers and found them delicious.

'Nate, have you thought what we oughta do yet?' she asked, when there was a momentary lull in the stream of customers.

'Yes,' he said, glancing about. 'I've thought. We must tell the Mayor. Likely he won't be so keen to have a mess o' Hanoverian English plotting on his island.'

'That sounds like sense. What's the Mayor's name, where does he live?'

'It's old Doc Mayhew, he lives on Orange Street.'

'Why,' Dido exclaimed, 'I'm jist a-going to fetch him to come and see Cap'n Casket who's got the raving fevers. Couldn't be more handy! I'll tell him the whole tale as we drive home. See you later, Nate.'

Doctor Mayhew was a fine-looking old gentleman with white hair and a frill of white whiskers all round his red face, so that he looked rather like an ox-eyed daisy. He wore a green coat with brass buttons as big as penny-pieces, and a snowy-white ruffled shirt.

'Hallo!' he said at sight of Dido. '*You're* a young 'un I've never laid eyes on before. Didn't bring *you* into the world! Living out at the Casket place, are ye?'

'That's it,' Dido agreed. 'I'm staying there, keeping young Pen Casket company till she's gotten used to her Auntie Tribulation.'

'Tribulation Casket? Has *she* come back to live on

the island? Why, I haven't set eyes on her since she was a young thing of fifteen. She went off to live with her grandmother, then, in Vine Rapids.'

'Oh,' Dido was disappointed. 'Guess you'll find she's changed a bit, then.'

'Lively young gal she used to be,' the doctor said reminiscently. 'Always one for a song or a bit of dancing or horseback riding.'

'Croopus,' said Dido. 'She ain't like that now. Doc Mayhew, can I ask you summat?'

'Why, certainly, my child! How can I help you?'

'Well, you see, it's like this, Doc. There's a whole passel of Hanoverian plotters on Nantucket and we think Miss Casket is one of 'em.'

'Hanoverians?' Doctor Mayhew seemed somewhat bewildered.

'Yes, sir. English Hanoverians. They're all a-plotting against the English king.'

Doctor Mayhew laughed heartily. 'Why, child, what an imagination you have!'

'It's true,' Dido said indignantly. 'I ain't bamming you!'

'Why, child, even if you were right, what harm could they do the English king over here? This sounds like pure fancifulness to me.'

'They've got a gun,' Dido said stubbornly. 'They're all a-camping in the Hidden Forest, except for Miss Casket that is, and they've got a mighty great gun about a mile long.'

'Oh no, my child. I have heard of those men. They are scientists, and that is not a gun but a telescope; quite a natural mistake to make. I believe they are ornithologists, studying our bird-life; somebody said they wished to see a black-crowned night-heron. English ornithologists, that's all they are.'

'Orny thologists be blowed,' said Dido. 'Ornery jail-birds is what they are, and they're here to do some piece of sculduggery; we heard 'em plotting it the other night in the wood; then they'll go back to England in their ship the *Dark Diamond*.'

'That's all right, then,' said Doctor Mayhew comfortably. 'And good riddance to 'em, whether jailbirds or bird fanciers. We've got no call to worry our heads about a pack of foreign English, even if they do put in a bit o' plotting in the evenings after they've finished bird-watching for the day. This is a free country, dearie. And we keep ourselves to ourselves on Nantucket, we've no truck with such highfalutin' nonsense as kings; even the president don't bother us much. Live and let live is our motto. And as for Miss Tribulation getting mixed up in such doings, that sounds like moonshine to me.'

'Maybe it does,' Dido said crossly, 'but it's true jist the same. You see she ain't Miss Tribulation. She's only pretending to be her.'

'Who the blazes,' said Doctor Mayhew, 'would want to *pretend* to be Miss Tribulation Casket? You've been reading too many fairy-tales, that's what's the matter with you! Now, you tell me what ails Cap'n Casket?'

Deciding that Nate might be a better hand at convincing the doctor, Dido abandoned the subject of the Hanoverians and described Captain Casket's symptoms and strange delirious remarks. Doctor Mayhew was very interested in the tale of the pink whale.

'Is that so?' he kept saying. 'That's mighty interesting. And why shouldn't there be a pink whale now? There's a-plenty pink fish, pink pearls, pink shells, pink seaweed in the ocean – why not a pink whale?'

'And why did she carry on so when she saw Cap'n Casket?'

'Oh, that's simple enough. Guess she was the little pink whale-calf he put back in the sea when he was a boy; he told me that tale once: he found her beached and dragged her back in. *And* of course, whales being warm-blooded, warm-hearted, long-lived critters – I've heerd of 'em living to a century or more – she'd naturally remember him kindly. They're kin to dolphins, ye know, and dolphins are right sympathetic to the human race.'

'Oh, I see,' Dido said. 'Kind of old childhood pals, like? Well, we'll be properly in the basket if he wants her to sit by his bed and hold his hand. Let's hope he's a bit better time we get back.'

Captain Casket did not seem to be much better, though, when they arrived at Soul's Hill. He was wild and feverish, rolled about in his bed, and kept throwing imaginary harpoons at unseen whales.

'He needs a dose of poppy syrup,' Doctor Mayhew said. 'That'll give him some rest.'

He administered a draught. Immediately Captain Casket fell back as if he had been pole-axed and began snoring loudly.

'That'll fix him for a good few hours,' Doctor Mayhew said with satisfaction. 'Powerful strong it is, the way I mix it. Here' – to Pen – 'I'll leave ye the bottle, but don't give him any more unless I'm delayed getting back to ye and he seems worse. Now, why don't I drive your mule on to Polpis, where I've another patient, and bring him back tomorrow, that'll save you an extra trip to Nantucket?'

Aunt Tribulation came into the room.

'Well, Tribulation,' the doctor said, 'I'd not have known ye, but I suppose we're all getting a bit long in the tooth. Remember when I pushed you in the creek and you were so mad at me?'

'Yes I do,' said Aunt Tribulation frostily. 'And it's not a thing to boast about. It was not the act of a gentleman!'

Doctor Mayhew laughed very heartily at this and took his leave, pinching Pen's cheek. As soon as the door closed behind him, Aunt Tribulation went off to her room for a nap.

The girls sat with Captain Casket through the afternoon, but he continued to sleep peacefully and never stirred. During this time Dido took the opportunity of telling Pen part of what had happened in the forest, and the conclusions that she and Nate had reached. But she did not mention their suspicions of Aunt Tribulation; she thought the news that Miss Casket might be a female English ex-convict would prove too much for Pen's new-found courage.

At last, when dusk was beginning to fall, Dido said, 'Maybe us'd better get the jobs done while Cap'n Casket's still quiet.'

Pen agreed that it would be safe to leave her father for a while.

As they were feeding the pigs Pen thought she heard cries from the bottom pasture.

'Dido, quick!' she cried, looking over the fence. 'There's somebody in trouble down there on the bog!'

At the foot of the hill was a small cranberry bog which had been neglected until it was half grown over with bushes and straggly trees. They could hear the cries for help clearly now, and see somebody floundering about among the crimson hummocks.

'I'll go,' Dido said, grabbing a long-handled wooden hayrake. 'You'd best stay here, Pen, in case your pa wakes.'

She bolted down the hill, calling, 'Hold on, I'm a-coming!'

When she reached the edge of the bog she saw that the person in distress was the little Professor Breadno. He was mired up to his knees, completely stuck; his eyes were bulging with fright and his ears stood out like wings.

'Well you *are* a clodpole, ain't you?' Dido said. 'How ever did you come to get into sich a pickle?'

'Is hoping seeing bird, seeing nat-herrn,' he explained humbly.

Dido crawled out with caution on to a fairly safe-looking hummock and extended the rake in his direction. He was just able to grab it.

'That's the dandy! Hold on between the spikes!' Dido said, demonstrating. 'Now I'm a-going to pull, so when I say heave, you shove off like an old bullfrog. Ready? – *Heave!*'

She threw herself back, pulling until every muscle in her skinny frame seemed about to snap. The professor came out of the mud a reluctant six inches, and fell forward on to his knees.

'Keep a-going, don't stop now, don't sink!' shouted Dido, throwing herself back again. 'Heave some more, come on, put a bit o' gumption into it. Don't pull *me* in!'

She dragged him slowly through the mud.

'If you've lost those boots I shan't half give you what-for,' she added. 'We've had trouble enough over them already.' He was so muddy that it was impossible to tell whether he had them on or not.

'Skrek verlige öfalt!' he exclaimed, looking at himself dolefully, and then, politely, to Dido, 'Is a much nick of time, treasurechild!'

'Yes, thanks, but don't kiss my hand again,' she said, retreating with haste. 'You better come up and get under the pump. Hope Auntie Trib's still asleep.' She beckoned him and he followed trustfully, dripping mud and ooze at every step.

'Mercy!' exclaimed Pen at sight of him. 'I'll put on a kettle.'

'Pump first,' Dido said grimly. 'It's *us* as'll have to scrub the kitchen floor if he walks on it in that state. Make him some o' your herb tea, Penny.'

The poor little man submitted meekly to being pumped over; 'I sank you; sank you!' he kept repeating piteously.

'I should jistabout think you nearly did sink me! Guess you're clean enough now, you can go into the kitchen. Don't make a noise.' She gestured towards the door where Pen had an old suit of Captain Casket's ready. It was far too big for the professor and they had to kilt it up here and there with lengths of string.

He drank the herb tea with loud expressions of

appreciation; they gathered it was something he had not expected to find outside his native land.

'Hjavallherbteegot! Wundernice! Gratefulness!'

'That's all right,' Dido said. 'Have some gingerbread. Now we don't want to get you into trouble with your friends, but we do want you to tell us about that gun o' yours, professor.'

'Gun?'

'Cannon. Pistol. Bang, bang!'

'Aha, königsbang! Is soon blowing up London.'

'*What?*'

'Is will be monstershoot, grosseboom, across –'

He looked about the room and saw an old, silvery globe of the world on one of the dresser shelves. With a finger he traced a course on it from the island of Nantucket up over Nova Scotia across the north Atlantic to London. 'Is shooting up palast – Sint Jims Palast, not?'

'Shooting right across the Atlantic? Blowing up St James's Palace. Is that what he means, Pen?'

'Goodso!' the professor said, delighted. 'Is fine shoot, not? And is all mine, Doktor Axeltree Breadno, mine mattematic kalkulätted!'

'But, Professor, blowing up London!'

'London – not. Sönmal Kungspalast.'

'Only the king's palace,' Dido guessed. He nodded. 'Croopus, that's mighty pretty aiming, I must say. But, honestly, Professor, you mustn't blow up the poor old king, must he, Pen? What harm's he ever done to you?'

'No indeed, it would be very wrong,' Penitence agreed.

But they seemed unable to convey this idea to the professor. 'Is cleverness, not?' he kept saying. 'Will being magnifibang!' He was so pleased with his amazing feat of having made a gun that would shoot right across the Atlantic and hit St James's Palace that he could not see any wrong in it.

'He's looking forward to the bang,' Dido said exasperatedly.

'Is being donderboom!' he agreed with an eager nod. 'And will pushing – lookso –' He made a gesture on the globe with his finger, from Nantucket to the New Jersey coast. It took them some time to see what he meant.

'You mean,' said Dido at last, 'that the what-d'you-call-'em – the recoil from the shot – will push Nantucket right back against that place, Atlantic City?'

'Is so!' he said in triumph. 'Is byggdegrit, not?'

'It certainly is! Just wait till the Mayor hears this! It ought to change his notions about not interfering. "We keep ourselves to ourselves on Nantucket," he said.' Dido couldn't help bursting into a fit of laughter. Then she sobered up. Pen was looking absolutely aghast.

'Push Nantucket all that way? But the houses would fall down!'

'That wouldn't be the half of it, I dessay,' Dido said. 'Think of the waves! Look, Prof, when's all this due to happen? When? Bang?' She pointed to the clock and a calendar.

He flew into a complicated explanation; they could understand only about one word in eighteen. They gathered there was some final calculation to be made, and then he kept saying, 'Expectness skepp coming.'

'Oh, I know,' Dido said at last. 'He's waiting for the ship, the *Dark Diamond.* She's bringing the cannonball.'

'So, is so!' He counted on his fingers. 'Tvo, tree day.'

'Three days? We've not got much time, then. Lucky Doc Mayhew's coming back. And then you sail away in the ship, do you?'

'Skepp awaits hjere.' He demonstrated on the map that the *Dark Diamond*, having delivered the cannonball, would hurry round to the other side of Cape Cod to avoid any tidal waves caused by the sudden displacing of Nantucket, and, when things had settled down, would collect the professor and take him home.

'Lucky thing!' said Dido with envy.

'You wishing withcome? I fixing.'

Pen gave Dido an anxious look but did not speak.

'Oh, goodness,' Dido said. 'Thanks, Professor, but I can't leave till Pen's fixed up. Anyway, I'd just as soon not sail along o' Mr Slighcarp.' Or Auntie Trib, she thought. 'Much obliged for the offer though.'

The professor now politely took his leave, indicating that he would return next day to collect his dried clothes. He offered handfuls of golden guineas to the girls, but they shook their heads.

'Not if they're your pay for blowing up poor old kingy,' Dido said; Professor Breadno beamed at her uncomprehendingly, kissed her hand again, murmuring, 'Excellenzchildren,' and trotted off down the hill.

'Well!' Left alone the girls stared at one another in amazement.

'I *said* they was a peevy lot,' Dido remarked at length. 'But I never thought they was as peevy as that. Blowing up St James's Palace!'

'And moving our island! Without so much as a by your leave!'

There came a tap at the door. Both girls jumped guiltily but it was only Nate.

'Anyone in?' he said, putting his head round the door. 'Say, girls! Guess the news! Guess who's turned up?'

'The *Sarah Casket*?'

Dido wondered if it could be the real Aunt Tribulation but did not say so.

'No, it ain't that. It's the old pink 'un!'

'The pink whale?'

'Where is she?'

'Off Squam Head, as plain as plain. She's a-diving and a-playing and a-carrying on like a porpoise; everyone from Polpis has been there watching all afternoon. Doc Mayhew's given strict instructions no one's to hurt her. Is Cap'n Casket awake?'

'I'll see,' said Pen, and ran upstairs.

'He ought to get a sight of her,' Dido said, 'as soon as he is well enough to go out. I dessay she'd do him all the good in the world.'

They tiptoed upstairs after Penitence.

'Papa,' she could be heard saying softly, 'Papa, are you feeling better?'

'Is that thee, Daughter? Why, where am I?'

'In your own bed at home, Papa.'

'Why, so I am. I have been having strange dreams.' He sighed. To Pen's fright, two tears formed in his eyes and rolled slowly down his cheeks. 'I dreamed that I had caught up with her at last,' he said sadly. 'And that she welcomed me.'

'Who, Papa?'

'The pink whale. It was but a dream, though.'

'No, Papa, it wasn't a dream! It was true! And she is waiting for you now, off Squam Head, waiting to see you, so you must hurry and get better,' Pen told him joyfully. But his response was disappointing.

'I know thee does it for the best, Daughter, but thee must not tell falsehoods. There is no pink whale. I have deceived myself for a long time.'

'But, Papa, other people have seen her too. They have said so!'

'They did but mock me.'

'But, Papa, truly she is out there now off Squam Head. Indeed she is!'

Two more tears stood in Captain Casket's eyes but he shook them away angrily, hunched his shoulders, and turned his face to the wall. To all Pen's protestations he would merely reply:

'I do not believe thee.'

Poor Pen came sadly out to the others.

'Never mind,' Dido comforted her. 'Maybe Doc Mayhew'll be able to convince him tomorrow. You make him some nice porridge or broth, summat strengthening, now. Nate'll help me with the chores.'

While they were feeding the animals Dido quickly told Nate about the abominable plan to blow up King

James III in his palace, and the disastrous effect this would have on the island of Nantucket.

He whistled in dismay. 'Heave Nantucket right back against the mainland just so's they can swap one king for another? Where's the sense in that? Why don't they stick with the one they've got?'

'Search me,' Dido said. '*I* never heard anything against old James Three. But they've got some George they want to put in.'

'Sounds like plumb foolishness to me,' Nate said.

'Anyway it proves we was right.'

'Did you tell the doc?'

'No,' Dido said crossly. 'He wouldn't listen to me. He thinks little girls tell fairy-tales. You'll have to tell him tomorrow, Nate. Maybe he'll pay attention when he hears Nantucket's going to end up in Atlantic City. I hope he'd know Aunt Tribulation was a faker, but she turned him off round her finger, smooth as pie, pretending to remember when he pushed her in the creek. He was fooled.'

'Does Pen know she's really Miss Slighcarp?'

'No,' Dido said. 'I ain't told her. Young Pen's not much on play-acting; she'd give the whole game away.'

'Oh well, I'll be along in the morning early before the doc gets here. 'Night!' Nate jumped on to his pony, which he had left tethered in the yard, and kicked it into a canter.

'Good night,' Dido called. She turned back into the barn to get a basket of eggs for supper – and stood still, petrified with horror. Aunt Tribulation was there, standing in the shadows behind the oil lamp. The upward-slanting light gave her face a most sinister expression.

'Oh!' Dido stammered. 'I d-didn't know – that is, I th-thought you was asleep.'

'I *was* asleep,' Aunt Tribulation said menacingly. 'But I have woken up now, as you see. And I have overheard the most curious conversation!'

As Dido still gazed at her, frozen with indecision – how much had she heard, would there be time to shout after Nate and warn him? – Aunt Tribulation turned her head sharply and said:

'Ebbo, deal with this one. And make no mistake about it – deal with her *for good*!'

A thick black bag came down over Dido's head, smothering her.

9

Kidnapped – Captain Casket is taken for a walk – Pen meets the doctor – the pink whale meets her friend – breakfast on the beach

Dido struggled furiously inside the sack, but somebody had thrust a gag into her mouth (it tasted like and probably was a muddy sock) and her hands were tied in front of her, so she was helpless. When she tried to run somebody tripped her and she fell to the ground and lay there winded and gasping.

Low voices were speaking near by. She heard Aunt Tribulation say:

'Did you get the boy too, Brother?'

The answer was a grunt which could have been yes or no.

'That miserable little Breadno has been blabbing,' Aunt Tribulation went on. 'You can never trust scientists or foreigners, curse them! They've no sense. We should have kept a closer watch on him. Luckily it's only got as far as the children; they were to have told Mayhew tomorrow. That has been stopped in time. But Breadno is too big a risk; he'll have to be dealt with too. Has he finished his final calculations?'

'He's just sighting the gun now, and calculating the charge, back at the hut,' Mr Slighcarp's voice said. 'We'll make him work right through the night; it shouldn't take him more than another three or four hours. But Sister, are you sure we shall be able to fire the gun without him?'

'Of course we shall, ninnyhammer,' she said impatiently. 'Anybody can let off a gun once it is aimed and the amount of charge is calculated. He'll be no loss. In any case I was planning to leave him behind on the island after the gun was fired; there'd have been little sense in risking our necks coming back to pick him up. I'll fire it, if you like; only mind you pick *me* up.'

'Very well.' He sounded relieved at this suggestion. 'The rest of us will go on board *Dark Diamond* as soon as the gun is loaded, and stand off round Cape Cod in case of tidal waves. Then we'll come back afterwards to pick you up, wherever you've got to. What shall we do with the prisoners, take them on the ship too?'

'Has she been sighted yet?'

'No, I can't think what delays her,' he said vexedly.

'Storms, perhaps. In any case,' said the false Aunt Tribulation, 'there'd be no point in taking the prisoners on board. We don't want to keep them; we want to get rid of them. Tie a rock to their feet and drop them over Sankaty cliff when the tide is high.'

Dido's hair stood on end when she heard this cold-blooded order. She struggled fiercely and bit her gag but in vain.

'Supposing the professor doesn't finish his sums till tomorrow morning? We can hardly toss them over the cliff in broad daylight. There might be people about watching for the whale.'

'Shut them in the lighthouse till dark, then,' she said impatiently. 'The lighthouse keeper goes off at dawn and you know where he keeps the key.'

'Yes, under one of the rocks. That would answer,' he said, considering. 'What about the third child – Casket's daughter –'

Dido held her breath.

'I heard the other girl say she knows nothing.' Dido breathed again, remembering how she had told Nate in the barn that Pen was unaware of Aunt Tribulation's real identity. Evidently Aunt Tribulation had taken this to mean that Pen knew nothing about the plot at all. Lucky for Pen, Dido thought.

'She had better be left here,' Aunt Tribulation went on. 'Doctor Mayhew, when he returns, would think it strange if she were not in attendance on her father.'

'On you, you mean,' Mr Slighcarp said sourly. 'Oh, yes, it's very nice for you up here, waited on hand and foot by those children, while we pig it in the forest!'

'Don't be ridiculous, Brother. You know it was quite out of the question that I should camp with you in the forest; it would be most unsuitable.' He made a sneering remark, but she ignored it and said, 'I will think of some story to account for the absence of the other two, should anyone ask.'

'Casket knows nothing about us?'

'Not he. His wits are clean gone.'

'It must have been a shock for you when he turned up.'

'In his present state, it was all for the best,' she said

calmly. 'If my own *brother* accepts me, no one else can have any doubts.'

'Suppose he recovers?'

'He is hardly likely to do so before we leave. He keeps jabbering blubber-headed stuff about pink whales.'

'That's not so blubber-headed,' Mr Slighcarp said drily. 'She's there off Squam Head. There were crowds on the shore yesterday watching her. If she comes farther south we may have to change our plans; we can hardly unload the stuff from *Dark Diamond* with a whole lot of jobberknolls watching.'

'In that case you'd better choose some other point to dispose of the prisoners.'

'It will be all right after nightfall,' he said. 'And we must be at Sankaty, anyway, to watch for the ship; we arranged to exchange signals there; then she'll heave-to a mile off the coast and we'll go out by boat, as if we were after bass, and collect the stuff.'

'Very well. Send me a message as soon as she is sighted. You'd better get back to Breadno now and see that he is kept to work and doesn't wander off again looking for night hawks or something else foolish. The sooner those prisoners are disposed of, the easier I shall feel; we don't want fuss and inquiries at this end spoiling our plans at the last minute.'

Dido was now rudely dragged to her feet, and forced to walk by repeated prods in the back. She could not see because of the sack over her head (it was a flour sack and she kept sneezing as the loose flour sifted down). Her bound hands were buckled on to a dangling strap. In a moment she realized that this was the pony's stirrup. So they must have got Nate, she thought dismally; he's probably on the other side of the pony. Now we are in the basket. How the mischief will we get out of this fix? What'll Pen do when I don't come back? Aunt Tribulation will tell her some tale, so she won't worry for hours. Will she have the sense to tell Doc Mayhew about the gun when he comes tomorrow? Yes, she'll probably have that much sense, but will Doc Mayhew believe her? And suppose Aunt Tribulation catches her at it? And even if he does believe her, that probably won't be in time to help Nate and me and poor old Breadno. We'll be feeding the fishes before they guess what's happened unless we can work ourselves loose somehow. Oh well; let's hope old Breadno takes a devil of a long time over those final calculations of his.

Immersed in these gloomy thoughts she trudged along. The going was much rougher now; they had left the track. Bushes and brambles caught her legs, so she guessed they must be approaching the forest. Presently they halted and there was a long wait while the pony stamped and shifted impatiently. Dido was desperately tired and longed to sit down, but the strap that attached her hands to the stirrup was too short to allow this; all she could do was to lean against the pony, grateful for its warmth in the chilly night air. In the end she did fall into a sort of doze on her feet, regardless of the awkward position. When she next opened her eyes she was surprised to find daylight filtering through the loose mesh of the flour sack. Presently footsteps approached and there were some faint protesting cries which ceased abruptly; evidently poor Professor Breadno had been added to the roll of prisoners. Dido felt sorry for him and remorseful that she had been the cause of the gang's decision to dispose of him. But, she thought, he shouldn't have invented the gun. I suppose he don't see the harm in it; he's like a child.

Now the procession moved forward steadily for a considerable distance; Dido, stiff and aching all over, thought they might have gone three or four miles when at length they halted again and their captors conferred in low voices.

'Too late to chuck 'em now; broad daylight and somebody might come along. Besides, it ain't full tide yet; no water at the foot of the cliff.'

Thank the lord Breadno's a slow worker, Dido thought.

'Any sign of the ship yet?'

'Yes, there's a sail to south'ards that looks like her.'

'What the blazes is she doing down thataway? No wonder she's behind schedule.'

'Gale blew her off course, maybe.'

'Has the lighthouse keeper left yet?'

'Yes, half an hour ago.'

'Bring them along, then; best carry them the last bit. Lucky we put them in flour bags and the weather's a bit thick; if anyone happens along, we're just delivering flour to the lighthouse.'

Mr Slighcarp laughed sourly.

Dido was picked up and slung over somebody's shoulder, carried about a hundred yards in a very jolting and uncomfortable manner, and then thumped down roughly on to a stone floor. Something – another body – fell heavily on top of her. She wondered if it was Nate or Breadno. Then she heard footsteps retreating. A door slammed. I'll count to a hundred, she decided; then I'll try to wriggle out of my sack. Dunno when I've been so tired, though.

Counting was a mistake. The numbers slipped by more and more slowly . . . tied themselves in knots . . . began to run backwards. Before she had reached forty, Dido was asleep.

The pony's footsteps had died away down the track. Aunt Tribulation turned and went back into the house. A delicious smell of broth filled the kitchen. She could hear the voice of Penitence upstairs in Captain Casket's room.

'Try to take a little more, Papa dear! To please me! Just a spoonful and a cracker. That's it – famous! Now you may lie down and sleep.'

In a moment or two Pen appeared, looking very white and fatigued, with the empty bowl and plate.

'Well, miss!' Aunt Tribulation snapped. 'I notice you make broth for your father but none for your poor old aunt who's had charge of you all this time. Fine gratitude, I must say!'

'I'm sorry, Aunt,' Penitence said tiredly. She pushed the hair off her forehead. 'There is plenty more broth in the pot if you would like it. I can heat it up in a moment.'

'Very well. Make haste!'

'Yes, Aunt,' and Pen added gently, looking Aunt Tribulation straight in the face, 'Poor Aunt, is your rheumatism very bad?'

'Mind your own business, miss!'

'Where's Dido?' Pen asked, as she put the broth pot on the stove.

'The sow got loose again. Nate offered to help her search and they may not be back for a long time. You had best go to bed when you have washed up those dishes.'

'I shall sit with Papa.' Penitence poured broth into a bowl, adding a pinch of herbs and spices, and set it before Aunt Tribulation.

Then she quietly said good night and went up to the captain's room.

Aunt Tribulation sat at the kitchen table, grim and erect; slowly, because it was so hot, she sipped at the steaming broth.

Captain Casket suddenly woke up and looked about his room. The whale-oil lamp was still burning brightly, but daylight was beginning to creep past the curtains. He saw his daughter Penitence sitting at the foot of the bed. She was very pale.

'How do you feel now, Papa?' she asked in a low voice.

'I am better, Daughter, I thank thee, after that excellent broth and the good sleep it brought. I feel myself again.'

'Do you *indeed*, Papa? Truly? Well enough to get up and take a walk?'

'Take a walk?' he repeated in bewilderment. 'Why, what o'clock is it, then?'

'Not long after dawn.'

'Strange time for a walk, Daughter.'

'No, Papa, it is very urgent – it is dreadfully important. Can you, do you think? Can you try?'

'What for, my child?'

'I will tell you when we are on our way. Please, Papa! I would not ask you if it were not so important. But if you cannot come I shall have to go on my own, and I do not like to leave you.'

Captain Casket sat up and found himself fairly strong. 'I shall do well enough, I thank thee, child,' he said, when Pen offered to help him dress, so she retreated to the kitchen and packed a bag of food.

'Why, who is this?' Captain Casket said when he came downstairs.

'Hush!'

Penitence laid her finger on her lips and dragged him to the door. 'I will tell you outside.' He followed her, puzzled but complying.

When they were well away from the farm Pen turned to the right and took the track leading towards Sankaty.

'Now!' she said. 'I will explain everything, Papa. But first, did you really not know that lady sleeping in the kitchen?'

'Never saw her in my life before,' declared Captain Casket.

'She is not my Aunt Tribulation?'

'That lady? No indeed, nor in the least like her! Tribulation is much shorter, with black hair and eyes.'

'Is she? I had not remembered. Well, Papa, that lady has been calling herself Aunt Tribulation and living at the farm for the last month.'

'I do not understand!' he said, passing a hand over his forehead. 'Passing herself off as my sister Tribulation? But that is infamous behaviour! Then where is my sister?'

'I do not know, Papa.'

'This is an outrage! We must go back at once and demand to know what she means by it, and where Tribulation is. Some harm may have come to her.'

'Wait, Papa, listen. I have not told you all yet. That is not nearly the worst. Yesterday Dido and I helped a man who had fallen into the cranberry bog. He is Professor Breadno, a foreign scientist, and he has made a gun in the Hidden Forest which is going to shoot a shot right across to London and kill the king of England.'

Captain Casket sat down abruptly in a clump of broom. 'I am *not* better,' he said mournfully. 'I am having wild delusions. I think my own daughter is telling me about a gun which will fire across the Atlantic. Next I shall be seeing pink whales.'

Pen pulled him to his feet.

'Yes, you will, Papa, but please listen, this is true! It is a wicked plot by the English Hanoverians to get rid of King James.'

'But why,' asked the father doggedly, 'not that I believe a word of this, mind thee, but why do they come all the way to Nantucket to fire at King James? Why not just do it across the Thames?'

'Why,' Pen said impatiently, 'because nobody over here will bother to stop them. Whereas in London I suppose the king's soldiers would grab them if they so much as showed their faces. But that is not the worst, Papa.'

'Speak on then, Daughter.'

'Last night,' said Pen breathlessly, 'I went out to the

barn for some eggs and what do you think I saw? The woman who calls herself Aunt Tribulation was there, and she and Mr Slighcarp put a sack over poor Dido's head and tied her hands up with rope, and I heard Aunt Tribulation say that Dido and Nate were to be thrown over Sankaty cliff.'

'Why should they want to do that?' asked Captain Casket in perplexity.

'Because Dido and Nate had found out about their gun and were going to get Doctor Mayhew to stop them. And that woman who pretends to be Aunt Tribulation is really Mr Slighcarp's sister. I heard her call him brother.'

'Slighcarp? Is he, too, involved in this? I always thought him a sly, foxy-faced fellow. I was glad enough when he failed to turn up for this trip.'

'Mr Slighcarp was helping get the gun ready in the Hidden Forest. Oh, Papa, I was so frightened when I heard the things they said! I nearly screamed out to them to let poor Dido and Nate go, but I knew they would only put *my* head in a bag too, and then there would be nobody to help them, or to look after you, Papa.'

'So what did thee do then, Daughter?'

'I crept away in the shadows – it is fortunate that I am not very big. And, then, luckily, Aunt Tribulation – I mean Miss Slighcarp – asked me for some of your broth. So I gave her some of the poppy juice that Doctor Mayhew had left for you in it, and she went off to sleep in the kitchen as you saw.' Here Penitence could not help giggling at the thought of having successfully put Aunt Tribulation to sleep.

'Dear me, Daughter. Was that judicious?'

'But, Papa, what else could I do? They are going to throw Dido and Nate and Professor Breadno off Sankaty cliffs unless we do something to stop them. So as soon as Aunt Trib – Mr Slighcarp's sister – was asleep and you were peaceful, Papa, I crept out of the house and went to the forest and warned the professor to take as long over his calculations as he possibly could. I do not think he precisely understood why I wished him to do so, but when I explained that the lives of my friends depended on it, and gave him some molasses candy, he agreed.'

'Thee went to the camp of these villains in the forest? But, Daughter, was thee not afraid?'

'Yes I was,' Penitence said in a low tone. 'I was dreadfully afraid.'

'And did the others not stop thee speaking to this man?'

'No, because they had left him alone in a little hut and were sitting outside round a fire. So I stole in very quietly and he was very surprised to see me.'

'Alack!' said Captain Casket. He had halted, leaning heavily on his daughter's shoulder. 'Child, I am not so well as I thought. I must sit and rest awhile. Perhaps thee had best go on to Sankaty without me. Yet what can one frail child do against such evil? I shall be in dread for thee.' His legs failed him and he sank into a clump of bayberry.

'Oh, Papa!' cried Penitence in distress. 'Can you really go no farther? Look, it is not much more than a mile now to Sankaty, you can see the white tower.'

'Child, I have outplayed my strength. The fever was a short one but sharp while it lasted.'

'Oh, what shall I do?' Penitence wrung her hands. 'I shall have to go on, Papa. I must try to help Dido and Nate. They have been so good to me.'

'Yes, thee must. I shall pray for thy safe return. Ask help of anyone thee may encounter – yet it is not likely that many will be abroad at this hour,' he said doubtfully.

'There may be some,' said Pen with more optimism. 'Because of the pi –' She checked herself, gave her father a tender kiss, and hurried on towards the foot of the slope at the top of which Sankaty lighthouse stood on the cliff edge like a pointing finger.

By great good luck Penitence had not gone far when she heard the thud of hoofs. Crossing her path ahead lay the road from Polpis to Sankaty; to her left she saw a cart proceeding at a smart pace. By running her fastest and waving a handkerchief she was able to attract the attention of the driver who slowed to a halt as she reached the road.

'Well, bless my soul if it isn't little Penitence Casket!' cried a cheerful voice. 'What are you doing out so early? Like all the rest of Nantucket, come for a sight of the pink whale? She's a bit farther up the coast, child, towards Squam, but heading this way. How's my patient this morning?'

It was Doctor Mayhew, driving Mungo.

'Oh, Doctor Mayhew!' cried Pen thankfully. 'I was never so glad to see anybody in all my life, never! Will you help me, please?'

'Of course I will, child. I was just on my way to visit

your father, soon as I've seen a patient in 'Sconset. I spent the night at Polpis and then, thought I, I'll just have another look at this famous pink whale and, if she's still there and old Jabez Casket is able, I'll take him to see her; a sight like that might be just the thing to put him on his legs again.'

'Oh yes!' cried Pen. 'It was what I thought, too! But when I told Papa that she had been seen he would not believe me.'

'He'll believe the evidence of his own eyes, I suppose. And ears. Listen!'

They both stood silent. Above the hushing of the sea beyond the cliff could be heard a strange noise – a most mournful bellow, rising sometimes to a whistle, then sinking again to a kind of discontented mutter.

'What is it?'

'Why, it's the old pink 'un, grizzling away out there in the ocean. It's my belief,' continued the Doctor, 'that she misses your pa and is a-calling for him. And the sooner he sees her the better, in my opinion.'

'Will you help me fetch him?' Pen said eagerly. 'He is not far from here. We started to walk to Sankaty but Papa's strength failed him.'

'Walk to Sankaty? Child, are you out of your wits? What possessed you to do such a thing?'

'Oh, sir, there are wicked men on Nantucket who are going to throw Dido and Nate into the sea off Sankaty cliff. They have shut them up in the lighthouse till this evening. Will you help me let them out?'

'Eh, bless my soul,' the doctor said in astonishment. 'What imaginations you young 'uns do have. Only yesterday that friend of yours was telling me about some gun in the forest. Says I, that's no gun, child, but the biggest telescope between here and California.'

'But it *is* a gun! They *are* in the lighthouse! If you come with me you will see!'

'Dear, dear,' said the doctor. 'Ah, well, I always say it does no harm to humour people in their fancies. What shall we do first, then, pick your father up or go to the lighthouse?'

'Oh, the lighthouse, please!' Pen said, clutching his arm in her anxiety. 'Every moment may be important.'

'Very well, we'll see how fast this canny old mule of yours can go if he's pushed.'

Mungo was co-operative and it took them only another five minutes to gallop up the hill to the lighthouse. The place seemed totally deserted. A chill wind blew the grasses and straggling shrubs which covered the sandhills round about; beyond the low cliff the ocean growled and whispered. The desolate bellow of the pink whale could still be heard farther north.

'Oh, quick!' whispered Pen, as the doctor tied Mungo to a railing. 'Suppose we are too late!'

'What about the key, child?'

'I heard Mr Slighcarp say that it was kept under a rock.'

'It'll be close by the door, I reckon,' grunted the doctor, and soon found it. 'Well, now, where's these poor castaway captives of yours?' He thrust the big key into the lock, turned it, and pushed open the heavy door. 'Anybody about?' he called, and walked in, with Pen close at his heels.

The round room was empty.

'You see,' Dr Mayhew said indulgently. 'All imagination, as I was say –'

Pen had darted in horror to a pile of flour-sacks and bits of rope. '*Look!*' White as a sheet she held up a length of rope. 'There's blood on this! Doctor Mayhew! Do you think they've thrown them over already?'

'Thrown – hey! Let's have a look at that rope. Yes, that's blood sure enough,' he muttered, inspecting it. 'And recent, too, it's hardly dry. What in tarnation's name has been going on around here? Can there be some truth in the child's story?' He stared at her in doubt.

'Hush!' whispered Pen with terrified eyes. 'What's that sound?'

They listened and both heard it: a step on the winding stair overhead.

Then all of a sudden a voice burst into song:

'As I was a-walking down Wauwinet way
I met a young maiden and this she did say:
Oh, Pocomo's pretty and Quidnet is quaint
But the swimming on Surfside is fit for a saint!

'And Madaket's modish and 'Sconset's sedate
And Shimmo is sheltered and Great Point is great –'

'*Nate!*' cried Pen. 'Nate, is that you?'

'It's never Penitence?' He came clattering down the stair and into sight. 'And Doc Mayhew too! Well, of all the luck! Chop me into chowder, how ever did you get here?'

'Where's the others? Where's Dido? And Professor Breadno?'

'Just a-coming down,' he said grinning. 'It's a powerful long stair. We'd been up top, trying to work out whether, if we tied all the bits of rope together, they'd be long enough to let one of us down to unlock the door from the outside. Dido thought yes. Professor Breadno thought not. I'm glad we didn't have to try. Hey!' he yelled up the stair. 'Pen's here with the doc. Come on down!'

'*Penny!*'

Dido shot down the last round of the spiral stair like a whirlwind, threw herself at Pen, and hugged her. 'How did you do it? How did you know we was here? You *clever* little girl, Pen!'

Doctor Mayhew was staring at Nate's wrists. 'So that's where the blood came from! Hey, boy, who's been gnawing at you?'

'Well, you see, sir, we was tied up. Dido and I managed to shuffle the sacks off each other's heads – that took a plaguy long time, I can tell you – but we couldn't get our ropes undone, not nohow. So I rubbed through mine on the edge of the bottom stair, but it left my wrists kind of chawed-up.'

'And then he undid me and the professor,' Dido explained.

'I'll put something on those wrists for you right away, my boy. But where are the miscreants now?'

'They sighted their schooner, the *Dark Diamond*. I heard them talking outside. They were planning to go out to her in a dory, as if they was after fish. Guess that's the dory you can see about a mile to south'ards now. We kept out of view in case it was them. You can get a famous view of the old pink 'un from the top of the tower; she's running down this way like a Saratoga winner – hear her bellow?'

'Ja – hwalnn!' exclaimed Professor Breadno enthusiastically. 'Ismistibiggn hwalln!' He had been more than a little subdued since his recent experience, but the sight of Rosie appeared to have cheered him up.

'Oh, this is Professor Breadno,' Nate told the doctor. 'He was going to let off the gun for the Hanoverians, but he told Dido and Pen about it, so his friends fixed to chuck him over the cliff in case he told anyone else. Nice lot, ain't they?'

'So there really is a gun, my boy? It is not a telescope, not a fairy-tale of the young ladies?'

'Oh no, it's there right enough, sir. And the Professor says it's capable of firing across to London.'

'Konigsbang, monstershoot,' the professor put in proudly.

'So we've got to stop them, haven't we?' Dido said.

'Well, but that ain't so easy, my dear,' Doctor Mayhew objected. 'For one thing, it's none of our affair if the English choose to blow each other up. For another, there's precious few able-bodied men on the island – every man-jack of them is off whaling and we've nothing but young children and old crocks like myself, and whale-widows.'

'But Doctor!' exclaimed Pen. 'You haven't heard the worst yet! When those wicked men let off the gun it will blow Nantucket right back against the mainland – right back to Atlantic City!'

Doctor Mayhew slowly turned purple. It was a fearsome sight.

'*What did you say?*' he bellowed. 'Just repeat that, will you?'

'It's true, Doc!'

There were maps and charts on the wall. Professor Breadno was pleased to demonstrate how, when the shot was fired across Nova Scotia, the back-thrust would send the island of Nantucket sliding south-westwards to bump against the New Jersey coast.

'She ain't so tight on her moorings, I guess,' Nate said. 'Being mostly sand.'

'Great guns! Why didn't you tell me that before? *Push our island over against that crowd of money-grabbing roustabouts and frauds at Atlantic City*? Why, we'd have a lawsuit from here to doomsday before we ever got it out of their clutches again. What would all the whaling captains say to me when they came back from their voyages and found Nantucket had moved? This puts a different complexion on the whole matter!'

'What'll we do, then?'

'We'll have to go into it very thoroughly,' Doctor Mayhew said, taking deep breaths to calm himself down.

Here Penitence said in a small voice, 'Please, what about Papa?'

The doctor started.

'Quite right, my dear, quite right. In the emotion of the moment I had forgotten about him. We must go to his aid at once. Nate, just run and make sure those scoundrels are well away so that we can leave the lighthouse in safety.'

Nate soon reported that both the *Dark Diamond* and the dory had shifted south; the *Dark Diamond* was almost out of sight round the corner of the island at Tom Never's Head, and the dory was pursuing her.

'Guess they don't want to get mixed up with the old pink 'un,' he said. 'She's middling close now; hear her whistle?'

Indeed the whale was now letting off regular blasts, like the siren of a lightship, almost as if she was trying to attract somebody's attention. With one accord the whole party moved outside to look at her.

'Why, there's Papa!' cried Pen joyfully. 'He must have felt himself sufficiently rested to follow me. Papa, Papa! Do you feel all right now? Are you sure that you have not overtired yourself?'

'No, Daughter, no,' Captain Casket said absently. He moved towards the group.

The hillside where they stood sloped up quite steeply past the lighthouse to the cliff-edge, so that it was not possible to get a view of the sea until one stood on the very summit.

'What is that sound?' said Captain Casket.

'Take care, Papa!' cried Pen anxiously. She darted to him and held his arm, supporting him tenderly. They moved on together and stood at the top of the cliff.

A great sigh burst from Captain Casket.

'Oh!' he said brokenly. 'I am dreaming again. I must be! But it is a beautiful dream!'

'No, Papa, it is no dream! We all see her too.'

'And ain't she half carrying on,' said Dido. 'Gosh-swoggle, ain't she got no *dignity*? You'd think a grown whale would be ashamed to act so.'

The pink whale was indeed giving an exuberant display of rapture at meeting her old friend Captain Casket. It was a beautiful and touching sight. She leapt clean out of the water a great many times, as if bent on demonstrating how high she could go; she repeatedly dived and came up, she rolled playfully from side to side waving her flukes and, as Dido said, 'ogling the captain like an orange-girl'.

'I must go down to her,' Captain Casket said.

'Pray be very careful, Papa!'

'Why don't we all go down?' Doctor Mayhew suggested. 'Didn't I see you with a basket of food, Pen? How about breakfast on the beach? Those ruffians are

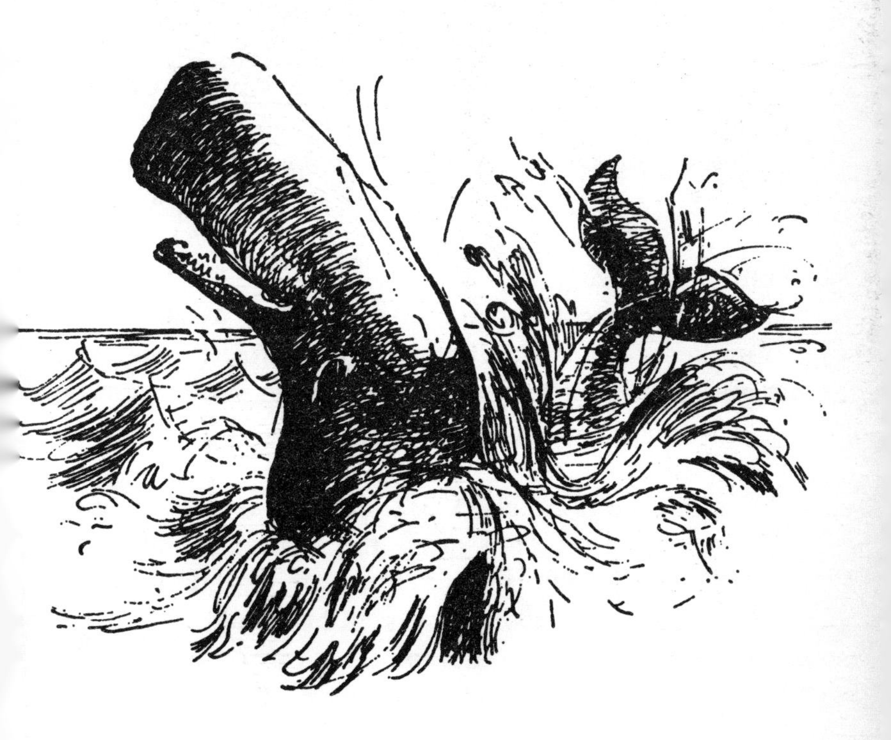

not likely to come back while *she's* out there. And it's not a sight to miss.'

So Pen fetched the food from the cart while Dido and Nate prospected for a path down the cliff, and then the whole party descended to the beach. Captain Casket made straight for the edge of the ocean, and Pen had much ado to prevent his wading in, so eager was he to approach as close as possible to the pink whale – who, luckily, saw his intention and swam in near to the land; and so these two friends gazed at one another with the utmost delight and mutual satisfaction.

'Could you give her a hint not to come too close, sir?' Nate said anxiously. 'It'd be the devil to pay dragging her off if she got beached; I dare say she'll weigh all of a hundred and fifty tons.'

'She is a fine figure of a whale,' murmured Captain Casket blissfully. But he roused himself to make some warning gestures, and the pink whale evidently understood these, for she swam to and fro parallel with the shore, letting out a series of loving bellows, without coming too near.

'Well, it's most uncommon I'm bound to say,' Dido remarked. 'But if I don't get summat to eat soon you might jist as well bury me on this beach, for I shan't be able to climb up the cliff again. What've you got in your basket, Penny?'

Pen had large numbers of hard-boiled eggs and buttered biscuits, molasses tarts, and a stone jug of broth for the Captain which Dido and Nate heated up over a driftwood fire. The broth was all he would take; after that he stood at the edge of the surf throwing hard-boiled eggs to Rosie, who caught them with the grace of a dolphin. Doctor Mayhew opened his black bag and brought out a large leather bottle of ginger-jub which he passed round for the party's refreshment.

'Never go on my rounds without it,' he said. 'If medicine won't help a man, this will. Many's the fellow digging clams today who'd ha' been buried long ago, but for a dram of ginger-jub.' It was indeed powerful stuff.

While they were eating, Dido said:

'Now, Penny, I wants to hear all about how you came to be trapesing over the moors at sun-up with your pa, a-rarin' to rescue us, instead of snoring in your bed like a good girl. How the mischief did you know where we was?'

Pen explained how she had overheard the scene in the barn.

'And you mean to say you bamboozled old Misery so she never guessed you knew? Why, Pen, I never thought you had it in you,' exclaimed Dido handsomely. 'You're a walking wonder, girl! And slipped a Mickey Finn in her skilly? She'll surely think she's got sleeping sickness! Oh, dear, I haven't laughed so much since Mr Slighcarp fell over the cutting-spade!'

'Order!' said Doctor Mayhew severely. 'Now, has everybody finished eating? Nate! stop throwing eggs at the whale. This is a serious occasion. We have got to think how to prevent those deadbeats from heaving our island into the middle of New Jersey!'

10

Ways and means – Penitence eavesdrops –
Aunt Tribulation is suspicious – the rocket –
the gun's last ride

'Now,' said Doctor Mayhew, absently tipping the last of the ginger-jub down his gullet, 'how are we going to stop them firing this gun?'

'Is not firing kungscannon?' exclaimed Professor Breadno woefully. 'Is not having bigbang?'

'Your big bang, my dear professor, would leave this island in a devilish undesirable location.'

'Could firing otherwards round world mayhaps?' the Professor said hopefully. 'I fixing nordwestbang.'

'No, no, professor, that would push us out into the middle of the Atlantic, right over to Spain probably. Can't you see, we don't want the gun fired at *all*.'

The professor's face fell.

'Besides,' Dido pointed out kindly, 'you really can't shoot poor old King James, you know!'

'Na, na, na, snat Kung Jimsbangen, 'sKung George-bangen. Kung George IV!'

'King George the Fourth?' said Dido, bewildered. 'But

we haven't *got* a King George! It's King James the Third, bless his wig!'

The professor shook his head and burst into a flood of refutal, mostly in his own incomprehensible language, which it took some time to disentangle.

'I see what it is,' Dido said at length. 'Those peevy culls have been leading him up the garden path, making him believe there was a Hanoverian king on the throne because he's really *against* the Hanoverians and they wanted him to make the gun for them. Talking about pitching the double! What a lot of swindlers! Can you explain to him, Doc?'

It took some time to get across to the professor that there was already the sort of king he preferred on the English throne and therefore no need to shoot anyone off it; in the end he was convinced but greatly disappointed.

'Firing at sönn, at mönn, at stare?' he suggested as a last forlorn hope.

'No, Breadno, that just *wouldn't do*. It would sink us. We'd go right under water. Have a bit of sense, can't you?'

Poor Professor Breadno sighed heavily and stumped away from the council down to the edge of the waves, where he stood skipping stones and gazing mournfully at Rosie, who, exhausted by her great aquabatic display, was resting comfortably in the swell, her tiny eyes fixed on Captain Casket with a look of great devotion.

'You say the gun is now all ready to fire, and the professor's presence is not needed?' Doctor Mayhew said to Dido.

'That's right. Aunt Trib – Miss Slighcarp said she

would fire it. They only need the cannonball and that's being delivered today. Then they plan to go back on board the ship, tipping us over the cliff on the way, I dessay, and skedaddle till the rumpus has died down, before coming back to pick up the gunner. They wasn't aiming to pick poor old Breadno up at all; I wonder if they'll leave Auntie Trib behind too?'

'So,' said Doctor Mayhew thoughtfully, 'as we haven't enough able-bodied men on the island to deal with a whole shipload of desperate ruffians, our best plan would be somehow to get rid of the gun itself before they can fire it.'

'But, Doc, it's *huge*! It's about a mile long, and as thick as a tree! I don't see how you'll ever get it moved if you've got no help but grannies and young 'uns and whaling widders.'

'No more do I at present,' Doctor Mayhew said frankly. 'But somehow it must be done, so we had all better set our wits to work.'

For a long time nobody spoke. They sat frowning in the silence of intense thought.

'We couldn't stuff the barrel full o' summat?' Dido suggested doubtfully.

'That might lead to a most disastrous explosion,' Doctor Mayhew said.

'Cut the gun into sections – no, that would take too long,' Nate muttered.

Several hours slipped by in fruitless discussion. Nate paced about the beach in circles, staring at the ground.

At last Pen said, 'Sheep.'

'Sheep, Penny?'

'There are such a lot on the island. Could they not

be put to some use? Harnessed to the gun and made to drag it away?'

'Dunnamany ropes you'd need,' Dido said kindly. 'Have another try.'

Nate, who had wandered near, strolled down to the edge of the waves and skipped stones with the professor.

'Or we could bury – no, that would not do,' Pen sighed in discouragement.

'Hallo, what's bitten Nate and the professor?' Dido suddenly said.

Nate, apparently galvanized by an idea, had grabbed the professor's arm and was talking to him earnestly, using a lot of gestures, sometimes pointing out to sea. They buttonholed Captain Casket, and brought him into the discussion. He nodded, at first doubtfully, then with confidence and animation.

'What's the lay?' called Dido. Nate came pounding back over the shingle with the others close behind him.

'We've got it! The very thing! We'll use the pink 'un.'

'Old Rosie?' said Dido. 'Why, o' course! She's just the article. Why in Pharaoh's name didn't I think of that meself?'

'But how? How do you mean?' said Pen.

'Why, it was your notion of the sheep that put it into my head,' Nate told her. 'Tie a rope to her flukes, don't you see, and get her to haul the gun into the sea. It'd be as easy as a greased slide.'

'But would it be *kind*?' said Penitence dubiously.

'We can fix a knot that'll come undone as soon as the gun's in the sea. Cap'n Casket's agreeable to the idea. Says he don't think it'd upset her too much.'

'We'd need an uncommonly strong rope, and a long one,' Doctor Mayhew observed.

'There's the lifeguard rope,' Nate said. 'That's best new five-inch Manila, and there's nigh on two mile of it.'

'We'll need all of that. Now let's think of how we'd go about this. One party would have to make an end of the rope fast to the gun, while Captain Casket and somebody else must row out to the whale with the other end. We can use the lifeguard's dory – I'll explain to him afterwards. I had best be with the captain, who must obviously remain here on the shore so that the whale does not swim away before we are ready. Nate, you had better go with Professor Breadno and tie the rope to the gun; the professor will know the most suitable place to make fast.'

Nate saw a difficulty.

'How're we going to shift the rope? That coil's powerful heavy.'

'In Mungo's cart,' Dido suggested. 'We can all lift it in, and then it will unroll as you go.'

'We can't take the cart all the way to the forest; if there's anybody left on guard they'd spot us.'

'No, but you'll have unrolled a lot of rope by the time you get there, it won't be so heavy. You can leave the cart about half a mile away and roll the coil along the last bit. There are sheepskins in the cart; put those on your shoulders and meander through the scrub a bit aimless-like and stooping; anybody watching from the forest'll think you're a sheep. I'll come with you to keep a lookout,' Dido volunteered.

'We really ought to try to find out when they aim to

fire,' Doctor Mayhew said. 'If Miss Slighcarp's going to do it, we only have to keep an eye on her movements, and as soon as she starts for the forest we'll know. Who could do that?'

All eyes turned on poor Penitence, who became rather pale, swallowed once or twice, and then said valiantly, 'I'll do it. I don't mind. That is if, Doctor Mayhew, you'll promise to look after Papa.'

'Penny you're a real bang-up hero,' Dido said warmly. 'I wish I could come with you, but if Aunt Trib was to see I'd got out of the lighthouse she'd twig the whole lay in a minute. But you can pretend you know nothing about anything and just act like a saphead – try to delay her from going to the forest if she seems liable to start before Nate and the cap'n are ready and we've got the gun away.'

'How should I delay her?' asked Pen nervously.

'Why, talk to her, distract her, ask her advice about summat – ask her how to make wedding-cake or some blame thing.'

'And supposing she wants to know where I've been and where Papa is, what shall I tell her?'

'Why, you can tell the truth. Say Doc Mayhew reckoned as how it would do your pa good to have a look at the pink whale and that he's a-sitting on Sankaty beach. That sounds innocent and harmless and will put her off the scent.'

'Very well,' said Pen, wan but resolute.

Everything was now in train. The whole party helped to lift the lifeguard rope, which was kept coiled in a chest at the foot of the lighthouse, on to Mungo's cart. Then Doctor Mayhew and Captain Casket returned to the beach, dragging with them one end of the rope, while Nate, Dido, and Professor Breadno drove slowly away down the Polpis road, unrolling the coil as they went. They took Pen with them for some way, and then she left them and struck off across the moors towards Soul's Hill.

'Poor Penny,' said Dido who waved vigorously as Pen looked back for reassurance. 'I reckoned as how I'd teach her to stand up to Aunt Tribulation, but I never figured things would be quite as rugged as this. But she's coming up smiling, I will say; I'd never a thought Pen had so much gumption in her. Reckon her pa ought to be mighty well satisfied with her now, considering what a little puny moping thing she was on board ship. If he could take his mind off that blame whale o' hisn for five minutes, that is!'

The whale was still just visible, rocking like a pink blancmange in the breakers, and Nate began singing softly:

> 'Sweet whale of Nantucket, so rosy and nice,
> As round and as pink as a strawberry ice –'

'That ain't stately enough,' Dido said. 'That don't give a proper notion of her at all.'

'All right.' Nate considered a moment or two, while a few more fathoms of rope unrolled.

'How about this, then?'

> 'Sweet Whale of Nantucket, so pink and so round,
> The pride of our island, the pearl of the Sound,

By Providence blest to our shores you were led,
Long, long may you gambol off Sankaty Head!'

'That's better,' said Dido. 'Though it was really Cap'n Casket she was led by, not Providence. I guess really, all the time he thought he was following her, *she* was following *him*.'

As Pen disappeared over a hill Dido said with a sudden pang of anxiety, 'Croopus, I do hope nothing don't go wrong when Penny gets to the farm. I wonder did we do right to send her?'

'Oh, I guess she'll be all right,' Nate said.

Dusk had begun to fall when Penitence reached the farm. Nobody was in sight. Penitence slipped quietly into the kitchen and then paused, as she heard voices coming from the parlour. The door was not quite closed.

'. . . should be loaded by now,' Mr Slighcarp's voice said. 'Thanks to that cursed whale and all the brats and old grannies swarming on the beach at Quidnet we were obliged to slip right round to the south side of the island, which meant the men had to carry the shot a great deal farther from the landing-place. We didn't want to risk anyone getting a sight of it.'

'No, you were very right,' his sister agreed. 'Where is *Dark Diamond* now?'

'Making northing again, back to Quidnet. Just coasting along she's innocent enough – might be going back for another sight of the pink whale. We've another boat beached at Quidnet ready to take us all off to her when the gun's loaded.'

'What delayed the ship so long?'

'They were chased all the way from Spithead by a perditioned naval sloop, the *Thrush*, which several times nearly caught them; in order to give it the slip they were forced to beat right down to Trinidad.'

'What happened to the sloop, then?' asked Miss Slighcarp uneasily.

'They lost her in the end; probably gave up and went back to report failure.'

'It's as well we are now ready to fire.'

'They could never have touched us on Nantucket; it's American soil. But we had best get away prudently and as fast as possible in case the sloop is still hanging about.'

'What time shall I fire the gun?'

Penitence drew nearer to the door and listened intently.

Mr Slighcarp did some calculating. 'Hmm, there's a fair south-westerly, say fifteen knots, plus the trip to Quidnet . . . Give us time to get away. Say six hours. Better make it eight hours. Don't fire before midnight.'

'Very well. I will fire at midnight exactly. Darkness suits us better,' she said. 'There is no risk of being seen on my way there. I don't want to be suspected before you come back to pick me up. As Tribulation Casket I am safe enough.'

'Come to think,' he said, 'where is old Casket and the child?'

'Lord knows. The wretched, foggy sea air in this place makes me sleep like the dead; when I woke this morning it was late and they'd gone off somewhere. To see the whale, I suppose. You'll deal with the prisoners?'

'We couldn't just leave them, I suppose?' he said.

'Fool! Use your wits! As soon as they speak to anybody, our whole plan comes crashing down. If the lighthouse keeper sees them – no, they must be dealt with.'

'I'll see to it, then. On the way to the boat. I must hurry. One last thing –'

'Yes?'

The voices were approaching the door and Pen looked desperately round for a hiding-place. There was just time to scramble into the grandfather clock.

'Should any emergency arise, so that it becomes necessary to fire *before* the time agreed, we will communicate by rocket. If we let off a rocket, do you fire as soon as possible afterwards. Likewise, if for some reason you need to fire earlier, send off your rocket first to warn us and we'll make for what shelter we can, wherever we are. But fire at all costs; we shall never have a better chance. The usurping Stuart monarch is bound to be in his palace tonight because tomorrow is the State opening of Parliament.'

'I shall not fail.'

She laid the rocket on the kitchen table and the two of them went out of the house, still talking.

Pen acted on a lightning impulse. She sprang out of the clock, seized the rocket, which was about the size of a french loaf, and dipped it, first one end, then the other, in a large jug of buttermilk. A bundle of lucifer matches lay with the rocket. She served them in the same manner. There was just time to climb back into the clock before Aunt Tribulation reappeared.

Pen was now in terror lest Aunt Tribulation observe the damp state of the rocket or should take it into her head to wind the clock. Fortunately she did neither of these things, but went upstairs. Seizing the chance Pen slipped out of the house, first cautiously reconnoitring to make sure that Mr Slighcarp had gone. He was visible in the distance, walking down the track to Sankaty at a great pace. Pen re-entered the house, making as much noise as possible, took a deep breath, and called up the stairs:

'Aunt? Aunt Tribulation? Are you there?'

'Penitence? Is that you?'

Aunt Tribulation – somehow Pen could not think of her as Miss Slighcarp – came downstairs, looking grim. To Pen's alarm she had exchanged her usual gingham for a black silk dress and a black, fringed shawl. She carried an awe-inspiring bonnet ornamented with small jet tombstones. She wore bottle-green boots.

'Well!' she said. 'What have you to say for yourself, miss? Where have you been all day? And where is your father?'

'With Doctor Mayhew, ma'am, watching the pink whale. You were asleep when we left – we did not like to disturb you. Doctor Mayhew is keeping Papa on the shore a little longer but they – they thought I should come home. Is Dido not back yet?'

'You can see she is not,' Aunt Tribulation remarked severely. 'Well, child, don't stand gaping – there are plenty of tasks to be done. What's the matter?'

'You are so fine, Aunt!'

'I shall be going out by and by,' Aunt Tribulation said carelessly. 'Hurry now – feed the animals and make some supper.'

'Yes, ma'am.'

As Pen fed the pigs and hens she was filled with anxious calculations. If Aunt Tribulation did not go off to fire the gun till midnight, that was excellent, for it should give Nate and the Professor ample time to secure the rope, and for the pink whale to do her part. But what would happen when Mr Slighcarp returned to Sankaty lighthouse and found the captives had escaped? Almost certainly he would let off his rocket and Aunt Tribulation, alerted, would start out to fire the gun much earlier. Could she somehow be prevented from hearing or seeing the rocket? Pen hurried back to the house, leaving half the pigs screaming with rage because they had not been fed.

Aunt Tribulation was seated in the kitchen rocker, grimly swaying back and forth while she stared straight ahead; from the expression on her face she might have been enjoying the spectacle of St James's Palace blowing sky-high. Pen began clanking pots and pans, putting bacon to hiss and splutter in a skillet, pounding sugar to break up the lumps.

'Don't make such a noise, child,' Aunt Tribulation said. 'I can't hear myself think. No, don't draw the curtains yet, it is too stuffy, and not quite dark, leave them.'

Reluctantly, Pen obeyed. She served Aunt Tribulation a large bowl of chowder and, taking some herself, began to eat it noisily.

'Don't gulp so, miss! You sound like a pig. And, talking about pigs, why are they squealing? I don't believe you can have fed them properly. Go and give them more to eat.'

While Pen was outside there was a short, sharp report

from the direction of Quidnet. A twisting snake of green light shot into the twilit sky and fell, scattering sparks. Oh my goodness! thought Pen. She hurried indoors.

Aunt Tribulation was hastily putting on her bonnet.

'Oh, please, Aunt, where are you going?'

'It's none of your business, miss. Mind you wash the dishes now.'

'Oh, but please – before you go – I want to ask you how to make wedding-cake –'

'Have you gone *mad*, child? Pass my umbrella – there, by the flour crock.'

'I mean,' said poor Pen. 'Not wedding-cake, I mean, please, would you give me some advice about my sampler? I should so like to do the sails in satin-stitch, but I do not know how. Would you be so kind as to show me, and then I can sew it after I have finished the dishes?'

Aunt Tribulation looked at her narrowly. 'What's all this about? Wedding-cake – samplers – *are you concealing something from me, Penitence*?'

'N-n-no, Aunt!'

Aunt Tribulation took a menacing step towards Pen, who winced back. But just at that moment the clock struck the half hour. Aunt Tribulation appeared to recollect that time was too short for questions.

'Make haste then,' she said. 'Fetch the sampler.'

Relieved, Pen ran up to her room, unaware that Aunt Tribulation followed behind with swift, silent steps. As Pen knelt to take the canvas from its tissue in her bottom drawer, she heard the key turn in her door. She had been locked in.

Darting to the window she saw Aunt Tribulation

walk into the yard and attempt to let off the damp rocket. After some struggles and furious exclamations, she finally abandoned the attempt. Putting the bundle of matches in her reticule, she set off with rapid strides for the forest.

'Be-e-e-eh!' bleated Dido in Nate's ear. 'Hallo! All rug?'

'Nearly done!' he whispered. 'We made fast, the prof's just taking a last look. I think he can't hardly bear to say goodbye to his gun. It was lucky we'd covered the rope with leaves and bits o' brush as we went – we'd hardly finished when two of those deadbeats came sloping past going towards Sankaty; on their way to drop our poor bodies over the cliff, I reckon. Wonder what they'll do when they find we're gone?'

'Get lickety-spit to blazes outa there I should think,' guessed Dido.

She added uneasily, 'Hope they don't run up agin Cap'n Casket and the doc, though. Here's old man Breadno. All hunkydory, professor?'

'Ja. Is fastmakingness,' he said sadly.

'Then we'd better be fast making tracks. Give the signal, Nate.'

Nate gave two vigorous tugs on the rope, to indicate to Doctor Mayhew and the captain at the other end that the gun was now attached.

'Now, scarper, cullies – follow me!' Dido said. 'We want to be well away from the rope after they fix it to old Rosie, or we're liable to have our feet scorched from under us. But keep low.'

Crouching under their sheepskins they hurried over the scrubby ground as fast as they dared to the hollow where Dido had left the mule-cart. Just as Nate was untying Mungo they were surprised by the report of a rocket, and its green light climbing up the sky illuminated their startled faces as they stared at one another.

'D'you suppose that's *them*?'

'Dunno, but whatever it is, we'd best hurry,' Dido muttered. 'Give Mungo a prod, Nate.' They scrambled into the cart and Mungo, who was not used to rockets, bolted away down the track towards Sankaty. They could see the lighthouse beam clear ahead of them.

'Shouldn't be far now,' Dido said. 'Wonder when old Rosie will start? They seem to be taking a pesky long time tying the rope to her tail. Oh, *Nate* – s'pose she acts up and won't have it, and skaddles off out o' reach?'

'Nonsense,' he said more stoutly than he felt. 'She'll do anything for Cap'n Casket, eat outa his hand.'

Just before they reached the lighthouse they heard a choking, panting voice which called to them from the side of the road.

'Dido! Nate! Is that you? Oh, stop, please stop, it's Pen!'

'Why, Penny!' Dido jumped out of the cart and lifted her in. 'Are you all right, Pen? What's happened?'

'She – Aunt Trib – she's started for the forest –' gasped Penitence. 'I can't – couldn't – stop her –' She had run so far and fast that her chest was heaving painfully; she pressed both hands against it but could not speak for several moments. 'Climbed out to tell you –' she got out presently – 'rocket – meant – fire –'

'Oh, poison,' Dido said. 'That rocket was their signal, you mean?'

Pen nodded, gulping in air. The others exchanged glances of dismay at this confirmation of their fears. 'So, any minute now –' said Dido. 'Croopus, what in tarnation's Cap'n Casket –'

But as she spoke her words were drowned by a vast, prolonged, ear-shattering bellow that seemed to make even the lighthouse tremble to its foundations. They heard the rope twang like a banjo-string as the slack was suddenly drawn up. They heard a shrill whistling hiss, like the whine of wind in rigging, as the rope flew over the uneven ground, cutting through sand, slicing off shrubs and sea-grass. They heard a wild shout of warning from the dory, which came in sight at this moment, Captain Casket and Doctor Mayhew rowing frantically for land. The tide was full and the waves struck at the very foot of the cliff.

'Great candles!' cried Dido. 'There she goes!'

As they strained their eyes seawards they had an instant's glimpse of the pink whale flashing across the lighthouse beam, half out of the water, arrow-straight and wild-eyed, with her flukes streaming behind her like pennants. Then she was gone, into the dark, heading north.

'Oh *dear*!' said Pen. 'I didn't think she'd like it! Supposing she doesn't forgive us and never comes back? Poor Papa will break his heart.'

'Don't let's worry about *that* yet,' said Dido. 'He can go arter her when things has calmed down and feed her some cream buns or corn-dodgers – the main thing is, now, will the rope hold? And where's Auntie Trib?'

Two minutes later her questions were to be dramatically answered.

With a low rumbling, which increased as it approached to a clamorous clattering din, the huge gun rattled into sight, lurching over the rough ground on its innumerable pairs of wheels, tipping and swaying like a log in a torrent but, by a miracle, remaining upright. 'Look, *look*!' gasped Penitence. 'There's somebody on it!'

The light from the rising moon showed a wild figure clinging to the gun-carriage – Aunt Tribulation, astride the chassis, mad with rage, fiercely striking match after match on the breech in a last relentless effort to fire the gun as it was dragged along. Not one of the wet matches would light.

'She'll be over the cliff if she don't take care!' Nate exclaimed.

Aunt Tribulation heard him. Observing for the first

time how near to the sea the gun had been dragged in its headlong course she abandoned the matches and flung them from her with a curse. Shaking her fist at the party on the cart, screaming imprecations, she leapt with frantic agility up on to the breech itself, and ran, balancing like a tightrope walker, along the barrel of the gun.

'She's got a knife!' cried Nate.

'She's going to cut the rope!'

'She'll never do it!'

'Yes she will, by thunder!'

But even as she sawed furiously at the tough five-inch manila rope there came a last crazy lurch of the gun; the muzzle dropped, the breech reared up into the sky and remained poised for an instant on the edge of the cliff – then the gun and its wild rider plunged over and down, disappearing without a sound into the white foam below.

11

Mr Jenkins returns – the civic banquet –
the Thrush *– another Aunt Tribulation –*
goodbye to the pink whale

Dido woke suddenly, and lay blinking in astonishment, not quite sure where she was. The sun was blazing in at the window, and somebody was perched on her chest, repeating over and over again in a patient voice:

'Your ladyship's bath is growing cold.'

'Mr *Jenkins*!' Dido exclaimed, coming to with a jerk. 'Why, you funny old bird, how did you get here? Is the *Sarah Casket* in port, then?'

'Your Grace's wig needs a little powder,' Mr Jenkins replied. Dido jumped out of bed and began dressing. 'Wake up, Penny!' she said, thumping the mounds of quilts on the other side of the bed. 'Look who's here! Wake up, we've got visitors to cook breakfast for!'

But when they hurried downstairs they found that the visitors were already doing for themselves. Nate had been out feeding the pigs, Professor Breadno wandered in with a hatful of eggs and a heron feather, while Doctor Mayhew was scientifically thumping away at a bowl of beaten biscuit mixture.

'Look who's come!' Dido cried. Mr Jenkins left her shoulder where he had been sitting, and launched himself like a loving rocket at Nate's head, crying, 'Oh, your Excellency, I am afraid your sword has got caught in the carriage door.'

Captain Casket's eyes lit up. He had been sitting in the rocker, looking a little sad and downcast, the only member of the party to do so; but now he brightened. 'Why, Nate! Thy bird has come back to thee! That must surely mean that the *Sarah Casket* has returned. We must set off for Nantucket town at once.'

'Ay, that we must,' Doctor Mayhew said. 'My patients will be wondering if I've gone underground. And there is much to organize – a service of thanksgiving for having been saved from Atlantic City, and a civic banquet for our noble preservers –' He chucked Pen under the chin, pulled Dido's ear, and tweaked a lock of Nate's red hair. 'Then we must send a warning about the *Dark Diamond* to the British navy. Those miscreants must be caught.'

'And I,' Captain Casket said, 'must find out the whereabouts of my sister Tribulation, in order that she may come and look after the children while I search for the pink whale.'

Penitence suddenly burst into tears.

'Why, Penny!' Dido exclaimed in concern. 'What's the matter, girl?'

'What ails thee, Daughter?'

'It's too unfair!' wept Penitence. 'I tried so hard not to be afraid of Aunt Tribulation, and now it turns out she was the wrong one and I've got to start all over again.'

'Never mind,' Dido comforted. 'The real one *couldn't* be any worse.'

After breakfast Nate hurried home to assure his mother of his safety. He found his pony straying in the forest; there was little other sign of the conspirators there, except for some broken bushes, for the gun had smashed their hut to fragments on its rush to the sea.

As soon as Nate returned they all went in to Nantucket town together and made haste to the North Wharf where the *Sarah Casket* was berthed. Great was the joy of the crew, particularly Uncle 'Lije, on seeing that Captain Casket and Nate were safe and not drowned, as had been thought.

'We reckoned as we'd make it a plum-pudding voyage, Cap'n,' Mr Pardon said, 'and come back with only half our barrels full, for, to tell truth, when we heard the pink 'un had been sighted off Nantucket I'd half a mind to wonder whether somehow you hadn't run aground here. I'm powerful glad we did come back. Hear there's been some everlasting rum doin's in the old place since we left. Guess you'll be glad to put to sea again, Cap'n?'

'Yes, Mr Pardon,' Captain Casket said rather mournfully.

'He's pining for the pink 'un,' Dido whispered to Nate, who nodded gloomily. However they all cheered up during the civic banquet, which was indeed a splendid affair. Professor Breadno, who had struck up a friendship with Doctor Mayhew, ate so many Nantucket Wonders that he was almost consoled for the loss of his gun, while Dido, Nate and Penitence were toasted so often for their part in saving the island from disaster that they became quite bashful and retired out on to the balcony of the Grampus Inn (where the banquet was held) in order to recover their countenances. However they had not been out there more than a few minutes when Dido came flying in to exclaim:

'Doc Mayhew, do come and see, there's a British man o' war beyond the harbour bar and she's lowered a pinnace and the pinnace is a-coming into the harbour!'

'If she's looking for the plotters she's come to the wrong shop,' Doctor Mayhew said. But he slung his mayoral chain round his neck again (he had taken it off for the easier consumption of scallops) and went out to greet the captain of the English sloop *Thrush* who now came ashore, saluted, introduced himself as Captain Osbaldeston, and asked permission to make some inquiries about a gang of English criminals who were thought to be lurking on Nantucket.

'You needn't bother, sir, you needn't bother!' Doctor Mayhew told him affably. 'Mind you, so long as they'd left us alone, we'd 'a left *them* alone, and you could have saved your breath asking for them. But as we found 'em to be a nest of plaguy varmints we cleared them out ourselves, there's not one left in the island. Instead of losing time here you should be out chasing their schooner *Dark Diamond* – she's probably halfway to Land's End by now.'

'Oh no she's not,' Captain Osbaldeston corrected him. 'She's lying in a hundred fathom of water in Massachusetts Bay.'

'Eh?' exclaimed Doctor Mayhew, much startled by this information. 'How did that happen, then? How did that come about?'

Captain Osbaldeston explained. He had just abandoned his fruitless search for *Dark Diamond* on the previous evening, he said, and was about to up anchor and make for home when, shortly after moonrise, he saw a schooner scudding along the Nantucket coast under full press of sail. He thought it was his quarry.

'We were in the lee of the land at the time and she didn't appear to see us; she was coming up fairly fast when suddenly the strangest accident befell her that ever I witnessed in all my life at sea.'

'What happened?' Dido and Nate asked in one breath.

'Why, a thing that looked in the moonshine like a great pink whale came tearing along the coast, dragging behind it what seemed to be a rope. It cut clean across the schooner's course and when this rope struck the *Dark Diamond*, such was the speed of the whale's progress, if you will believe me, sir, that this rope sliced the schooner clean in two, and she sank in a matter of moments. It was an awesome sight, sir, it was indeed! Of course we searched the waters round about, but we were unable to find any survivors.'

'Then the world is well rid of a pack of troublemakers,' Doctor Mayhew observed cheerfully. 'But won't you join our celebration, sir, since your task is at an end? Come in and drink a toast to our young friends here, who succeeded in getting rid of this nest of cockatrices for us.'

Captain Osbaldeston observed that he would be very pleased to hear the whole story leading up to the mysterious destruction of the *Dark Diamond*, so that he could include it in his report to the First Lord of the

Admiralty. He came in and drank a great many glasses of ginger-jub while the tale was told.

'So this young lady is a British citizen, is she?' he inquired, looking at Dido when he had heard it all. 'Do you wish to be repatriated, madam?'

'To be whiched?'

'Would you like a passage back to England, my dear?'

Dido choked over a pickled tamarind. The temptation was almost irresistible. But she saw Pen's imploring eyes fixed on her and summoned the resolution to say, gruffly:

'That's mighty civil of you, mister, and I thank you kindly, but I guess I'd better stick in Nantucket yet awhile. I made a promise I'd stay with a friend till they were fixed up right and tight, which they ain't yet. So thanks, but not this time.'

'In that case,' Captain Osbaldeston said, 'I'd best be on my way.' And he bowed to the company and returned to his pinnace. Dido went out to watch it flit across the harbour, and to take several deep breaths and rub a slight mistiness away from her eyes. As she stood on the balcony, reluctant to go back to the gaiety of the banquet, she noticed the sails of another ship, a three-masted whaler, approaching Brant Point.

'Sail-o!' she called. 'There's a-plenty traffic today.'

The new ship, which presently revealed itself as the *Topsy Turvey*, came to anchor at length against the South Wharf, and everybody ran out to gaze at her in curiosity, for she was not a Nantucket vessel. The moment she was berthed a stout lady who stood on deck had herself slung ashore in a barrel-chair and came bustling along the wharf in a state of great excitement.

'Can anybody give me news of Captain Jabez Casket?' she asked. 'Is he 'live or drownded? – Why, there he *is*, his own self! Jabez! Brother Jabez! I declare, I never thought to see you more. I'd heard you was swallowed up by a pink whale!'

'Why, Sister Tribulation! I am amazed to see thee! Where has thee been?'

'And there's Mr Pardon! And my old friend Enoch Mayhew – ho, ho, do you remember when you pushed me in the creek, you wicked old fellow!'

'Good gracious!' whispered Pen in Dido's ear. 'Can *she* be Aunt Tribulation?'

The stout lady was cheerfully, even fashionably dressed in pink-and-grey striped sarsenet, with flounces, and a pink satin parasol, and cherries on her bonnet. She had black curls and gay black eyes, and her face was round and rosy and soft, like a pink frosted cake. She smelt strongly of lavender.

'Oh, don't call me Tribulation please, Jabez, I have quite got out of *that* habit,' she said laughing. 'Sam always calls me Topsy. Only fancy! I am married, Jabez! This is my husband, Captain Sam Turvey. We got married all of a sudden last fall, and I went off to sea with him. That was why I wrote my second letter saying that I should not, after all, be able to take care of Penitence in Nantucket. But of course when I heard you had been swallowed by the whale –'

'Second letter? But I had no second letter,' he said, bewildered.

'Did you not? I sent it to Galapagos with Captain Bilger; I made sure you'd have had it by now. But where *is* Pen, then? How have you managed?'

She turned gaily round, exclaiming, 'Now, which is my niece? Let me see if I can pick her out!'

'Here I am, Aunt Tribulation,' Pen said shyly.

'Topsy, love, Topsy! Never call me Aunt Tribulation!' cried Aunt Topsy, enveloping Pen in a warm hug. 'Yes, and I can see your mother in every inch of you but how you've grown, bless you! I'd not have known you.'

'I'd never have known *you*,' Pen murmured.

'No, *that* you wouldn't,' Dido muttered to herself, amazed at the difference between Pen's five-year-old memory of her aunt and this cheerful, pink-cheeked, sweet-scented, bustling reality. Pen's ma must have had some right silly ideas, she thought, to call her a dragon. Oh dear, why did this Auntie Trib have to go to sea? If only she'd stayed on shore, everything would have been all hunky-dory. Pen's taken a fair fancy to her, anyone can see that with half an eye.

It was true. Penitence was leaning happily in the circle of Aunt Topsy's arm, her eyes shining like stars.

'. . . so as I've decided that a life at sea doesn't suit me,' Aunt Topsy was saying, 'I'm going to stay right here in Nantucket and build me a house out at 'Sconset, for Sam to come back to between trips. And you'll keep me company there, won't you, Penny, when your Papa's at sea?'

'Oh yes!' Pen cried joyfully. 'Oh yes, Aunt Topsy!'

'Oh no!' groaned Dido involuntarily. 'Oh, why the blazes couldn't you have sailed in an hour ago instead of *now*? Then I coulda been snug aboard the *Thrush* at this very minute, a-sailing back to London River.'

'Oh, Dido!' cried Pen remorsefully. 'What a shame!

But you can stay with me and Aunt Topsy till we find you another ship.'

'It's all right – never mind.' But Dido bit her lip.

Suddenly Captain Casket shook himself out of his sad reverie.

'Nay!' he exclaimed. 'But we'll up anchor with the *Sarah Casket*! A Nantucket whaler can soon overhaul that lumbering English craft. We'll put thee aboard!'

'Oh!' cried Dido. '*Could* you?'

Captain Casket was already rattling out orders: sails were shaken loose and the anchor was whisked up; half Nantucket town crowded on board to see Dido on her way.

The *Thrush* had a considerable start but was still in view, and the *Sarah Casket* rapidly began to gain on her as they crossed the Gulf of Maine. Then it could be seen that the *Thrush* was hauling her wind and bringing to; soon they saw the reason for this. Out of the north-east, arrowing through the ocean in a shower of spray like a broad piece of sunrise-coloured ribbon, came something that could only be the pink whale herself.

'It's Rosie!' Dido cried. 'It's Rosie come back to look for the cap'n!'

'Come back to see you off,' said Nate.

'Come back to forgive us,' said Pen softly.

Rosie frolicked round the *Sarah Casket* like a flying-fish, and the blue-jackets on board the *Thrush* crowded the rail to gaze in astonishment at this phenomenon.

Captain Casket hailed the *Thrush*.

'Hey, there! Can you take a passenger? Miss Twite would like to sail to England after all.'

'And welcome!' the *Thrush* replied. The captain's gig

was sent across for Dido. She hugged everybody on the *Sarah Casket* goodbye. Now that she was really leaving she found herself sad; but just the same she was happy – very, very happy – to be homeward bound at last.

'Come back soon, *dear* Dido!' said Pen. 'Come and stay with me and Aunt Topsy next summer.'

'Forvandel, blisschild,' said Professor Breadno, who had accepted an invitation to stay with Doctor Mayhew and study snowy owls.

'So long!' said Nate.

'You'll always be welcome in Nantucket,' said Doctor Mayhew. 'You saved it from a fate, far, far worse than death.'

'Thee is a good child,' said Captain Casket.

'Your ladyship's carriage stops the way,' said Mr Jenkins.

Dido jumped down into the gig and was rowed across. When she reached the *Thrush* they piped her on board as if she had been the Queen herself, and the captain invited her to sit at his table. But she waited on deck, watching and waving until the *Sarah Casket*, escorted most joyfully by the pink whale, had started back to Nantucket and was out of sight.

When Dido went back next year to visit Pen she found that Captain Casket had given up seafaring. Since the pink whale had returned, his only wish was to live on Nantucket and watch her every day as she sported and frolicked off its shores.

And, as whales and sea-captains are both notoriously long-lived, it is possible that if you go to Nantucket today you may still have a sight of them.

Dear whale of Nantucket, so pink and so round,
The pride of our island, the pearl of the Sound,
By Providence blest to our shores you were led,
Long, long may you gambol off Sankaty Head!